Praise for J.T Greathouse

'Sublime prose and pin-sharp characterisation combine to produce a captivating epic of conflicted loyalties and dangerous ambition' Anthony Ryan, *New York Times* bestselling author

'[This] is not the gentle story of a boy's rise to power; instead, it digs its fingernails into the layers of an empire that would consume and erase half that boy's identity. Brilliantly told and immediately engrossing, filled with magic, mistakes and their merciless consequences'

Andrea Stewart, author of *The Bone Shard Daughter*

'An original fantasy filled with magic and culture, the story of a character torn between two names, two loyalties and two definitions of good and evil'

Kevin J. Anderson, *New York Times* bestselling author

'A great coming-of-age story about a foolish boy who seeks to unravel the secrets of magic and maybe do something good in the process. I absolutely loved it'

Nick Martell, author of *The Kingdom of Liars*

'Sometimes a book comes along that is truly special. J.T. Greathouse is about to take Patrick Rothfuss's crown with *The Hand of the Sun King*. It's a beautiful tale about someone trying to discover the magic within themselves, in a world where they'll never truly fit in. Be prepared to be swept along on a unique journey where the consequences of choice echo through an empire' Mike Shackle, author of *We Are the Dead*

'A coming-of-age narrative with the energy of a modern fantasy and the gravity of a classic, sure to hit with readers who like their prose vivid and their worldbuilding lovingly textured'
M.L. Wang, author of *The Sword of Kaigen*

'Well written, thought provoking and enjoyable, *The Hand of the Sun King* is an impressive debut novel that left me eager for more' Lisbeth Campbell, author of *The Vanished Queen*

'Entertaining, richly imagined and full of conflict'
Anna Stephens, author of *The Godblind Trilogy*

'Greathouse casts and engrossing spell, establishing himself as an exciting new voice in epic fantasy' *SFX*

'A spellbinding debut with terrific characterisations, immersive worldbuilding, and prose that swept me away . . . this is one of the best debuts I've ever read' Novel Notions

'Exquisite . . . Greathouse's characterisation, his prose and worldbuilding are an absolute triumph' The Fantasy Hive

'An excellent mix of classic and modern fantasy with a grimdark undertone' *Grimdark Magazine*

'A staggering fantasy debut with poetic prose and near-flawless characterisation' FanFiAddict

THE PATTERN OF THE WORLD

J.T. GREATHOUSE

This edition first published in Great Britain in 2024 by Gollancz

First published in Great Britain in 2023 by Gollancz
an imprint of The Orion Publishing Group Ltd
Carmelite House, 50 Victoria Embankment
London EC4Y 0DZ

An Hachette UK Company

1 3 5 7 9 10 8 6 4 2

A CIP catalogue record for this book
is available from the British Library.

ISBN (Mass Market Paperback) 978 1 473 23297 6
ISBN (eBook) 978 1 473 23298 3

Typeset by Deltatype Ltd, Birkenhead, Merseyside

Printed in Great Britain by Clays Ltd, Elcograf S.p.A.

MIX
Paper | Supporting responsible forestry
FSC® C104740

www.gollancz.co.uk

To those who would sacrifice to build a better world.

Introduction

You have heard, now, the tale of my rise and my fall. Of my father's garden and the Temple of the Flame, of Usher and Oriole and Atar, of the factionalism that nearly tore our rebellion asunder, and of the culmination of that rebellion in my greatest, most world-shattering mistake.

The emperor survived, and yet I broke the world.

As the ragged edge of a garment begins an unravelling that, in time, creeps inwards to unmake the whole – a single thread, pulled and pulled until the warp and weft of the cloth collapses – so the ragged edges of the world unravelled. Monstrous claws scraped at barricaded doors, and all of us – even those who had never once tasted magic, that most thrilling wine that made all the world more vibrant for an instant – felt the tremors through the pattern.

And now, I sit and write.

It is what I have always done best. Magic was ever my obsession, but I now give myself over to my truest talent to leave some record of what we have done.

There will be a world, and I will have played a terrible and wondrous part in creating it. I would have those who endure long after we are gone understand, at least, my final, most devastating, most liberating choice. If those who come after us would love me, they must love me in the full knowledge of all that I am, all that I have done. If they would hate me, I would at least have them hate me honestly.

That is all any of us, in the end, can ask.

PART I

City

I

A Better World

Foolish Cur

Not since my childhood had the forest been so full of mystery and terror. A cry twisted in the brittle air – perhaps a fox yowling for its mate, perhaps some monster on contorted limbs signalling, with eerily human voice, that it had at last caught our scent. Okara loped ahead of me at Doctor Sho's heels, his hackles high with the same creeping dread that clutched at me. A dread that gradually faded as dawn turned to morning and the cries of beasts no longer closed my throat with horror. As shadows became only shadows, no longer the frayed tears in the pattern of the world.

Doctor Sho set down his pack and lowered himself onto a fallen log. 'We should be safe to rest,' he said, massaging his calves. 'The pattern hasn't worn thin here yet.'

I collapsed in the roots of a tree, my limbs leaden after my flight from Eastern Fortress and the rebuilding of my body after my battle with those ... things ... in the forest. Doctor Sho had called them 'unwoven'. He had said that they were drawn to magic like spiders to the struggling of a captive fly.

Okara snuffled around the edges of our makeshift camp, little more than a space between two gnarled trees. Satisfied, he flopped to the ground beside me and rested his scarred head on my knee. I searched those scars for any flicker of light, any sign that Okara the god was still with us, still inhabiting this dog who was only his namesake. Any sign that he was still an ally.

The emperor had called me a fool for trusting this god who had led me, by dreams and premonitions, away from happiness in An-Zabat. To Hissing Cat, and thence to that fateful moment in Voice Golden-Finch's garden when, in desperation, I had wielded forbidden magic against the emperor, giving the gods the excuse they needed to rekindle their war.

The Wolf of Guile indeed.

I reached out to ruffle the dog's ears. My hand shook, then shrank away. It was not his fault. Forces beyond his awareness, beyond his ability to comprehend, had made use of him. Yet when I thought of Okara, I thought of this dog's face.

'Where are we?' I asked, mostly to draw my attention away from the dog and how badly we had both been used. 'We should be near Eastern Fortress, but I don't recognise these woods.'

'You fled far.' Doctor Sho searched the drawers of his medicine chest and produced a handful of dried mushrooms. 'And you look exhausted. Here. Eat some of these. Not particularly tasty, but nourishing, with potent medicinal qualities.'

I took the mushrooms, distinct for their yellow stalk and red cap, and ate mechanically. 'I need to get back to the city. Hissing Cat will need my help to ... Well, I ought to help her, in any case. This is my fault.' My voice hitched. I ate another mushroom, settling myself before I pressed on. 'And the battle wasn't over. I should be there, not hiding in some forest.'

Doctor Sho's gaze felt different somehow, more penetrating, but of course I understood him now better than I had. He was not only Doctor Sho, my erstwhile companion, but Traveller-on-the-Narrow-Way, a man who had been preserved across eons of time, like the emperor and Hissing Cat, though he possessed no talent for magic. A scholar whose ideas had formed the foundations of the Sienese Empire and had shaped so much of my own thinking. No mere doctor but the most revered – and hated – mind in the world.

'Hissing Cat is more than capable of sealing the bulk of the city from the pattern's fraying, but that protection comes at the cost of magic,' he said. 'Are you a skilled enough swordsman to single-handedly defeat what remains of the Sienese Army? No? Then leave that work to soldiers and their captains. We have another task.'

'I caused this.' My throat ached at the words, but I forced them into the world. 'I have to fix it.'

'And how will you do that?' he asked, leaning towards me, his elbows on his knees, his gaze burning bright as a furnace. 'Will you, as Tenet – your emperor – did, force the gods into some uneasy peace, brittle as glass?' He leaned back and took a deep breath. 'Why is order valuable? Why is it preferable to chaos?'

I opened my mouth to speak, but hesitated. My mind had darted instantly for the dogma of empire, dogma I had learned to question and come to reject. Yet here was its architect, asking me this most foundational question.

'When everything is in its place, there is harmony and life can flourish,' I answered, 'to quote … well … you. When there is disorder, life's energies are consumed by the effort to survive it.'

'Close enough,' he muttered. 'And has the empire created order? Was there harmony under Tenet's reign?'

'No.' The answer came easily. 'The empire's order had to be maintained with the edge of a blade. The rebellions here and in An-Zabat and the destruction in Toa Alon speak to instability.'

'Because Tenet has no faith.' An acid bite seeped into Doctor Sho's voice. 'He does not trust the pattern. Does not trust people to find their place, does not trust in harmony. It is difficult to blame him. He lived through such days of chaos . . .' He shook his head sharply. 'But he strayed from the path. Refused to do what was necessary.'

He looked away, the muscles of his jaw tense under his wispy beard. 'Tenet could have saved us from this, but he wanted his empire, a world shaped as he desired, cultivated and pruned like a garden. He had wielded power too long to abandon it.'

'What of the classics?' I asked, feeling adrift. I had long understood this man's words as the foundation of the empire he now spoke of with open loathing.

He answered with a brittle laugh. 'My writings were as wind-calling or battle sorcery, a tool Tenet took and twisted to his own purpose. There are glimpses of the truth to be found, but only glimpses. No, when I learned what he intended to make of my writings, I left the imperial palace and swore never to return. And he, in turn, promised that I would live to see the world he meant to build.'

Perhaps it was exhaustion, or the vertigo of so many sudden revelations, or the dregs of the nightmarish wake that seemed to permeate the world around me, that put up my hackles, drying my mouth, and turning my stomach. The sky wheeled above me and I would have collapsed if Doctor Sho had not caught me by the arm. We sat there for a moment, the bark of the tree digging roughly into my listless back, Doctor Sho's hand firm on my elbow. The edges of my vision began to churn with colour, yet when I looked towards the strange, swirling lights, they danced away, holding ever in the periphery.

'Now listen to me,' Doctor Sho said, his voice thin. 'The pattern is in tatters, yes, and there will be suffering, but you must not despair. Order is preferable to chaos, but chaos creates opportunity, a chance to get things right this time. But I can't do this on my own. I need you to promise that you will help me and do what is necessary when the time comes, no matter how it pains you.'

My gaze found his face and penetrated through layers of wrinkled, greying skin to the sagging ropes of muscle underneath and the angled planes of his skull. 'Help you do what?' I murmured.

'Help me make a better world,' he said, his voice ringing in my ears as sleep took me. 'A pattern free from the curse and yoke of magic.'

Doctor Sho's words resounded as my own first thought upon waking. *Free from the curse and yoke of magic.* The chill, dewy air bit at my face and hands. The leaves overhead shimmered in the bright blue light of dawn. For a moment, the last few days seemed no more than a terrible dream, a premonition, the pattern's injunction against wielding the power that Hissing Cat had warned against. I would sit up and find a smouldering campfire nearby, Clear-River curled up in his blankets beside it or fetching water for morning tea. Soon Torn Leaf and the others would join us to continue their practice with the canons I had carved in strips of bone. Hissing Cat would lurk nearby, watching it all with a scowl, the ravens' skulls in her hair clattering, and Running Doe would walk—

A tear tumbled from my cheek. A sharp hook caught within my chest. Had I been happy then, towards the end of our long march to war? I remembered the night before the battle, the bonfire, Running Doe's eyes dark in the moonlight …

'Good, you're awake.' Doctor Sho said gruffly, emerging from the forest. He set down his pack and studied me, his eyes rimmed with dark bruises of fatigue. The flesh around them hung slacker than I remembered, as though he were being slowly pulled apart by some invisible force. It was a sight that at once captivated and repulsed me.

'Awake, but still feeling the effects of that medicine, it seems,' he went on with a gentle smile. The maddening geometries of his teeth sent a fresh wave of nausea through me. 'Don't worry. The side effects will fade as you develop a tolerance.'

'I've long thought you something of a miracle worker with your herbs,' I muttered, 'but I'm beginning to doubt my judgment.'

He fished one of the red-and-yellow mushrooms from his pocket and flourished it. 'Witch's eye,' he said. 'So named in ancient days for its ability to open the eye to the world's deepest mysteries. Or so it was believed. In fact, it does the opposite. The gods move freely in the world again, and they will be wary of you, if they do not already hunt you. I have long moved through the pattern like a snake through tall grass, disturbing not a blade, leaving no wake or ripple. This' – he gestured with the mushroom – 'will allow you to do much the same, by stifling your magic.'

His words echoed between my ears. Despite my knowledge that wielding magic would draw the horrors that had so nearly killed me, I delved into the pattern. My awareness was as broad and keen as ever, and the world redoubled in its brightness and texture as power filled me. I cupped the palm of my hand and conjured a flame.

Not even a wisp of smoke appeared in answer, nor the warming wake by which I had first felt magic.

Stunned, I reached for battle sorcery, and produced neither a spark nor the sharp heat down my limbs. Neither did the wind come at my call, its brittle chill failing to suffuse my lungs. I had awoken to find my arms and legs bound, my voice gagged, my ability to affect my world stripped away. I poured power inwards, hunching my shoulders, willing my arms to twist and reform into the broad wings of an eagle hawk.

The creases of my palm were a vast, empty expanse, its ridges like the dunes of the Batir Waste, the jagged diamond scar where I had cut away the imperial canon a bleak desert. I stared down at that emptiness, powerless and terrified, fragile as I had never been before.

'Come now, it isn't as bad as that,' Doctor Sho chided. 'You're alive, aren't you? And there is work to be done.'

All my terror reared up and bared its fangs. 'You did this to me!' My voice cracked like rotten ice. 'You took away what even the emperor could not!'

'He could, and did,' Doctor Sho corrected. 'By more invasive means. You needed a night of sleep, and while the unwoven are unnerved enough by me to shy away, eventually their hunger for one who has done so much to rewrite this world would overwhelm their fear, and what little protection I can offer would fail. I saved your life, as we must save the world.'

I stared at my featureless hand, and at the pink stump of my right arm, the latter a loss I could once have restored on a whim, blending the magics of veering and healing. I had left it untouched for months, considering it not a wound but a reminder of the path of tragedies that had carried me from my father's garden to Greyfrost Keep. Now, stripped of my power, a sudden, aching longing for that missing limb swept through me. 'Give me whatever medicine counteracts this poison. *Now.*'

Doctor Sho shook his head. 'It will wear off on its own in time, and you will need to take another dose before then. Listen to me. Those beasts will be upon you—'

I stood, turned away from him, and began to walk. The angry heat behind my eyes burned away any thought for the forest around me, or which direction I was going. My sole aim was to leave Doctor Sho behind.

'Wait!' he called after me. I heard the rattle of his medicine chest as he jogged to catch up.

I ignored him and kept walking. He had taken away the *one*

thing that had been my guiding light, my hope for any control of my life in a world where so many forces had driven me to their own ends. My father, the empire, my grandmother, the rebellion, the gods – even Atar had manipulated me. I saw that now. She had used me to further her own end of An-Zabati rebellion and liberation. The one meaningful choice I had made, to betray the empire and join the rebellion, had been motivated by guilt for my mistakes and made at Okara's prodding. I should have stayed in Hissing Cat's cave, drunk deep of the knowledge I had always longed for, and given up on the rest of the world.

I saw the tree root through a misty blur the moment it caught my foot and sent me sprawling on the forest floor, freshly scraped and bruised, staring up through the forest canopy at the grey dome of the sky, half expecting shrieking monsters to flock down, hungry for my flesh, or – worse – one of the inscrutable, many-winged gods to unfurl and, with a gesture, burn me from the world, unprotected and powerless as I was.

'What is your plan, exactly?' Doctor Sho leaned his elbows on his knees, taking heavy breaths that puffed out his whiskered cheeks. Despite his unnatural lifespan, he showed the occasional sign of age. 'Walk back to Eastern Fortress defenceless? Likely get yourself killed by some Sienese soldier fleeing the city, if not the monsters actively hunting you? *Think.* What reason do I have to take away your power, other than to protect us?'

'A world without magic,' I replied bitterly. 'You said as much yourself.'

'A *world*, yes. But magical ends can be achieved only by magical means. I will need your help, and your power, to make the world what it should be. To make it safe at last and give humanity a chance to live in harmony.'

A world without magic. When I closed my eyes, I could still feel that first flush of my grandmother's conjured flame, could still remember the thrill of the world coming into focus in all its richness and all its detail. The sudden blossoming of hope for freedom.

It was a gift not equally given, for there were so few witches of the old sort in the world, and the pacts and the canon offered no true freedom. In truth, magic had done much more harm than good. It was the foundation on which Tenet had built his empire. Every act of imperial cruelty and degradation – the poverty of An-Zabat, the massacre of Setting Sun Fortress – sprouted from roots of magic. And now, thanks to my ambition and ignorance, the world had been plunged back into war with the gods.

Perhaps Doctor Sho was right. If harmony depended upon all things aligning to the pattern's will, it stood to reason that magic – which tore apart and rewove the pattern on a whim – could breed only chaos. Perhaps the cycle of horror, whether on the scale of empires or of gods, could never end while magic still rippled through the pattern.

But it was a gift infinitely precious to me, despite everything. I loved it as a calligrapher loves his hand, a singer loves his voice or a dancer loves her feet. More, it had filled the world with beauty and wonder. Without it, An-Zabat could never have flourished as an oasis in the desert, a bridge across the Waste, founded on mastery of wind and water. I thought of my dance with Atar, when we had first embraced, and of silver-threaded scarves and conjured fire twining in a helix of woven wind. And in that moment, in my weakened state – full of fear, desperate to control a world unravelling around me – I rebelled against the very thought of giving it up, even to save the world.

I could fix this, I told myself. If all things had their place in the pattern, that must be true of magic as well. Doctor Sho was only afraid of it, never having wielded it himself. He did not know the meaning of the sacrifice he demanded. The world could surely be put right again by less painful means.

'I will go to Eastern Fortress,' I told him. If anyone in the world could help undo the damage I had done, it was Hissing Cat. With luck, she still stood in Voice Golden-Finch's garden, holding back the unravelling of the world. I levered myself to my feet as Okara emerged from the undergrowth with a squirrel in his teeth, studying us. 'Follow if you must.'

Ignoring Doctor Sho's muttered protest, I found my bearings from the growth of lichen on the trees, using a skill he had taught me during our first months of friendship while we followed the Sun Road north. With Okara at my heel I headed east, my fist curled tight, the stump of my wrist aching, feeling as lost as I had ever been.

2

A Beast from the Sea

Pinion

Pinion woke to the taste of sand and the crash of the surf. A groan crawled up from his numb toes – still trailing in the receding waterline – along the length of his spine, to bubble from his parched throat and salt-chapped lips. Memory flooded in after.

The many-winged *thing* hovering in the air. The flames coloured like the sheen of oil, washing down to carve through the *Ocean Throne*. The halves of the ship's hull collapsing into the sea like the ribs of some massive, desiccated corpse. Kicking and clawing at the sea, fighting to keep his head above the waves. Lashing himself to the spar at Huo's insistence, though he had moments before been ready to sink beneath the waves and embrace his end.

Huo.

Bits of broken shell cut into his palms as he crawled his way up from the edge of the surf. He pushed himself to his knees, swooning as blood rushed out of his head and towards his numb extremities. A length of rope, heavy with salt and water, still clung around his waist. He pawed at the knot, casting about for the spar it had been tied to and to which Captain Huo had clung.

Dawn had blossomed into morning and filled the blue sky with wisps of mingling cloud and smoke. While he searched for the captain, Pinion's eye lit upon – and darted past – a strange shadow against that blueness. Not a cloud, and darker even than the inky smoke that roiled up in columns, marking the position of Eastern Fortress. He put it from his mind. Questions of the madness Wen Alder had unleashed upon the world could wait. First, he needed to survive.

At last, some dozen or so paces down the shore, he spotted a length of mast. He shuddered at its broken edge – not splayed and torn as shattered wood ought to be but cleanly cut, as though sliced through by some enormous blade – and blinked away a vision of the winged beast and its oily flames.

Pinion worked saliva into his cheeks and lumbered to his feet. His limbs dragged at him like leaden weights, but he staggered towards the broken mast and made himself shout. His voice emerged at first as a dry whisper, but soon became a sharp cry that rose above the crashing waves. Movement answered him. Captain Huo's head lolled, his shoulders rising with the swell of the surf, as he sought the voice that called his name.

'Captain!' Pinion went to his knees and levered Huo onto his back. The tatters of his blue-and-gold undertunic clung to him like seaweed. His sword jutted upwards at a crazed angle, its hilt buried in the sand beneath him. A knot of bruises down his right side spoke to broken ribs. Sand and bloody shreds of tunic were pasted to his chest, obscuring what seemed a deep puncture.

Pinion gritted his teeth against a curse. Only days ago, he might have relished seeing the captain – a thorn in his side all the way from Greyfrost to Eastern Fortress – brought so low. Now, in the aftermath of catastrophe, he needed whatever help the world saw fit to offer. And despite Huo's toeing the line of mutiny countless times, the man still believed in the hierarchies of empire and in Pinion's right to command, not only because Pinion was Hand of the emperor, but because the emperor himself had summoned Pinion to the *Ocean Throne* to offer him a place at his side.

This fact Pinion had entirely failed to reconcile with his own burgeoning hatred for the empire, a hatred born on the march south from Greyfrost in the shattered bodies and spraying blood of innocents outside the walls of the city of Setting Sun Fortress, where the army he had led in flight from Wen Alder's rebellion turned on the Nayeni refugees they had, until that morning, been charged to escort and protect, and who had been promised sanctuary behind the city's walls.

Much as he had come to despise the empire, a deeper hatred burned in him for Wen Alder. He would make Alder suffer as Alder had made him suffer – no, as Alder had made the world suffer. The severed Hand was due payment for Oriole's murder at Iron Town, for the death march from Greyfrost and the slaughter of thousands in the battle for Nayen's capital, and for the terror Alder had unleashed by inviting the gods back into the world in some mad bid to destroy the emperor and free Nayen.

Such hatred and questions Pinion cast from his mind. None would be settled here, on this beach. None would ever *be* settled if he died of exposure, or was captured by some Nayeni patrol.

The captain's injuries were severe, but healing magic could quickly put them right. Pinion reached out with the phantom limb of his magic, hoping against hope that his connection to the network of Voices and the emperor's canon – severed during the nightmare that had unfolded when the gods appeared above Eastern Fortress – had been restored. Yet where he ought to have found channels bearing the effervescent flow of power, he felt a cold, expansive emptiness.

On the *Ocean Throne*, the second time the winged creature

called down its flames, he had reached for magic, almost instinctively, unthinking, though the canon had vanished from his mind. He remembered sheets of light descending, enfolding him, shielding him from the flames even as the ship collapsed into dust around him. An impossibility …

A cough bubbled up from Huo's lips, and with it a dribble of red froth.

Pinion put his hand to Huo's brow and shut his eyes. Either this would work or the captain would die, leaving Pinion on his own, without magic, in a forest full of rebel war camps, his nearest shelter the city Alder's army had put to the torch.

Like a man rendered suddenly sightless, Pinion reached out into the darkness, towards where memory and instinct told him the source of healing magic ought to be. Tranquillity trickled through him, dulling a panic that had filled his chest since waking. And with that quietening of his terror came the certainty that all he had ever been taught of magic was wrong.

'Sorcery is the emperor's gift,' his father and teacher in magic, Voice Golden-Finch, had told him after Oriole had failed the imperial examinations. It had been but one lesson in the flurry of books, tutorials, and lectures to which Pinion was subjected – a gauntlet meant to prepare him to take his brother's place. 'By the emperor's grace alone, we are permitted to reshape the world. Without the canon, we are powerless.'

And yet now, as he reached out into the darkness, unaided by the emperor's will, he found power waiting. This fact alone should have left him paralysed by doubt and confusion, yet the wake of healing sorcery washed away those feelings too. A profound calm descended in their absence, which allowed his mind at last to indulge a horrible curiosity sparked by his first glance at the sky.

No ever-unfolding wings met his eye, nor any strange holes in the fabric of the world. There was only the sun, crawling its way up past the peaks of Nayen, and even it was obscured by drifts of black smoke. Yet the sky was not as it should have been. Above the sea, where the *Ocean Throne* and its fleet had met their end, hung a terrible cloud – a perfect sphere, black as a drop of thick ink, that ate the light of what little sky peeked through the clouds behind it.

Old poems flitted through Pinion's mind. Verses meant to capture the strange terror of an eclipse, of heaven's orbs coming into unusual alignment. Others that cast the sun and moon as opposites, the one radiating heat and warmth, the other the cold light of midnight. Yet the moon still cast a light; hanging above the sea was the sun's opposite. Opposite in all things, in fact, for the sun crawled each day across the heavens, and this sphere of swallowing blackness hung motionless, less an object in the sky than the lack of one. Like a hole burned through a painting.

Huo gasped and arched his back, drawing Pinion's detached attention back to the task at hand. The strange darkness in the morning sky was one impossibility; the fact that, on his own, without the canon of sorcery, he had wielded magic to knit the captain's chest was another. Gently, Pinion wiped sand and dried blood away. What had once been a hole wide enough for two fingers had shrunk to the width of a brush handle. Despite the wake of the magic he wielded, Pinion felt a tremor through his calm.

Huo groaned and pawed at his flank. Time enough for mysteries later.

'Huo?' Pinion leaned close to the captain's face. 'It's Hand Pinion. We're on shore. You've been badly wounded. I'm doing what I can, but fully sealing the wound will take time, and we're exposed. If you can walk, we should make for the shelter of the trees. Do you think you can try?'

Huo nodded weakly. Grimacing, he managed to lever himself

up until he sat with his elbows on his knees. 'What happened?' he muttered, his voice dry as sand.

'Don't worry about that now.' Pinion draped the captain's arm over his shoulders and helped him to stand. Sudden fatigue swept through him – the cost of the magic he had worked – yet he kept his feet. 'I'll explain as well as I can later, when we've found shelter.'

Pinion's own scrapes and bruises complained as they made their way up the sloping beach towards the treeline. Huo grunted with every step, effort twisting his face, but the trees grew nearer and nearer, and Pinion began for a moment to believe that the nightmare had ended, or at least come to a pause. But at that moment a sharp splash drew his eye back to the sea.

A limb, black and wriggling, reached up from the surf and clawed at the sand. Another followed, and a third. Ridged, boneless tentacles dragged a mass as sleek as sealskin, white as pale flesh, ribboned with purple veins. The mass split, like a boil rupturing, yawning open to reveal a maw lined with hook-barbed teeth.

Pinion's stomach clenched, disgust and horror warring for dominance with a third feeling, muted beneath the wake of healing magic: a deep ache, like a broken heart in the pattern of the world.

A tongue flicked out of the maw, tasting the air. In a surge of limbs, the mass of flesh hauled itself onto the beach, dragging its bulk towards them with threatening speed.

Pinion clenched his teeth, shifted Huo's weight on his shoulders, and pointed. Heat pulsed down his spine as thunder boomed and scattered sand. A fork of lightning speared the hideous creature through, casting up a gout of hissing steam. The tentacled monstrosity shrieked, hurled itself further up the beach, and collapsed. Its limbs and ragged mouth fell slack.

The surf receded, frothing around a dozen more churning

limbs. Three more monsters – no two alike, but all hideous, twisted from the bulbous, distended shapes of sea creatures – crawled onto the beach, baring their teeth, filling the air with inhuman cries that shredded what remained of Pinion's nerve. He hurled lightning, carving through the surf. Monsters collapsed into hulks of charred flesh, only for others to emerge, howling and thrashing, in their wakes.

'We have to run,' Huo wheezed.

Pinion looked to the still-seeping hole in the captain's chest and the purple knots along his flank.

Huo answered his concern with a scowl. 'If you keep me on my feet, I'll keep up.'

Though the captain had been on the edge of death only moments ago, Pinion wasted no time arguing. Together, they managed a shuffling run, Huo wheezing and dragging one foot. Bestial cries and the scraping crawl of strange limbs hounded them. Alone, Pinion had a better chance of escaping to the shelter of the trees, even a chance of outpacing the slow, hitching gait of the monsters, yet he pressed on, half-dragging the captain over the sand, then onto a field of jutting rocks and muddy earth – the last stretch of open ground between them and the forest.

A dozen paces now. They could throw themselves down amid the roots and underbrush or make a stand behind some fallen trunk, an obstacle that would surely impede the monsters with their heavy, bulbous bodies and limbs unused to land.

Huo gasped and twisted, his hand clawing at Pinion's back as he fell. Pinion stumbled forwards, his feet sliding on gravel, while Huo collapsed onto his back. The nearest monster lunged, its maw gnashing the air. Pinion regained his feet as Huo's sword flashed in the morning sun. Thick, dark blood sprayed from pallid flesh, soaking into the sand. The monster recoiled even as another surged forwards to take its place.

Pinion planted his feet and took a deep breath. Without the canon, the reins on his magic felt loose, and he would not risk a fork of lightning arcing wild and killing Huo. Instead, he fumbled with his phantom limb where memory told him the magic of An-Zabat should be. A brutal, sudden chill seized his lungs and he hurled a spear of wind that punched through pallid flesh and sent the monster tumbling back towards the sea, buying Huo enough time to scramble to his knees. Pinion ran to him, skidding on loose stones.

A cry like that of a strangled hawk split the air.

Above them, three dark shapes circled against the billowing sky. One flattened four wings against a serpentine body. Pinion reached again for magic as it dived, though his mind had grown sluggish, as though drawing power without the guidance of the canon took a greater toll.

Before he could hurl lightning, however, the creature shrieked as it was struck by an arrow, then banked back towards the sea, trailing ropes of blood.

'Run for the trees!' a voice shouted in Nayeni. 'We'll keep the bastards off!'

This statement was punctuated by a flight of three more arrows, two of which sank deep into the nearest monster, which gurgled and hissed, its strange, boneless limbs pawing at its wounds. Pinion threw Huo's arm over his shoulder and hauled him the last dozen steps up the beach into the shelter of the trees.

The monsters followed, smearing the rock and sand with their viscous blood even as another flight of arrows riddled them. They pressed on, heedless of pain like no creatures Pinion had ever known. Their limbs tangled in the roots and branches where the thick forest met the edge of the beach. Arrow after arrow punctured their bodies and roars of incoherent fury rumbled from them until, finally, they collapsed, leaking putrid ichor from their maws and dozens of wounds.

The distant cries of their flying cousins reached down through the forest canopy, then faded as they went in search of less troublesome prey. Pinion heaved a sigh and leaned against the trunk of a tree. A tremor seized him, pulsing down his limbs, shaking off the terror that had gripped him since waking.

'What were those bloody things?' Huo gasped weakly, hugging himself tightly with one arm, the other gripping his sword. He prodded the nearest monster, sprawled and tangled in the roots of a tree. Gelatinous flesh rippled, then collapsed, spilling gore and meat and emitting a noxious putrescence that made Pinion gag. Huo backed away, muttering a string of curses, then grimaced and clutched at the still-seeping wound in his chest.

'I'd not disturb the corpses,' the Nayeni voice that had called out to them said, nearer now. Pinion turned towards it. A few leaves and ferns swayed, as though a wind had passed through the underbrush. 'Their blood does strange things to human flesh. Though I've not seen these sort before come crawling out of the sea. What d'you think they were, before the change took 'em? Squid?'

There was a pause before a young woman's voice answered. 'Jellyfish, maybe?'

'Who there?' Huo called out in poor, barking Nayeni – a vocabulary and tone useful only for cowing villagers. 'Show you self!'

'Put the sword away first, little soldier,' the first voice said. 'And you, Hand. Can't really do much to stop you blasting us to pieces, but I doubt you'd make it far on your own. Rumour has it witches draw the monsters' attention when they wield magic out here. By the look of that scuffle on the beach, I'd wager the same holds true for your Sienese sorcery.'

'What are they saying?' Huo hissed.

'Sheathe your sword.' Pinion peered into the undergrowth,

seeking bent ferns or rustling leaves, anything that might help him guess where and how numerous the Nayeni were. He raised his voice and answered in their own tongue. 'We thank you for rescuing us. We were at sea when the ...' *When the sky opened and filled with fire and forgotten gods* felt accurate, but the words snagged on barbs of their own impossibility. '. . . when we were caught in the catastrophe. We want no trouble, only to make our way back to Eastern Fortress.'

'Oh, aye?' A thick-bearded Nayeni stepped out of the undergrowth, a bow held loose in his hand. 'A pair of Sienese, one carrying a sword and the other a sorcerer, and ye think we'll let you just wander on back to the city?' The Nayeni sucked his teeth and shook his head. 'Would you lot offer our kind the same kindness?'

Pinion showed his tetragram. 'You know what I can do. You're a fool if you think you can stop us. I'm offering to let *you* live.'

The Nayeni scratched his beard and scowled. 'Ignore my warning. Burn me to ash if you want. Throw a fucking tantrum. As I said, you'll only call more of those twisted beasts, and this time without our help to fight 'em off.'

A bolt of lightning would burn away that beard and melt the scowl behind it, but the man's words prodded at Pinion's mind. He had never before seen – never even heard of – monsters like the ones he had just fought. Monsters that had grown more numerous as he'd fought them, a new mass of roiling flesh and grasping limbs rising to replace each one he cut down with wind or lightning. Perhaps they'd been drawn only by the scent of blood and sound of battle. Yet the first had appeared only *after* he'd begun to heal Huo's wounds.

'So you're more than an idiot child after all. I see the mind's brush working behind those eyes.' The Nayeni toyed with the red braid down the centre of his beard, seeming far too relaxed for one staring down an imperial tetragram. 'You noticed, didn't you? There're some dozen names for them floating around – in our tongue, at least. Twisted Ones. Magic-Eaters. The emperor's maggots.' A few titters of nervous laughter rose from the forest around him. 'That last is only a joke, mind. Hissing Cat says your emperor still lives. You'll be on your way to see her shortly. Just waiting for those flyers to move on. They're drawn to magic, but they'll snack on any meat for want of it.'

Pinion wondered, while the Nayeni spoke, how these rebels could already have known so much about the monsters, which surely must have appeared alongside the return of the gods to the world mere hours ago. Yet something else the man had said caught Pinion's attention.

'The emperor lives?' Pinion blurted. For a moment, his simmering hatred gave way to a wave of relief. Brutal the emperor might be, but his survival meant some vestige of the world Pinion understood still endured. But how? He reached again for magic but felt only the expansive void, unstructured, teeming with unbridled power. Perhaps the absence of the canon meant only that no Voice had survived the battle and the fire of the gods, leaving Nayen isolated. Yet this notion did nothing to answer the most pressing question: how *had* he, lacking the canon, wielded magic?

'So t'would seem, the bloody bastard.' The Nayeni peered up at the sky. 'Hands behind your backs now so my lads can bind you up.'

Huo stepped forward, brandishing his sword.

'All right, then,' the Nayeni muttered. 'Not the move I'd make, but what can ye do?' He whistled sharply, and in a clattering of branches five archers dressed in cloaks stitched with leaves and moss appeared suddenly, like figures in a trick painting whose image changes when viewed from a slanting angle. Their arrows gleamed in the dappled light.

'Your sorcerer friend, Hissing Cat'll want,' the Nayeni leader said. 'You, I think we can leave for the beasts.'

Pinion touched the flat of Huo's sword. 'We'll come peacefully. Please.'

Huo glared at him. Pinion met his stare and pushed the ichor-wet tip of the sword towards the earth. 'To quote the great sage, "The foolish merchant trades a stable future for the slim chance at sudden wealth,"' Pinion whispered in Sienese. 'Whatever you're hoping for, it won't happen if these bastards shoot you dead.'

'That's the other thing.' The Nayeni leader approached, playing out a length of rope. 'No chatter. We move quiet, and if you can't manage on your own, I'll gag you.'

With another roving glare that fixed on each of the six Nayeni in turn, Huo wiped his blade on his salt-stained tunic, leaving streaks of black gore on the blue-and-gold linen, and sheathed it. The Nayeni leader smiled warmly, then forced Huo's hands behind his back. Huo grunted as the Nayeni tied first one knot, then another, then a third for good measure. The Nayeni then took the sword from Huo's belt and slipped it through his own. Pinion offered his wrists willingly, and suffered far less.

'A bit funny to tie you up, I think,' the Nayeni muttered while he finished Pinion's bonds. 'You could kill us all with a thought, no? Remember, though: you'd be dooming yourself just the same.'

The words chilled Pinion, though the Nayeni might have been lying, of course. They wanted him as a prisoner, or at least this Hissing Cat person they seemed to serve did. Was she the leader of the hunters, perhaps? Or one of Wen Alder's captains? Besides Alder, the only names he knew were Harrow Fox and Frothing Wolf, though much may have changed since Greyfrost Keep. Regardless, if the rebels meant to hold him captive, they had to find a way to stop him from wielding magic – a feat that even the deaths of Nayen's Voices had failed to accomplish. The monsters were terrifying and *had* seemed drawn to magic. It was a simple enough lie to craft – if lie it was – and a believable one to a mind already rattled by shipwreck.

Yet it was an unnecessary one, for the moment at least. The Nayeni intended to take them to Eastern Fortress, which suited Pinion. Once there, he would free himself and find Wen Alder: the traitor, the Severed Hand, Oriole's killer and – Pinion would bet whatever inheritance might be left to him – the fool responsible for these monsters, the opening of the sky, and the black emptiness that even now hovered above the fraying world.

3
Finding a Course

Koro Ha

Days passed on the *Swiftness of the South Wind* as it carried Koro Ha away from the Black Maw – or from where the Black Maw had been before the island reared up from the ocean floor and strode towards the mainland, leaving whirlpools wide enough to swallow cities in its wake. No one aboard the *Swiftness*, from the deckhands to Captain Yin Ila herself, had spoken of the occurrence since. Koro Ha could hardly close his eyes without seeing the jutting slopes of rock rolling over, casting up monstrous waves as skeletal, serpentine limbs of stone heaved up before crashing down again, shaking the earth and churning the sea.

The sight had troubled him nearly as much as had the last words of his teacher, Uon Elia, the last stonespeaker of Toa Alon, who had spent the dregs of his strength to save the *Swiftness* from imperial pursuit. 'There is deep lore,' Uon Elia had whispered, 'passed down, generation unto generation, from the first stonespeaker, buried in the roots of the Pillars of the Gods.'

Whatever this deep lore was, however, Uon Elia had kept secret, even as he had taught Koro Ha all he could of magic in those last fraught months of the stonespeaker's life. Koro Ha ran his tongue over his teeth, remembering the sting of the needle that had marked his gums with a blue line of ink, a mark that had brought with it a deeper awareness of the world than he had ever known and access to the ancient powers of cultivation, healing, and dowsing passed down by the stonespeakers. Only a few years ago, he would have baulked at the sight of such a mark, and likely reported the one wearing it to the nearest Sienese authority. He had spent his life as a tutor, educating the sons of the wealthy to take the examinations that were the gateway to the upper reaches of Sienese society, examinations that selected for the young minds best suited to becoming scholars, magistrates, generals, and sorcerers in service of the empire.

Koro Ha himself had passed them, attaining the first and highest degree. But his wiry, curled hair and dark skin marked him out in a way that could never be overwritten by any achievement. And so he had become a tutor, living comfortably on the margins of wealth and success. Such a life had suited him well enough, even in its dullness, reaching its peak when he educated the Nayeni prodigy Wen Alder to success as Hand of the emperor. Well enough, that is, until Orna Sin – Yin Ila's employer – had offered an opportunity to leave an even greater legacy: not just one student raised to success, but a school of them, all of Toa Aloni blood. A chance to prove that his people were just as capable as any in the empire.

Orna Sin had begun the school with an agenda of his own: to find a worthy successor for the stonespeakers, a pupil for Uon Elia, who lived in the buried ruins of Sor Cala, near Orna Sin's estate. His plans had shattered, however, when word reached Toa Alon that Wen Alder had thrown away success to join his family in rebellion, leaving Koro Ha instead the unlikely successor to his people's magic, burdened by his teacher's shrouded secrets and final command.

Now Koro Ha leaned on the rail at the bow of the *Swiftness*, listening to Yin Ila and the ship's quartermaster mutter over the ship's ledger. Even before the chaos at the Black Maw, the *Swiftness* had been running light, evading imperial patrols on a mission to extract Uon Elia and Koro Ha from hiding. Whatever Yin Ila had been planning to do after that, the sudden changes in the world and the rumours that drifted from ship to ship, written in a code of coloured kite tails glimpsed by the watchman atop the mainmast, had wrenched those plans awry. Now the *Swiftness* darted about, just beyond sight of the mainland shore, while Yin Ila struggled against her own uncertainty in an effort to decide on a place to land.

'We should go to Sor Cala,' Koro Ha called over his shoulder, not bothering to turn away from the heaving seas. He knew little of ocean-going, but enough to recognise that the sudden swells and whorls of wind as if from nowhere, and the bursts of ball lightning from a clear sky, to say nothing of the nerve-rattling silhouettes of sea beasts that from time to time circled beneath the ship, went against the common course of nature.

'We've spoken of this before, tutor,' Yin Ila said. 'The risk is too great. At a glimpse of the *Swiftness*, every cutter in Sor Cala will be upon us with grappling hooks, if not battle sorcery and grenades. We must put in, aye, but I'd rather die drinking saltwater than willingly give myself to the empire.'

Her words rankled Koro Ha. He was no tutor. Not anymore. A year ago, he would have quailed under Yin Ila's hard stare, but a great deal had changed since then. Uon Elia had marked him and entrusted him with the greatest burden in all of Toa Alon.

'If you have any love for your people, you will take that risk,' Koro Ha said, wielding the firm voice he had used countless times to admonish unruly students. 'There are secrets buried in the old city. The heritage of our people. Secrets Uon Elia charged me to find.' As, in the same dying gasp, he had charged Koro Ha to seek *them* – whoever *they* were – among the windcallers, the witches of Nayen, and the Stormriders. Perhaps whatever he was meant to find beneath Sor Cala would guide him.

Or perhaps those words had been only the dying ramblings of one who had spent decades in the darkness, apart from the world. If only Uon Elia had explained these things while he had yet lived. There had been time, Koro Ha was sure, during their months of isolation on the Black Maw. Why, then, had the old man kept his secrets?

'Buried where in the old city?' Yin Ila matched him stare for stare, her sharp eyes boring into his. Her face had been toughened by the sun, sea wind, and salt spray until it resembled flesh less than it did leather armour. Yet there was a twitch of fear and uncertainty there. 'Orna Sin excavated only a few tunnels and domes. Whatever it is you seek is likely still buried beneath tons of rock and rubble. Old stories say the stonespeakers had a gift for finding things, but how will you dig it out, assuming you can even reach Orna Sin's tunnels? Let me remind you, his estate was seized, given over to a Sienese merchant family, occupied by *their* guards. It will be a wonder if they have not yet found the tunnels and filled them in!'

'I can do none of those things from the deck of this ship,' Koro Ha snapped. 'And what do you plan to do, Yin Ila? Sail to some safe harbour – if there is any left – and wait for the empire's interest in you to fade? How long will that take? What will be left of Toa Alon when you are finally ready to act?'

Yin Ila set her jaw. 'Yes, tutor. My life is as shattered as yours, but I still have this ship and this crew. They are my responsibility, and we will make a *new* life for ourselves, as we have done countless times before.'

'I am no one's tutor now,' Koro Ha said. He took a breath. Yin Ila was a hard woman. If he tried to batter her down, she would only meet him with resistance. He'd had students like that – Alder had been one – and with them a different tack had been needed. 'You saw what I saw, Yin Ila. The strange shimmer in the sky. The Hand of the emperor's magic flickering out like a candle. You know the rumours written in the message kites. Know them better than I, for I must hear them second hand while you can read them yourself. The sea is empty of Sienese patrols. News no longer travels as it once did, from Voice to Voice. Entire provinces, it seems, are cut off from the emperor's will.'

Yin Ila grimaced. The watchman was not shy about shouting the news down to the decks whenever he spotted a sail kite – a practice that might come to threaten morale if that news turned much darker and stranger.

'Perhaps the Sienese will hunt us down the moment we approach Toa Alon,' Koro Ha pressed, 'but it seems to me that they have greater concerns. Something shakes the foundations of the empire. We may never have another chance to return to the buried city and seek out whatever it is Uon Elia meant us to find.'

Yin Ila glared up at him, her arms crossed tightly until their corded muscles bunched and twisted. 'Promise me this, then, stonespeaker,' she said, tilting her head, her eyes hard and determined. 'If we return to Sor Cala and the chance presents itself, you will do what you can to save Orna Sin.'

Koro Ha baulked, though guilt gnawed at him. How much would Orna Sin have risked to save Koro Ha if their roles had been reversed? Despite his flouting of the law – something Koro Ha still struggled to accept, despite having become a fugitive himself – Orna Sin had been a good man, kind and caring, spending his fortune in a bid to shepherd Toa Aloni culture into an uncertain future – a responsibility Koro Ha now felt heavy on his own shoulders. With Orna Sin a prisoner and

Uon Elia dead, who else was left now to take up the dream of a restored Toa Alon?

'How would we accomplish such a thing?' he demanded. 'I would like to see him freed as much as you—'

'Not as much as me,' Yin Ila snarled.

Koro Ha threw up his hands. 'Fair enough, but my point stands. He languishes in an imperial cell – *if* he still lives. If we are to reach the buried city, we will need to *avoid* detection. Would you have us begin our effort by assaulting the garrison?'

'He lives,' Yin Ila said firmly, 'and old stories tell that stone-speakers could find the only vein of gold in a mountainside. I've sprung men from cells before, and with your help we'll have no trouble finding him. We both want impossible things in Sor Cala. If I'm to help you seek yours, you'll help me seek mine. Those are my conditions.' She cocked her head towards the steersman, who stood at the tiller, awaiting her order. 'And I'm the one with a ship.'

Koro Ha rolled his shoulders back, trying to match the captain stare for stare. He still knew little of the hard life Yin Ila had lived, but it was not difficult, in that moment, to imagine her cutting throats and ordering men to their deaths. In contrast, the poverty of Koro Ha's childhood seemed as soft as a cushion – not to mention the decades he had spent living in Sienese gardens. 'That you are,' he said, sighing. He was not used to so much danger. What she asked of him was good and right, which unfortunately did little to ease his fears. 'Very well, Yin Ila. If – if! – Orna Sin yet lives, and if my aid will help to free him, I will do what I can.'

Yin Ila nodded sharply, then wheeled away and began barking orders. Sailors – many scarred, and all at least wearing tattoos of intricate Toa Aloni knotwork – leapt at her words as Koro Ha could only ever have dreamed his students might heed his. The ship's sky-blue sails furled wide and it canted to port, turning sharply with the wind back towards the south and west, towards Sor Cala, where danger and secrets lay in wait.

4

The Eye of the Storm

Ral Ans Urrera

The storm is far from over, but every storm has its eye.

It lingers, now, in a growing war camp beyond the walls of the Skyfather's Hall. Winds of change and chaos whip across the plain, churning the air into howling gusts at the edges of the camp, beyond the barrier of the Skyfather's protection. A shimmering line etched on the earth marks the end of his blessing and the edge of chaos. Every war band that arrives from beyond it brings word of strange beasts – wolves and vultures pulled apart and rewoven into monsters – and stranger visions in the sky. The stars are wrong, the elders say when Ral Ans Urrera visits their fires. The guidestar no longer points north but draws all who survive upon the steppe here, to the eye of the storm.

Ral has no answer for their questioning eyes. They look to her because she too is a strange, new, impossible thing: a Stormrider, the first in a generation, though she does not wear the marks of her power. They were lost – as her people believed all their magic must be lost – when the empire conquered the plains.

The empire is gone now, scoured from the Skyfather's Hall

like so much grime by the wind of Ral's fury. The skeletal corpses of Sienese merchants and bureaucrats hang on thick ropes from the walls, the smallest repayment in kind for the years of oppression and horror the Sienese brought to her people. Ral intends to bring them to a full account, to lead her war band south, into the Sienese heartland, and burn Centre Fortress to the ground. Not even these rumours of strange nightmares twisted from the broken bodies of beasts will cow her, nor those, stranger still, that the empire has retreated from its own northern border, as though inviting an invasion – or, as some of the elders speculate, collapsed inwards upon itself.

If the empire falters, Ral will seize the opportunity to shatter it. If it feigns weakness to set a trap, Ral will spring it and break those who think themselves clever enough to snare her. She is Ral Ans Urrera. She is a storm, and a storm cannot be trapped. Not when the Skyfather himself drives its wind.

She has told the elders of her dreams. Of the face in the clouds, watching her, urging her to act. Of the voice in the back of her mind. The Skyfather's blessing, she knows, is what has kept the chaos tearing through the Waste away from the edges of her camp, holding back the wild winds and monstrous beasts beyond that shimmering silver line. But how long will that blessing last if she lingers here, a spear unwilling to be thrown?

Not yet, she tells herself as she watches the southwestern horizon. Twenty days ago she sent the windcaller Atar back to the Batir Waste with an offer for her people: join the storm or be broken in its wake. Long enough for her to reach them on her windskiff. But the An-Zabati settle nothing without debate, and in that time everything has changed.

Chaos sweeps now across the world. Perhaps the windcallers, too, have been shattered by its fury. Without them, it will be a long, hard ride into the heart of the empire. Even in disarray, Sien commands magics stolen from every corner of the world and a trained army that encloses those corners within a single, sinuous border. Enough of her people have died. The thought brings with it flashes of butchered flesh and bone, among it a face like her father's, heaped in hideous display. Once, she had nearly broken herself to deliver vengeance, but she will not break her people. Not if there is another way – which, if Atar and her ships do not soon return, there may not be.

<I will be your shield as you are my spear.> The voice thunders behind her eyes. She closes them, revels and quakes in the presence of the god. <But my patience is not endless, Stormdaughter. If your people are to have a place in the new world, you must help to scour this one clean.>

She shivers. The winds surge within her. Lightning burns beneath her fingernails. *Not yet.* The effort to hold still, to preserve this eye in the midst of the storm just a little longer, sets an ache in her teeth.

'They saved me, once,' Ral whispers. Not a prayer – no burning tallow and wailing at the sky – but a demand. Where was the god when her people were dying? He owes her for those years of neglect, and for her suffering. 'They deserve a place in the world to come.'

'Are you all right, Stormrider?'

A jolt runs down Ral's spine. The horizon, and her hope for the sight of sails or signal kites, so absorbed her that it stoppered her ears against footsteps whisking through the grass. Her father would tap her forehead and shake his head in shame.

She turns to face the speaker – Garam Yul Teppo, iron-haired above his leathery face, which is seamed by two fresh scars from the fighting to retake the Skyfather's Hall. The son of a band chieftain, reduced by imperial conquest to a tradesman making saddles to sell and send south to cushion the arses of imperial lords and merchants. Yet the fire in him smouldered long, and the wind of Ral's coming stirred it to a blaze. Garam wears armour of his own make, stitched with scraps of gilded steel broken from the helms and breastplates of Sienese captains he's killed. He and his children – a son and daughter, flanking him, wearing their own armour and weapons – dip their heads and touch their chins in obeisance, but the question lingers behind Garam's eyes.

'Only consulting with the Skyfather,' Ral says, and they nod. Why shouldn't she, who is herself a miracle, speak directly with the gods, despite their being silent for countless generations?

'Another band has arrived,' Garam says, straightening. 'They wish to speak with you.'

'They had word of me, then?' Ral asks. After the rout of the Sienese, riders set off for the four corners of the plains bearing word of Ral's coming and the toppling of the empire. The first war bands – with their herds and families trailing behind – had come to answer that summons, until chaos gripped the Waste and the river of new arrivals faded to a trickle, each speaking in terror of the nightmares they had endured in coming. Ral has long assumed that those messengers not yet returned fell prey to the long-loping wolves and monstrous vultures that stalk the edges of her storm's eye.

Garam exchanges a glance with his daughter, who wears a worried frown beneath her fur-lined helm. 'They did not say so, Stormrider,' he says. 'They were shocked to find themselves at the Skyfather's Hall, and to find so many here. Their elders refused to meet with anyone else until they spoke with you. We can send them to the audience hall to wait—'

'Am I Sienese, that I waste time on decorum?' Ral shakes her head. 'I will go to them, Garam. Lead the way.'

A flicker of amusement lights Garam's eyes. He and his children turn on their heels and guide Ral through the growing encampment that spills from the Skyfather's Hall. Pitched tents stand in clusters surrounded by herds of horse and cattle, or flocks of sheep and goats, all gathered as near the walls as possible, like children beneath a mother's skirts. There are over a dozen bands now, marked out by fluttering banners, some little more than a hastily dyed strip of hide bound to a spear. It has been decades since the Girzan rode to war, but the elders remember the old sigils – words written in circular script, pictographs of running horses. One flutters above the gate itself, depicting the black silhouette of a woman wreathed in curls of white lightning. A new sigil for those who, like Garam, have lost their band.

It is Ral's sigil now, whatever her ancestors might have flown when they rode to war. Her elders are dead, and all that they remembered with them. The truth of this gnaws at her even as she looks upon this new sigil – that of her new people, of the Skyfather's Hall – with hope. It will not be only hers, she knows. It is the sigil of the new world.

No sigil flies above the newcomers' camp. They have pitched their tents away from the others, as near to the strange, shimmering edge of the Skyfather's protection as they dare. Men and women – some wearing bandages, some still in bloodstained armour – sit horse with their bows across their saddle horns, eyeing the plains, the fear burning in their eyes stifled only by the exhaustion that makes their shoulders sag and faces droop. A herd of only a few dozen cattle, still crusted with sweat, mills about, cropping hungrily at the long grass. Most unsettling of all, no children run between the tents, or ride alongside their parents, or keep watch over the herds. Ral hopes that they are all sheltering in the tents, sleeping perhaps after days and nights of flight.

One of the sentries rides near. He shows his hands in the gesture of peace. Ral does likewise and dips her head. 'I am told your elders wish to speak with me,' she says.

The sentry looks to Garam. 'This woman leads you?'

Garam shrugs and says simply, 'She is the Stormrider.'

Disbelief quirks the corner of the sentry's mouth, but he gestures towards the central tent. Eyes follow Ral as she crosses the camp. Garam keeps his hands folded but ready to draw his looted Sienese sword. Ral wishes he had left it behind. These newcomers may not know her yet, but they are her people. The days when bands raided and warred with one another are long past. There is but one enemy worth baring steel against, one enemy with blood worth shedding.

Furs, skins, and rugs woven with geometric designs cover the floor and walls of the vast tent, holding in the heat of a low burning pit fire at its heart. The skulls of bears, wolves, and wide-horned elk hang from the framing poles. The light catches on the resin-darkened planes of those skulls, casting deep shadows in the hollows of their eyes. Beneath them, in a ring, sit the nine elders of the band: four men, four women, and one who wears a beard and the twin braids of a maiden. Two of the men and one of the women lay sprawled out and bandaged, attended by two youths wearing the silver-stitched jackets and belts of herbs that mark them out as healers. One stained bandage in need of changing encircles the stump of a severed arm. All talk between the elders ceases at Ral's entrance. One of the women pauses with a copper tea kettle held ready to pour.

Ral touches her chin and bows deeply. 'You sent for me, honoured ones?'

The tea kettle rattles against its stand as a shaking hand returns to motion. Eight pairs of eyes scrutinise Ral. The man with the missing arm does not stir.

'This slip of a woman?' one of the men snarls. 'This is the Stormrider who gathered such a host?'

Ral feels heat behind her eyes but swallows her anger. 'The host gathers itself, Elder. I am only the star that draws it in.'

'Since arriving, we have heard the rumours of you.' The

bearded maiden strokes the iron streak below her chin. 'A Stormrider ... yet I see no mark of power on your cheeks and brow, as the stories say you should wear.'

Her words stun Ral to silence. Her own elders had forgotten those stories, else they would have marked her. Instead, she learned her power strapped to a horse's back beneath the driving rain, sitting on a flake of shale while lightning burned the sky around her.

'My elders found other means to teach me,' Ral says. 'Mine is a gift not of heritage and ritual but of the Skyfather himself, meant to shatter the empire and scour the Sienese from the world.'

A woman with close-cropped hair scoffs and dumps her cup of tea onto the coals. She glares through the puff of steam. 'You wield magic, girl, but you wear no marks. Your power is no gift of our gods but some witchcraft of your own making. It *angers* the gods. How else do you explain the chaos that rages upon the Waste? The saw-toothed wolves that took Alad Dor Enden's arm? The dozen-taloned hawks that tore out Ka Alsa Allon's eye?'

One of the women winces, her hand rising to the bandage that wraps the right side of her face and the blood that still plasters her cloud-white hair.

'I have held my magic long,' Ral counters. 'Wielded it many times. The chaos did not rise until days after we chased the Sienese from our lands. Surely you do not believe the Skyfather resents us that victory?'

The short-haired woman sneers but has no answer. Ral considers telling them of the Skyfather's voice in her mind, of his demands for the swift destruction of Sien, but swallows the words. It is one thing to hear a rumour that the Stormrider sometimes whispers at the sky; it is another for her to claim that she hears a voice from nowhere.

'Nevertheless, the coincidence is inauspicious,' the bearded maiden asserts, tilting her head and narrowing her eyes. 'We followed the north star, and yet it led south. A journey of days – brutal, hard days – but we arrived to find nearly a month had passed here, since the unfurling of chaos upon the plains.'

'This is a thing we have heard from others,' Ral says. 'Time floods its banks, it seems, and flows in strange directions.'

'Perhaps your power was but the first such overflowing,' the short-haired man says. 'Old boundaries – those that bind time and the stars and define the shapes of beasts – are broken. Why not those that once bound magic?'

'Or those that once bound the gods?' the bearded maiden observes. The others shift uncomfortably, as though this treads near some idea they wish not to discuss. Questions bubble within Ral, but the bearded maiden cuts her off with a smile. 'We must apologise, young Stormrider. We have not shared our names. I am Elsol Url Tabr, herbmistress of the Red Bull band.'

The others mutter and grumble but speak their names, giving Ral the pride of sharing hers last. When the simple ritual is done, Elsol leaps ahead with her next question.

'My fellows may question whether your power is an ill omen or a gift. I know better. No plant is only medicine or poison, a boon or a curse. All depends upon how it is used. We have seen well enough how you have used your magic. To chase the Sienese out of the steppe is a boon to all Girzan, Ral Ans Urrera. For that you deserve our gratitude, and you have it. As you deserve our gratitude for this shelter from the storm of chaos.'

'No,' Ral says. 'For that, you owe the Skyfather thanks. It is no work of mine.'

Another ripple of discomfort passes through the elders. The one-eyed woman – Ka Alsa Allon, huntmaster of the band – mutters a word for fending off evil. Only Elsol retains her placid smile.

'We understand that you intend to wage war in the south,' Elsol continues. 'That this is no mere gathering but a war band. If what you say is true and the Skyfather touches the world again, then it may be he twists the stars themselves to draw the Girzan in and build this host.'

Ral blinks. She has not considered that, assuming the strange position of the stars as being a product of the same chaos that has twisted beasts into terrible nightmares.

Elsol's smile shifts, losing its placidity, becoming the comforting, mournful expression of one who bears tragic news. 'How much did your elders teach you, child, of the Skyfather and when last he touched the world?'

Ral remembers stories of the Skyfather's wrath and the elders burning, in his honour, the stomach, brain, and kidneys of the first kill from any hunt. Remembers, too, the An-Zabati speaking of their own goddess, Naphena, who lost her life to the Skyfather's jealousy. But the sky brings rain as well as wind and lightning, the shade of clouds as well as the blazing sun.

'You would have me afraid,' Ral says simply. 'As you are afraid.'

'How are you not already?' Ka Alsa Allon blurts, pounding a fist on her thigh. 'You would know fear well if you had ridden as we—'

Ral opens her hand and reaches out into the world. A flush of fever burns through her, and a single spark of lightning sizzles from her fingertips, casting the old bones that decorate the tent in stark relief as it arcs to the iron kettle stand and down into the languid coals of the pit fire.

The elders exchange another flurry of frightened glances. Ral shakes her head and lets her shoulders sag in disappointment. 'I would benefit from your wisdom, elders,' she says, 'but I will not be turned from my course. What fear dwelt in me has been burned out. If the Red Bull band will join with mine and ride to war, you are welcome.'

She searches their faces, all but Elsol's now frozen in wrinkled masks of terror. They know now how easily she might have killed them rather than entertain their absurd, tortuous conversation. Their willing cooperation would have been better, but this is not the first time Ral has conjured lightning to cow a prideful, reticent band. Only the bearded maiden does not wear open fear. Her face has hardened, her smile gone, her eyes burning their own coals.

'If you will not fight, stay here,' Ral says. 'Though I doubt this will be a place of safety. The Skyfather, and his protection, will ride with us.'

'These are truly dangerous times,' Elsol says, her voice flat and sharp. 'We will ride with you, Ral Ans Urrera. It seems we have no choice. I only hope you remember that a storm destroys the just and unjust, the deserving and the innocent, alike.'

Ral bows her head once more. 'Then we should drink tea together, that you might learn to trust—'

The rustle of hides thrown hastily aside interrupts her. The elders' eyes go wide at the intrusion as Garam steps backwards into the tent. 'I apologise, elders,' he says, his back still turned. 'There is news the Stormrider should hear, and it cannot wait.'

Elsol flicks her wrist dismissively, though her face remains troubled. 'What is an intrusion upon the elders' tent when compared to the deceit of the stars? Speak your news, man.'

'Sails and kites spotted on the southern horizon,' Garam says. 'The An-Zabati, at last, have come.'

Ral resists the urge to bolt from the tent and run to confirm this news with her own eyes. She does as she ought, instead, and bows to the elders. 'I would still drink tea with you,' she says, 'if you would welcome me back.'

'Go, child.' Elsol all but shoos Ral from the tent. 'Tend to your affairs. I'm sure they are many.'

Ral dips her head once more, then rushes out into the bracing chill of the early evening, Garam at her heels, his quiver rattling. A half-dozen curious watchers already line the ridge at the camp's southern edge. She joins them, shading her eyes. She remembers Atar's promise, her voice bright in anticipation of the vengeance Ral's power made possible. 'I will bring the Waste,' she said. 'Dozens of ships, if not hundreds, and every soul aboard thirsty for Sienese blood.'

The ships are distant still, their angled sails little more than shards of white against the blue sky. Seven ships, Ral counts. This must be the vanguard. More must follow, still too far for the reach of the eye.

A dark blur passes in front of one of those white sails, little more than a speck at this distance but enough to put Ral back on her heels. Then another, darting down to the deck before lifting away, lurching in flight as though weighed down. More of the dark shapes flit around the other ships. Ral's heart aches, heavy as a fist of lead.

'We could ride to them,' Garam says. His jaw works back and forth. Neither he nor Ral has fought the twisted creatures that stalk the plains, but they have heard stories and seen the wounds of those who have. 'A hundred horse, to escort them in.'

It will not be enough, Ral knows. If the windcallers are already overwhelmed, a hasty war party will fare little better.

<You need not worry over them.> The voice thunders within her. <What use will their ships be once you leave these grasslands? What purpose will they serve in the forested hills of the south?>

Ral grinds her teeth. Useful or not, these people saved her. She will not see them destroyed by her storm. Her eye fixes on the shimmering line at the edge of her camp.

'Give them a path,' she whispers. Garam leans close, but she shakes her head and looks to the sky, her voice rising. 'Shield them as you shield us.'

<They are not my people,> the voice answers. <They worship a pactbreaker instead of their rightful gods, who languish. They are as deserving of death as your enemies.>

The words mean nothing to her. 'They broke no pact with me,' she mutters, and turns to Garam. 'Stay here. Watch the line of safety and be ready to lead as many as you can into the Hall.'

Before he can question her – before her mind can begin to doubt – she acts. The sentry answers with only a baffled stare when she demands his horse and is quickly glared into submission and out of his saddle. She fears the young colt will baulk at the shimmering line of the Skyfather's protection, but he surges over it, into the chaos, as though it does not exist. Yet, passing from safety into danger, she feels a pulse of fear, as though some distant predator's eye has locked upon her, watching for its chance to pounce.

A hundred hoofbeats until, from the corner of her eye, she sees the shimmering line shift, snaking beneath her. As the Skyfather enfolds her within his shield, the sense of threat fades.

<Foolish girl,> the voice rumbles. <I should have let them tear a few pieces from you. You could use the lesson.>

Ral twists her mouth but does not speak. The shimmering line races just ahead, only ever a stride quicker than her horse's gait.

The dark shapes that flit around the ships resolve into monstrous birds, many-winged and with snapping maws where beaks should be. Some fall, shrieking, skewered by flights of arrows or darts of conjured wind, yet more always appear from behind the clouds. They dart down, tearing sails and flesh, carrying men and women over the rails and dropping them to tumble and break upon the earth as the ships race on.

The shimmering line sweeps out to encircle the first ship. Like motes of dust carried on the wind, the monstrous birds flee its edge, tumbling through the air in their haste to escape it. Soon, all seven ships are enfolded within the Skyfather's shield. They begin to slow, their hulls and masts creaking as the stress of long and hard-pressed flight eases.

An-Zabati clutch their bows and watch the monstrous birds circle the edge of the Skyfather's protection. A few look down at Ral, murmuring among themselves in confusion. She recognises the third ship, the *Spear of Naphena*, which rescued her from Sienese capture, and rides up alongside it. A familiar bearded face appears, and beside it stands Atar, her shoulders heaving, blood dripping from a bandage that encircles her upper arm.

Ral shows her hand in greeting and catches Atar's eye. The winddancer answers with a grim expression. She has brought her people, but at what cost?

An ember of guilt burns in Ral, but she stamps it out. The world has changed, and it was none of her doing. Together, at least, the An-Zabati and the Girzan might seize the opportunity for revenge. Together, they will carry the storm to the south, to the very palace of the emperor, and scour the stain of him from the world.

5
Captivity

Pinion

The rope chafed Pinion's wrists. Thrice already he had tripped over a root or loose stone and had nearly toppled, unable to throw out an arm to catch himself. Once, his feet had slipped out from under him and he had stumbled a dozen steps before colliding with a tree. Only the threat of summoning another horde of twisted monsters forestalled him from calling lightning to cut away the rope, and with it his Nayeni captors.

Darting Buck – the heavily bearded captain – had laughed aloud at Pinion's humiliation, then threatened to carry him the rest of the way to Eastern Fortress. 'Maybe your people should have learned a spot of woodcraft before invading a bloody forested island, eh?'

The insults meant little. Pinion and Oriole had bandied worse back and forth in childhood behind the backs of their father and their tutors. It was the indignity of it all that dragged Pinion to the edge of idiocy. Worse, Huo, despite his injuries, had yet to stumble once. He walked proudly and as straight-backed as his bound hands allowed, glaring daggers at their captors all the while.

While they marched through the afternoon, following a

deer trail that cut up- and downhill with disorienting randomness, Pinion planned out their arrival at Eastern Fortress. The moment the city wall was in sight, he would free himself and Huo and kill their captors. The Nayeni's sentry lines and defences would have their guard down after the recent capture of the city and there would be gaps large enough, hopefully, for them to slip through unnoticed. Then it would be a matter of hunting rumours and pulling threads until they discerned Wen Alder's location and a means of taking him unawares. Once he was dead . . .

In all likelihood, Pinion and Huo would be captured and killed. The thought did not trouble him, however; only Alder's death mattered now. Perhaps the world would return to normal, the gods fading back into the space between the stars, the twisted beasts chased back into the shadows, and that hanging sphere of blackness above the sea scoured away. He could hope, at least. But that, too, did not matter. Killing Alder was a worthy end in itself, not the means to making a better world, nor even to fulfilling the emperor's will.

Pinion barked a laugh. Darting Buck glared at him, but Pinion only rolled his aching shoulders. Let the Nayeni captain wonder what had so amused his captive for the short while he had left to live.

As twilight like a blot of ink in water darkened the blue of the sky, Darting Buck put up his fist and their small column came to a sudden halt.

'You'll want to keep your eyes on the ground,' Darting Buck said, 'or, better yet, shut them until we're through.'

'Through what?' asked Pinion. Not a dozen paces ahead of them, the undergrowth began to thin and the light seemed brighter, even for early evening. The edge of the forest, then. Soon they would reach the city.

Darting Buck stroked the braid in his beard. 'Even hardened woodsmen have heaved up their guts the first time, and I hear tell witches get it worst of all.'

'What is he saying?' Huo hissed, speaking Sienese.

'He suggests shutting your eyes if you don't want to vomit,' Pinion said.

Huo frowned. 'Some kind of trick? To hide something?'

'Quiet, you two,' Darting Buck snapped. 'Save your words for Hissing Cat. She'll have plenty of questions.'

Pinion matched the Nayeni captain's glare but kept his mouth shut. Huo was surely right: the Nayeni had laid some trap or meant to keep secret the details of their sentry lines. Oriole might have had a better idea of their intent, from the heroic romances and tactics manuals that had obsessed him. Regardless, Pinion had no intention of doing as Darting Buck advised. They could blindfold him if they wanted, but he refused to cooperate. Soon enough, he would burn them all to ash.

'Whatever it is, I'm sure we've weathered worse,' he said.

Darting Buck only shrugged. 'Have it your way,' he said, and led on, but locked eyes with the soldier who followed close behind Pinion, giving some unspoken order.

Here was the moment of highest danger. Pinion would free himself and Huo and dispatch as many of their captors as he could before they reached the denuded field between the forest and the city. Yet if he acted too early, he risked calling down a flock of twisted birds or a pack of monstrous wolves. Readying himself to run – and hoping Huo would have the good sense to follow – he reached out with the phantom limb of his power, towards where memory told him the magic of imperial battle sorcery should be.

Just as he felt the first flush of power and feverish heat down his limbs, it vanished. Like a foot failing to find the next stair, his mind lurched, grasping at emptiness. The sensation was so disorienting that he barely processed the sudden shifting of the world around him. The forest seemed to compress and then unfold. His stomach flopped against his ribs and he went to his knees, gagging and swallowing against his rising gorge, until his gaze fixed on a fern that seemed to bend suddenly at a right angle, as though the world were painted upon a partially folded silkscreen.

He heaved his guts onto the fern and shut his eyes tight.

'Bloody sages,' Huo muttered, sounding queasy himself, though he'd felt only half of the surge of nausea that had afflicted Pinion.

'Warned you, didn't I?' Darting Buck muttered. Rough hands grabbed Pinion beneath the arms and hauled him to his feet. 'We're past it now. Just don't look back the way we've come.'

'What was that?' Pinion asked when his stomach had settled enough to speak. A deeper, more burning question pried at his tongue – *What has happened to my magic?* – but he dared not ask. Likely, Darting Buck would not know. Better to let his captors believe he could still call lightning at a moment's notice and went along with them willingly.

Darting Buck looked back at him, eyebrows up and mouth twisted in a bemused smile. 'Hissing Cat's seal. Keeps things in the city stable. No twisted ones, no strange shimmers, no days passing in a span of hours.' The smile shifted from bemusement into gloating. 'No magic, either. Be grateful. You're safe now.'

Pinion felt a spike of panic. *No!* The Nayeni had to be lying. By rights, his power should have vanished the moment the emperor had disappeared, the moment transmission from the Voices of Eastern Fortress – his father among them – had evaporated like so much mist. Yet he had been able to shield himself, conjure lightning, and call the wind even without the guidance of the canon of sorcery. Surely this was no different. Surely …

He flexed that invisible muscle in the world by which he had navigated the canon, by which he had wielded magic even on his own. He felt the fever of battle sorcery. It surged through him, begging to be unleashed. But as he opened his hands to burn away his bonds, not even a spark lit his fingertip.

'Wait, Buck.' One of the Nayeni escorts – the younger woman who had bantered with Buck during the ambush – tilted her head. 'Don't a few witches still walk the city? Just a few, mind, but ain't that part of why Burning Dog's people have their claim—'

'Gods, Vole, didn't your mother teach you to keep your mouth shut?' Darting Buck snarled. 'What, you think they need some ideas how to escape and where to run, eh? Damn fool of a girl.'

Vole's face turned bright red. She adjusted the arrow nocked to her bowstring and muttered under her breath. Pinion could have wrapped her in his arms and planted a kiss on her filthy, sweat-stained cheek, and to hell with propriety. If that rumour held true, someone in the city still wielded magic. If Pinion could find them and convince them – or force them, unlikely as that may be – to tell him how, he might yet muster enough strength to fight his way to Alder and see justice done.

Darting Buck cut a path that circled wide around the city towards the harbour. Pinion had expected to find the field still foetid with corpses, yet evidence told of a battle fought days ago rather than hours. A few charred divots scarred the earth where chemical grenades had struck, and the abandoned shafts of broken arrows littered the ground. The earth in places still held the black stains of spilled blood, but there was not a body in sight.

No days passing in a span of hours. Darting Buck's words reverberated, now, within Pinion's skull. He swept his gaze across the field, searching for the piles of corpses, the soldiers digging hasty graves. There were a few mounds of fresh-turned earth but not even a single bone, as though the field had not only been cleared but left for scavengers to carry away what remained. Scavengers! Fresh nausea clutched at his stomach. There should have been vultures, crows, ravens, wolves, and wild dogs wandering the field, carrion eaters drawn by an easy feast. Instead, only the occasional raven hopped about, pecking for scraps.

'What madness is this?' Pinion muttered.

'They've hidden the corpses,' Huo replied in whispered Sienese. 'Thrown them into the sea, surely. Not enough time to burn them, even with their witch fire.'

The captain's eyes were wide and wild, his posture rigid as though making ready to flee. He knew battle well, and its aftermath.

'What's he jabbering about?' Darting Buck demanded.

'The bodies,' Pinion answered, hoping Huo was right, that there was a reasonable answer for this latest impossibility. 'He wonders what you did with them.'

'Burned them and buried their bones, of course.' Darting Buck gestured towards the earthen mounds. 'A few days' hard work, that, and dirty.'

'A few days . . .' Mad laughter bubbled like a mountain spring, but Pinion stoppered it.

Darting Buck massaged his shoulders. 'Aye. Last thing we all did together before … well, shouldn't speak of that. And a while's passed since then, to my eye. Wouldn't have left the barrier, but there's a need for hunters—'

'Oh, he tells *me* not to run my mouth,' Vole snarled, 'then jabbers like a merchant looking to sell off shoddy wares. Excellent leadership, Buck.'

Buck put up his hands and grinned. 'That'll show me, eh, young one? We must all watch our lazy tongues when the uncanny sets them to flapping for comfort. Listen here: if you've any more questions, you put them to Hissing Cat and she'll decide what you ought to know. Until then, not another word.'

Pinion shook his head. These rebels were fools, entirely without discipline, yet he had fallen into their hands. He should have fought his way free while he still could have called lightning. The few books of Sienese military doctrine that Pinion had read told that chaos always reigned in a recently conquered city, that the violence of conquest gave way to the unbridled brutality of looting, rape, and petty vengeance, until the conquerors could re-establish order. Eastern Fortress had been conquered by rabble with little discipline, if Darting Buck and this Vole woman were a representative example. The city would still be in tumult, certainly. There must be a way to slip past the walls unnoticed.

Then again, how recently had it truly fallen? At least days. Weeks? More? When had this Hissing Cat woman risen to prominence, high enough that Darting Buck should mention her dozens of times without once naming any rebel leader known to the empire, neither Harrow Fox, Frothing Wolf, nor Wen Alder himself? Such questions sent Pinion's thoughts spiralling again into panic as the Nayeni led him across the empty field.

They rounded the city wall and came to a narrow gate. By Pinion's reckoning, it opened into what had been the imperial garrison. Darting Buck rapped his knuckles in an odd, rhythmic pattern. A hatch in the tower above slid open, then shut, and the gate groaned on its hinges.

'Buck!' A young man appeared in the gateway, clapped Darting Buck on the shoulder, and ushered them into a long, dimly lit tunnel lined with arrow slits. 'We thought one of the twisted beasties had bit your head off by now!'

'Sadly, no. They left that task for you, Newt,' Buck said, his voice echoing from the stone walls and low ceiling. 'But no game, either. Seems whatever deer managed not to get twisted into monsters are keeping themselves scarce.'

The young man – Newt – spat and sucked his teeth, then turned an appraising eye on Pinion. 'Where'd these two come from? Sienese deserters?'

'They say they're from the fleet.' Buck stroked the braid in his beard. 'That is, the fleet that isn't there anymore. Fished 'em out of the surf just before something that was probably a squid at one point got its grip on 'em—'

'Jellyfish, more likely,' Vole said with a sniff. 'Didn't look much like a squid.'

'Didn't look much like anything,' Buck snapped. 'Anyway, this one's a sorcerer.' He jabbed a thumb at Pinion. 'The other one's his bodyguard or some such. Carried a decent enough sword for an officer, and looked to fight well. Taking 'em both to Hissing Cat.'

'A sorcerer?' Newt's appraisal took on a hard, threatening edge, like the gaze of a starving predator. It drifted towards Pinion's bound hands. 'Army of the Wolf still pays a bounty for 'em. Pay in rice and dried meat.'

Buck shook his head sharply. 'They go to Hissing Cat. She's the only one likely to get us out of this bloody mess.'

Newt's gaze lingered on Pinion while he led them, walking backwards, towards a closed door outlined in dwindling sunlight. Pinion met his stare, trying to project his displeasure at being reduced to a bargaining token. 'True, true, but stores run low. They've got us on half rations now. Harrow Fox woulda made the trade, I wager. Doubt Hissing Cat'd mind a few extra measures of fodder in the—'

'That's as may be,' Buck said firmly, 'but I leave that decision to her.'

Another mention of this Hissing Cat woman, who by the

sound of things had replaced Alder as the rebellion's leader, or perhaps led a faction of her own.

'Of course.' Newt dipped his head, then threw open the door, which led into a walled courtyard, as broad as any public square and tiled in plain ceramic. Several dozen tents stood along the walls, where men and women lounged in their armour with weapons near to hand. A squadron drilled with spears, working through compressed formations, practising advancing through a winding channel of dowels laid flat on the ground. A simulation of city streets, Pinion realised.

'Is the fighting in the city not ended?' Pinion wondered aloud.

'You're worse than she is,' Buck snarled, pointing his chin at Vole. 'I said to save your questions, didn't I?'

Curious eyes in gaunt, haggard faces followed them on their way across the yard. Pinion took note of the watery cookpots and spitted rats hanging over their fires. If things were as bad as this, perhaps the rebellion had collapsed into infighting for want of food. But the thought felt wrong. The city's granaries should have been well stocked in preparation for a siege. How much time had passed here, in the few hours since the gods' arrival and the destruction of the fleet, that they were nearly emptied? Buck had said weeks, with no mention of how many.

Despite its victory, the Nayeni rebellion was in a sorry state, a fact that evoked neither sympathy nor disdain in Pinion. These were no innocents, like those slaughtered before the gates of Setting Sun Fortress, but soldiers who had followed Wen Alder and taken up arms for him, plunging their homeland into chaos. The commoners in the street might evoke his pity, but not these, who were as guilty as the most brutal imperial official.

Except there were no commoners to be seen. Darting Buck led their party from the garrison yard out into abandoned streets. Market stalls stood empty and hasty barricades and boards covered most doorways and windows, as though every home and craftsman's workshop had become a fortress unto itself. A frightened pair of eyes watched from a second-floor window, then vanished the moment Pinion caught sight of them. Darting Buck kept them to the edge of the street, moving through alleys whenever their route allowed, and Vole and the other archers kept careful watch on the rooftops, arrows nocked to their bowstrings.

Pinion had never lived through the aftermath of a siege, but Eastern Fortress seemed less gripped by the aftershocks of battle than it was by fear of present danger. That Darting Buck had been so violently reluctant to speak of the city's present troubles only cemented that impression. The question, then, was how to use that danger to his own advantage.

Pinion's train of thought was brought to an abrupt and jarring halt as they rounded a bend to find, jutting above the central square, the blackened, broken wall of his father's estate. A hollow opened up in his stomach. Flames had scoured the white and red paint, leaving soot-stained scars. That gate itself still stood, though hammers and rams had left splintered scars on the bronze-banded planks. Above, behind the blackened crenellations, Nayeni archers surveyed the city streets.

Again, Darting Buck rapped his fist on the gate, summoning a guard to open a hatch before the gate swung open, just wide enough this time to admit their party single file.

The hollow in Pinion's stomach deepened and twisted as they entered the courtyard garden. Every stand of bamboo had been cut – for spear shafts and to bolster barricades, he reasoned, but also to create an open killing field between the gatehouse and the reception hall. There, at the top of the marble stair, a pair of iron-banded ballistae fitted with cups for hurling grenades had replaced his father's ornate sculptures of lion serpents. Even the pavilions had been put to martial use. Some of the harvested bamboo had gone to fit walled platforms to the pavilion roofs, where lone archers held position. The estate – his childhood home – had become a fortress.

Worse, the fortress of his father's and brother's killers.

That thought took the strength from him, and he collapsed to his knees. The last time he had walked these paths, mounted that stair, visited that reception hall to answer his father's summons, he had left the bonds between them frayed, if not eroded completely. That rift between them could now never be healed. The raw wound it had left would bleed him, and bleed him his every remaining day.

Could he lay that wound, too, at Alder's feet?

'You Sienese put that much stake in your gardens, eh?' Darting Buck said, prodding Pinion with the end of his bow. 'Get up. You can mewl and whine once I'm through with carting you around.'

Pinion let out another slow breath while Darting Buck growled, jabbing with his bow as though Pinion were a stubborn mule instead of a man whose world had been upended. He glared at the Nayeni captain, hauled himself to his feet, and carried on. Huo watched with a subtle nod and an approving look, then went back to studying their surroundings – committing the Nayeni defences to memory, Pinion assumed, for when the time came to escape, either by sneaking past sentry lines or fighting their way free.

Relief eased the pit in Pinion's stomach as they skirted around the reception hall and towards the inner courtyard. The destruction of the inner garden was less obvious, though many trees and stands of bamboo had been reduced to stumps and jagged shoots. No carp swam in the pond – likely they had all been fished to supplement the rebels' diet – and no kingfishers darted from the porous stone. The stone itself was a stabilising presence, something solid left behind from Pinion's earliest memories, though all the rest lay in tatters. But such relief lasted only until Pinion saw what had become of Oriole's plum tree.

Fractal scars of flaking ash as thin as ribbons ran up the length of the young tree. The heat and wind of conjured fire had torn away its late-winter petals, leaving the branches naked and skeletal. A few bricks of Oriole's grave gate yet stood on the face of the hill, but most lay shattered and charred.

An old woman sat beneath the blackened branches with an array of cracked shoulder blades spread out before her like pieces on a Stones board. She glared up at a short man dressed in simple robes, the wild curls of his hair held at the nape of his neck by a leather thong.

'She does realise that, without me, the madness that circles this city will claim it?' the old woman snarled. 'If not, then bloody well *make* her understand.'

The wild-haired man planted his hands on his hips and heaved a sigh. 'I almost think she would prefer that. It would give her the chance to flush the Sienese holdouts from the inner city, at least.'

Pinion gaped at that voice. He knew it, though he had last heard it speaking Sienese, and with a far more servile tone.

'Stupid girl.' The old woman scowled and shook her head, rattling the dozen ravens' skulls threaded through the grey cloud of her hair. 'She understands nothing, and – worse – would rather let us all starve than admit I can't give her what she wants. The only reason the Sienese haven't boiled out from their holdfast and ground her to paste is because they know we'd march straight up their arses if they tried it. You tell her that, boy.'

'And what should I tell the Sienese?'

The old woman harrumphed. 'The same. We'll see how stubborn they are when unwoven wolves come howling through their streets.'

The wild-haired man – Clear-River, once the magistrate of the small town of Burrow, a fact that beggared belief – nodded sharply and let his arms fall slack. 'People are starving. We need their grain, Hissing Cat, and they don't respond well to threats.'

'Only because they don't understand them,' Hissing Cat snapped. 'I've lived through this before, and I intend to live through it again. Out of the kindness of my dusty, withered heart, I mean to keep as many of you alive as I can, but I've no patience for all this idiocy, Clear-River. Tell them *that*.'

Clear-River shook his head. 'Very well, Hissing Cat. Do you care to hear their reactions, or is there any point? You've one cudgel and you seem determined to crack it over all our heads.'

This, then, was the new leader of the rebellion, this old, cantankerous woman with skulls threaded through her hair.

Hissing Cat glared up at Clear-River, then waved him away. With a defeated sigh, Clear-River took something from the pocket of his robe. Cramps seized Pinion's calves and shoulders, and with them came the familiar – and impossible – rush of sensation in the wake of magic. Sharp colour, bright sound, the furious texture of his salt-stained robe scraping his back and shoulders. In a swell of cinnamon scent, Clear-River transformed into an eagle hawk and darted over the garden wall. Hissing Cat watched him go, her expression sour, before finally turning her hard gaze on Pinion.

'Who the hell are you?' she snarled. 'I asked for a meal. We're not at the point of eating our prisoners yet, I hope.'

Stunned into silence, Pinion only stared back at her.

Darting Buck gave a wry chuckle. 'Not yet, lady, no. These two are Sienese. The only survivors to wash up as yet from the fleet.' He went on, relating the brief battle with the twisted creatures on the beach and their march through the forest, but his words were only an incoherent buzzing in Pinion's ear. Clear-River had wielded magic, though he was no sorcerer, nor a witch. Not unless he had been made one in the half-dozen months since Pinion had left him at Burrow.

Again, Pinion reached out into the pattern of the world, hoping that something had changed, that his power had returned. Still, no matter how he drew on his power, no matter how the feverish wake filled him, he found the well of battle sorcery as dry as it had been since crossing the uncanny barrier in the forest.

Yet, though Pinion could not, Clear-River had wielded magic, and this Hissing Cat woman – more obviously a witch than any person Pinion had ever encountered – had seemed unnerved by his veering.

'I'm too tired for a bloody interrogation,' Hissing Cat snarled. 'Take them to a cell. Do you know what weeks without sleep does to a person, Buck?'

'Nothing good, I'd wager,' Darting Buck conceded.

'No.' Hissing Cat's voice took on a flattened edge. 'Nothing good. Now get the hell out of here.'

Darting Buck snapped a salute and led their small company towards the back of the garden. Pinion followed in a daze. He and Huo were deposited into the same room, a narrow cell once meant for a servant, now with its windows and door reinforced with bamboo bars. Darting Buck snapped shackles around their wrists, then tugged on the chains that bound them to the wall.

Darting Buck fixed them with one last, lingering stare. 'Would rather have caught a deer or a brace of rabbits,' he muttered, then shut the wooden door. A sharp *click* announced a bolt sliding home.

'Well?' Huo whispered when Darting Buck and his party's footsteps had faded. 'A bit of lightning should melt through these chains before too long. What are you waiting for?'

Pinion tamped down annoyance. The captain was no sorcerer. His ignorance was not his fault. 'I can't,' he said. 'Something in this city – something that woman Hissing Cat is doing, I'm sure – keeps me from conjuring as much as a spark.'

Huo shook his head. 'But that half-breed traitorous bastard turned into a bird not ten feet from us.'

Pinion nodded slowly. 'A question without an answer.'

Huo slumped in frustration, then began casting about the room, surveying their pitiful furnishings. A pair of threadbare pallets. An earthenware chamber pot in the far corner of the room, reeking of foetid waste. Huo tugged on the chain that bound his ankle to the wall and studied the iron fixture, held to the brick by four heavy bolts. Dust trickled from a gap between the fixture and the wall as he prodded at it, trying to force the tip of his finger into the opening, then scowled. 'Then we'll have to find another way,' he muttered and crawled across the room towards the chamber pot. 'Terracotta. Hopefully not too thin. If they ask, we got into an argument and I threw this at your head.'

Pinion yelped in surprise as the pot shattered against the floor, but soon understood the captain's intention and set to work gathering up reeking shards of pottery, despite the stench, despite the nausea that churned in his stomach when his fingers brushed against unspeakable slime. What was a little disgust when measured against a chance at revenge?

6

The Gates of Sor Cala

Koro Ha

The harbour of Sor Cala overflowed with ships bearing port flags from cities up and down the Sienese coast that hung limply in the still air of mid-morning. The Sienese would have a hard time picking the *Swiftness* out from the crowd, if the hunt for a single smuggler's ship occupied them at all.

On Yin Ila's order, they dropped anchor just within the southern arm of the bay, far from the vessels that clustered like frightened hens near the docks. Only she, Koro Ha, and a hand-selected group of ten sailors went ashore in a longboat – the only one they had left after abandoning the other in their haste to be away from the Black Maw and, with it, Uon Elia's corpse.

They rowed along the shoreline until they were out of sight of the city, then put in on a secluded beach. Koro Ha clung to the gunwales while Yin Ila and her sailors leapt into the surf and dragged the boat, scraping and rocking, onto the gravelled shore.

Yin Ila offered him a hand and a salty grin. 'If you're to be a man of the sea,' she said, 'you'll need a sturdy pair of trousers rather than that stupid robe. I can have the quartermaster sew you some.'

Koro Ha grunted, took her hand, and hopped down, holding the hem of his garment above his knees. He had to brace himself against the gunwale for a moment while his wobbly legs adjusted to land, but he could have wept. Not a jagged island in the mouth of a slumbering beast, nor the deck of a swaying ship, but solid ground, sturdy and constant. 'No, thank you,' he said. 'If I had my way, I'd never set foot on deck again.'

Yin Ila laughed. 'Planning to take Uon Elia's place in those catacombs, are you?'

'Only to find whatever secrets he left behind,' Koro Ha said flatly. 'I hold some power, but not nearly enough understanding to survive as he did.'

Uon Elia had taught him two of Toa Alon's three powers: dowsing, which allowed him to sense the presence of a desired object so long as he had access to its like, and healing. His only lesson in cultivation, the magic that had been the source of Toa Alon's prosperity and the means by which the stonespeakers fed themselves while buried beneath the earth, had been upon the sea, when Uon Elia sped and shaped the growth of a patch of seaweed to grapple with a Sienese ship and slow its chase.

'Either way, we'll have to break into Orna Sin's old garden,' Yin Ila said. 'No easy task, I should think. Though not as difficult as springing Orna Sin from a Sienese dungeon. First thing, of course, will be making it into the city without alerting the Sienese.'

Yin Ila and half of her sailors unpacked and distributed chests of tools and supplies, among them barbed, broad-bladed knives, while she sent the other half inland to scout their route into Sor Cala. Koro Ha, yet again, found himself with little to do, having no experience in preparing for subterfuge and impending violence. When Yin Ila offered him a knife, he gently pushed it away.

'You may need to defend yourself, tutor,' she said, bemused.

He prickled at her words. 'Perhaps, Captain,' he said, 'but I doubt I would fare any better in a knife fight than you would in a poetry contest. As useful to put that in my hand as a brush in yours.'

A flicker of offence touched her face, then she barked a laugh and tucked the blade into the top of her boot. 'Fair enough. If we've a need to talk our way past the bastards, I'll leave it to you, and if there's a need to stab 'em, you leave it to me. The beginnings of a grand partnership.'

'I suppose it is.' Koro Ha returned her grin, though his stomach turned at the thought of being involved in any stabbing, whether directly or only as an accomplice. But what did he expect? That a well-phrased petition would see Orna Sin set free and his garden restored? That the Sienese would simply give them access to the tunnels beneath Sor Cala, where the secrets of the stonespeakers waited? He had learned better than that by now. Yet knives still made him uneasy, and the thought of killing burned like a coal in his mind.

Late afternoon had filled the forest with sweltering heat by the time the sailors sent to scout had returned. They told of a river of travellers on the road into Sor Cala. Entire towns and villages had emptied themselves, it seemed. Most had fled rumours of monstrous beasts in the woods and valleys, while a few who remained told tales of wolves stepping out of shadows or neighbours howling and tearing each other apart. Sor Cala, they all said, was the only place of safety, where the Sienese had found a way to keep the monsters from the gates.

Yin Ila scratched her chin thoughtfully. 'Assuming the Sienese welcome this lot, we'll have an easy enough time slipping into the city in their company.'

Koro Ha shuddered. 'If these stories they tell are true, they can't be the first wave of refugees. Weeks have passed since we left the Black Maw.' The memory of that island rearing up and walking across the floor of the sea had been enough to silence any doubt in him at the villagers' tales. 'The city must be as full as the harbour by now.'

'An unenviable situation, for empire and refugee alike,' Yin Ila mused. 'For us, though, an advantage. An overcrowded city means crime, which means the Sienese will be well occupied.'

'And on higher alert, surely,' Koro Ha said.

Yin Ila showed a golden tooth. 'Oh, aye, tutor, but once Orna Sin is free of their dungeon, it'll be far simpler to spirit him away.'

Koro Ha did not raise the question of whether Orna Sin yet lived. He saw that same fear in Yin Ila's eye, despite all her effort to mask it beneath bravado.

'At any rate, the first step will be easier,' Yin Ila went on, taking the gold studs from her ears as she led the way north through the forest towards the road. 'Hunch your shoulders, tutor, and slacken your jaw like you've been walking for a few sleepless days.'

Before they reached the road, Koro Ha heard the low murmur of voices, the exhausted wails of children, the creak of over-loaded cart wheels, and the arrhythmic scrape of countless feet on the cobbles. Toa Alon's roads cut through the forest, with low walls of stone keeping the undergrowth at bay, and Koro Ha had to lean on one such wall and gape at the seemingly endless stream of humanity crawling by.

The crowd packed itself tightly, hundreds of people at a glance huddled in a slow-flowing stream of refugees more willing to rub elbows with strangers than stand within arm's reach of the forest shadows. And that was only a quick estimate, on this stretch of road. The line continued backwards and forwards without thinning, certainly unto the gates of Sor Cala, and judging by the exhaustion in the bent bodies with leaden limbs passing him by it likely stretched into the forested hinterlands for leagues. More people, packed more tightly together, than Koro Ha could fully comprehend. The nearest thing he'd seen to such a spectacle had been on the day of his imperial examinations, when thousands of young men from across the southern reaches of the empire had gathered, but that gathering had been as much anxious as hopeful, full of energy and excitement at the possibilities that awaited them. Such traits were missing from this sad trail of huddled refugees carrying the long-burning terror of recent trauma, evidenced by the stained bandages, limping gaits, carts and stretchers bearing the sick and wounded, and the vacant gazes of countless haunted eyes.

Koro Ha's heart broke at the sight of them. These were his people – his responsibility, now, as their last stonespeaker. Even knowing that the time was not yet right, he longed to reveal himself, to offer them what comfort he could, yet he knew that even healing a festering wound or lending strength to a flagging, exhausted child would put everything Uon Elia had entrusted to him at risk.

A few stared as Yin Ila led Koro Ha and her sailors over the wall to join the stream of bodies, but no one paid them any mind once it became clear they were, like all the rest, only ordinary travellers making their way to Sor Cala. These people were too weary to wonder where a few newcomers hailed from, or why one of their number wore faded scholar's robes rather than the baggy trousers and jerkin of a Toa Aloni commoner. The next step forwards was all that mattered, forcing a tired body on towards the promise of safety.

The column began to slow as they rounded a bend and came in view of the gate – an archway of marble blocks carved with the intricate knotwork that was Toa Alon's writing and greatest art form. The first time Koro Ha had seen the gate, he had been able to read only a few snatched phrases. Now, after Uon Elia's tutelage, he marvelled not only at the scale and splendour of the construction but at the depth of poetry written in the carvings: an intertwining blessing for comings and goings, a welcome and a parting wish, a declaration of peace within and without the walls.

That final benediction had been made false a generation ago, when the empire had conquered the city and turned its public gardens and temples into estates and palaces. If the Sienese understood that writing well enough to read it, they would have destroyed the gate and replaced it with one of their own, carved with lion serpents and other symbols of their power. Instead, only a pair of red banners stitched in golden thread with the imperial tetragram – the four logograms that formed the emperor's never-changing name – hung from the lintel of the gate, draped over the heads of all who passed through.

'Don't like the look of *that*,' Yin Ila muttered.

Koro Ha followed the line of her gaze to see several ranks of soldiers with spears and crossbows to hand flanking the gates, admitting refugees a few at a time. Near them, a trio of figures wearing the caps and long hair of Sienese scholars worked a collection of merchants' scales. A family stepped forwards and offered up one of the bundles they carried. The scholars fussed over the contents of the sack, then selected one of several weights. They poured grain from the sack into the wide bowl of one of the scales, placing the weight in the opposite bowl, until the two hung even. Only then did they return the sack to the refugees and motion for the soldiers to let them through.

'A gate tax,' Koro Ha said. 'Which makes a cruel measure of sense. There will be no produce coming into the city for some time if the countryside has been emptied.'

Yin Ila swore under her breath and began fishing in her pockets for the studs, rings, and other jewellery she had stashed away. 'All right, lads. Hand over whatever you're wearing.'

The sailors grumbled but did as ordered. One of the men removed his coat to make a bundle that soon bulged with all manner of trinkets. Yin Ila cocked her head at Koro Ha. 'It wouldn't be too much to hope you've got a few taels' worth of valuables stashed about your person, would it?'

Koro Ha shook his head, which prompted a grumble and another round of donations from the sailors to cover him. It felt foolish, but he promised them all he would pay them back as soon as he was able. His assurances were met with steady, cynical glares.

Twilight had crept over the forest by the time their turn came at the gate. Koro Ha hesitated at the back of their party, afraid that his robes might be recognised and prompt unwanted questions. Yin Ila stepped forwards to offer up their bundle of trinkets to the tax assessor.

The assessor glared up at her over the glint of gold and silver. 'Taxes must be paid in foodstuffs, livestock, or textiles,' he said in clipped, heavily accented Toa Aloni.

Yin Ila stared in disbelief. 'This must be worth twenty times what you lot took from that couple who just passed through, and there are only twelve of us!'

'Worth?' The assessor coughed a laugh. 'A month ago, perhaps. Now, nothing is more valuable in Sor Cala than grain. Step out of the way.'

Yin Ila's eye twitched and her mouth flattened into a rigid, furious line. Koro Ha feared she might twist the bundle up until the baubles made a heavy mass and bludgeon the assessor with it, guards or no guards.

'Fine, then. We'll be back with grain,' she snarled through her teeth and led their party away, back down the column and off to the side.

'Best hurry!' the assessor called after them. 'The gates close at nightfall!'

Koro Ha had only a moment to note the horror of that sentence – at the prospect of hundreds of refugees left to camp overnight within sight of the walls, braving the horrors they had fled, many of them too impoverished to pay their way past the gates – before dread at their own predicament overshadowed it. There was no telling what violence might descend upon the column in the darkness of night, whether brought by monsters or by desperate men.

'Don't fret, tutor,' Yin Ila said, her voice harsh, still fuming from her conversation with the assessor. 'We'll send the boat back to the *Swiftness.* Our stores are running low, but there'll be no hope of resupply at all if we can't get into the city.'

Koro Ha gestured to the darkening sky. 'You want to brave the forest at night? After hearing what hounded these people?'

She shrugged, her eye twitching again, while the sailors redistributed their gold and silver, with more than one sigh of relief. 'Want's got nothing to do with it. I don't see another choice. If these trinkets won't buy passage through the gate, they likely won't buy much beyond it. Which means they'll be little use to desperate farmers fleeing their homes. And say we did talk some poor, uninformed idiot into trading his grain, and with it his life. What might he do when he realises we've tricked him? You'd best hope we're through the gates before he does.'

Koro Ha did not point out that they had all been just such idiots only moments ago. At any rate, he had no desire to take food or hope for passage through the gate from any of the refugees.

'Don't you have smuggling routes into the city?' he ventured.

'If by "smuggling routes" you mean a handful of paid-off officials who didn't look too closely while we unloaded the *Swiftness*, then yes,' Yin Ila said.

Koro Ha's dread threatened to collapse into despair. At least Yin Ila and her sailors had their knives, whatever good they might do against monstrous wolves and all the other nightmares that kept the refugees from the forest's edge.

'Wait a bloody second,' Yin Ila whispered. She leaned close and jabbed a finger at Koro Ha's bottom lip. 'Bloody hell, that mark's too well hidden. I always forget you're a blasted stonespeaker. They made gardens to feed everyone in the city in their day! You can magic us up enough to pay a few taxes, can't you?'

Koro Ha ran his tongue over his gums, feeling the slight ridge of the blue-green mark Orna Sin had tattooed there. His face warmed with embarrassment. 'I never really learned how,' he said softly.

'Well, can you bloody *try?*' Yin Ila snarled. 'Else we'll need to spend the night on a hike neither of us is particularly looking forward to.'

'I can't conjure food from nothing,' Koro Ha snapped back. He knew that much. The one time he had witnessed Orna Sin wield cultivation, it had been to accelerate and shape the growth of plants that already grew on the sea floor. 'We'll need to find something growing wild, or some seed.'

Yin Ila snapped her fingers with a jubilant grin, like she'd just found a bit of gold in her bowl of congee. She spun around to face her sailors. 'The lot of you, go offer those farmers a handful of gold for a handful of seed. Not enough to cost them their passage into the city, mind. We shouldn't need much.'

'It needs to be *seed!*' Koro Ha called to them as they turned to go. 'Not grain for eating, grain for planting!'

Nervousness rattled through him while they waited for the sailors to return. This plan was much more dangerous than smuggling, and they were carrying it out within only a few hundred paces of a company of Sienese soldiers. If they discovered that he was a stonespeaker – the *last* stonespeaker, in fact – well … he preferred not to think of what would certainly happen, regardless of Yin Ila and her knives.

Before long, the sailors began to trickle back. Most returned empty handed, the refugees evidently having a good sense of what awaited them in Sor Cala. One brought a handful of rice, which would prove entirely useless; Koro Ha was no farmer, but he had read enough picturesque tales of rural life to know that rice had to be planted in a paddy and required enormous quantities of water to thrive. Another brought dried beans – also useless. Koro Ha had all but given up hope until one sailor, a young woman, returned with a single yam that had grown a dozen thin sprouts from one end.

'My mother kept a garden,' the young sailor said. 'She used to keep one yam back every harvest. Once it grew slips like this, you could plant them and—'

'You know how to use that to grow more?' Yin Ila prodded.

The young woman nodded, measuring the sprouts with her eye. 'We just need a patch of dirt. Better if we had some mulch, but—'

'Very good, Goa Eln, but you don't need to teach me how to grow a bloody yam,' Yin Ila muttered. 'Come along. You set the stage and let the tutor here work his magic.'

Koro Ha winced, wondering if the guards were close enough to hear, and followed Yin Ila and her sailors back into the forest. The shadows were longer and deeper now that the sun was beginning to set, and a thin trickle of fear worked its way down his spine while the young sailor, Goa Eln, found a likely plot of dirt without too many tree roots and began digging with her knife. After she had dug a hole half a handspan deep, she cut away one of the sprouts and a chunk of yam with it, then buried the chunk of yam like a seed with the sprout jutting just above the surface of the soil. Goa Eln went on until all twelve shoots had been planted, then stood back, surveying her work with a frown.

'Been years since I've done that,' she murmured. 'Almost

makes me think of leaving the sea.' She wiped the dirt from her knife and made it disappear somewhere up her coat sleeve. 'Almost.'

'Your turn, tutor,' Yin Ila said. 'Let's pay our bloody tax already.'

Koro Ha knelt over the sprouts, trying to recall what Uon Elia had done. The magic had carried a deep, vital feeling, like the first time his skin had brushed a fellow student's hand, sending shivers of delight and sublime fear down to his bones. The rush of too many cups of tea surging in his blood while he frantically hammered the classics into his skull in the weeks before his examinations. Feelings of maturity, of growth, of the sudden awareness, in early adolescence, that he was no longer and would never again be a child.

He reached out into the world, gathering that feeling in, embracing it, transferring it, through his hands and the soil, into the shoots. A shiver worked through him, settled in his ribs, and *pulled.* Strength seeped out of him, leaving his limbs leaden. With a gasp he recoiled, releasing the magic, blinking against a dizziness from nowhere. Something soft, like limp feathers, brushed against his hands.

'Bleed me!' Yin Ila murmured. 'I saw what Orna Sin managed with seaweed, but that was in the dark and during a storm. Seeing it up close and personal is … well, still bloody difficult to believe.'

Koro Ha opened his eyes, reeling from sudden exhaustion. The thin shoots had unfurled and burst into life, becoming a thicket of fern-like greens. Goa Eln, her hand shaking, dug up a yam as wide around as her forearm and twice the length of her hand – and then another, bound to it by thin yellow roots. And another. In all, one shoot had become seven hearty yams – enough to feed a family.

Yin Ila thumped Koro Ha on the back while the other sailors

set about digging up the rest of the yams. One took off his coat to make a bundle, grumbling about the dirt.

'Well done, tutor,' Yin Ila said. 'And here you thought—'

A snapping twig interrupted her, followed by a low, throaty growl. Yin Ila whirled to face the threat, knives appearing in her hands. Fear darted through Koro Ha's limbs, already exhausted by the magic of cultivation. A strange mirage captured his eye, seeming to blend the undergrowth and the earth and roots, till he could hardly pry them apart. Behind it, a shadow moved in the twilight between the trees.

'Get back to the road!' Yin Ila shouted. Her left arm snapped out and her knife flashed through the air. A guttural voice howled in pain, terribly human, as Yin Ila grabbed Koro Ha beneath the shoulder and dragged him to his feet. '*Run*, tutor!'

A shadow burst from the undergrowth, unfolding into a dark feline shape with spindly limbs and burning eyes. It pulled one of the sailors screaming to the ground. Blood sprayed against the green of the forest. Goa Eln appeared beside them, her knife dripping something thick and black, a gash on her forehead spilling blood into her eye.

The forest gave way to the road and the staring eyes of terrified refugees, most murmuring frantic questions. Some surged towards the gates with sudden shouts, fleeing from the terror that had chased them from their homes.

'Fuck!' Yin Ila spat, casting about herself. 'Where are the rest?'

Goa Eln shook her head, then winced and patted at her wounded brow with the back of her hand. 'I saw An Sala with his throat open. Rik Petr tackled the one that caught me with a claw, the bloody lunatic.' She shuddered. 'Can't speak for the others.'

A fresh chorus of screams erupted from further down the column. Everyone was running now, pushing and shoving, leaving carts and bundles behind.

'Where did they all come from?' Koro Ha wondered aloud. 'And what *are* they?' The shadowy beasts were not, to his eye, anything like the monster of jagged stone that had been the Black Maw.

'Does it matter?' Yin Ila drew the knife she had stashed in her boot. 'They're here now, and if we don't get on the other side of those walls, they'll rip us apart. Come on!'

'The others?' Goa Eln cast a glance backwards.

Yin Ila only grunted in answer, then elbowed her way through the panicking crowd. What had been a column had become a jostling press as the refugees, shouting for help, pushed towards the city. Koro Ha clawed his way forwards, following her, the shock of the monster's sudden appearance blossoming into desperate, thought-annihilating terror. Somewhere deep in his mind he knew that pushing past an elderly couple clinging to each other, or the father desperately carrying his child, or the young siblings calling for their mother, was as good as condemning them to a bloody fate – the gates would close soon, and only those few nearest the front would make it through – yet his panic overrode his guilt as he dug his way through the throng. There would be time enough for shame later, if he survived.

'Order!' the Sienese assessor roared. 'Yes, night is falling, but one more night on the road is far better than a spear through the belly, which is what you lot will earn if this riot keeps up! Order, I say!'

The company of Sienese guards held the shafts of their spears across their bodies, shoving the crowd back as it surged in desperation, a hundred voices all shouting for the assessor to let them through, howling incoherent warnings of the beasts from between the trees. To which the assessor answered with only another call for order and a sharp command. A rank of crossbowmen levelled their weapons.

The crowd surged backwards. Someone's elbow caught Koro

Ha in the stomach and he doubled over with a grunt. Another heavy body shoved past him, knocking him to the ground. Darkness swallowed him, the sun little more than glimmers of light through the press of flesh. A foot clipped the side of his head. Someone stepped on his calf, crushing muscle against bone like dough under a rolling pin. He shouted in terror and pain, his palms scraping the tiled road as he tried to push himself to his feet.

A hand found his elbow and hauled him upright. 'Stay up, tutor!' Yin Ila shouted in his face. He gritted his teeth as he found his footing, leaning on her as he tested his leg, hoping it was not broken.

'To hell with this,' Yin Ila snarled. She raised her elbows, shoving aside the people around her, and readied her knives. 'I'll put a blade through that assessor's eye. It'll spark a bloody riot, but as I see it we've no better chance to slip through.'

'Wait!' Koro Ha grabbed her elbow. 'You'll get all of these people killed!'

'And us with them, otherwise.' Yin Ila jerked her arm away. 'You've got a better idea, tutor? Tutor? What are you—'

Her voice faded into the roar of the crowd as Koro Ha began shoving his way to the front of the mob. He squeezed between sweat-drenched bodies, using his elbow as a wedge, keeping his feet planted, each sidling step sending a fresh wave of pain up his trampled leg. The cries of the crowd became the roar of a storm at sea, drowning out his thoughts even as he tried to collect them. The assessor had backed up behind the wall of spears, his twitching fingers signalling that he was on the edge of panic.

'Honoured sir!' Koro Ha called, casting his voice into the high formality of Sienese scholarship. 'Honoured sir!'

The assessor only stared wide-eyed at the crowd simmering on the edge of a riot. Koro Ha gritted his teeth and surged forwards, dragging himself past an old, emaciated man and a wailing child until he was at the front of the crowd. The nearest soldier shouted and shoved his spear shaft against Koro Ha's chest. Koro Ha rocked back on his injured leg to keep his balance and bit his tongue to keep from screaming.

'Honoured sir!' he howled again in pain and desperation.

At last, the assessor met his gaze. Hope burned through Koro Ha, nearly striking his mind of the argument he had meant to make.

'What is a public servant's duty to the citizenry of the empire?' Koro Ha shouted.

The assessor worked his mouth, as though chewing on his own confusion.

'It is a simple question!' Koro Ha fought to make his voice even. Stately. Like a proctor hearing an oral examination. 'Surely you answered its like to earn your commission, or have years of self-indulgence in your ministerial post emptied your mind of doctrine?'

'What is the meaning of this?' the assessor snapped. 'Who are you?'

'A scholar of the first degree,' Koro Ha snapped back. 'Now answer the question!'

A ragged, monstrous voice howled behind Koro Ha, but he kept his face forwards, watching the assessor's eyes bulge. Everything depended upon this man's sense of duty and how it weighed against his fear.

'If you are who you say you are, what are you doing with this rabble?' the assessor shouted. 'Get back! All of you!' He made a gesture and shouted an order. The front line of soldiers levelled their spears, prodding at the press of refugees, who stumbled backwards. A spear point hovered dangerously near Koro Ha's chest and he fought to keep his gaze away from it. Either he would win this argument or he would die anyway, either crushed by the frantic crowd or torn apart by monsters. Around him, shouts of desperation became howls of outrage. Farmers hefted sickles and spades. Young men reached for stones.

'Ought an elder brother leave his younger siblings to face terror and death alone?' Koro Ha shouted over the din and the thunder of his heart in his ears. 'Or, worse yet, ought he to slaughter those who depend upon his grace? You know the answer, honoured sir. You are a minister of the Sienese Empire, a master of the Classic of Living and Dying. You know every word written by Traveller-on-the-Narrow-Way. Do what you know must be done, else shame yourself and the doctrine you swore to uphold.'

The assessor stared over Koro Ha's shoulder at the horror consuming the column and his face blanched. His lip quivered and his hand rose, teetering on the edge of some fateful order. His chest swelled with a deep, steadying breath.

'Form columns to either side of the road!' he ordered. 'Protect the citizenry! Keep the gates open as long as you can, for as many as you can!'

The soldiers hesitated, their expectations clashing with their orders.

'Do it!' the assessor roared. 'In the emperor's name!'

Slowly, the spearmen moved forwards, opening the way into the city. Koro Ha did not wait to observe their battle with the monsters but rode the tide of bodies through the marble gates. The gateway opened into a broad plaza, where the crowd split and began to flow into the city streets. Koro Ha cut across the current, wincing with every step, and took shelter in a narrow alleyway. He sat on an empty barrel, stretched out his aching leg, and watched the crowd, hoping for a glimpse of Yin Ila, Goa Eln, or one of the others, his stomach knotted around the terrible thought that they had been too far from the gates to make it to safety.

At last he spotted Goa Eln, her short curls slicked with sweat and blood, and behind her Yin Ila. He waved and shouted, eventually drawing their attention.

'That's twice in one day you've managed to surprise me, tutor,' Yin Ila said when she reached the alleyway. She walked with a limp and held one arm across her body. 'Though I'd like to remind you our goal was to enter the city *without* being noticed. Now let's get somewhere I can lie the hell down before I pass out.'

'What of the others?' Surely Yin Ila had not seen them all taken by the beasts?

She only grunted. 'If they made it through, they'll know where to find me. Now come on. That bit about passing out wasn't half a joke.'

Koro Ha looked once more to the gates, where howls of pain spoke of the desperate fight still raging beyond. The urge rose in him to go to them, to heal the wounded passing through, as a stonespeaker ought, but he knew that the gesture, however it might ease a bit of suffering and balm his soul, would only see him captured by the Sienese and the last bastion of Toa Aloni magic and legacy lost. And so, with a heavy heart, he turned to follow Yin Ila, all the more determined to make good on his promise to Uon Elia to uncover those secrets that might – that *must*, he had to believe – rid the world of the horror that gripped it.

7
The Cat and the Dog

Foolish Cur

The swirling lights in the corners of my eyes grew fainter as the day wore on. From time to time, I reached for magic to conjure a spark of flame or a curl of wind – enough to prove that Doctor Sho's poison had worn off but not, I hoped, enough to draw the unwoven. Yet though I could feel power within my grasp, it ever slipped between my fingers.

All the while, I refused to acknowledge Doctor Sho. At first he pleaded his case over and over again, using new arguments that all circled around the same point: magic had done nothing but harm to the world. Far better, he claimed, for humanity to live as the beasts did, without the power to reshape the pattern at a whim. When it became clear that he may as well have been shouting at a stone, he took to muttering under his breath, and finally fell silent, his footsteps and the rattling of his medicine chest the only reminders that he yet followed.

Magic itself was not at fault, whatever Doctor Sho believed. Even now, touching it but unable to wield it, the sharpness of it filled the world, bringing every detail to life in transcendent beauty. How could he even dream of destroying such a thing? Perhaps it had been misused, but that was no reason to rid it from the world. He saw only its harms, while I knew well its beauty – the gift of water in An-Zabat, the joy of flight on veered wings, a dance of twining fire and wind, and so many other wonders and possibilities I had yet to experience at first hand.

Knowing the truth, now, that he was Traveller-on-the-Narrow-Way, I could begin to understand his desperation. His aphorisms and philosophy were themselves like magic, beautiful and potent yet twisted to terrible ends. Perhaps his determination to see magic scoured from the world was but a reflection of his guilt, his regret that he had ever written the classics, which had given Tenet the cornerstone on which to build his empire. Undoing his perceived sins of the past was of course an impossibility, yet perhaps in his mind he saw stripping the empire of its most powerful tool as a means of redemption for such an act. If such guilt and need were his motivation, I could sympathise, but they had surely blinded him to other, less destructive possibilities.

As the sun began to crawl down from noon, we emerged from the forest onto the battlefield around Eastern Fortress. Not far from us stood the blackened, smoking scar left by my first meeting with the unwoven. Though only a day and a night had passed since then, all that remained of the roaring flames and bursting trees were charred logs and a wash of grey-and-white ash.

Had I, in my flight, had the presence of mind to extinguish those flames? My memory of that night felt loose. There had been such chaos, such desperation, and memory rarely captures every moment at the best of times. Or had I slept longer than I thought? While it was true that a mild hunger gnawed at me, it was surely only that of a morning spent walking on an empty stomach.

Doctor Sho emerged from the forest, took one look at the

battlefield, and spat a curse. 'It can't be this bad already,' he said, stalking off towards the city. He knelt over a patch of churned and blackened earth where a grenade had struck and ran his fingers through the char.

I bit back a question – there was little reason to think a man who would steal my magic could be trusted to answer honestly – and instead watched him wander back and forth, muttering to himself. Okara loped out of the forest and sat beside me, cocking his head.

'They've already collected their dead,' Doctor Sho muttered. He looked toward the walls. 'How many days have passed within the barrier, I wonder?'

Frustration and confusion at last overwhelmed stubbornness. 'This is some kind of trick, isn't it?' I demanded. 'Your drug kept me asleep for days and now you're play-acting to put me off balance.' It was exactly the sort of thing Voice Usher might have done when he had been my teacher.

Doctor Sho's glare could have withered an oak. 'And spooned soup into your mouth while you slept? None of this is an act, boy. Hissing Cat and I both told you of these days. Distance and time were the first to start unravelling.' He looked to the sky, towards the black, spherical cloud hanging over Eastern Fortress. My eyes had skirted away from it, remembering when it had first appeared, and with it the many-winged gods. 'Not long now until the gods' battles birth new mountains and boil the seas,' Doctor Sho went on. 'We have little time and much to do, yet you insist on petulance and self-pity.'

A chill of fear washed through me, but I scowled it down. 'You mean to say that a day passed for us while nearer a week passed here? And more within the city? What about in the Batir Waste? Or Centre Fortress?'

'Who can say?' Doctor Sho shrugged. 'Last time the world was broken, it seemed that perception played some role in holding distance and time together. Time flowed much the same for you and I because we observed it flowing from the same vantage, and observed one another observing it. But some unknown follower just behind us in the forest might traverse the same distance and arrive here to find that a month had passed, or mere hours.' He stepped towards me. 'The fabric of reality is fraying. Little that you once understood still holds.'

I wanted to reject what sounded like madness, but Hissing Cat *had* warned against the fraying of the world when the gods had last waged war. Had spoken too of fragments of reality held stable but separate, each with its own flow of the pattern behind seals of magic such as the one she had built around Eastern Fortress – and the terrible cost of releasing those seals, letting each fragment crash into the rest, unleashing a second cataclysm in the aftermath of war.

All of it was happening again, because of me. Because I had been desperate to destroy the emperor, to liberate Nayen, to put behind me the awful burden of guilt I felt for my years of service to Sien, to transform myself from misguided fool to triumphant hero.

Instead, I had worked an even greater evil upon the world: a rekindling of the war between the gods, with humanity pawns at best, ants at worst, trampled underfoot by their struggle. The very evil that the empire had been built to guard against and, ultimately, destroy.

Yet it could all be put right. I would find Hissing Cat, and together we would work to undo what I had done. The gods had made a truce once. They could be forced to do so again.

I set off at an angle across the shattered ground towards the Sun Road and the city gates, Okara at my heels and Doctor Sho rattling and muttering behind.

Just as the road came into view, its tiles shattered by grenades and a farmer's cart abandoned where its axle had broken, I felt suddenly light-headed as though layers of thought had been stripped away, and then a stomach-wrenching chill, a breath of deepest winter, reaching down from the upper air to rake my bones. Gasping, I staggered forwards a pace, clutching at myself for warmth. The chill passed as swiftly as it had come. I swept my gaze along the wall and the road, wondering if this was some forewarning, a wake in the world left by some horror like the unwoven, or the gods themselves.

Something was wrong with the cart, to my eye. It seemed to have rotated slightly, as though some great hand had picked it up like a child's toy and turned it. Not only the cart – the angle of the road, too, seemed to have changed subtly, as did the line of the wall.

The shadows had shifted too, I realised. They stretched out as though the sun had advanced by three or four hours in that single footstep. A glance at the sky lent evidence to this theory and deepened my terror.

'I tried to warn you,' Doctor Sho said. He shifted his weight uncomfortably and squinted. 'I'd nearly forgotten how off-putting that is.'

Only Okara seemed not to notice the twisting of time and space around us. He padded to the road, paused to sniff at the cart, and then emptied his bladder on its wheel – a moment of incongruous normalcy in the face of such unnerving strangeness.

One last shudder worked through me, though I now knew what that chill meant: that we had crossed the line of Hissing Cat's seal, that most potent weapon against the gods – the only thing able to destroy them, in fact – which carved out a piece of the world from the rest of the pattern and made it immune to the influence of magic. The unwoven could not reach us here, with or without Doctor Sho's mushrooms. But neither could I wield my power.

A thought struck me and I studied Doctor Sho, his deep

wrinkles and stooped shoulders. 'Will whatever has kept you alive so long wear off now?'

He harrumphed. 'I bloody well hope not.'

His words worried me. Since my return to Nayen, Doctor Sho had been my most constant companion. He had deceived me, and meant to use me – as everyone else in my life had used me – to serve an agenda of his own, yet I found that none of that had destroyed my affection for him but only complicated and confounded it.

'The unwoven leave you alone,' I said. 'You should stay out there, where it's safer for you.'

'I've taken greater risks.' The glimmer of some unspoken thought flickered in his eye, but he said only, 'Well? Let's be about it. Hopefully your rebels have secured the city. I'd rather not have to dodge arrows and explosions on our way.' He adjusted the straps of his medicine chest and set off toward the gates. An observer might have believed that our return to Eastern Fortress had been his idea from the beginning.

The gates stood shut, as though the city were still besieged. Frothing Wolf's banner hung from a guard tower. A pair of hard-faced Nayeni peered from the battlements, bows in their hands.

'Declare yourself!' one called when I was a few paces from the gate.

I paused, shading my eyes with my hand. 'I am Foolish Cur, the witch. Open the gate. I would join council with Frothing Wolf and my uncle.'

The guards exchanged a sideways glance. One said something to the other, his voice too low to hear at such a distance. The second guard disappeared into the tower. A moment later, the gate began to creak open.

'Something isn't right,' Doctor Sho muttered.

I had made that same observation myself. The soldiers of the

Army of the Wolf had little reason to love me, but this reception seemed particularly cold in the aftermath of victory. Soon the door stood wide enough to admit us. I strode forwards, Okara at my heel and Doctor Sho grumbling along behind me.

A dozen soldiers met us, half with their hands on sword hilts, the other half with strung bows and nocked arrows. They made two columns with space for us to walk between. None were witches known to me. The battle had cost all our cadres deeply.

'An honour guard seems needless,' I said to their leader, a young man whose bruised knuckles showed white on his sword hilt. 'The city has fallen, has it not?'

The man did not blink, only turned and began to lead me between the columns of soldiers. My gut twisted. I hesitated just inside the gate and put out a hand to stop Doctor Sho. The young guard turned back to face me, his expression grim. Okara lingered between us, his hackles high.

'Before I go with you, I would know how things stand in the city,' I said.

The soldiers shifted uncomfortably till I thought they might bare steel. On instinct I reached for the power to call the wind and conjure flame, but of course the power slipped my grasp – doubly so, as Doctor Sho's mushrooms and Hissing Cat's seal conspired to keep magic from me.

The young captain's expression soured. 'Burning Dog will apprise you of the situation. We will bring you to her.'

Burning Dog? A dozen questions darted through my mind. 'I would speak with my uncle, first.'

'To hell with this,' one of the soldiers – a grizzled, scar-seamed woman – muttered. Steel rasped out of her scabbard. 'Orders are to bring you to Burning Dog alive, but that dinnae mean unbattered. Keep your hands where we can see them! We'll take you senseless if we—'

I dropped low, lunged towards her, and drove my elbow into

her diaphragm – a sequence from the middle of the Iron Dance, drilled into me by my grandmother across dozens of moonlit nights. The woman buckled, her sword clattering to the street. I grabbed Doctor Sho by the straps of his medicine chest and shoved him past her towards an alley.

'Run!' I shouted, ducking the flat of a blade and kicking out my attacker's knee, which crunched and buckled at the blow. Doctor Sho did not need any more encouragement. His chest rattled against his back as he dashed away. I followed, dodging blows and striking at knees, stomachs, and elbows with my feet and my good hand, leaving one guard winded and two more on the ground nursing cracked joints. Surprise alone had been my advantage. The six with bows soon drew down on me, waiting for an open shot. I turned and ran, wincing at a bruise where my heel had met a kneecap.

A hand caught the back of my robe. I gagged, lurching backwards, turning and twisting, swinging an elbow, desperate to free myself. A snarl sounded, then a scream of pain. From the corner of my eye, I watched Okara gnaw a man's wrist to the bone as I ran, blood spurting between his teeth. Two of the archers levelled their arrows.

I forced myself to turn away, forced my legs to carry me further into that alleyway. A blade of wind or a lance of lightning would have been enough, but I had only my body – little good against a dozen men and women with swords and bows.

A yelp echoed. My eyes blurred. I sobbed aloud while a hook tore at my heart.

'In here!' Doctor Sho hissed. I nearly ran past him, but he caught my sleeve and pulled me through a doorway into the ground floor of an abandoned house, then into the shadowed corner of a room. Feet pounded in the alley outside. Doctor Sho waited until they had faded.

'Not the reception you were expecting, I hope,' he whispered. 'We have to get to Hissing Cat. Where will we find her?'

A shudder worked through me. 'They killed Okara.'

Doctor Sho grimaced, his hands balling. 'Bastards,' he muttered. 'You can't set a thing right that some idiot won't break again. A shame, but it doesn't change anything.'

'I left Hissing Cat in the governor's estate.' My words sounded distant, my mind busy replaying the moment Doctor Sho and I had found Okara by the side of the road, beaten and bloodied, the days we had spent nursing him back to health. 'Then again, I left my uncle and Frothing Wolf allies.' And the guards had mentioned neither of them. Though they flew Frothing Wolf's banner, they had spoken of taking me to Burning Dog. What had happened, in however much time had passed in the city?

'Well, we can't stay here,' Doctor Sho said, tightening the straps of his medicine chest. 'They'll start sweeping these houses as soon as they realise they've lost us. Had I my way, we'd leave this bloody city, but I doubt we'll manage to get back through that gate. The estate it is, and you'll have to lead the way.'

'Do you feel nothing?' I snarled, forgetting to lower my voice.

He stared down at me, his expression shrouded by the thin light slanting through the boarded windows. 'Of course I do. As much hurt as you, I wager. Who doesn't regret the death of a loyal friend? All the more a loyal beast. Kindness uncomplicated by ideology or ambition . . .' His eyes took on a distant cast and he sighed. 'But I've lived through this before, and there'll be worse to come. On your feet, now, and get a move on.'

I glared back at him, then heaved myself to my feet. We waited a few moments more, then slipped out of the house and back the way we had come down the alley. At the first turning, I took the lead and we made our winding way towards the inner city, keeping to alleys when we could.

An oppressive air held in the city. Every window we passed

had been boarded up; every eye we glimpsed peering between the boards held hostility and suspicion. Whatever had happened since the battle, it had left deep scars.

When the echo of booted feet or shouted orders found us, we ducked into what cover we could find – into doorways or behind piles of refuse – until it faded. Not all were out hunting us, certainly, but until we knew more of the situation in the city, it felt foolish to risk any confrontation.

On occasion I glanced backwards out of habit, expecting to see Okara padding along behind us. The empty street tugged at the hook in my heart. Another death adding to the burden of my guilt – a small one when set against all I had done, but it weighed heavy.

Our slow but steady progress brought us at last to the western gate to the inner city. We expected to find it closed, as the main gate had been, but it stood wide open. More surprising still, a steady stream of ordinary folk moved through it: old men and women with children – mostly Nayeni, though I was surprised to see a few Sienese faces – flanked on either side by men and women with spears.

'Each adult to take *one* ration bundle,' one of the soldiers repeated, his voice loud but toneless. 'Any disturbance will be met with force and the loss of ration rights. Each adult to take *one* . . .'

'Keep your head down,' I murmured, and stepped out into the meandering line. A few people eyed Doctor Sho and me, resenting our joining the line so near the gate, but said nothing. The soldiers' threats were taken seriously, it seemed. I felt a prickle down my spine as we passed through the gate, but aside from a few glances at the ornate, worn carvings on Doctor Sho's medicine chest, the guards paid us little mind, and none seemed to recognise us.

We were nearly through the gate when a cramp lanced down

the lines of my limbs and the faint scent of burnt cinnamon tickled my nose. My gaze snapped up. An eagle hawk swept over the city in wide, lazy circles.

It couldn't be … but it was. Again, I flailed for magic. The poison mushrooms' grip had weakened. With a swell of triumph, I caught hold of the power to veer, swallowing a cry of relief as the world sharpened around me. Colours burst to their fullest brightness. The faces of the guards and city folk leapt out to me like paintings of infinite detail, every nuance of their bored, frightened, or desperate expressions as clear to me as language.

I clutched my magic dearly, waiting until we were a few steps further. The rest of the line meandered on towards a granary tower, but I slipped into an alley between two looming houses with high walls and Sienese roofs. Doctor Sho's muffled protests followed me but touched me no more than mist.

Shadows enfolded me and I reached into the pattern. As a brush might rewrite a logogram, I rewrote my body, willing my limbs to crack and break and bend, my flesh to twist and shrink and expand, until I might leap into the sky on eagle hawk's wings.

Except no change came.

The eagle hawk above us continued to circle, as though taunting me. Every cramp I felt in its wake carved questions deeper and deeper.

'That should be impossible,' I snarled.

And if it wasn't, how had I – a witch of the old sort, among the most powerful to wield magic in generations – been constrained by Hissing Cat's seal while another had not? As ever, magic held secret mysteries, and the need to unravel them dug at my mind.

This time, I could only hope that that need would not lead me to disaster.

Doctor Sho came rattling into the alley, his face a storm cloud. 'You might be able to slip in and out of crowds, but we're not all so unburdened,' he muttered. 'What's got into you?'

Doctor Sho knew almost nothing of magic. Only two people could offer the answers I needed and one of them had vanished, presumably back to his citadel in Centre Fortress. I stood, tried to put the constant, cramping wake from my thoughts, and continued on towards the governor's estate.

A short while later, the eagle hawk descended, landing somewhere on the east side of the city. The cramps had faded, and with them the lingering scent of cinnamon, but the memory of them dug at me like a splinter. My mind gnawed incessantly at the question – *how* had someone veered within Hissing Cat's seal? – generating and discarding theories, hardly paying attention to where I was going beyond following alleys to the south and slightly east.

Always my thinking circled back to Hissing Cat's explanation of the seal she now held over the city. It was the same power I had used to shatter the imperial canon in Voice Usher's mind in my first success with magic of the old sort, an alignment of the will to the pattern and a reassertion of the pattern against any magic meant to reshape it. But trying to hold the pattern in mind had been like pouring an ocean into a teacup. The boundaries of the seal were far more manageable, and the potency of the seal more certain, because the mind had to hold a smaller, contained version of the pattern. In much the same way, unravelling a complex treatise spanning volumes is much easier than rebutting a simpler, more straightforward argument within a single paragraph.

There had to be some strange loophole unknown to me, some means of evading Hissing Cat's will or tricking her – and with her, the segment of the pattern within her seal – into accepting certain magic, yet I could not imagine any such means.

I had stood within the boundaries of such a seal and plunged my sword into the emperor's chest. The *completeness* of it had been overwhelming. Then, as now, wielding magic had been as impossible as writing on a stone tablet with a single strand of dry hair. Only when the blackened, shattered gate of the governor's estate came into view did my mind retreat from its hopeless questioning.

'Foolish Cur!'

My gaze snapped up to find Torn Leaf standing before the gate, astonishment to equal my own splitting his face into a broad grin.

'Burn me, we'd all but buried you.' He was at my side in a bound, laughing and pulling me into a tight embrace. 'Hissing Cat will just about shit when she sees you.'

I smiled with the first true relief I had felt since waking from Doctor Sho's poison. Once, the impropriety of a man who had been my student and a member of my cadre throwing his arms around me would have put a rigid chill in me. Now, I returned the embrace as warmly as he offered it.

'What's happened, Leaf?' I asked as he led us through the gate with a quick salute for Doctor Sho, who answered with only a grumble. My eyes swept the ramparts for Harrow Fox's banner but saw neither flag nor symbol. 'Tell me everything.'

He whistled through his teeth and scrubbed at his hair. 'A hard order. It's been a damned strange and busy two weeks.'

I nearly tripped over my own feet. 'Two *weeks?*'

'Ah, you've been out of the city.' Torn Leaf winced. 'I heard things get … odd, out there. The unwoven, of course, as Hissing Cat calls those freakish monsters, and patrols and hunting parties that go out in the morning and come back who knows when, saying in every case they were only gone from sunup to sundown. But things in the city are stable enough. Well, time's passing is, anyway. Can't say the same for … anything else, really.'

Even Doctor Sho's eyes had widened in astonishment. We knew time had slipped in strange ways, but if two weeks could pass in what had been for us only a day and a half, who could say what else had transpired in Nayen, or elsewhere in the empire for that matter? How much time had the emperor had, relative to us, to react to the gods' return to the world?

'It seems your little alliance has dissolved,' Doctor Sho said. 'We were met with a good deal less welcome at the main gate.'

Torn Leaf grimaced as he led us along paths I had walked countless times during my years as a guest in Voice Golden-Finch's garden, though the scenery had since been stripped of all familiarity. A few levelled stands of bamboo and fortified pavilions were of little concern, however, beside the explanation for them that Torn Leaf offered.

'Frothing Wolf is dead,' he said stiffly. He had fought for her before joining my cadre, and the shadow of mourning darkened his eyes. 'It isn't clear to us how, but of course Burning Dog blames you for it. There was a good deal of chaos in those first minutes after the ... Well, you saw.' His gaze darted upwards at the strange black moon that hung above us like a heavy drop of ink on a sheet of blue silk. 'Your uncle, too. He was on the wing when Hissing Cat made the seal, it seems. It forced him out of his veer. Tawny Owl, too. They didn't survive the fall.'

He paused, watching me, obviously uncomfortable with delivering news of a death in the family. Perhaps it reveals a flaw in my character – a lack of proper filial piety – that I felt no grief, only a regret for the loss of my uncle's leadership. His death had surely contributed to the chaos that now gripped the city, but in truth the news that Frothing Wolf had died troubled me more. Burning Dog had wanted my blood as badly as her mother had, but she had been far less willing to cooperate. If she commanded half of the Nayeni forces, there was little hope for the unity we would need to rout the Sienese and restore order.

'Go on,' I prodded Torn Leaf. If I was to begin making plans and taking action towards repairing the damage I had done, I needed all the information he could offer.

'With the seal up, the tide of the fighting turned,' Torn Leaf said. 'We had the advantage until our witches lost their magic, which let the Sienese regroup and fortify the eastern garrison house.

'For a while the armies of the Wolf and Fox hung together, trying to prise the Sienese out of their defences, settling the city, burying the dead. Until Burning Dog got it into her head that we were hiding you, and that the seal was your doing. The alliance didn't last long after that. We've fought a few skirmishes, but both sides know the moment we go for each other's throats, the Sienese will boil out of their garrison. So it's been a stalemate for about a week. Bloody miserable.'

'What of the rest of the cadre?' I asked.

'Running Doe is at the western garrison house, and I'm here. The rest ... well, the rest that survived went over to Burning Dog's side. The Sienese captured the canons of those who fell.' He shook his head in annoyance. 'If not for that, it would be simple enough to force them out, but they've got a few people who seem to know enough about conjuring fire and wind, at least, to mount a solid defence.'

Another wave of relief accompanied the news that Running Doe, too, had survived the battle, after I had left her at the edge of death, bloodied and burned by the emperor's sorcery. I felt a sudden, irrational urge to find her, to reassure her that I yet lived, and a warm, stirring hope that I would see my own relief mirrored in her face. Yet that relief soon gave way to a dawning realisation.

'The canons? You mean the canons of witchcraft? Why should they matter?'

Torn Leaf reached to a pouch at his belt and withdrew a strip of bone no wider than my thumb. Four carvings decorated its surface: a campfire, a wing, a whorl of wind, and the logogram for *medicine.* It was one of the canons I had made, binding structures in the deep layers of the pattern – the patterns of the mind and the soul – to the marks on the bone. Anyone who touched those marks would find their mind filled with walls guiding them to a single magic, either conjuring flame, veering into an eagle hawk, calling the wind, or healing. A canon to rival imperial sorcery, but mimicking the method of the ancient pacts with the gods rather than the emperor's transmission into the minds of his Hands and Voices.

I gaped at him. 'Impossible. The seal should reassert the pattern here against any magic.'

Torn Leaf only shrugged and pressed his thumb to the first mark. A feverish wake washed through me, burning away my disbelief as he called a tongue of flame to dance in the palm of his other hand.

'Except for the canons of witchcraft,' he said. 'Couldn't tell you why, but I can tell you it's made them heavy weights on the bloody balance of power here in Eastern Fortress. At least, pact-marked witches like Burning Dog and your grandmother can't wield magic, and neither can the surviving Hands of the emperor – so our scouts and spies tell.'

That explained the veered eagle hawk I had felt and seen, yet it was an explanation that prompted further, more complicated questions – questions it seemed that Hissing Cat herself had yet to answers. Unless she had decided, for whatever reason, to keep those answer from Torn Leaf. I would have a chance to ask her soon enough.

'Where is my grandmother?'

We had rounded a bend in the path that led past an arrangement of columnar basalt. Oriole's plum tree, blackened and skeletal atop a low hill, loomed over the scrap of scarred path where my cadre and I had battled the emperor. Hissing Cat sat beneath it, where I had left her. She leaned the back of her head against the tree, her eyelids fluttering, her flesh drawn and wan as I had never seen it. Though ancient and deeply wrinkled, her face had always been full of vitality and life. The sight of her, frail and exhausted, paired with the damage wrought to Oriole's grave and tree, written clear in the afternoon sun, cut me to the heart.

'She's fine.' Torn Leaf's voice had taken on an agitated edge, as though he were nervous, or frightened, to be in Hissing Cat's presence. 'Her orders were to bring the two of you to her, and I've done that. Now I should get back to the gate.' He saluted us and turned to go.

'Two bloody weeks, eh?' Doctor Sho muttered, studying Hissing Cat from a distance. 'And she's kept this up all that time?'

'Should we let her rest?' I wondered aloud.

'It'd be kind of you, but pointless,' Hissing Cat snarled down from the hilltop. 'I'm not sleeping. Haven't really slept since you left me here. Been working on a solution to that, but it gets harder and harder to think straight every day.'

Slowly, her eyes opened. A rheumy weakness had settled into their edges, but they still burned with fury. 'Come up here, boy. I would stop yelling to be heard and start yelling for bloody impact.'

8

Two Confrontations

Foolish Cur

I knelt beside Hissing Cat beneath the blackened plum tree. An arc of animals' shoulder blades fanned across the ground before her – oracle bones, meant for reading the pattern of the world. It was a habit of hers I had never really understood.

A growl rumbled in her throat. 'Get on your feet. I'm not an invalid, just tired.'

'I'm sorry, Hissing Cat,' I said, rising as she had instructed, though looking down on her felt profoundly wrong, like staring down at a mountain top. 'I should have heeded your warning.'

She grunted in agreement. 'You should have. But we all have our regrets, Cur. What matters is what we do from here. Have you had any contact with the dog?'

Her words prodded the raw wound of Okara's death. 'No. Not since before the battle.'

She heaved a sigh. 'If he won't talk to us, we'll need to find a way to reach Tenet. His plans are blasted to pieces, but his little army of Hands and Voices is the best weapon we have against them. If he transmits the power to make these seals, we might be able to force another stalemate and rebuild the pacts.'

'Is that what you really want?' Doctor Sho cut in. He had

followed me up the hill and unslung his medicine chest. Almost absent-mindedly, he plucked handfuls of herbs from the small, palm-wide drawers and began filling a paper sack. 'After all of this, no more than a return to where we stood before it began?'

'You're backing the emperor's madness now?' Hissing Cat wheezed a laugh. 'Things are bad, Sho, but I didn't think they were bad enough yet to send you back into his arms. And it's a little late. We forced him to loose the arrow early, before the bow was fully drawn. He's lost the twin advantages of surprise and the gods' passivity.'

Doctor Sho glowered at her, then waved to one of the archers standing guard atop a pavilion that had once played home to so many of Usher's lessons. 'You there! Bring a teapot and boiling water!' The guard glared at him, but at a nod from Hissing Cat he descended the ladder from his platform and stalked off towards the main house. 'I don't intend to help Tenet kill the gods, if that was ever his true aim.'

'Then what?' Hissing Cat demanded.

'He intends to destroy magic,' I said before Doctor Sho could answer. He turned his glower on me, but I ignored him and pressed on. 'He told me as much in the forest on our way here. Or he wants *us* to do it for him.'

'Rather than kill our enemies, you would throw away our only weapon against them,' Hissing Cat muttered. 'An unwillingness to take up arms yourself is one thing, but that is cowardice of a higher order, Sho.'

'Call it what you will' – Doctor Sho began combing his fingers through his wispy beard so fiercely I feared he might pull out its roots – 'but wait until you have the whole of it. *Destroy magic* is a terribly simplistic explanation, and the boy hasn't even heard my reasoning, or my notion of the means, nor how it would solve our damned problem!'

'The world is, in fact, unravelling around us just beyond the walls of this city.' Hissing Cat leaned forwards and seemed to regain an echo of her old ferocity. 'Our food supplies are running low, with no way to replenish them. People are going to starve. But before that happens, Burning Dog or the bloody Sienese are likely to spark another round of fighting, which will leave who knows how many more dead. We don't have time to listen to wild speculation and esoteric theorising. Explain, or leave and let the boy and I solve this.'

'Happily, if you will let me speak.' He swung his gaze from Hissing Cat to me and back again until, apparently satisfied that we would not interrupt, he continued: 'What are the gods, Hissing Cat? Do you know?'

She drew her mouth into a tight line, her eyes boring into him.

He threw up his hands. 'You can answer questions, obviously!'

'Bloody bastards, is what they are,' Hissing Cat snarled.

'Are they creatures like us? Of flesh and bone, like beasts? Or are they something else?'

We both stared back at him blankly.

'They are the gods,' I said, thinking of the wolf statues that guarded the Temple of the Flame, who had seemed to watch me from the very first time my grandmother brought me out into the forest to name me. Thinking too, with a pang of grief, of Okara the dog and the flicker of ember light in his scars.

'But what *is* a god?' Doctor Sho pressed. 'Not beasts, for – unless they descend to inhabit the bodies of lesser beings – we never see them, nor touch them, nor even hear them, save when their voices echo in our minds rather than the air or they deign to manifest themselves. They shape and shake the world, but at a distance, and only ever through the exercise of their power.' He pushed his palms together. 'Not physical bodies acting upon one another, but magic acting upon the pattern itself.'

'They're spooky bloody bastards, then,' Hissing Cat said. 'What's your point?'

Doctor Sho bristled at the interruption. 'I contend that the gods are, in many ways, our opposites. We are creatures of flesh and blood who touch the deeper layers of the pattern, of mind and soul, more than lesser beasts – deeply enough, in cases such as yours, to inscribe our will upon the pattern itself. The gods, in contrast, are beings of soul. They dwell not here, in the realm of earth and wood, water and fire, but in the shadowed places our minds brush in dreams. The same layer of the pattern where the pacts were made, from which you draw your power to wield magic.

'That is why the seals, like the very one that shields this city, terrify them and are the only true weapon that can wound them. They seal the world from the influence of magic. Ordinarily, no sorcerer can overpower them, but locked within a fragment of the pattern they are reduced and made powerless, perhaps even destroyed.'

We stood in silence, absorbing his wild conjecture.

'Speaking of which,' I said, uncertain how to respond to Doctor Sho but full of questions of my own, 'Torn Leaf told me that the canons of witchcraft still function within your seal. How can that be?'

Hissing Cat glared up at me. 'How would I know that, Cur?' she demanded. 'No one's ever made anything quite like them before, and I haven't exactly had time to experiment, have I?'

The archer returned and, grumbling, delivered a kettle of steaming water before trotting back to his post.

'Could we bring the conversation back to the topic at hand?' Doctor Sho said, tossing a handful of leaves into the water. 'There can be no true end to this war with the gods without cutting ourselves off from magic entirely, as I see it. You two, like Tenet, might not be able to accept that, but it is the truth.'

He seemed then as far from my imagination's conjuring of Traveller-on-the-Narrow-Way as he could ever be. Not the calm, well-reasoned scholar of human nature and society but a raving madman.

'So, what? You want us to make seals to cover the whole world?' Hissing Cat asked. 'Is that not *exactly what I just suggested?*'

'No! Don't you see?' Doctor Sho threw up his hands. 'We can't hope to defeat them in a contest of power. *They are power itself!* We may not be able to destroy them, but we can isolate them. Banish them to their own layer of the pattern and remain in ours – and not just by agreement, either. No mere exchange of promises – yours to contain the old magic, theirs not to interfere. We could lock them away, cut our layer of the pattern off from magic, and thus from their influence, for ever.'

Hissing Cat barked a laugh. 'A wild idea, Sho. Any suggestion for how it might be done?'

'No,' Doctor Sho admitted, letting his hands fall back to his sides. 'As you well know, Hissing Cat, I have never possessed any talent for magic. Tenet was working on such a method. He was aware of the possibility, at least, or so he told me. But he loved his power too much to give it up, even to save the world from the threat of the gods, and so the dream of his empire was born.'

'Then what you suggest also seems little more than a dream,' I said. Doctor Sho's brow furrowed at my words, and I felt the weight of his centuries and my deep-trained respect for the wisdom of Traveller-on-the-Narrow-Way. Who was I, after all? In my brief life, my own attempts to meddle in these higher affairs had brought us to this moment of chaos. Still, I pressed on. 'Were it possible, it would be well worth considering, but if neither I nor Hissing Cat have any notion of how it might be done, it seems better to fall back upon the method that worked before.' I looked to Hissing Cat, giving her a chance to interject if she had, indeed, discerned how to accomplish Doctor Sho's strange, terrifying goal. Her tired eyes did not meet mine but gazed instead at some distant, inward point. 'Better the world as it was under the pacts than as it is now, no?'

Doctor Sho stared at me a moment longer, then bent to his kettle and began filling a ceramic cup taken from his chest of drawers. 'I don't hope simply for a *better* world,' he said softly. 'I hope for a good one.'

'Either way, we'll need Tenet,' Hissing Cat murmured, blinking slowly. She rubbed a hand across her eyes. 'Though I doubt he'd want to speak with any of us. And none of this will solve the immediate problems of starvation and war.'

'Drink this,' Doctor Sho said, offering Hissing Cat the cup of tea. 'It won't replace sleep, but it will keep your strength up.'

I felt a twinge of suspicion – my trust in his medicines might never fully recover – but she took the cup and quaffed it without a blink of hesitation.

'I could take the burden from you,' I said. 'Hold the seal a while, give you a chance to sleep and think.'

Hissing Cat bobbed her head. 'A good thought, that, but not yet. There's a little bastard of a prisoner I've been meaning to interrogate, but you might be better suited to it than me. They've got him locked up in the servants' quarters. He might know something that could help us against the Sienese. They're hoarding the empire's strategic reserve of grain in the eastern garrison house. If we're to feed the city, we'll need to either seize those silos or cow the Sienese into cooperation. Find out what he knows, get your own night's sleep, and we'll deal with the delicate business of handing off the seal tomorrow.'

I frowned. 'What prisoner?'

Hissing Cat only chuckled and waved me towards what had once been the servants' quarters. 'Go, boy. And Sho, pour me another cup of that tea.'

Confused, I left her and Sho and traversed the brutalised

landscape, winding my way around the pond, its porous stone now devoid of kingfishers. I rubbed the stump of my right wrist, feeling the smouldering worry that I might never have a chance to heal it. Such fear was irrational, though, I knew. Even if we somehow pursued Doctor Sho's strange plan, there would be time and opportunity to wield magic again. I would not spend the rest of my life within Hissing Cat's seal or dosed by witch's-eye mushrooms.

I forced my hands to my sides and my thoughts to other things, particularly Hissing Cat's strange request. Had one of the Hands or Voices survived? If so, why did Hissing Cat want *me* to interrogate him? Perhaps in the hope that my understanding of Sienese propriety and doctrine might give me the insight needed to unravel his defences?

A pair of guards flanked the servants' quarters, bows in their hands and swords on their hips. The small one-room apartments themselves had been converted into prison cells, with heavy iron bolts on the doors and bamboo bars across the narrow windows. The guards snapped sharp salutes as I approached. Whether they recognised me or not, they had seen me speaking with Hissing Cat atop the hill, and proximity to her had evidently come to indicate authority.

Muffled voices and a soft, muted scraping sounded from beyond the bamboo slats. One of the guards set down her bow, turned a key in the lock, and put her hand on her sword hilt before easing the door open.

A hideous stench wafted from the room. I stepped through, and my heart thundered in my throat. There, in the thin blade of light falling through the doorway, crouched Pinion, his long hair tangled, his feet bare and filthy. I hardly noticed the second man, who sat rigid, his heavy muscles coiled tight and ready for any chance to pounce.

Golden-Finch had said that his son had been on his way

to meet with the emperor. I had nursed a quiet hope that he had survived the gods' attack on the Sienese fleet but had never expected to find him here. He should have been drowned, or killed by magic, or aboard a ship racing back to the mainland. Astonishment, coupled with an undercurrent of grief to see him – his face so like Oriole's – imprisoned and covered in filth, robbed me of words.

His eyes, bright and wild as a hunting cat's, fixed on me. His mouth opened a hairline, showing the tips of his teeth, and then twisted into a snarl.

'You!' His feet shifted beneath him and his hands flexed into claws, the tetragram on his right palm glimmering in the shaft of light. Yet he held back, studying me as though I were a threat. 'I thought I'd have to search the city, but here you are. You're never quite what anyone expects, eh, Alder?'

'Why are they covered in filth?' I demanded of the guard.

'Broke the chamber pot, didn't they?' The bearded guard scowled. 'Seemed one of 'em threw it at the other in a pique.'

I looked then to the other prisoner, who wore fury to match Pinion's. A single chain ran from a mount in the wall through first Pinion's manacles and then his cellmate's.

'See that they have a new chamber pot at once,' I said.

The bearded guard grumbled in his throat but made a quick salute and slouched off to follow my order. His companion touched her sword nervously and eyed the prisoners.

'How kind of you,' Pinion snarled. 'Where was that pity for my brother before you led him to his death? Have you seen what's become of his grave, Alder? The way they've desecrated it?'

'That was the emperor's doing,' I said, stepping into the room. The guard stiffened and moved to follow me, but I gestured for her to wait outside. I would have sent her away if I thought she would have obeyed the order. I wanted Pinion to hear me, to understand me, not to worry that a wrong move might lead to a beating. 'It pains me, too, though not as much as it pains you, I'm sure. I want to help you if I can, Pinion.'

'Help you the way he helped Voice Usher at Greyfrost?' the other prisoner cut in. He shifted in the shadowed corner, his hands curled tightly into fists. 'This one is a traitor, Hand Pinion. Every word from his mouth is a lie or a trick.'

'I'm past lies and tricks. What is your name, soldier? I would help you, too, insofar as I am able. A great deal in the world has changed since the battle we fought here.'

The soldier glared back at me and did not answer.

'You would offer me freedom from this cell, then?' Pinion said. The chain that bound his wrist rattled as he shifted. 'To what end? My family is dead. Monsters roam this godsforsaken island and the sea. Where would I go? What would I do?' He shook his head, a soft chuckle dripping from his throat. 'No, Alder, there is only one thing in the world that I want, and you have brought it to me.'

Pinion lurched. The chain snapped taut, then with a *crack* tore free of the wall. Stunned, I backpedalled a step and reached for magic, meaning to wrap him in wind. Power slipped through my fingers as the end of the chain whipped out, lashing for my face.

The young guard bowled into me, knocking me off my feet and out of the chain's path. Steel rang against iron as she knocked Pinion's attack aside with her sword. Pinion's cellmate surged from the darkness, reaching for me, but I scrambled backwards, lashing out with a kick that swept his legs from under him. His hand clamped down on my ankle and dragged me deeper into the cell. Panic surged within me and I kicked wildly at his head and shoulders, trying to wrench my foot free of his grip. Already I felt fingers digging into my flesh, ready to tear me apart.

Steel flashed. A sharp cry cut through the fog of panic. The young guard's foot slammed into my attacker's stomach, then cracked him across the forehead. His hand spasmed open and he writhed, gasping for breath and clutching at his gut, while the guard dragged me by the arm out of the cell. She threw the door shut and drove the bolt home, then leaned, panting and wild eyed, against the door.

'You all right, mister?' she asked.

I blinked up at her, taking deep breaths of my own to stifle my fear. 'Did you kill him?'

Her mouth hung open for a moment before she shook her head. 'Just smacked him with the flat. Hissing Cat doesn't want them dead, for some reason. Maybe as bargaining chips, Darting Buck figures, to trade to the Sienese.'

Darting Buck was the other guard, I assumed, whom I had foolishly sent to find a chamber pot. I stood on shaking legs. 'I need to speak with him again. Open the door.'

She barked a laugh. 'Excuse me, mister, but no. There's a window over there. Feel free to shout through it to yer heart's content, but they'll be on their feet in a minute, and without even a badly secured chain to slow them down next time.'

I leaned against the wall, limbs still shaking, and peered between the bamboo slats of the window. Pinion lay sprawled on the floor, the chain coiled beside him, his shoulders heaving with muffled sobs. His cellmate groaned and massaged a blossoming bruise that already mottled half of his face.

'I did not want our reunion to go this way, Pinion,' I said. His heaving shoulders stilled. Tension ran down his slumped back and curled limbs. 'You have good reason to hate me, but not for Oriole's death. For your father's, yes, and for the damage I've done to the world, but not for Oriole. His dying blood washed over my hands, but because I cradled him and did all I could to heal him, not because I dealt the blow.'

My voice caught. I cleared my throat, the memories surging within me. 'I killed the woman who opened his throat. Frigid Cub. Frothing Wolf's daughter. I took the vengeance you so hunger for, but it did not soothe me. His death still grieves me, as does hers, and the rebellion might still be unified if she yet lived. Vengeance only piles tragedy atop of tragedy.'

'Why should I believe you?' His whisper was a quiet dagger, driving for my heart. 'You have taken everything from me.'

'I don't know,' I replied just as softly, leaning my forehead against the bars. 'I know only that, after all I have done, if I could trade my life for his, I would.'

Pinion raised his head. His eyes met mine, still sharp and full of hatred. Then, after a long, hitching breath, he lowered himself back to the floor and said nothing more.

'See to it that they have their new chamber pot,' I told the young guard. She spluttered, her expression incredulous, but managed a salute before I turned away and set off back towards Oriole's grave, to speak again with Hissing Cat.

She was slumped against the scarred plum tree, teacup in hand, eyes glazed over and vacant. Doctor Sho and his medicine chest were nowhere to be seen. He would be off with the wounded, no doubt, wherever they might be found.

At that moment, standing beneath the blackened branches of Oriole's tree, I felt overwhelmed by the task ahead of us. I sympathised with Doctor Sho and could not doubt his motives – not truly. He believed his plan would help to heal the world, though whether it could ever be more than a theory remained an open question, and one I could not begin to imagine how to answer.

Yet I would not let myself be paralysed. There were other wounds, just as deep, that I could start to soothe now, while I muddled through the problem of putting an end to the war between the gods. I had broken the world, and in its brokenness thousands stood to starve. If the rebellion were to stand any chance of scouring the last of Sienese control from Nayen, of seizing the means to feed the people of Eastern Fortress, the fractures riven between its factions had to be mended.

'Hissing Cat,' I said. She started at my voice, mouth falling open to growl some retort. I pressed on, knowing that any delay might sap my courage. 'I need to meet with Burning Dog.'

9

The Journey South

Ral Ans Urrera

The ships are not the blessing Ral Ans Urrera had hoped they would be, no vast fleet to bear her war band to the walls of Centre Fortress. They carry supplies and non-combatants who would have otherwise ridden horse-drawn sledges, freeing up more mounts for her warriors, but they do not lend her storm more speed. More, their presence draws the ire of the Skyfather.

Ral has not dreamed of his face nor heard the thunder of his voice since testing him, riding out to meet the An-Zabati and enfold them in his protection. In the days after their arrival, while the An-Zabati tend to their wounded and the war band begins its preparations to ride south, Ral searches the clouds and the fall of rain for any sign. She dares not ask the elders to read the omens. The silver line that encircled the camp and now wraps around the trailing column, shielding them from the chaos of the changing world, yet holds. It is enough assurance to keep her moving. Enough for her to trust that the Skyfather still rides with them and will, through her, strike down the Sienese and their blasphemous emperor.

She has more immediate concerns, though, than the silence of a god.

The An-Zabati have suffered terrible losses. Thirty-one ships lost. Some abandoned after the attacks of the ravenous, twisted beasts reduced their crews to a wounded handful, others vanished in sandstorms as though consumed by the Waste. Still others have been swallowed by sudden rifts in the earth, their hulls shattering and tumbling into the depthless abyss.

Atar, who was before a bright if serious soul, now walks under a heavy shadow. Dark circles ring her eyes, as though sleep has long eluded her.

'We will see this through,' she told Ral on that first day, after the arrival of the An-Zabati, blood pouring from a torn shoulder to pool on the deck beneath her feet. 'If it destroys what remains of us, we will see this through.'

A high price to pay, Ral thinks, for a new world scoured free of empire. Yet what choice is there but to pay it? The windships will sail on, arrows in the Skyfather's quiver.

When her wounds are bound, Atar spends an afternoon walking beside Ral, sharing all her people know of the empire, of their tactics and resources. 'Though it is true we fought them only in An-Zabat, a colony, and when our ships raided theirs after the city's fall,' she says. 'Fighting them in their heartland will prove a different challenge, I am sure.'

Sien is a land of fortress cities, after all, with leagues between the edge of the steppe and the capital, where they might hope to find the emperor and put an end to the horror he has wrought upon the world – leagues that are well garrisoned and well fortified. Yet there is hope, Atar points out, that those garrisons might be emptier than they would once have been.

'I told you, once, of the witch Firecaller,' she says.

Her words stir unease in Ral, who remembers the conversation clearly. Remembers, also, her rage in its aftermath, for this man Firecaller's words kindled Atar's doubt and fear. It had been their last conversation before Ral stole Atar's windskiff and rode her rage and rising stormwinds to the Skyfather's Hall.

If she notices Ral's discomfort, Atar does not show it. A light burns in her eyes, excitement and anger mingling into a fierce determination. 'Firecaller leads his own rebellion in Nayen now,' she says. 'They fight, as we do, for the right to their own way of life, to control of their own future. And I am sure there are others in the world, too, doing the same. In Toa Alon. Even within the heartland of the empire itself. If we can find a way to speak with Firecaller again, we might unite our separate wars. Strategise. Take advantage when the empire's attention is drawn southwards, or draw it to the north to create an opportunity for the Nayeni. Even bid him reach out to others who might join our cause.

'I am sure that every corner of the world, even Sien itself, holds those who begrudge the empire its cruelty. We might have more allies than we know, if only we can find a way to reach them, to tell them they are not alone, to stoke their hope for freedom and vengeance.'

'A sound strategy,' Ral agrees. 'If only we had a way to contact this Firecaller. He spoke to you in a dream, you said?'

Atar frowns. 'Something like that, yes.'

'And you do not know how to reach out to him?'

Atar's silence is confirmation enough.

'Then we must hope he finds your dreams again,' Ral says, putting an end to their conversation. 'Until then, we must focus on our own war. Agreed?'

Atar mutters assent and is quiet until she returns to her ship, frustration lingering in her expression. Ral tamps down rising guilt. She does not mean to stifle Atar's fire, nor cut the throat of her idea, but she cannot afford to pin the future of her people, let alone the world, on the uncertain magics and unpredictable motives of strangers.

*

On the fifth day of their southward journey, Ral finds Elsol Url Tabr, herbmistress of the Red Bull band, seated on her roan mare atop a ridge near the edge of the Skyfather's protection, watching the windships. Ral joins her, for the Red Bull remain aloof from the rest of Ral's war band. Their old and young do not ride the windships but still walk beside the packhorses and sledges, and their warriors do not intermingle with those of other clans, sharing neither bedrolls nor cookfires as the custom of fellowship demands.

Often in the last few days Ral has considered returning to the tent of the Red Bull's elders, to do what she can to weave them into the greater whole. An arrow or a spear with a crack splitting its shaft will hardly fly true. Yet always she has hesitated and found some other task to occupy her. She senses a skittishness among the Red Bull and fears that they might break away. Their distance is no threat to her divine mission, of course. No hindrance to her storm. She would merely rather not drive these people into the waiting chaos beyond the Skyfather's protection.

She eases Falling Star, her silver-grey gelding, in beside Elsol's mare. The elder's gaze remains fixed upon the windships, but she dips her head in response when Ral bows in the saddle and touches her chin.

'How fare you, Elder?' Ral asks.

Elsol runs her fingers through her beard with a veiled, distant expression. 'What a question,' she mutters, shaking her head. 'How fares anything in this day, war leader?'

Ral bristles. Elsol is an elder, and deserving of respect, but the flippant response is an insult. Yet she swallows her pride. Elsol is agitated, perhaps troubled by the same lingering doubt or fear that keeps the Red Bull apart from the rest of the war band. Maybe if Ral can soothe the herbmistress, it will begin to soothe the band.

Before Ral can muster words, however, Elsol carries on: 'You have seen the faces of these An-Zabati, yes? They are like ghosts. Like the unsettled, vengeful dead – little more than husks driven by terrible purpose towards an inescapable end.'

'They are as alive as you or I,' Ral answers. 'They eat and drink the same as we do.' Then adds, perhaps too hastily: 'And for each of our herds they take for a cookfire, they fill our waterskins twice over.'

Elsol nods slowly, jangling the bells braided into the twin tails draped on her shoulders. 'I do not mean to say that they *are* dead, war leader, only that they seem it. My people suffered losses and privation in our brief flight through the chaos upon the plains, until we reached you and shelter – a flight of only days, yet there is not a family among us untouched, whether by death or grievous injury. I have spoken with the An-Zabati they call Katiz – do not look surprised; I must know the trading tongue well to buy medicines for my people. He tells me their journey lasted *weeks*. That the sun seemed to hang unmoving in the sky, stretching out the days. That the nights were marked by frigid hail in places that had never felt a drop of rain.'

The elder's eyes drift to the sky. 'Have you noticed, at night, that the guide-star still holds position above us, though we have ridden five days south? As though all the dome of the sky is fixed in place. If the terrain beyond the Skyfather's protection had not changed, I might wonder if we have truly travelled at all.'

Falling Star, perhaps sensing Ral's disquiet, whickers and stamps. Elsol's roan mare whips her tail and eyes him warily.

'The chaos is terrible, yes,' Ral says, shifting in her saddle, 'but it is part of the storm that will shatter the empire. Change cannot come without chaos, Elder. I regret that the An-Zabati and so many of our people were battered by those winds, but I welcome them all the same.'

'You think the empire is worse than this?' Elsol muses.

'The empire destroyed my family,' Ral says firmly. 'They slaughtered thousands of us, defiled the Skyfather's Hall, destroyed the city of the An-Zabati. They would have enslaved the world.'

'How many thousands have died in this storm, as you call it?' Elsol says, gesturing towards a black shape swooping back and forth just beyond the shimmering line of the Skyfather's protection. 'How many cities has it scoured away?'

'It is the gift of the Skyfather.' Ral breathes deeply against the heat that rises behind her eyes. Her anger will do nothing but drive these people away, and into terrible death. 'As my power is his gift. A chance to free ourselves. A chance to make a better world.'

'I'll not spit in the face of freedom, of course,' Elsol says. 'Tell me, war leader, do you know the tales of when last the gods walked freely in the world?'

Her words stun Ral. Twice now Elsol has spoken of things her elders never did. The elders of the Red Bull alone, who have ranged farther than any other clan, to the very edges of the empire's reach, remember the marks of a Stormrider's power. Now she speaks of legends Ral has never heard whispered, let alone told freely around the cookfires.

Elsol does not wait for an answer. 'Before there were Stormriders, before the Skyfather fell silent, before there were even a people who called themselves *Girzan*, the world was as it is now, full of monstrous beasts and uncertain forces. Time and the stars left to wheel without shape or rhythm. Impossible creatures hungry for flesh, and people contorted into monstrous forms. Beasts of stone and earth, wind and fire. All products of a war between the gods. A war that shook the world, tearing apart nature's warp and weft, leaving all in tatters.

'I wonder if this is the Skyfather's *gift*,' Elsol muses, her voice growing gentler. 'I wonder if it is but an accident – a product of the gods' return to war, as the legends tell. I wonder what shape the new world you claim to herald will take.'

'A world free of the empire,' Ral says, a wilful antidote to the venom of doubt. 'A world where our people can offer sacrifices to the Skyfather again, raise Stormriders again, *thrive* again.'

'Perhaps,' Elsol says with a slow, considered nod. 'If any of us survive.'

Falling Star whickers and sidesteps away from Elsol's roan, his legs whisking through the tall grass of the ridge. Ral should call the elder down, summon her to answer for her blasphemy, for her treason to the war band. Even an elder is not above reproach. If a verdict of guilty would cost only Elsol her life, Ral might have done just that, but she is not yet so hard hearted to doom an entire clan – and the humiliation alone would drive the Red Bull away.

She reins in her outraged mind, eases it, seeks some alternative, some punishment that the Red Bull will be able to endure. For she cannot abide this, not at the risk that the Skyfather – his favour already strained – might withdraw his protection.

As Ral considers, Elsol watches the windships placidly as though her words are nothing but acceptable, even ordinary. Until suddenly her expression twists in surprise and concern.

'Look there!' She points a finger at the second windship from the front of the column, the *Dunecleaver*. 'The ship lists!'

Ral peers into the distance and sees the truth of Elsol's words. The vast sails of the *Dunecleaver* no longer stand at their correct angle to the ground but have tilted. She digs in her knees. Falling Star rears and whinnies, then leaps for the slope, hooves pounding. Visions of the ship toppling onto its side, crushing the column of riders at its flank, spur her to speed. *Get away from the ship!* The words rise in her throat but fade as a sharp *crack* sounds and issues the order on her behalf. The ship's belly falls to the earth. Its sails bulge on swaying masts like lone pines in a windstorm. The crew who have kept their feet dash about, pulling on flapping lines to furl the sails and bring the ship to a shuddering, creaking halt.

The Girzan flanking the ship ride clear, and the An-Zabati slow the other windships. By the time Ral reaches the *Dunecleaver*, its captain and carpenter have descended a rope ladder to squat over the broken runner, surrounded by a half-circle of other An-Zabati – the winddancer Atar of the *Spear of Naphena* among them. A wide, jagged crack bisects the thick spar at an oblique angle, and as the ship fell the broken edge has caught against the earth. Momentum has torn the back half of the runner from its supports, scattering splinters and shards of wood while the hull carved a deep furrow in the soil.

Sulon, the captain of the *Dunecleaver*, stares stone-faced at the wreckage while his carpenter explains all of this. Even Ral, who knows nothing of ships, does not need to hear his verdict. Still, because she must say something, she asks what has happened.

'She's lame, but if I could hoist her off the ground, I could replace the runner,' the carpenter replies, scratching his scraggly beard, a stony hopelessness in his eyes. 'But we're far from an elevated harbour, and without dismantling one of the ships for wood I don't see a way to build a proper crane.'

'Unfortunate to lose the ship,' Ral says, stepping down from Falling Star's saddle. The An-Zabati do not appreciate being spoken to from horseback, she has learned. Sulon presses his hand firmly to his eyes – to stifle tears, Ral suspects, but does not shame the captain by drawing attention.

'Not unfortunate,' the carpenter corrects her, his voice sharp. He digs his fingers into the earth between his feet, scraping at the soil. 'Inevitable. We ran these ships hard to reach your people, and they were never meant to sail over this sort of terrain. The earth doesn't flow like the sands of the Waste. The ships are heavy enough that we hardly feel the jostling, and the grass provides some cushion, but every plank, every joint, is under far too much strain. The *Dunecleaver* broke first, but she won't be the last.'

The winddancer Atar's expression has soured while the carpenter was speaking. She exchanges words in the An-Zabati tongue with Sulon, whose shoulders begin to shake. Laughter bursts from him and his hand falls from his face.

'Let her hear.' Sulon shifts back into the trading tongue. 'Let her know. You say there is room on the other ships for my people? Well, let them go to the other ships. Let them delay their end a little and sail as far as they can.' He jabs a weathered hand at the *Dunecleaver*. 'My home lies there, shattered upon unwelcoming soil. I will remain with it.'

The ship's carpenter nods at the captain's words and a chill runs through Ral, a brisk cross-current to the raging storm. If the crew of the *Dunecleaver* remains, they will eventually lose the Skyfather's protection as the war band moves southwards. In a matter of days, the ship will be swallowed by the chaos that scours the world.

'You cannot be serious!' Atar pleads. 'Ships are lost, Sulon. It has happened before. Crews are broken and scattered. It is no cause for you to throw away your life!'

'We lost the city, Atar!' Sulon roars, his voice breaking. 'We have lost *everything!* Do you think these seven ships are enough to restore our people? Enough to carry our legacy? No. We are already destroyed. What remains of us when this war, this chaos, has ended – if anything does – will be joined to these Girzan, our ways swallowed by theirs in time, leaving only scraps and fragments, half remembered. You know this, yet you speak to me of survival.'

Atar bristles. 'The only way to save our people – to save *any* people – is to destroy the empire. If that means joining with the Girzan, then so be it.'

'We have no desire to swallow your people,' Ral says, trying to keep her voice gentle. 'We are not the empire.'

'No, you are not, but it doesn't matter,' Sulon says. 'That you will, whether you intend to or not, is as certain as the heat of the sun – though I suppose even that is uncertain, in these days when the stars stand still.' Another burst of softer, more aching laughter. 'We are here at the end of the world, Atar. When my sails were full and momentum carried me, I could force myself to move forwards, but my runner is broken, my home is crippled. It has stopped here, never to sail again, and I will stop with it, whatever that means for me.' He heaves a sigh and lowers himself to sit on the broken runner, like a traveller resting their aching bones at the end of a tortuous journey. 'Let those who still have leagues in them scatter to the other ships. I stay here.'

'I cannot promise that the Skyfather's protection will linger with you.' Ral can see the pride in the man's eyes. It is all he has left: pride of home, pride of purpose – both lost to him if he abandons his ship. 'It follows the war band, and the war band moves south.'

'Protection, is it?' Sulon glares back at her, pride kindling defiance. 'You know what I think it is, Stormrider? A noose around our necks, dragging us southwards to serve your god's purpose.' His gaze cuts towards Atar. 'This is the god who destroyed Naphena, winddancer. You know our legends better than anyone.' He points his chin at Ral. 'And Firecaller warned you about this one, didn't he? You should never have asked us to sail—'

'If we had not, we would all be dead,' Atar says, her words a cudgel beating down Sulon's accusation. 'As *you* will be dead if you let grief anchor you here.'

'Well then,' Sulon says flatly. 'I suppose I'll die.'

The carpenter barks a laugh and crosses his thick arms across his barrel chest. 'I'm sure there are plenty who will take the offer, winddancer, and join the other ships. But I think I'll stay here, with the captain. I've been patching *Dunecleaver* since she first crawled out of the construction yard. I'll not abandon her now.'

'You would throw your life away?' Atar demands, her voice strained, on the edge of furious tears. 'Other ships could use your skill.'

'Perhaps,' the carpenter agrees. 'There will be other damage, I'm sure, in this mad dash. Maybe some of it will be reparable. But soon enough I'll have to watch another ship crippled, and another, until we all walk or ride the last leagues to Centre Fortress.' He shakes his head. 'Not a future I'd like to see. Too much pain in that.'

'You are thinking only of yourselves,' Atar seethes, her eyes cutting from one man to the other. The carpenter scratches the back of his head and looks away. Sulon's gaze never leaves Atar's face, but there is a fog over his eyes – the blindness of fixed purpose. 'Is this who we have become? Cowards? Children? Do you think there is one person who fights the empire and is not afraid? If we gave in to fear, An-Zabat would have been lost long ago. Windships would sail only under the empire's banner. Any choice but to fight is weakness, and—'

'I understand,' Ral cuts Atar off. Further argument will do nothing but agitate the two men. She can see in the hard, hopeless cast of their eyes that they have already accepted death. A sad thing. She will mourn them once the new world is born, but until then the storm cannot linger, not even to mourn its lost and dead. 'We will leave you supplies. You will not starve or die for want of water.'

The carpenter nods. Sulon works his jaw back and forth,

chewing a retort. He only nods and turns his face to the sky and the burning sun. There is, perhaps, no point anymore in bandying words. He contends now only with time, death, and himself.

The day is spent moving passengers and cargo from the *Dunecleaver* to the other ships. Several dozen of its sailors, skilled men and women all, choose to stay with their captain and carpenter, one of the two windcallers aboard among them. Atar tries to convince the man to join another crew – his skills are too rare and useful to abandon – but the young windcaller is as hard and unyielding as iron. 'I will stay, and my bowl with me,' he says. 'There are no sails here to fill, but I'll not leave them to die of thirst, winddancer.'

The sky has already darkened towards twilight when the war band continues on its way. Ral pushes them on into the night, sailing and riding by the light of the stars. The storm surges within her, frustrated by the lost day, by the damaged ship, by the captain's doubt. She will not let her war band camp in the shadow of the *Dunecleaver*'s corpse, where Sulon's words might spread from fire to fire, darkening the hearts of the other An-Zabati, or even those Girzan – like the Red Bull – who question the Skyfather's gift and their divine purpose.

A storm to scour the world. A storm is an imprecise thing. Not a weapon like a blade or an arrow, but a wild force. It is inevitable that some innocents will be caught up and destroyed in its passing.

Perhaps not so innocent, Ral ponders as the war band's path winds between a pair of hills. Outriders stalk the ridgelines. They travel through Sien now, albeit its barren fringes. Still, they are wary of being spotted, or of ambush, and already the certainty of looming battle is on the wind, like the scent of lightning soon to strike. Old habits when passing through hill country. Perhaps, also, a sign of doubt.

It was doubt that condemned Sulon and his ship, Ral decides. Not doubt of her – plenty have doubted her, and still do – but doubt of the Skyfather. Doubt of the better world to come when the empire is no more. They were unworthy, she decides, to see that new world. That is why the Skyfather allowed their ship to break.

She shares these thoughts with Garam, who rides with her beneath the lightning-wreathed woman on her sigil flag. The jagged white lines stand out starkly in the night. The woman at their heart is little more than a suggestion, a shape defined by the greater power that surrounds her.

'That may be, Stormrider,' Garam muses, idly thumbing one of the plates of blood-stained Sienese armour stitched to his jerkin. 'Could also have been nothing more than an accident, like a horse stepping in a marmot's den and snapping a leg.'

The notion makes Ral shudder. *No.* The storm carries them onwards. The Skyfather guards their passage. Any failure, any harm must be a withdrawal of his protection.

'The other ships have fared well enough,' Ral retorts. 'You did not hear Sulon's words. He questioned everything. Conjured up old An-Zabati stories in which the Skyfather plays the villain. He and his ship were never truly a part of the storm.'

Garam only shrugs. 'As you say, Stormrider.'

At the next curve in their passage between the hills, the wreckage of the *Dunecleaver* will vanish from sight. On the hilltop, her silver-threaded scarf fluttering in the wind, stands the winddancer Atar. A torch burns on a pole beside her, casting her in flickering light and writhing shadow. Slowly, with deliberate movements, she begins to dance.

Ral watches, mesmerised. She has seen Atar's dances before, during her brief time among the An-Zabati, but never this performance. It is a gentle dance, with no dramatic leaps or flourishes. Her arms entwine above her head; her hands drift downwards like snow, falling leaves, the setting sun. Her feet carve wide, interlocking circles into the earth, then return to the centre of the pattern, beside the burning torch.

Suddenly, with a wail, Atar collapses, letting her arms and legs fall at wild angles, and then lies still. Ral's heart lurches into her throat. She spurs Falling Star to the top of the hill, wondering if the dancer has trodden on a serpent or scorpion, or if her outriders have failed to flush out some stalking bandit or Sienese patrol who have taken the opportunity to plant an arrow in such an obvious target firelit against the dark sky.

Atar lies at the centre of the interlocking circles. As Ral reins in beside her, Atar stirs, her eyes fluttering open, glistening with tears in the torchlight. She bears no wound save a toenail torn from one foot by the hard, unyielding ground – hardly an injury to make Atar, winddancer and warrior, wail and collapse.

'What happened?' Ral asks, sliding down from her mount.

Atar stares up at her, chest heaving – with sobs or exertion, Ral cannot say.

'The *Dunecleaver* is lost,' Atar says. 'My people are lost.'

'Not all of your people,' Ral points out.

Atar closes her eyes again and rolls to face away from Ral and towards the distant silhouette of the shipwreck, little more than a sharp-angled blur against the plain blotting out the lowest stars. Just beyond it, the flickering veil of the Skyfather's protection still holds. For how much longer, who can say?

Shame washes through Ral. She knows the agony of loss as well as anyone. Atar is in mourning. An argument will not ease her pain. She lowers herself to the ground, hugs her knees to her chest, and watches the war band pass them by.

'What was that dance?' Ral asks gently. 'I did not recognise it.'

'One performed at funerals for great leaders,' Atar answers.

Ral lets the silence linger. It is easier than finding something else to say. She sees her father in her mind. His face, smiling and vibrant, and the butchered head that was so much like it, sharing its shape and structure, and yet so horribly strange. Comparing her grief to Atar's will accomplish little, she knows, but she can hold her own suffering in her heart and let it resonate. Feel, for a moment, at least an echo of another person's pain. Otherwise, she fears she will try to argue Atar's grief away, pointing out that those who will die with the *Dunecleaver* chose that death, that the An-Zabati have suffered no worse than any other people in the world and are indeed fortunate that a remnant survive to serve the Skyfather's storm. Such words she knows will only wound Atar more deeply, and so she swallows them – though they are true – and only does what she can to join Atar in her grief.

'After we left the *Swiftness* together, what feels like an age ago,' Atar says, 'Firecaller spoke to me, conjuring words in my mind from leagues away. I told you of his warning then.'

Ral remembers those fraught days, flying over the Waste upon Atar's windskiff, with a twinge of guilt. Recalls, too, the strange little dark-complexioned man who accompanied them, always jotting notes and sketches in his little book. 'He told you that I threatened to anger the gods,' she says. 'Yet here I am, a favoured servant of the Skyfather. He was wrong, Atar, as we knew he must be.'

Atar raises herself on her elbows and faces Ral. The tears still flow, but when she speaks there is no hint of sadness in her voice, only a dark, seething anger. 'He warned me that you might shatter the world and bring about an age of death and chaos,' she corrects, each word sharp and jagged as a knife, and heaves herself to her feet, swaying. 'I'm beginning to think he was right.'

She turns and stalks down the hillside, back towards her ship. Ral's conjured grief is forgotten, replaced by indignation and outrage. Her face burns. She stands, shoulders quivering, hands curled into fists. Lightning crackles within her, ready to flare out and burn Atar from the world, and with her all these miserable, dying, doubting An-Zabati.

'I am the servant of a god!' Ral roars. 'The only peace left in this world surrounds me, *because* of me! You spit on the Skyfather's gift?'

Atar pauses, looks over her shoulder, the tight curls of her hair whipping in the wind. 'Do you remember Jhin, Stormrider?' she says flatly. 'The Toa Aloni scholar who helped you return to your home and begin this war?'

'Of course! What is the—'

'He was among the first to die.' Atar's voice is a cold rain, dampening the fire in Ral. 'Whether you broke the world, or the emperor did, or the gods, or Firecaller himself, I see only one way forwards,' she says firmly, mastering her rage. 'We will sail to Centre Fortress and drive our swords through every imperial heart we can find. But if we fight alone, if we depend on the whims of gods instead of those who would stand beside us, we are doomed as surely as the *Dunecleaver*.'

The winddancer turns back to her ship and walks on, soon fading into the darkness beyond the circle of torchlight.

Jhin. Ral held no special affection for the man, with his scrawlings and his strange questions, but she knew him. She remembers his inquisitive mind, his kneeling over every new plant or unusual stone with his little notebook and his sketches. And he helped her, albeit in a small way.

If the Skyfather punished Sulon for his doubt, what cause, she wonders, did he have to punish that simple, sweet, curious man?

She looks to the sky, to the fixed stars and the absent moon.

She can only have faith, she reminds herself. She is the storm.

Yet she feels then, in the starlight, the first cold, creeping question that will blossom into doubt.

IO

To Seek and Find

Koro Ha

'I'll show you where to find me,' Yin Ila explained while they picked their way downhill through backstreets and alleyways. She nursed her injured arm, though her limp had eased somewhat. Koro Ha still stepped gingerly on his right leg, but the throbbing pain had faded and he no longer feared that the bone had been broken. 'Then you can head off to find your family if you want. Things have changed in the city. It's worth making sure they're still all right.'

Things have changed was a startling understatement. Makeshift shelters of stretched canvas or piled crates lined every road. Haggard people with hollow cheeks and bright, desperate eyes watched their passage, kept from holding out their hands for alms only by Yin Ila's scars and the bloody wound on Goa Eln's brow.

'So many refugees,' Koro Ha murmured. A nagging worry needled him, like a nest of hornets stirred by Yin Ila's words. But a visit to his father, sister and niece would have to wait until he, Yin Ila, and Goa Eln found their bearings in the city. 'All of Toa Alon hides behind these walls, it seems.'

'And not a Sienese face on the streets,' Goa Eln pointed out. 'Not even a patrol since we left the gateway plaza.'

Koro Ha hadn't noticed, and the young woman's observation stunned him. For his entire life, Sor Cala had been a city sharply divided. Even a modest Sienese merchant enjoyed a life of unimaginable wealth compared to the Toa Aloni, who could, at best, hope for a life of meagre comfort as skilled labourers or tradesmen. Yet this quarter near the city gates had been one of the places where those worlds overlapped, where Sienese overseers came to hire Toa Aloni workers and where those Toa Aloni with a few coin to spend might buy a small luxury from a Sienese shop. No longer. The chaos that roiled outside the city had frightened the Sienese back to their estates and mansions.

'It might be easier to move around than we'd hoped,' Yin Ila murmured. 'Though making our way into Orna Sin's garden, or the dungeon where they're keeping him, will likely prove a bit more challenging than in ordinary times, I'd wager.'

Koro Ha's worries redoubled in ferocity. A city overstuffed with desperate people hardly seemed a safe place. His father; his sister, Eln Se; her husband, Yan Hra; and their daughter, Rea Ab lived in an old district far from the estates. The Sienese were conquerors, yes, but the city had reshaped itself around them. If they had ceased patrolling the Toa Aloni neighbourhoods, what would keep the peace?

'What's this foolishness, then?' Yin Ila muttered.

Decorated archways had always divided Sor Cala's districts, though few save those that opened to the Sienese neighbourhoods had been equipped with gates, let alone ever stood closed and guarded. The archway to the Runoff, the harbourside district where Yin Ila kept her safe house, was worked from planks of salt-stained wood eerily similar to the shipwreck structures of the Black Maw. A wooden gate of much lighter, newer wood had been hung on a central pivot. It stood open but was flanked by a pair of Toa Aloni men wearing the heavy aprons and leather sleeves of blacksmiths. One held a hunting bow, the other a sickle affixed to a broom handle. The one with the makeshift spear sized them up, lingering on Yin Ila and Goa Eln's injuries. 'What's your business in the Runoff?'

'Our business?' Yin Ila barked a laugh. 'A few drinks and a whore or two. What's it to you? Do the Sienese know you've posted up like this? Think they'll be keen on a militia popping up inside the city?'

The man sneered. 'Seen any patrols? The imperials stopped caring what happened outside the Voice's Wall weeks ago, beyond their gate tax.'

Koro Ha suppressed a groan. Things sounded even worse than he had feared.

'The Voice's Wall?' Goa Eln asked. 'You mean the wall of the governor's estate?'

'You'll know it when you see it,' the man said, leaning on his spear, the sickle blade flashing as it caught the evening light. 'Cuts the district around the garrison and the governor's mansion off from the rest of the city. They say the monsters can't cross it. Can't speak to that, but we haven't seen many of them in the city since the wall went up. Suppose that makes it a boon, though I shiver every time I catch a glimpse of the damn thing.'

'Well, it's doing little good beyond the city walls,' Yin Ila said, bristling. 'I'm guessing the freakish dogs that did this to us are your "monsters". A whole mess of 'em attacked the refugees on the road.'

The two guards exchanged a sour look. 'Ill news, that. Does explain your injuries, though.'

'We're in from the countryside,' Goa Eln stepped towards the man, making her eyes wide and frightened. 'My cousin has a place by the harbour. We ...' She reached towards the wound on her forehead, then clasped the hand to her chest and turned away. The guards had fixated on her, drawn in as though her gestures were the finest, most captivating poetry. 'Please,' Goa

Eln went on with a quivering lip. 'We need rest and shelter. It's been such a long journey, with such a terrible end.'

The guard with the bow coughed and nodded sharply. 'Of course. We're not here to stop folk getting to their people, just to keep the peace. Sorry for the trouble, miss.'

Goa Eln let her shoulders droop, play-acting a wave of overwhelming relief. 'Oh, thank you. We won't forget your kindness, or your bravery.'

Despite the worry gnawing at him, Koro Ha had to suppress a wry smile as they passed through the gate. His preference had always been for other men, but he doubted even he would have been immune to Goa Eln's performance when his blood had run hottest in his youth.

As soon as the guards were out of sight, she cackled and flashed a sharp grin at Yin Ila. 'Works as well on jumped-up militiamen as it does on customs agents, it seems.' She pouted her lip and fluttered her lashes. 'Please, boys, we're a breath away from collapsing from blood loss.'

'Yes, yes, well done,' Yin Ila snapped, 'but a pretty cheek and a soft word will only get you so far.'

'My charms at least bring a comely lad to my bed from time to time. Have you had much success bullying lovers into submission, Captain?'

Yin Ila glared at her. 'I've always had better bloody uses for my time. Go on, keep up your clever banter. See how well it serves you when we're back on the *Swiftness* and I've got you manning a bilge pump from sunup to sunset.'

Goa Eln laughed again but took Yin Ila's suggestion. They made their way through the Runoff, soon leaving the thick, cart-rutted thoroughfare for a narrow side street. The harbour was little more active than the gateway plaza. There were a few clusters of refugees beneath tarpaulins or huddling in the shelter of lintels, but most of the streets were empty save a few men and women moving with a purpose.

Once, they glimpsed a patrol of Toa Aloni carrying make-shift weapons. In the absence of imperial protection, the Toa Aloni had taken peacekeeping into their own hands, which gave Koro Ha little comfort. It stood to reason the same people who had held power within Sor Cala's underworld would be well positioned to organise militias and petty fiefdoms. Koro Ha doubted the rest of Sor Cala's criminals would prove as benevolently minded as Orna Sin and Yin Ila.

A dishevelled staircase of wobbly boards led to a ramshackle apartment above a dockside warehouse. Dust motes floated in shafts of pale evening light shining through holes in paper-covered windows. The few pieces of furniture were bare wood, and the only decorations were faded paintings and a pen-sketch map of the city on the far wall. If Koro Ha had to guess, the heavy iron lock on the door was by a fair margin the most valuable thing in the room.

'It isn't much, but it's a start,' Yin Ila grunted. She crossed to a heavy chest and threw it open, revealing piles of linen bandages and small glass bottles. She selected a bottle of some kind of liniment, wrapped it in a bandage, and tossed the bundle with her good arm to Goa Eln. 'We'll fix ourselves up, take the night, and get to gathering information in the morning. Just you wait, tutor. In a few short days, this place will be bursting at the seams with the talent we need to pull Orna Sin out of whatever hole the Sienese have stuffed him in.'

Goa Eln pulled the cork of the bottle with her teeth and made to daub liniment on the bandage.

'Wait,' Koro Ha said. Nervousness fluttered in his stomach, but he was a stonespeaker now. 'My magic can do more than conjure up a handful of yams.'

'Oh, I'm well aware, tutor,' Yin Ila said, looping a bandage over her shoulder to make a sling. 'Trust me. I'd rather these bruises just vanish than wince every time I want to move my bloody arm, but as I understand things the Sienese sorcerers can feel your magic at work. They may be hiding away behind this Voice's Wall, whatever it is, but I'd rather not risk discovery. Particularly because that bad business at the gate has likely drawn a Hand or two out of hiding to put the monsters down.' Yin Ila cut through the bandage with her teeth, then tied it off, binding her right arm tightly to her body. 'Besides,' she went on, 'you've your own business in the city to see to, haven't you?'

Koro Ha was taken aback. It was as though she had seen through him to the gnawing worry at his heart.

'I'll go with you,' Goa Eln said, tying off her own bandage around her brow and wiping the dirt and blood from her cheek. 'This is really just a scratch. One that stings like a bastard, but I'm still handy enough with a knife.'

Yin Ila looked Koro Ha up and down, frowning at his faded, salt-stained scholar's robe. 'You're not going in that. You'll want to blend in, not stand out, and I get the feeling anything that reminds folk of the Sienese will cause trouble.' She rifled through another chest. 'And hurry back. If any of those idiots we left behind at the gate make it into the city, they'll wind up here, likely battered halfway to death and in enough need of your talents we'll have to take the risk.'

'Of course,' Koro Ha said. 'Thank you.' Gratitude towards the two women warmed and settled him, even as Yin Ila's words reminded him of the dangers they had faced and those that still threatened them. Despite the horrors of the day, despite witnessing companions brought down by terrible beasts, they understood his simple fears.

'Aha!' Yin Ila pulled a shirt and trousers from the chest, tossing them to Koro Ha. 'Put those on, and then be off with you. The light's fading and I don't suppose the city will get any kinder in the night.'

By the last light of the sun and a lantern salvaged from the safe house, Koro Ha led Goa Eln up from the Runoff, thankfully by a route that took them past a different archway than the one they had entered, though it too was under guard by men with makeshift arms and armour. Gradually, they wound their way uphill towards the gravestone of the ancient city: the jagged, treeless mound left behind when the emperor had brought his wrath down on Sor Cala. They passed a Toa Aloni patrol, whose leader shouted for them to take shelter before nightfall. Goa Eln dipped her head and smiled in thanks for the kind suggestion, then rolled her eyes and grimaced as soon as the patrol was out of sight.

'He may have a point,' Koro Ha said. 'You can return to the safe house if you wish. I can spend the night with my sister's family.'

Goa Eln produced a knife from some hidden pocket of her sleeve, twirled it in her hand, then made it disappear, as though she were only occupying idle hands. 'Of the two of us, I think you've far more reason to fear the city streets at night.'

Koro Ha took her point. If they ran into trouble, he would be the one looking to her for protection. Toa Aloni magic, after all, was not particularly dangerous – at least, Koro Ha did not know nearly enough to make it so.

As they left the lowlands of the Runoff, the towers and private walls of the Sienese estates that dotted the highland districts came into view. At a glance they seemed normal, but if Koro Ha looked too long his head began to throb. The angle at which they stood seemed *wrong* somehow. They appeared straight enough, but his eye struggled to trace their vertical lines without drifting to one side or the other. Whether or not the strange rumours of the Voice's Wall the Toa Aloni guard had spoken of proved entirely accurate, it was true that something odd gripped the Sienese districts.

Not his concern, now. He shifted his gaze to the west, towards the neighbourhood of merchants' estates where Orna Sin had built his garden mansion and tunnelled his way into the ancient city, and breathed a sigh of relief. Whatever strange phenomenon gripped the Sienese districts, it had left Orna Sin's neighbourhood alone – which meant, Koro Ha hoped against hope, that the Sienese had abandoned that part of the city just as they had abandoned the Runoff.

'It might prove easier to reach the tunnels than I'd feared,' he told Goa Eln, then explained his observation and his theory.

'Fortunate for you,' she said. 'Of course, any guards pulled back from other parts of the city will be in the garrison, which is where they're most likely holding Orna Sin.' She held out her hands like unbalanced scales. 'The easier the one task becomes, the harder the other. We might be able to find whatever Uon Elia left behind in the buried city, but even if it's some kind of powerful weapon, we'll need leadership and unity if we're to chase the Sienese out of the city. Yin Ila doesn't show it, but she's in over her head. One ship, she can manage. To run a fleet, or a large-scale smuggling operation, or a rebellion, we need Orna Sin.'

A fair enough point, which smothered what little hope Koro Ha had allowed himself to feel. He wanted to rescue Orna Sin. Perhaps not as desperately as Yin Ila and her crew, who thought of the old smuggler like the patriarch of their strange family, but Orna Sin had been a friend. More, he had helped to open Koro Ha's eyes to the importance of preserving their people and their way of life, even if there could be little hope of scraping the empire out of Toa Alon. He was a good man, and he deserved rescue. But he had been a captive of the Sienese for the better part of a year. If he still lived, who could say what condition his mind and body might be in?

Justice and compassion demanded they free him if at all possible, but freeing him meant striking out at the Sienese, agitating them, endangering the effort to uncover whatever secrets the ancient stonespeakers had left behind, which Uon Elia and his fellows had sought during their long decades buried in the ruins. Was freeing a single, broken man worth endangering the legacy of their people? It was a question Koro Ha felt ill equipped to answer.

The patrols thinned as they entered the maze of streets that made up the Tanneries, a district that crawled along the western side of the mound that marked the ancient city. The nose-wrinkling aromas Koro Ha knew from his childhood were weaker than they should have been. Half the doors and windows they passed had been nailed shut; the others had been abandoned too quickly for such precaution. The homes and alleyways were empty. No one, it seemed, was desperate enough to take refuge here. Rats watched them from doorways left open. Cries and howls echoed through the otherwise empty streets.

'Bloody eerie,' Goa Eln observed. 'What happened here, d'you think?'

They had their answer soon enough as they passed an alleyway littered with what Koro Ha took at first for bundles of rags. Only when the rot-sweet smell of old corpses reached him did he recognise them for abandoned bodies, ravaged by wild beasts. Old bloodstains spattered the walls and street with black.

They hurried on, their eyes drawn to every alleyway and shadow, then cringing away from unmoving, contorted shapes. The same horror that had struck at the gate that afternoon had run rampant here. Koro Ha found himself muttering old words he'd not thought of in years: Toa Aloni prayers, taught to him by his mother, begging the stone-faced gods to protect his family – too late, he could not help but fear.

The door to his father's house stood unlatched, cracked open beneath the slate tiles that bore the stone-carver's chisel and the seamstress's needle and thread. Weakness gripped Koro Ha's knees at the threshold. His hands shook and his shoulders hunched inwards, as though they might shield him from the sight of his sister's huddled corpse, or his niece's blood, or his father's sightless eyes.

'I'll go first, if you want,' Goa Eln said gently.

Koro Ha swallowed and nodded, but found his feet had rooted themselves. Goa Eln stepped past him, pushing the door open only far enough to slip through, shielding him from whatever lay beyond. Endless moments pounded at the base of his skull, each breath coming more shallowly than the last.

At last, Goa Eln returned. 'Empty,' she said, and Koro Ha nearly collapsed from sudden relief. 'Looks like they left in a hurry, though.'

'Thank the stone-faced gods,' Koro Ha murmured, and followed her into the house. It looked to have been torn apart. Chests and drawers stood open, clothes lying abandoned in piles on the chairs and table. Upstairs was no better, the beds having been stripped of blankets, likely to bundle up what few possessions Yan Hra, Eln Se, and Rea Ab were able to carry on their backs.

'It's getting dark,' Goa Eln said. 'I'm sorry, Koro Ha, but we should head back.'

He nodded, feeling half awake as he drifted through the wreckage, hoping against hope that his family had left some sign of where they had meant to take shelter. But no. They would not have expected him to come looking for them. As far as they knew, he was still in hiding. He brushed his fingers through the dust that had settled on the tabletop, which his mother had kept fastidiously cleaned and polished all her life, a habit Eln Se had picked up after their mother's illness and death.

His fingers brushed a comb of carved horn, one of the dozen scattered objects forgotten in their haste, decorated with a knot of Toa Aloni scrollwork, and his hand closed around it. He did not recognise it, and wondered whether it had belonged to his sister or to her daughter.

It was something. A bit of hope to cling to.

A lump filled his throat. He rapped his knuckles, turned, and followed Goa Eln back out into the street. With luck and by the grace of the gods, he would find them, but both seemed in short supply in Sor Cala.

II
A Bargain

Pinion

The pain was nothing compared to the humiliation.

Pinion lay on the floor of his cell, stinking of his own waste, his fingers still clenched tightly to the length of chain. He stirred only once, when the heavy bolt slid aside and the door swung open just wide enough for one of the guards to place a fresh chamber pot inside. He stared at the crack of late-afternoon light that speared through the gap. The desperate urge to stand and dash for it, to throw his body against the open door, swept through him but faded beneath the pain and nausea that churned in his gut.

'Next time, do us all a favour and brain the other bastard, would ye?' Darting Buck snarled, then slammed the door shut and rammed home the bolt. Pinion let his head drop back to the floor.

Alder had been within arm's reach. A mere handspan away. Huo had taken him to the ground. Another dozen heartbeats and it would all have been over, at last. Alder would be dead. Oriole, his father – the entire empire, as far as Pinion could tell – avenged. And then, his self-imposed duty done, Pinion could walk into the sea and let the waves or the beasts that haunted their depths take him.

He fought down despair. There would be a second chance, he promised himself. His hands were free. Alder's idiotic, arrogant guilt – as though his *remorse* did anything to salve Pinion's wounds or make good all the harm Alder had done – would draw him back to that window, surely, and next time Pinion would not miss his opportunity.

Gradually, the pain in his abdomen faded. That guardswoman, Vole, must have been wearing steel plates in the toes of her boots. Thank the sages that she had missed his ribs. Huo had not been so fortunate. The left side of his face, from forehead to just below his cheekbone, was a single mass of swollen bruise, so dark it seemed black in the evening light that filtered between the bars of their narrow window, and his breaths were punctuated by low groans. If Pinion had his sorcery, or whatever strange echo of it he had been able to wield outside the damnable seal over the city, he could have set them both to rights, made them ready to spring for the door when the guards brought the pitiful bowls of watery congee that passed for their daily meal each morning.

'Huo,' he managed to wheeze, when the blades of light falling through the bars had thinned and turned the pale red of twilight. 'Try not to sleep, if you can manage it.' He remembered that much from the medical texts he had read as an apprentice Hand while studying to perfect his use of healing sorcery. Those with head wounds were in danger of dying in the night if permitted to fall asleep. Stifling his own groans, he shifted onto his back and nudged the captain with his toe. 'Keep awake, Huo. We're not finished yet, you and I. Not until the severed Hand is dead.'

Huo coughed a shallow laugh. Good: he was still awake. It would be a long night, but Pinion would rather endure those sleepless, painful hours than face the rest of his life, however short it might be, alone and imprisoned by his enemy.

'Quite a way we've fallen, eh?' he said, to fill the silence and keep Huo from drifting into sleep. 'From the deck of the *Ocean Throne* to a stinking, piss-soaked cell. Hard to believe. It's funny, I was certain my father would have me imprisoned, if not killed, when I burned the emperor's summons. Instead, I was offered a place at the right hand of the emperor himself, just before the world ended.'

Huo's right eye opened a crack. 'You did what?'

Pinion chuckled, but his mirth faded as he met the captain's steady gaze. 'I was upset after Setting Sun Fortress. You know this – you were there. In that last audience with my father, I let my outrage get the better of me. That's all.'

Huo's gaze pierced through the darkness filling their cell. 'Outraged? At duly given orders?'

'They had you slaughter children, Huo. Innocents. It wasn't right. You knew it. I saw it in your face that day.'

'And yet I did it. As I followed *your* orders. Every one. Even when you seemed to be going mad.'

'Perhaps you shouldn't have.'

Huo levered himself upright, leaning on his elbow. 'You are Hand of the emperor, Your Excellency,' he snarled. 'I do not deny doubt. I embrace it. It reveals the truth of the world. That I am only a soldier. That I understand nothing. That it is best for me to stay in my proper place and follow the orders of those who *do* understand.'

A sudden swell of fear threatened to close Pinion's throat. He tightened his grip on the manacle chain. 'We all have doubts, Huo.'

Huo's teeth flashed in the moonlight.

There was another *clunk* as the bolt was thrown open. Pinion started, rattling the chain.

Four figures dressed in heavy cloaks, two with clubs to hand, stood silhouetted in the open doorway. One put up his hands. Pinion recognised his young, hardened face.

'Easy now, sorcerer,' the young man said in Nayeni. By his voice, Pinion knew him: Newt, the gate guard who had welcomed Darting Buck's party back into the city. 'Why don't you put down that chain so we can talk? You and your friend there don't look to be in fighting shape, anyway, and it'll go better for us both the fewer bruises I have to add.'

'What is this?' Pinion demanded, still clutching the chain, bracing himself and making ready to lunge. He would get only one swing. 'Did Alder send you?'

'Can we hurry this along, Newt?' one of the others muttered. 'Hanging might not be worse than starving to death, but I'd still like to avoid it.'

Newt put up a hand to quieten the speaker, then turned back to Pinion. 'No one else knows we're here. We aim to bring you to your people. The Sienese have some full granaries left, see, and I'm tired of the knot in my belly. They'll want one of their Hands back, I'm sure. Probably enough to give us safe harbour and a few meals. What say you? Come quietly and get your freedom, or do we knock you senseless, stuff you in sacks, and haul you off?'

Doubt clawed at Pinion. If he were Nayeni, he would never have imagined aiding a Sienese Hand, whether or not that aid might have earned relief from starvation. More likely, he thought, this Newt and his fellows meant to avenge themselves on him and Huo for whatever pain the empire had dealt them – perhaps, even, for the massacre at Setting Sun Fortress.

More, much as Pinion wanted to be free, he wanted that freedom for a singular purpose, one he could little achieve from the Sienese partition of the city. Perhaps he would have an opportunity to return, this time armed and with allies. Or perhaps his best opportunity would come again if he waited patiently for Alder's foolishness and guilt to overwhelm and weaken him, prompting a second visit and a second chance.

'Newt!' the soldier who had spoken earlier hissed. 'If they won't come easy, knock them over the head and let's get on with it. The wall patrols won't be turned away much longer.'

Newt offered his palm. 'What say you, Hand?' His gaze drifted to Huo, who glared up at the soldiers through his good eye, his breath whistling through his broken nose. 'Rumour is the Sienese have a few of those strips of bone the witches use to work their magic. We'll get your friend the help he needs, and me and mine get our grain, all right? We both stand to benefit. Let's do this the easy way.'

Pinion gritted his teeth. Whether these Nayeni intended to murder him or deliver him to the Sienese, he had little choice but to go with them. Fighting back would only invite another beating, one that might leave him as battered as Huo.

'Fine,' Pinion said, 'but I am injured too. You lot will need to carry him.' Then, to Huo, he said in Sienese, 'They say they want to free us in exchange for food and shelter in the imperial quarter. We'll not have a better chance to escape.'

Huo grunted. 'I'll not let down my guard, Your Excellency.'

'Are we understood?' Newt asked.

At a nod from Pinion, two of the soldiers slipped into the cell. They hefted Huo to his feet, covering his mouth to stifle a groan, then slung his arms across their shoulders and half-dragged him out into the night. Pinion followed, uncertainty churning in his stomach. His gut still ached from Vole's kick, and his head swam for want of food and water. Whatever these Nayeni had planned for him, he saw little chance of fighting back on his own, let alone grabbing Huo and making a run for it.

They followed the line of the garden wall, keeping to shadows, pausing when the light of lanterns moved along the parapet or down a nearby path. One such lantern swept suddenly towards them. Newt grabbed Pinion's arm and pulled him into an alcove shielded by a standing stone, a simulacrum representing one of the Pillars of the Gods.

'Wait here,' Newt whispered, gesturing for them all to crouch down and stay hidden. He trotted out to meet the bobbing lantern light. Pinion's core ached as he squatted, listening to the muted exchange between Newt and the passing guard. A sudden burst of laughter punctuated their conversation, and the voices began to fade away. Finally, Newt returned.

'Cost me my last few sips of liquor,' he muttered. 'Come on. The way's clear to the servants' gate.'

Soon they came to a small door in the wall, guarded by a single soldier who nodded at Newt's approach, opened the gate, and followed them out into the city. Another defector. If five were willing to steal a prisoner and exchange him with the hated Sienese, the Nayeni must indeed be suffering. Pinion saw the hunger, now, in their gaunt faces. Perhaps the scarce meals of thin congee had not been a callous cruelty.

By moonlight, the streets of Eastern Fortress were a dim, winding maze made all the more treacherous by abandoned barricades and the strewn rubble of shattered buildings, broken by magic or chemical grenades. For the first moments of their escape, Pinion's heart thundered in his chest. They passed shadowed alleys and abandoned homes, and each time he wondered whether Newt would drag him into the cover of darkness. He tensed in anticipation of the flash and bite of knives.

Yet they walked on, making their way westwards, Pinion tracking their course by the position of the moon and stars, though he had never been an expert navigator. They avoided the few patrols they passed, and he let himself believe that Newt had told a semblance of the truth. He turned his mind to the next problem he would face.

The Sienese still held territory in Eastern Fortress, but they would be cut off from the emperor, both for want of Voices and because of the seal over the city, and paralysed for want of his commands. An attack on the governor's estate was an enormous risk, one Pinion would consider not worth taking if his only concern had been the preservation of imperial power and the destruction of the Nayeni rebels. Fortifying a defensible position and allowing the Nayeni factions to whittle away at one another was sound doctrine. Attacking either faction would only unite them, as they had been united in their assault on the city.

But the world had descended into chaos. A defensive posture might see them all devoured by monstrous wolves or cast into the sea by the glittering flames of a god suddenly birthed from between the stars. Or that strange black mass that hung above the bay might ... well, he could little imagine what, but it haunted the corner of his vision as he followed Newt through the city, and he found himself again wondering what had caused it and what it would do. Another unpredictable threat; another reason he could ill afford to gamble on a defensive strategy. The fight had to be taken to Alder's faction, and fiercely, if Pinion was to have his vengeance.

Newt put up a hand. Feathers of lantern light spilled from an upcoming bend in the road. Another Nayeni patrol, Pinion assumed. They had crossed no boundary or barrier that he had observed. Certainly no manned barricade or defensive line. He tensed but waited for Newt to lead the way to some sheltered, shadowed corner.

'Wait here,' Newt said and made a sharp gesture to one of the other soldiers, who clamped a hand just above Pinion's elbow. Pinion jerked away, as much from reflexive surprise as genuine fear.

'What is the meaning of this?' Pinion demanded, trying to

keep his voice low and quiet, only to turn back to find that Newt had already crossed the street towards that illuminated corner. 'Why did you bring us here?'

'Like Newt told you,' the soldier holding his arm said. 'We mean to trade you.'

Voices rose from around the bend. Voices speaking Nayeni.

'To the other faction,' Pinion murmured, realisation dawning as memory of Newt's words in the tunnel at the garrison gate swirled up.

'What are they saying?' Huo snarled, twisting in the grip of the soldiers supporting him. 'Your Excellency, what are they—'

A fist to the jaw left his head hanging, dazed to silence.

'You'll be found out.' Pinion's heart thundered.

'Likely they will find us out,' the soldier holding his arm allowed, squeezing tighter. 'Won't be hard, really. We aren't planning to go back. We were in the Army of the Wolf, not the Fox, or whatever Hissing Cat leads now. Stuck with her for a while, seeing as how she's the only reason the mess beyond the city walls hasn't leaked in yet, but that won't matter if we all starve, will it? And Burning Dog's people have food, too. Not as much as the Sienese, I hear, but enough to keep our strength up and fight.'

'A few granaries and stockpiles,' Pinion rambled, his mind scrambling for any argument that might convince the soldiers to take him back to his cell. Better Alder's prisoner than a prisoner of his rival. In the governor's estate, he had at least been near enough to lash out should the chance arise. 'You'll eat through your supplies, and what then? Farms can't survive in that madness out there, with time itself unhinged and the world overrun with beasts. This city will starve and you know it!'

'Quiet,' the soldier snapped, tugging on his arm. 'Why should I be first to suffer, eh? If I'm to die, I'll put it off as long as I can, thank you. Now keep your jaw *shut* or I'll break it. Burning

Dog's people said nothing about delivering prisoners whole, just alive.'

'But you—' The soldier's fist thudded into Pinion's aching gut, doubling him over and forcing him to swallow his words.

'Enough talk, I said,' the soldier snarled, menacing Pinion with his fist.

Newt reappeared, and with him a pair of Nayeni, one with ravens' feathers sewn into his hair. Newt's hand clamped down on Pinion's wrist and twisted his arm, showing his palm and the tetragram branded there to the lantern light.

'There, see?' Newt said. 'And the other one's a captain of some sort. We don't want anything for 'em, understand? Just a show of good faith to get us back in Burning Dog's good graces.'

The new arrivals said nothing. One spun Pinion around, wrenched his arms behind his back, and clamped heavy manacles around his wrists. A shove sent him stumbling until he found his gait. Bruised muscles pulsed with pain at every step.

His mind swam through fog, enduring occasional shoves of encouragement. He could have laughed. It seemed the world had determined to revoke whatever good fortune had seen him born into wealth and power. The disaster at Greyfrost, the brutality at Setting Sun Fortress – product of his own mad, half-considered plan – his disillusionment with the empire: all had been knives in his heart. Now he lived only to deal a single death and then die, and still the world took from him, dragging him away from his desires, driving every knife deeper and *twisting*.

They passed over a bridge, through a guarded gate, and beneath the lights of rooftop sentries, drawing a few curious eyes. This had once been one of the city's poorer districts, where minor Sienese merchants and Nayeni labourers made their homes. More lamps burned in the windows here. There were still scars of battle, but evidence of repair too: scaffolding raised to reinforce cracked facades; rubble piled neatly in the mouths of alleys rather than strewn across the street. The faces of the men and women who peered out into the night for a glimpse of the captives were not so gaunt, a fact that Newt and his fellows appeared to take note of, judging by their hopeful glances.

Huo began to stir, moaning and squirming against the pair of soldiers who still held him up. Pinion searched for an avenue of escape but found none. There were too many onlookers, now, and he doubted he could run far before exhaustion and his abused muscles gave out on him. Even if his own escape were possible, he would never be able to bring Huo with him; the captain hung unconscious between two rebels. And despite the long-standing tension between them, Huo had saved his life twice over. Could he repay that loyalty by abandoning him?

As the first light of dawn brushed the underside of the clouds, they came to a broad, squat warehouse. Figures armed with bows walked the rooftop and a pair of Nayeni in armour with swords on both hips met them at the wide cart door. More words were exchanged, but Pinion could little concentrate on them. His attention had fixed, in abject horror, upon a pair of corpses strung from spars of wood that jutted from the edge of the roof. Crows perched on the bodies, cawing at the newcomers between jabs of their hungry beaks. A dozen arrows sprouted from one, pinning silken robes to bloated flesh. The other wore fragments of Sienese armour that hung battered and blasted apart – one leg ended in a ragged stump at the knee. Both of their right arms had been folded up, their hands nailed to their chests to show their palms. The tetragrams branded there glimmered in the sunrise.

Pinion's bowels threatened to loosen. One of the soldiers escorting him shouted and caught him by the arm before he collapsed. His manacles bit into his wrists as the soldier heaved him upright. In the same moment, another shout and then a sudden furious *crack* sounded from a few paces away.

One of Huo's escort lay on the street, his arm twisted backwards and broken at the elbow. The other grappled with Huo, who, wild eyed, drove his forehead into his opponent's nose. The guard collapsed, blood spurting from his nostrils. The other Nayeni stared, shocked into stillness. For a moment, Huo and Pinion locked eyes. The captain's furious, swollen, half-dazed expression made him seem not a man, not a soldier of the empire, but a beast woken from sleep to find itself in danger and desperate for safety.

In that moment, any hope that Huo might free them both withered and died. The captain turned on his heel and ran into a shadowed alley. Bowstrings twanged. Arrows chased him into the darkness.

'Well?' Newt roared. 'After him!'

The soldier holding Pinion shoved him to the ground and drove a knee into his back while boot heels echoed down the alley after Huo.

Newt muttered curses under his breath. Pinion twisted beneath the knee between his shoulder blades, straining for a glimpse of the alley.

'It doesn't matter,' Newt spat. 'Get him up. Burning Dog's bounty is for Hands and Voices, not battered soldiers. Go on, get him up!'

Rough hands hauled Pinion to his feet and dragged him into the warehouse. Braziers and lamps hanging from wooden columns lit the open space, emptied of whatever merchandise had occupied it before Wen Alder broke the world. Nayeni sprawled against the walls on bedrolls or low cots, cleaning swords or fletching arrows. All wore the same fetish on their uniforms: a bone carved into the shape of a wolf's skull.

A wide table dominated the centre of the space. Behind it,

in a heavy chair carved with flowers and twining serpents that looked to have been dragged from some lesser official or wealthy merchant's mansion, lounged a young, broad-shouldered woman. A fresh scar stretched from her hairline to the edge of her right eye.

'What's this?' the young woman said, her voice rough, like the serrated edge of a blade. She stood, her palms on the table, and leaned towards Pinion. 'And what the *bloody burning hell* was that shouting about?' Her dark eyes fixed first on Pinion, then on Newt, and narrowed. 'Come crawling back, have you?' she said, a snarl twisting her voice. 'Tired of the gardens, eh? Or ready at last to finish the fucking war?'

Newt put up his hands. A strange gesture, to Pinion, who would have been bowing to the floor in his place.

'You can't blame us, Burning Dog,' he said. 'It was chaos. We were on Hissing Cat's side of the city and didn't know whether it would be safe to travel even a few blocks. By the time the dust settled, word had spread you were cutting heads off any defectors you caught, so we had to wait until we'd snagged ourselves a gift that might win back your trust.'

'Oh? *Had* to wait, did you?' She jerked her chin at Pinion. 'That's him? Your *gift?*'

'A Hand of the emperor,' Newt said. 'But not just any Hand.'

Stunned disbelief gripped Pinion. How could Newt have known he was the governor's son? More, why should Burning Dog care at this point, when his father was already dead? Dizzy, stupid thoughts born of simmering terror.

'Hissing Cat's people found this one on the beach,' Newt went on. 'A survivor from the fleet. The very same that went down in flames when those winged bastards filled the sky. Might be he knows something about what happened out there, and what the Sienese were planning – and might still be planning.'

Burning Dog regarded Pinion. He flinched away from her

gaze, which shone with a rabid, feverish hatred. Her hands curled into fists on the table.

'Get out of my sight, Newt,' she sneered. 'You've earned my pardon, but nothing more.'

'Thank you,' Newt said, bringing his fist to his chest. 'You won't regret—'

'Get the *fuck* out,' Burning Dog roared, pushing away from the table, her hand darting for her sword.

The sound of Newt's hasty footsteps echoed in the air, every eye in the warehouse watching his retreat with piercing disdain. The warehouse door slammed shut behind him and those eyes drifted back to Hissing Cat, and to Pinion, who knelt before her, his wrists bound at the small of his back. She strode around the table, one hand curled around the bone hilt of her sword. The other reached out and with a jagged fingernail traced a fiery line down Pinion's jaw.

'I don't give a damn about your fleet, or what you lot have planned for my island,' she said in a slow, venomous whisper. 'You Sienese bastards killed my family. First my father, when I was just old enough to see it and understand but too young to do any-bloody-thing about it. Then my sister – the first of that traitor Wen Alder's countless sins. And now my mother.'

Her fist tightened around the bone hilt and Pinion felt a sudden, impossible warmth spread through his body, and with it a wafting cinnamon scent. She brought her finger from his jawline to hover between his eyes. Wet blood stained the tip of the nail. A tongue of flame burst to light, flashing blood to steam.

'But Hissing Cat stole your magic away with ours. Only these bones hold any power, now, and I have one.' Her teeth were bright in the flickering light of conjured flame. 'What will Wen Alder say, do you think, when he learns I've been using his little toy – his canon, his little scheme to keep magic for himself after stealing away the pacts – to torture his Sienese friends? It can't hurt as much as the pain he's dealt me, but I hope it stings him just a little.'

Alder! Hope surged beneath terror.

The flame drifted closer, angling towards Pinion's right eye. He fought the urge to flinch away. Instead, he met her gaze, tried to match its depth of ferocity. 'Wen Alder killed my father,' he said, his voice quavering, but he pressed on. 'He led my brother into death. As much as you hate him, I hate him more.'

Burning Dog laughed – a cold, sharp sound – and still she held the flame to his face. 'Doubtful,' she said. 'His allegiance drifted back and forth in his little quest for power, didn't it? Always another lie with him, and another layer of betrayal. Putting your eye out may not pain him, true. I doubt anything but the agony of his own flesh will reach that stony heart.'

'You overestimate him.' Pinion's eye had begun to water, but he refused to turn from Burning Dog's gaze. 'He hasn't masterminded any of this, just blundered his way from one crime to the next. His heart is as twisted and conflicted as any man's. But he does feel something for me. Just today he came to my cell, full of teary-eyed apologies, begging me to forgive him. Twice now he has had the chance to kill me, and twice he has sent me away. I remind him of his crime against my brother, whom he loved.'

'So, hurting you will hurt him,' Burning Dog said, and brought the flame a hair closer. 'Good.'

'You would throw away your best advantage by torturing me to death?' Pinion blurted. 'You want revenge. So do I. And I disarm him, don't you understand? We can set a trap for him. Agree to a meeting. Offer them a parlay. Then take me with you, and when he lets down his guard at the shock of seeing me, you can strike!'

The burning finger drifted away. Burning Dog studied him, something more than fury lighting her dark eyes at last.

'Interesting,' she muttered, the flame fading, becoming only a subtle flicker on her fingertip.

'This is the best chance either of us will have to take our vengeance,' Pinion said, feeling sweat drip into his eyes but unwilling to blink lest she take it for a show of fear or weakness. Only the emperor's mind leafing through his, dragging free the half-formed plan that had led to the horror at Setting Sun Fortress, had been more terrible than this. 'We have the same goal, Burning Dog.'

'We have the same goal,' she agreed, leaning back against the table. 'And perhaps you could help me lay a trap for him, as you claim.'

'You know he spent time in the governor's garden as a youth,' Pinion said, giving in to hope, sagging into its embrace. 'I was there with him. My brother, Oriole, and I were his only friends. I have seen him weep for Oriole and grovel for my forgiveness. Let me help you, and we can both get what we want.'

'But we can never be allies, Hand.' The edge in her voice returned, and with it the flame burst to sudden, roaring ferocity. 'You are Sienese. You are a plague upon this island that must be burned away.'

'No! No!' Pinion finally flinched away, toppling backwards onto his arms, wincing in pain as his elbows and wrists twisted beneath him.

She planted a foot on his chest. 'My mother once said that in war, even the foulest of all things has its uses. A plague, too, can be useful, if it weakens an enemy. So I will not kill you, yet.' She leaned down, the blazing finger moving steadily, like a surgeon's knife, towards his eye. 'But neither can you be left unpunished.'

12
Penance

Foolish Cur

Dawn light filtered through the oiled-paper screen that covered my window. For a moment I lay there, wrapped in a thin blanket, letting the cool morning air brush my face.

Distant, muted shouts dragged my mind from the fuzzy quiet of waking and cast it back into the tumult. Sleep had come quickly, despite the gnawing of my burdens and worries, but my mind resisted the need to wake. *Let me lie here*, some simple, heartbroken, childish part of me begged. *Let the world, in all its pain and all its need, wait a moment longer.*

I kicked off the blanket, dressed in simple trousers and a tunic provided for me, and pulled on sturdy soldier's boots. That pain was my fault. Those needs were my responsibility. I could indulge in moments of comfort only when the world was whole again.

More for my own security and less from any notion that I deserved privacy and solitude, Hissing Cat's people had given me quarters in what used to be the children's wing of the governor's estate. Not Oriole's room – I had been careful of that – nor Pinion's. A servant's cubbyhole, big enough for a cot, a window, and a single chest of drawers. Nonetheless, an aching, sorrowful nostalgia gripped me as I walked those familiar halls where once I had come to visit Oriole for bottles of wine and games of Stones.

Would I know such peace, such friendship again?

Loneliness prodded me to seek out Running Doe, who Torn Leaf had told me could be found in the western garrison house. I took comfort in the thought that she was still alive, that there was someone in the Army of the Fox who still cared for me, despite my mistakes and all they had cost the world – assuming, of course, that the wounds she had suffered in our battle with the emperor had not curdled her affection. The notion sickened my stomach. I wanted to find her, wanted to believe that whatever had been between us on that night before the battle – whether love or friendship mixed with fear, desperation, and need of comfort – still remained. Yet I feared, too, that I would find her cold and distant.

It was easier to turn the other way, towards the hill and Oriole's tree, where duty waited, though that duty called for a confrontation with a woman I *knew* wanted me dead.

There was some comfort to be had in certainty.

The sight of the scarred plum tree still dug at me, yet only for the moment before I saw the figure at Hissing Cat's side – a short, sturdy man in a plain robe, his wild hair tied at the nape of his neck.

'Clear-River!' I blurted.

He turned towards me and smiled tightly. 'So it was more than a rumour,' he said, crossing his arms across his chest. I was unsure what else I had expected, but the cold rigidity of his posture pained me. 'I'm to understand you want to speak with Burning Dog, which is convenient. She wishes to speak with you.'

Though the words were what I wanted to hear, the menace dripping from his tone made me shiver. 'Word spreads quickly, I suppose.'

'Two men, one missing a hand, the other with a medicine seller's chest, accompanied by a dog, tussled with guards from the Army of the Wolf at the city gate,' Clear-River said. 'Your face may not be known to the ordinary soldier, but Burning Dog's people make their reports and she knows you well. At least she finally believes Hissing Cat hasn't been hiding you.'

'Good, then,' I said. 'I appreciate your efforts to arrange the meeting.'

'I didn't say I would arrange it,' Clear-River said sharply. 'Alder, think about this. Frothing Wolf died in the fighting. Burning Dog blames you for that, as well as for her sister's death. She doesn't want to talk with you; she wants to run a sword through you and burn you to char and bone for good measure.' He withdrew the strip of bone carved with my canon from his sleeve. 'She has one of these. Scavenged in the chaos of the battle. Plus two more in the hands of witches loyal to the Army of the Wolf. Even if I take a side and go as your escort, and you take Torn Leaf and Running Doe with you, it will be an even match, and don't think for a moment she'll hesitate for fear of her own life when she sees the chance to have her revenge.'

The bone disappeared back up his sleeve, and as he put it away I too put away the impossible question it raised: how did the canon of witchcraft still function when all other magic in the city fell silent under Hissing Cat's seal? Hissing Cat herself did not know, though, so there was little chance Clear-River held some secret insight when her millennia of knowledge offered nothing.

'Meeting her will accomplish nothing more than your death,' Clear-River went on, 'and we need you alive. As I understand these things, you're one of the few people in the world who might be able to fix the mess the gods have made.'

I felt the sting of his words, though he had elided the truth.

A mess the gods had made, perhaps, but only because I had played into Okara's hand in my naivete and desperation to free Nayen.

'I owe Burning Dog,' I said firmly. 'How can I face the damage I have done to the world if I cannot face the pain I have caused her? More, the rebellion will fail if we cannot stand united. The Sienese will simply wait while we pick and snipe at each other, then surge out from behind their walls and put what remains of us to the sword. The sage Rushes-in-Water wrote that division in a community is a sickness that saps all strength. The healing must begin here, Clear-River.'

'A noble attitude,' Clear-River said with a shake of his head. 'One that will see you killed and nothing accomplished.'

I felt the truth surge within me, desperate to be told. Clear-River, for all his compassion and all his commitment to peace, might sympathise but would never understand me. Perhaps there was no one in the world who would, not even Running Doe. Yet silence would condemn me to isolation. Was I still, after everything, too much of a coward to tell a simple truth?

'It hurts me, too.' I held out my hand, palm upwards. The diamond scar of my tetragram was a pink plane in the morning sun. 'Some nights I dream of Oriole's death, but not that alone. I dream of Frigid Cub, too – her knife flashing, and the searing hatred within me, and the lightning I called to burn her life away.'

Clear-River's mouth twisted in distaste, and I felt that willingness toward vulnerability, towards honesty, retreat within me. The truth I would express was not only incomprehensible to him, I saw, but horrifying.

'Burning Dog's pain is worse, I know,' I pressed, in spite of mounting shame. 'That's why I need to speak with her. Not to explain myself or defend myself, but to beg for her forgiveness. And if she can forgive me, maybe the rest of the Army of the Wolf can too and we can finally bring this war to its end.'

Clear-River heaved a sigh. 'You won't get forgiveness, Alder. She'll only do to you what you did to her sister. Or worse.'

'Maybe. Pain begets pain. Suffering begets suffering. We stab at each other, hoping, if not believing, that when our knife strikes home some of our pain will leak out into the one we hate, hoping the world can be made right with the thrust of a blade.' I thought of the emperor's blood, his gasping breath, and the shattering of the pattern around us. 'But it can't. I may not be able to heal the world or force the gods to a stalemate – it took every witch of the old sort, last time, and there were dozens then. Now we have only Hissing Cat and I, and the emperor, if he can look past the sword I put through him. And the Girzan woman, if we can find a way to reach her. Only four, and no way to know if it will be enough. But I can do this, Clear-River. I can break the cycle of vengeance and fear. Perhaps not in all the world, but at least here in Nayen.'

'By throwing your body in the path of Burning Dog's blade?' The disgust in his eyes had faded, but the wry twist of his mouth remained.

'Do I wish I owed this to someone less delighted by violence?' I muttered. 'Of course. But I owe it to her.'

Clear-River scrubbed a hand through his hair. 'You won't get to speak a word. The sight of you will drive her into a rage. I tell you, Alder, this is foolishness.'

'It is,' I agreed. 'It is also necessary. The first step I have to take if we are to accomplish anything else.'

He studied me for a long while, his body rigid, his face twitching through a series of fraught expressions – annoyance, giving way to anger, building to break into a quiet, baffled admiration.

'Fine, then,' he said. 'I will set the meeting. Only promise me you won't go alone. Take Torn Leaf with you, at the very least.'

'No,' I said. 'I will bring no fighters with me.'

'I guarantee you that she will.'

'That is her choice.'

Clear-River shook his head and chuckled. 'Gods, Alder, you hardly seem the same person I knew, however briefly, as a boy – let alone the terror that swept through Burrow. Still arrogant to a fault, of course.'

I did not argue with him, though to my mind little had changed, only my perspective. Always I had longed for some third path through the world, neither the empire's grasping cruelty nor my uncle's fatalistic resistance. I had long hoped that magic would provide such a path, but of course magic was only a tool, not an end in itself. Pursuing it had only entangled me deeply in the very conflict I had shunned and deluded myself into believing I might avoid.

This, though, was a true step of independence. No doctrine, no strategy, no brutal calculus of empire or rebellion or vengeance had led me to this decision, only Pinion's desperate rage and his weeping. Only the guilt I carried with me, and the understanding – my first, and perhaps only, mote of wisdom – that the world could not be made better by following those old, well-trodden, blood-soaked paths.

'Thank you, Clear-River,' I said.

'I only hope those thanks won't turn to curses when this is done,' he muttered and, at last, clasped my hand. Then, with the shifting of his grip on the strip of bone, a gust of cinnamon scent, and a sharp, familiar cramping down my limbs, he veered and launched himself over the garden wall.

For a wistful moment, I regretted my lack of magic and my inability to follow him. Despite my resolve, the raw emptiness where power should have been ached as badly as my missing hand.

'Bleed me, Foolish Cur,' Hissing Cat muttered, her eyes half shut and her body slumped as though on the edge of sleep – but of course, though she sat a few paces off, she had heard everything. 'You're bloody desperate to earn that name thrice over, aren't you?'

'I don't expect you to understand—'

'Good, because I don't, and never will,' she snarled. 'Just don't get yourself killed trying to salve guilt and bruised feelings. More than your sense of moral sentiment is at stake, boy. Loath as I am to admit it, I can't do what needs to be done on my damned own.'

A glib comment sprang to mind, but those half-closed eyes and tightly drawn mouth spoke of more than exhaustion. True fear hid beneath her stony expression.

'I will be as careful as I can,' I said. 'This is far from the most dangerous thing I have done.'

'Perhaps,' she conceded, 'but not, I'd wager, without magic. Don't forget, boy, a sword in the gut can kill you easily enough now.'

Her warning weighed heavily and made the stump of my right wrist itch. I thanked her for the advice and left the garden. There were other conversations to be had, other hurts to try to salve and guilt to assuage, before I would be ready to face Burning Dog.

Torn Leaf insisted on sending an escort with me to the western garrison house. It felt absurd to be flanked by six soldiers with bows and swords, and I was certain that Doctor Sho had been allowed to move about Hissing Cat's territory on his own, however chaotic the city might be. The bitter irony of being treated as precious cargo when I had, at last, begun to break down my own sense of self-importance had me caught between laughing aloud and grumbling with irritation.

The escort proved unnecessary, of course. The streets were empty, save for the occasional patrol and a few wide-eyed, hollow-cheeked observers peering down from windows above us, perhaps wondering who I was that I warranted such care. The people of Eastern Fortress – those who had not gone to join the forces of one of the three armies occupying the city – remained in the shelter of their homes. Only one or two from each household ever ventured out to the granaries for food, or to scrounge scraps from the abandoned markets, or to hunt vermin in the streets.

When we reached the garrison house, my escort exchanged salutes and quick words with the guards at the gate before handing me off like a Sienese bride brought to her husband's household. Two of the gate guards made to follow me into the courtyard, as though even here I required delicate handling. I chased them back to their posts with a hard glare, and immediately regretted it when they had gone. I had failed to ask where I might find Running Doe and my grandmother.

Soldiers crowded the courtyard of the garrison house, their tents and lean-tos sprawling across the tiled parade ground. Greasy smoke rose from fires where soldiers roasted spitted rats and other vermin to fortify their meals of thin gruel. After the first dozen people I asked for directions rebuffed me with a glare and a cold shoulder, at last a young woman, her right cheek and eye wrapped in bandages, pointed the way to the northern wing of the barracks, now the garrison hospital.

There, and not in the least to my surprise, I found Doctor Sho among the cots and blankets. He knelt over a young man, whose eyes stared wide and wild at the ceiling from sockets like dark, sunken pits. The sight of the young man sent terror scuttling through me – an animal reaction, as to a decaying, diseased corpse. Doctor Sho muttered under his breath, his fingers probing the young man's bone-thin wrist for a pulse.

'What's wrong with him?' I asked, my mouth dry.

Doctor Sho looked up, startled. At the sight of me, his

expression took on an almost accusatory cast. He turned back to his patient, and I thought I might not get an answer.

'This one, and a few of the others here, are from a hunting party,' he said at last, shifting his fingers to the side of the young man's neck. 'One of the first to go out. They came back a few days later, from the perspective of the people here. A few days that they, so I have been told by those who heard their tale on their return, experienced as nearly three weeks. The forest shifted around them. The trails they were following appeared and vanished at random. The sun and the stars led them in circles. Three weeks spent fighting off the unwoven, eating their twisted flesh when no better game showed itself.'

He rifled through the drawers of his medicine chest, plucking out herbs and dropping them into a waiting mortar. 'It does things to you, the longer you spend in it. Sometimes in hours, sometimes years, depending on the person. We're more resilient than ordinary beasts, of course – a benefit of that same spark that gives you witches the power to reach out and twist the world. A will can hold itself together, hold its body together, against the distortions in the pattern for a time, but even the strongest will eventually gives way.'

Terror clawed at the base of my skull. I fought against a rising nausea and forced myself to say the words aloud. 'He was becoming one of them. One of the unwoven.'

Doctor Sho nodded. For a time, the groans of the wounded and the scrape of his mortar and pestle were the only sounds between us.

'Something not dissimilar had happened to you when we first met, as you may recall,' Doctor Sho said. 'Not a consequence of the gods' churning the pattern to a froth, but no less destructive. If he is lucky, I can do for him what I did for you and restore his body's internal pattern. But I cannot help those beyond this city. Nayen may be free of the empire, but outside Eastern

Fortress it has become a waking nightmare. And beyond, unto the four corners of the world.'

Anger flared to my defence, casting light that, for that moment, burned away the shadow of my horror. 'You've no need to remind me. Not of what I did, nor of its consequences. Hissing Cat and I will restore the pacts and—'

'And a thousand years from now, some talented fool will fall for another god's tricks and unmake them again.' Doctor Sho jabbed the pestle at me, flecking my shirt with bits of crushed root and leaf. 'And once again a million souls will be cast into chaos, until the cycle repeats, and again, and again, and again. *Think.* There is only one way to truly put an end to the nightmare once and for all – not to contain it or control it, but to end it. Break the cycle. Shatter the wheel that weaves this horror into the pattern of the world. Don't simply push it on to its next turning.'

'I don't need to hear this again,' I nearly shouted, and felt ashamed for disturbing the wounded. 'If we knew of a way to do what you propose, I would do it, but all you have is philosophy and theory.'

His eyes narrowed. 'Would you truly?' I hesitated, and he leapt into the gap. 'Would you give up your power – your magic – to give the world a chance to truly heal?'

Yes! I wanted to shout the word in his face. To scrawl the logogram on his forehead. To carve it into the cornerstones of the earth. But I swallowed it.

Yes meant giving up the rush of life and texture, the sharpening of scent and light, the heady thrill of bending the world to my intent. It meant giving up the foundation of the obelisks of An-Zabat, the windships of the Waste, the miracle of healing sorcery, the wonder of flight on eagle hawk's wings. It meant giving up the only thing I had ever pursued for its own sake.

A pursuit that had led me from mistake to mistake, leaving ruined lives and a broken world in my footsteps.

I swallowed the word, and Doctor Sho scowled at the conflict that played itself out upon my face.

'For a moment, I hoped you were a better man than Tenet,' he muttered, then jabbed the pestle towards a door at the far end of the room. 'You're looking for Running Doe, I assume? You'll find her through there, with the freshly wounded.'

His words were a stone in my throat, choking off any argument I might mount in my own defence. I had never created an empire, slaughtered nations, crushed cultures beneath my heel, yet Doctor Sho's young patient testified in his agony to the horror I had wrought – a horror that was even now only beginning. That my misdeeds had been accidental hardly seemed to matter. I left them there, carrying that stone with me, my guilt deepening but, with it, my resolve to put right what I could or exhaust what remained of my life in the effort to do so.

My thoughts so absorbed me that I nearly stumbled over Running Doe before I saw her. She knelt on the floor, one hand on the shoulder of an older woman who lay swaddled on a thin blanket, her other clutching her canon of witchcraft, thumb pressed firmly to the symbol for healing. A wake of sorcery wafted from her, like a pleasant, calming incense. The weight of Doctor Sho's words remained, but in the presence of that magic the lingering agony of guilt faded. A good thing, that, for the sight of her, still bearing the scars of our battle with Voice Golden-Finch and the emperor, might have doubled me over in pain.

She looked up at me, her dark eyes wide with astonishment. One eyebrow arched upwards. The other, like her hair – I could remember that short fall of reddish curls dancing around her ears so clearly, could almost feel my fingers twining through them – had been burned away by lightning. In its place she wore a fractal weal of pinkish scar that crawled down the side of her face, disappearing beneath the high collar of her tunic. There would be more like it, I knew. Healing sorcery could restore a great deal, even rebuild a severed hand, but I had taken her with me before she had mastered the art and then abandoned her, gasping in pain, to heal herself from the emperor's brutal attack. Now, like my grandmother's arm withered by Voice Usher's torture, Running Doe would forever wear a mark of her suffering.

I fell to my knees beside her.

'Foolish Cur,' she murmured. 'I thought you must be dead.'

'Perhaps I deserve to be,' I answered, my voice as weak as I felt.

She turned away from her patient, seized my arm, and shook me. 'Never say that!' She wrapped her arms tight around me. The corner of the canon of witchcraft dug between my shoulder blades. She said nothing more, only held me as the calming wake of her magic faded. The stone in my throat clawed its way at last to my tongue and the corners of my eyes and I wept like a child, clinging to Running Doe as though she were my mother and I in need of no more than a kind word and comfort.

My mother! Another layer of guilt atop all the rest. Not worse than breaking the world, but more deeply felt, piercing both the natural, infantile love all children carry and my most hard-trained Sienese moral sentiments. My mother and father were out there, on their estate – or perhaps at sea, in my father's case – hunted by unwoven beasts, or being sickened and transformed themselves by the rending of the pattern. Their deaths, too, would add to the weight of crimes I carried.

'I'm sorry,' I blubbered, my tears soaking the shoulder of Running Doe's tunic. 'I'm so sorry. But that will never be enough.'

'Is this how you plan to parlay with Burning Dog?' another, too-familiar voice asked. I looked up, my eyes still stinging with tears. My grandmother loomed in the doorway, her withered arm twitching, her face a thunder-cloud ready to spit lightning. 'By throwing yourself on her and weeping? By bawling apologies for killing her sister? Running Doe's soft heart might find forgiveness for you, but Burning Dog will sooner sear away your tongue than listen to a word.'

I staggered to my feet, disentangling myself from Running Doe's arms, trying to muster my composure and stanch the flow of tears.

'What is she talking about?' Running Doe asked, still kneeling beside her patient.

'You've heard, then,' I said.

My grandmother scoffed. 'Of course I have. My son is dead, but there are still those in the Army of the Wolf who carry more loyalty to him than to Hissing Cat. You discuss your plans with her in the middle of a garden, surrounded by soldiers on rooftops. Absurd to think word would not trickle out. In all likelihood, word of your desire to meet will reach Burning Dog before Clear-River does.'

I took a step towards her. 'Grandmother, I'm sorry—'

'Don't try that with me,' she snapped. 'You ignored my warnings and my advice, and now you come crawling for forgiveness. I won't have it. I thought you at least had a spine, Foolish Cur. Now you whine and weep and apologise to your enemies.'

'Would you rather we cut each other's throats while the world collapses around us?' I protested.

'And who collapsed it, eh?' she growled. 'From the first, you reached too far, too quickly. Tried to do things you didn't understand. I should have known this would happen and stopped you. I tried to, at least, but I let myself hope we could benefit from your power without suffering for your foolishness. And now look where we are.' She jabbed her chin at Running Doe. 'Where is the brutality you visited on the emperor? The ruthless willingness to risk the rebellion, Nayen, the world itself, for victory? Even your little plaything's suffered for your idiocy and ambition. You dragged her to ruin and the edge of death, and now you do her the dishonour of *apologising* for your choices instead of owning them, instead of *committing to a course.*'

'No one *dragged* me,' Running Doe protested, rising to her feet. 'I fought for my right to fly beside him, to go where the fighting was thickest. He does me no dishonour, Broken Limb, but *you* do, speaking as though I did not take every step with full knowledge of where it might lead.'

'Then you're far wiser than he is,' my grandmother snarled. She turned her hard eyes back to me. 'Do what you want, Foolish Cur, but do not expect me to weep for you after Burning Dog tears you apart. I've wept myself dry already.'

She left me stunned, standing amid the wounded, feeling the blade of her words in my chest.

'You mean to turn yourself over to Burning Dog, then?' Running Doe said softly.

I nodded, my body moving as though through water: numb, slow, and distant.

'Don't.' She set her jaw, fierce and determined, her hands balled tightly at her sides. 'Do you think your life is worth a few sacks of grain?'

'Any number of people have a right to take vengeance on me, but I don't intend to die,' I said, though in that moment I might have welcomed it. How much could a single heart endure before crumbling? 'But this is the right thing to do, Running Doe. Perhaps all the more so because it is dangerous. An act of penance that cost me nothing would hardly mean anything, after all.'

Doubt flickered across her face, but she gave it no voice. 'Dying won't fix anything, Foolish Cur. It will only hurt those of us who still care about you.'

Warmth spread through me, but as the wrong heat at the

wrong moment in its forging can make a blade brittle, I felt my resolve crack and my heart begin to break, and I turned away from her. 'As I said, I don't intend to die.'

'Then take this.' Her hand found mine, opened my fingers, then closed them around the strip of bone. 'And prove me wrong.'

I brushed my fingernail down the carvings in the bone. Three intersecting lines for fire, three swooping lines for flight, a whorl for wind, and the *medicine* logogram for healing. Each was a key to a fragment of the power I had lost. Together, they gave me a chance to meet Burning Dog not on my knees but on equal footing, to negotiate from a position of strength rather than begging for forgiveness.

'I can't,' I said, yet already my thumb trembled, desperate to press against those carved lines, to feel the rush of power they promised, even here within Hissing Cat's seal. 'The wounded need healing sorcery. If I go armed, she will never listen to me and it will all certainly be for nothing.' *Shatter the wheel*, Doctor Sho had said. *Don't simply push it on to its next turning.* He had meant the war between humanity and the gods, but the same principle held true here. The armies of Nayen had been kept apart by the competing ambitions of their leaders. If I met Burning Dog as a rival in power and magic, that would only be more of the same foolishness. Unity required more of me. 'I won't fight her, Running Doe.'

'Then don't fight her,' she said. She closed both hands around mine, tightening my grip on the canon of witchcraft. 'Even still, take it.'

'But your patients—' I murmured.

'I've already helped the worst off,' she said. 'The others will be all right with rest and medicine, especially now that Doctor Sho is here. Take it, Foolish Cur. You gave it to me once, and now I'm giving it back.'

I took a slow, steadying breath and tucked the strip of bone up my sleeve. 'Thank you.'

'Just make sure you come back to me,' she said with a worried smile.

I wanted to promise that I would, but the words caught in my throat and lodged there while we studied each other – her pain written in the scars that seamed her body, mine tearing through me like invisible claws – until a cramping wake of sorcery drew me to the doorway and my eyes to the sky.

An eagle hawk landed in the garrison courtyard, then veered into Clear-River's familiar, wild-haired silhouette. He spotted me and crossed the courtyard, a hard frown on his face and a worried cast to his eyes.

'I should have known you would be here,' he said. 'Hissing Cat nearly bit my head off when I asked. Burning Dog has agreed. You and her, while I serve as mediator. No guards.'

I swallowed against the stone of fear in my throat. 'Good,' I managed. 'When?'

'Tonight,' he said. 'But, Alder, when I told her to bring no weapons, she laughed in my face. You may imagine this a parlay, but she thinks it a duel. And there's more.' He shook his head. 'Hand Pinion escaped the governor's estate last night – or, more accurately, was stolen. She has him as her prisoner now, and she intends to bring him to the meeting.'

The stone in my throat dropped into my stomach. 'How … ?' How had Pinion and Burning Dog wound up aligned in this when her sister had killed his brother? No. It didn't matter. 'That's good,' I said, trying to sound confident. 'I tried to express my contrition to him once. He should hear what I have to say to her as well.'

'Or he may hold your arms while she cuts your throat,' Clear-River said wryly. 'One last time, I advise you not to go. I'm sure, with enough time and cooler heads, I can negotiate an arrangement with her. The way she is now, nothing but a bundle of rage and violence, she'll lash out at the sight of you.'

'Then she lashes out,' I said, and fought the urge to cross my arms inside my sleeves, to run my finger along the carvings in the bone. 'We don't have time to wait and see if she forgets her hatred. I doubt she ever will. Her mother agreed to work with me before, and now she is dead. If Burning Dog is to trust me, if we are to unite against the empire, I need to show that I understand her pain and her doubt of me, and I must put myself in her power. Surely the freedom of Nayen, the end of starvation in this city, and the salvation of the world is worth that risk?'

Even to my own ears, I sounded pompous. It was that sort of thinking – the belief that I could save the world – that had led to my greatest mistake. Yet I felt the truth of the words in my bones.

Clear-River scrubbed his hand through his hair and grimaced. In his eyes I could see our argument from that morning playing out again while he sought some angle, some line of attack that might turn me from my course and towards some other way the rebellion might be reunited and the empire finally overthrown. The same sharp mind that had excelled at the imperial examinations now turned to the task of saving me from my own need for an absolution Burning Dog would never give. And he must have seen, in my eyes, my unbending need to face her – and, through her, to face and account for the damage I had done.

'Thank you, Clear-River,' I said. 'Once, I thought we might become friends, only for the paths of our lives to twist us apart. I know I cannot ask it of you now, not after what I have done, but—'

He clasped my hand and pulled me into a tight embrace, a shattering of the limits of propriety. 'When this is over, we might be friends again,' he said. 'For now, I'm only the mediator for this *extremely* dangerous negotiation you seem determined to hurl yourself into.'

I laughed and felt something loosen in me. *When this is over.* I ran my fingers along the edge of the bone strip tucked into my sleeve and felt a shudder of anticipation.

If I could survive this without layering violence upon violence, vengeance upon vengeance, I might endure anything, accomplish anything. Restore the fractured rebellion. Overthrow the Sienese occupation, at long last. In that moment, even the broken pattern of the world seemed a small thing as I hoped to mend Burning Dog's shattered heart and, with it, my own.

13

Atonement

Pinion

A twitching, clinging darkness gripped the world. Pinion's remaining eye longed to let in the reddish light that played against his lid, but any movement conjured waves of agony.

For the hundredth time, his hand hovered over his ruined flesh, trembling with a morbid desperation to explore what remained of the socket, the cheek, the brow. To know, if only with the brushing of fingers, what Burning Dog had made of him. He let one finger touch and felt only the crust of a scab. Beneath, it felt like thousands of ants danced on his flesh. She had healed him only for the fractional moment required to keep him alive and left him in itching anguish. A mercy, she had called it, and one offered only because he might be of use to her. He deserved to be nailed to the warehouse wall like the other Hands she had ensnared.

As hateful and raving mad as she was, Pinion felt in a twisted, pus-filled pocket of his heart that he deserved the pain and loss, whether for the brutality at Setting Sun Fortress or for doubting the necessity and mission of the empire. Who better understood, now, the barbarism of these Nayeni, who had slaughtered his brother and father and subjected him to torture? Somewhere buried deeply within him, below sorrow and outrage and unspeakable horror, rested a self-hating satisfaction. This was what *should* become of men who let doubt and some deranged internal sense of injustice blind them to the cruel realities of the world.

'Get up.'

Pinion squinted, wincing at the pain. A tall Nayeni in a dark coat loomed over him. The ravens' feathers stitched in his hair brushed the harsh geometries of his cheeks.

'Stand,' Burning Dog said from somewhere behind the figure. 'If we have to carry you, we'll leave your legs behind.'

The gaunt Nayeni frowned at that and offered Pinion a hand. Pinion took it and let himself be pulled to his feet.

'He should have a bandage,' the gaunt man said.

'It doesn't matter,' Burning Dog snarled. She wore her armour of overlapping leather plates and her battle harness with the bone-handled sword in its sheath. 'We need to hurry. Give him the medicine.'

The gaunt man grumbled but offered Pinion a pill wrapped in paper. 'To dull the pain,' he said. 'It should last long enough.'

'For what?' Pinion croaked, studying the pill.

'Foolish Cur has invited *me* to parlay,' Burning Dog said, her voice almost gleeful. 'No need to even set a trap. He'll walk right into my open jaws.'

Pinion laughed deep in his throat, not caring for the wave of agony it caused, nor for Burning Dog's glare. He was being brought along only to unsettle Alder, to give Burning Dog her chance to strike, not to take his own revenge. Yet even after everything, the thought that Alder might suffer for his crimes was a balm. Nothing could be worth what he had endured at Burning Dog's hands, but perhaps, while the two were distracted with one another, he might find the chance to put a knife through both their hearts.

He swallowed the pill. While Burning Dog and the gaunt man led him from the warehouse-turned-fortress and towards the centre of the city, a hazy numbness descended. Soon, the jarring of his footsteps no longer sent the flesh beneath his wound into spasms of pain. He fell into the rhythm of walking. The early-evening air was cool and refreshing, almost pleasant. Enough, at least, to raise his spirits ever so slightly while his mind pawed its way through fog, indulging in imagined victories, in seeing both Alder and Burning Dog's faces carved to ribbons and twisting in death's agony.

A giggle bubbled in his throat. He swallowed it, forced what remained of his face to seriousness, and walked on, his head hanging down like the prisoner he was.

'Here,' Burning Dog said, snapping Pinion back to the present moment. They stood in what had once been a market square. To their right loomed the inner wall of the city, where torches moved along the ramparts against the falling dark.

The gaunt man pointed to a shrouded alley. 'Get their backs facing that if you can.'

Burning Dog dragged an abandoned bench from the edge of the square. Stone scraped on the tiled street as she angled it just so and sat, her posture open but her hand still on the bone hilt of her sword. The gaunt man gave a sharp nod, then crossed the square and vanished into the shadows of the alley.

Burning Dog thumped the bench beside her. 'Now we wait.'

Pinion nearly obeyed, yet something caught him and held him back. His gaze – narrowed and dizzying for want of half its usual field, even in the muffled calm brought by the pill – locked on Burning Dog's piercing eyes, full of smouldering hatred and a sparking glee, an echo of his own innermost feelings.

He wanted to vomit. Another effect of the pill? he wondered distantly. Or was it the product of the detachment the drug had granted him, of his newfound perspective – of being able to look into himself from outside, to perceive the rot within, not blinded for once by the need for catharsis and release promised by an eruption of vengeance and blood?

'I said *sit*,' Burning Dog snarled.

Pinion made himself move towards her and sat, waiting as the stars wheeled into view overhead. Burning Dog shifted beside him, her fingers drumming on the bone hilt of her sword, brushing the lines carved there that promised power. Could he wrestle that sword away? Arm himself with lost magic? Use it to burn a path away from the hatred, from the pain, from the blood and bile while this strange, unsteady clarity held?

Burning Dog's fingers stopped their drumming and gripped the hilt tight. She leaned forwards, her teeth glinting in the moonlight. A torch moved at the far end of the square, bobbing towards them.

'At last,' Burning Dog snarled. 'Sister, Mother . . .' Her voice hitched. She swallowed hard and growled low in her throat, wrestling with some internal struggle of her own.

For a moment, Pinion felt towards her only a disquieting pity, but the moment was broken as the circle of torchlight drew near and she stood to face it.

'You're no coward,' she said. 'I'll credit you that.'

Pinion squinted. His burn had begun to itch again and needles of pain dug up from deep beneath the drug fog that muffled his senses. Two silhouettes, like hazy, standing shadows emerged from the torchlight.

'But I have been, Burning Dog.' The voice sent ice down Pinion's spine. 'I have been a coward for many, many years.'

The urge to lunge, to claw for Alder's eyes, to bite at his throat swelled and faded. Pinion clenched his fists. They trembled, aching and weak. His limbs moved slowly. A consequence of the drug wearing off, he wondered, or taking firmer effect?

'And now you've found a spine,' Burning Dog spat. 'Well?

Your friend there said you had words for me. Out with them.'

The second figured tensed, his hands folded in his sleeves. Pinion had to stare for a moment, but that wild mane of hair and spray of freckles surely belonged to Lu Clear-River. What was the magistrate of a fallen township doing here, and at Alder's side?

Wait. Clear-River had been in the garden, hadn't he? When Pinion had been taken prisoner. His thoughts churned, grasping at memories, finding no hold. He doubled over and vomited on the tile.

'What have you done to him?' Alder's voice held an aching, angry note, which only layered confusion atop confusion. What had he to be angry for? No one had hurt *him*.

The memory of when last he had seen Alder's silhouette, in the doorway of his cell, speaking some plaintive nonsense about Oriole and his father and guilt. Begging for forgiveness. Pinion wiped his mouth and laughed, still bent over his own bile.

'Nothing he didn't deserve,' Burning Dog shot back. 'Nothing *you* don't deserve tenfold.'

'The purpose of this meeting is not to exchange threats,' Clear-River said firmly. 'There are people starving in this city, and we can ill afford to spill so much blood over old grudges. We are here to make an agreement.'

'Like the one he made with my mother?' Burning Dog's voice rose to a roar. 'The one that saw her *killed?*'

'As it saw my uncle killed.' Alder's words still held an edge, but a blunted one, like a fist desperate to strike but held back, trembling. 'I own his death, too, as much as I own your mother's, and your sister's, and the thousands – tens, hundreds of thousands more – who will die before the world can be made whole again.'

Still he spouted these apologies, and to a woman armed and ready to cut him to ribbons and burn what remained! Pinion wanted to laugh at the absurdity, at Alder's raw arrogance. To think that his words could bring back the dead or salve the wounds dealt by their dying!

Burning Dog clutched the bone hilt of her sword and leaned forwards, an image of brutal menace. 'If you own those deaths, accept justice for them. The penalty for murder, under the rule of the Sun King, is death. Kneel so I can cut your head from your shoulders, and Hissing Cat can have what she wants from my granaries.'

Alder's knees buckled, as though desperate to bend, and he bowed his head forwards, showing the nape of his neck ready for a blade.

'I can't,' he said. 'Not yet. This is only one of many wounds I must repair, and though it might be easier, my death will not heal the rest.'

'Then why have you come here?' Burning Dog bellowed, throwing her left arm wide. 'You know what I want from you, Cur. Are you taunting me? Is that it? Or do you think you can twist my head around with slippery words?'

Alder straightened. His gaze met Pinion's for an instant that held quiet and fixed, like a scene captured in a perfect painting.

'I was taught – perhaps for unworthy reasons – to honour my responsibilities, Burning Dog,' he said, his gaze drifting back to her. 'That is all I am trying to do, as well as I can. Perhaps in doing so, I can soften your heart and achieve my aim of a united Nayen and an end to the skirmishing and siege. If not …' He took a deep breath and shook his head gently. 'If not, then at least I will have done the right thing by my own sense of justice. Too often I have chased a distant goal without considering the steps along the way. No longer. Now, I do the right thing, even if it costs me, even if—'

'Enough talk,' Burning Dog snarled and drew her sword, tilting it so the blade gleamed in the torchlight.

Pinion's heart leapt to his throat – not in excitement, though if he had described this scene to himself mere minutes ago he would have shuddered in anticipation. *Let him speak!* he wanted to shout. There had been something in Alder's words, something that resonated in the deepest, cracked and damaged chambers of Pinion's heart, where he held the pain of Setting Sun Fortress, of his brother's death, of his father's blindness to all the wickedness of the empire they served. Where he held fast the memory of Oriole as a child standing before their father, arguing against the unjust punishment of a servant boy. *Let him speak!*

'We agreed to a peaceful parlay.' Clear-River stepped between Burning Dog and Alder, his hand clutching something within his sleeve. 'Put the sword away, Burning Dog, or I cannot guarantee your safe passage from this place.'

A shadow moved in the alley behind Alder and Clear-River. It drew a knife, stark in the moonlight. Clear-River, his face twisted in confusion, followed the line of Pinion's gaze and turned on his heel. In that moment the gaunt man who had accompanied Burning Dog, wrapped in the lung-chilling wake of windcalling, darted out of the shadows.

A second wake of windcalling roiled out from Clear-River, slamming into the gale the gaunt man had sent against him. The clash created a vortex that spun through the square, filling the air with dust, hurling abandoned bits of wood and loose stones. Still the gaunt man charged, his knife slicing through the churning winds.

Alder kept his gaze locked on Burning Dog, his mouth twisting in disappointment, his eyes full of sorrow.

Burning Dog only howled in answer and thrust her sword at him, calling a flame as white-hot as the sun. Its feverish wake wrestled with the chill in Pinion's lungs and the disorienting fog of the drug, sending him reeling, paralysed, watching as she hurled the flame at Alder.

Pinion braced in anticipation of another wake of sorcery, for the deeper chill in his lungs as winds cast the flames to the earth or cramps racing down his limbs as Alder veered to fly above them, but Alder only flinched backwards a step while the fire washed over him. Disbelieving – elated, horrified – Pinion watched Alder's skin blacken, flake, and blister. Only then did a wake ripple out from him, soothing and calming, settling the wild flailing of Pinion's mind.

When the flames had passed, Alder stood, breathing heavily, contortions of agony rippling beneath the skin of his face. Smoke rose from his smouldering tunic and steam from his swiftly healing wounds.

'Did that bring you satisfaction?' Alder said through gritted teeth.

Burning Dog snarled and hurled another gout of fire, then held it, filling the square with heat and churning light as the flames danced in the winds of the gaunt man's furious assault on Clear-River. Pinion stood in place, trembling, his nose and mouth filling with the sweet, sickening smell of burning flesh. This was what he had wanted, to watch Alder suffer as he had suffered. Better to call the flames or wield the knife himself, but to witness his agony should have brought at least some satisfaction.

Clear-River loosed a sharp, pained cry as the gaunt man's blade sank into his shoulder. The once-magistrate growled, caught the gaunt man by the wrist, and called a wheel of wind between his fingers. The gaunt man's arm came apart, his hand still clutching the hilt of his knife while blood sprayed.

Pinion should have rushed into the fray, tackled Clear-River or seized the knife in his shoulder and rammed it again and again into his flesh, yet he only stared in horrified fascination at Alder's flame-wreathed body – naked now, the clothes long since burned away, along with the skin, the eyes, the hair, leaving only a skeleton wrapped in blackened flesh. Pinion's own flesh crawled and recoiled at the sight.

Do something! He wanted to scream. *Fight back! You can't endure this. No one can!*

Yet Alder's thumb still pressed firmly to the strip of bone, and as Burning Dog's fury seared his flesh away, he rebuilt his body, his healing racing against her flames. As Pinion watched, dumbfounded, Alder's limbs regained their muscle. Blackened weals knitted into pink, healthy skin.

Other flames burst to life, clashed, and filled the square with swirling shadows as Clear-River and the gaunt man continued to duel.

'Stop this, Burning Dog!' Clear-River roared between panting breaths, leaping away from a gout of flame that turned the street tiles white hot until they burst into molten shards. He landed, grunted, and went to his knee, gripping his injured shoulder.

'No,' a voice rasped from within the roaring fire. Alder's eyes slowly opened, black as coals in the heart of a furnace. His lips and tongue, still flecked with jagged cracks of black and red, dragged their way through the words. 'If ... this ... is what ... she must do ... let her do it.'

A cry tore itself from Pinion's throat. His hand went to his missing eye, where a ruined tear duct itched and spasmed. He remembered the heat of Burning Dog's magic, the pressure of her finger in the globe of his eye until it burst and burned away. Alder endured that same pain, dozens – hundreds – of times over. Justice might have seen his head under an executioner's sword, but this ... this was a sickening sort of vengeance, a gorging on meat and blood. Yet Alder welcomed it. Invited it. Endured it. Believing, perhaps in madness, perhaps in self-hatred, that his pain could somehow atone for the wounds he had dealt and reunite the rebellion.

No doctrine, no propriety had ever demanded so much. If the empire had betrayed its own philosophy at Setting Sun Fortress, then Alder had surmounted that same philosophy here, bowing to the needs and will not only of his father or elder brother but of his own greatest enemies. He could not bring back the dead, but he could share in the suffering of their survivors.

To think that Pinion had doubted him when he came in contrition, desperate to voice his own guilt, his own anguish at Oriole's death. He wanted to throw himself into the flames beside Alder – for the father, his skull shattered as he sheltered his children with bleeding arms; the woman who would have fought a legion with a pair of shears; the family trampled by chasing cavalry. All the dead at Setting Sun Fortress. The pain and guilt Pinion had stuffed away, unwilling to grapple with it any longer while the world came apart, clinging instead to hatred of Alder, whose crimes were so much worse, whose brutality, whose inhumanity, must eclipse Pinion's own and render it meaningless. Who now, in kneeling to accept the fire of Burning Dog's wrath, made Pinion's hatred seem little more than a thin, crumbling veil.

The flames vanished. The heat of them, both on Pinion's face and in the feverish wake in his blood, faded. Clear-River and the gaunt man had long since paused in their duel to watch, wide eyed and stunned, each stanching the blood that seeped from his wounds.

Burning Dog's whole body heaved with each panting breath. Sweat poured down her face and dripped from her outstretched arm. The blade of her sword glowed in the sudden dark in the absence of her conjured flames. Across from her, Alder rebuilt his ruined flesh, knitting muscle to bone, restoring all as it had been, even to the last strand of tightly curled hair, down to the puckered stump of his right wrist. He stared at her, unspeaking, and she howled in fury.

'Is this a joke?' she demanded, letting the sword fall to her side. 'Do you mock me, Cur? Offering your life only to cling to it?'

'If I . . .' Alder rasped, then cleared his throat, swallowed, and pressed on. 'If I could give you my life, I would. But I have too much yet to do. All I can offer . . . all I can give in payment for the agony I have caused you, is my own pain. As much of it as you need to extract. And then we will be done here, our bargain sealed.'

'You're a madman,' Burning Dog breathed. She shook her head and looked to Pinion, her eyes wild with laughter. 'He's a madman, isn't he?'

Pinion had, in all his life, never heard anything more sane. Here, at last, was someone willing to answer, and to pay, for the hurt he had left in his wake, the lives he had ended, the agony he had caused. Something the emperor himself had been unwilling to do.

Burning Dog took a long, shuddering breath. 'Toy with me, will you?' She stepped forwards, raising her blade high. 'Let's see you knit together a severed head!'

'No!' The word burst from Pinion like water through a breaking dam. He lunged, caught Burning Dog's arm, and hauled it backwards, pulling her off balance. Her hold on the sword faltered, and Pinion grasped for it. She tightened her grip, catching his fingers between her palm and the bone hilt.

'What the *fuck* are you doing?' Burning Dog snarled. She drove her fist into Pinion's gut, reawakening the bruises he had suffered the night before. Nausea swept through him, but the pain-killing drug kept it at bay as her hand crushed his and her fist moved from his abdomen up to hammer at his missing eye. His scab split in a bright flash of pain. Still he clung.

'Don't do this, Burning Dog,' he begged through the pain and gritted teeth.

'He killed your brother! Your father!' She shifted her grip, meaning to crush Pinion's hand more tightly against the hilt. He felt an edge bite into the meat of his palm, like the bevel of a coin, and with it a frigid rush like a first breath of winter air swept through him. He grasped for it, though his phantom limb felt weak and unsteady, its grip slippery – from underuse these last few days, or from the drug?

'What happened to that bloody Sienese familial propriety or whatever the fuck?' Burning Dog roared. 'Let. Go. Or I will rip out your—'

He called a wind and slammed it into her midriff, driving the breath from her lungs and doubling her over. Pinion jerked at the sword, ripping it free of her grasp, and staggered backwards, holding it before him. Burning Dog snarled. The hatred that had fanned her conjured flames blazing in her eyes.

'Stand down, Burning Dog,' Clear-River shouted, eyeing Pinion warily. 'Without the canon, you haven't any hope of winning, here.'

'Stand down and do what?' she spat. 'Fight the Sienese alongside these traitors?'

'No, Burning Dog—' Clear-River began, but she gave him no chance to finish.

Her mouth twisted. She stood. 'I would rather die,' she said, and charged at Pinion, who in a moment of panic reached for the wind and felt his grasp on power slip. Burning Dog's hands, curled like claws, reached for his bleeding eye. Pinion screamed and threw all of his will into a single act of magic. Wind burst from him like a bolt from a ballista. Burning Dog grunted, slid backwards a pace, and looked down at the weeping hole punched through her chest. With a final, gurgling snarl, she collapsed.

'No!' Alder breathed. He crawled towards her, his arms and legs trembling, exhausted after enduring so much pain and expending so much to cling to life. His hand touched her heel and another wake of healing washed from him into her. But healing sorcery could not restore the dead. He let his hand drop to the cobbles.

Pinion's grip trembled on the hilt of the sword. He stared down the length of the blade at Alder – vulnerable, now, in his nakedness and weakness. A burst of wind, or even a step forwards and a thrust with the blade … An hour ago, he had lived for nothing more. Now, he saw in Alder the memory of Oriole, standing before their father, demanding justice from an unjust world. He steeled himself, readied the blade.

'I'm sorry,' he breathed. 'I … I only meant to push her away. She drugged me, and …'

Excuses would change nothing. She was dead, by his hand, when Alder had endured agony and the edge of death in an effort to make peace. The sword clattered on the tiled square. Alder looked up at him and nodded slowly.

'I understand, Pinion,' he said simply. He struggled to his feet and offered Pinion a hand. 'Let me see what I can do for that wound.'

'No!' Pinion's fingers darted up to brush the weeping burn, the puckered ridge of his eye. He could not go back to the way he had been before, full of hatred – for himself, for the world – but unwilling to look it in the face. Alder still wore his missing hand, evidence of his break from the empire. Pinion would wear his missing eye just the same. Too much, in that moment, to put into words, to express clearly. He said only, 'I want to remember.'

Concern flickered across Alder's expression, but he nodded.

'I suppose we should take this as well,' Alder said softly, and took the sword from where it had fallen.

'And find you some clothes,' Clear-River said, still bleeding from the knife wound in his shoulder. His gaze was fixed on the gaunt man, who only stared blankly at Burning Dog's corpse. For a moment, Pinion feared the gaunt man would lunge for them, calling fire and wind to rip them apart and avenge his fallen captain, but he only curled his shredded arm to his chest and wove healing sorcery to seal the wound and restore his hand. 'We'll send people for her body,' he grunted, 'and an emissary to Hissing Cat in the morning.'

'You surrender, then?' Clear-River muttered.

The gaunt man shook his head. 'I accept Foolish Cur's offer. Cooperation. Burning Dog was our leader. Loyalty demanded that we follow her. With her dead, I will be the leader, and ...' His mouth worked, as though trying to find words to express something more, then shut firmly. Pinion was not alone, then, in being moved by what Alder had done. Yet they were both too shaken, too raw and tender, to give those feelings their full voice. 'I think we have killed enough of one another,' the gaunt man said at last.

Alder, his eyes glazed, slumped as though another layer of weight had settled on his shoulders. He turned away from Burning Dog's corpse, handed her sword to Clear-River and walked back towards the centre of the city.

'This was not your fault!' Pinion cried. 'I killed her, not you.'

Alder paused, a moonlit statue. 'Neither of you would have been here if I had never gone to Iron Town,' he said, and continued walking, each step like the last stroke of the final logogram of an essay, the issue closed and the question answered.

'As much use to argue with him as with a mountain,' Clear-River advised, then held out the sword to the gaunt man. 'I will take the canon, but I can remove it from the blade.'

'No,' the gaunt man said. 'We will join you, but there are those among us who still love Burning Dog, if only for her mother's sake. Her body, once properly burned, might offer them closure. Her weapon would only serve as a reminder.'

'Fair enough.' Clear-River knelt and pulled the scabbard from Burning Dog's sash, sheathed the sword, and propped it against his shoulder. Then he made a beckoning gesture. 'You are welcome with us, Pinion. I doubt Alder would have thrown you in a cell to begin with if he'd had his way. Now, I can guarantee you protection, I think. However you feel about the outcome here – or how *he* feels – you saved both our lives.'

Somewhere in a deep crevasse of Pinion's mind, a laugh echoed, stirred up by absurdity. The greater part of him – the part that had recoiled in horror at Setting Sun Fortress, that had risked everything to challenge his father in an impotent gesture, that clung to that earliest memory of Oriole above all others – wondered if, perhaps, absurdity might be a defence, a shield conjured to protect from painful truths. *We laugh because to look the world in the eye and act on what our honest appraisal reveals is too painful and difficult.* He had wanted to kill Wen Alder only moments before saving his life, yet he did not feel ashamed. To change, he decided, is to reckon with oneself, find oneself wanting, and be willing to become better.

With his first step, he trembled from heel to head, but Clear-River seemed to have forgotten the arrogant, terrified Hand who had nearly executed his loyal guardsmen at Burrow, and Alder did not turn around and remind him of the lashing chain and howled hatred. As the scorched walls of his father's estate came into view, he realised that the trembling had faded, and the footsteps came easily.

PART 2

Empire

14

Battle Upon the Plain

Ral Ans Urrera

Dust swirls across the abandoned palisades. Goose-feather fletching catches the breeze, making arrows abandoned in their ammunition barrels rattle in a nervous dance. Armor, shields, swords, and spears hang on stands. There are no corpses in the courtyard or the stairwell of the watchtower. No human bodies, living or dead. Only the stables bear bloodstains, but even they are empty of bone and sinew.

Falling Star huffs and stamps the dry earth, shifting uneasily beneath her. Ral strokes his mane and whispers reassurances. There are no dead here, no ghosts of Sienese watchmen torn apart.

She shudders, which only further unsettles her mount. The beasts of chaos she has seen resemble wolves or birds of prey. Is there any reason to think men could not be so twisted?

She thinks of the captain and carpenter of the *Dunecleaver*. Wonders if they are among those monsters that stalk the edges of the Skyfather's protection.

Garam returns to her in the courtyard of the outpost, the stained plates on his jerkin rattling as he thumps a fist to his chest. 'There are grain stores. Enough for a dozen men to last months. Not much, but better than nothing.'

Little better. Though there is plenty of fodder for the herds in these grasslands, dependence upon their meat has reduced their number by half already. Weeks remain between the storm Ral leads and Centre Fortress. There is a point at which a herd has been culled too severely ever to repopulate fully. A point that will be passed long before this war is over.

Not that it matters. They need only reach the emperor and shatter his walls – a conquest already begun by the capture of this watchtower, even if, in the chaos, it was abandoned undefended. The tower marks the northern end of the imperial road, which their storm will flow down, into the southlands. Soon they will meet the empire's armies and crush them. Then, when the chaos and terror the Sienese have wrought upon the world is at an end, the Girzan will rebuild from the riches of the southlands. New, stronger herds taken in spoils from the Sienese – repayment, as much as could be made, for generations of stolen tribute.

Until then, though, they need another source of food, else arrive at Centre Fortress not as a raging storm but as a starving band seeking refuge. She sees in the flinty cast of Garam's eyes that he knows this, and that he is not alone in that knowledge.

'Better than nothing,' she agrees. 'Far from enough, but we have crossed into the Sienese heartland. A fertile land, rich with grain. There will be other outposts, other villages, other granaries. Arrange for scouting parties to ride ahead of the column, to search for such places and to guard against ambush. A Hand might shield a legion by magic as the Skyfather shields us.'

Scepticism crosses Garam's face. 'Scout beyond the Skyfather's protection? Our warriors are fierce, but there are things they cannot defend against.'

'They will have protection,' she promises.

Garam nods in salute, then pulls himself onto his mount. In

a drumming of hoofbeats he is away to spread her command.

<Bold to promise what is not yours to provide,> the Skyfather's voice thunders in her skull.

Ral looks to the grey churn above: heavy clouds that promise rain but have offered none for near a week. A product of the chaos, or the Skyfather's taunting her after she tested the limits of his gift by riding out to save the An-Zabati?

'We are your spear,' she replies. A few in her entourage of guards and outriders glance away. It is now considered a sacrilege to look upon the Stormrider while she communes with their god. 'Would you deny us the sharpening stone? Would you let our shaft crack so that it shatters at the first blow? To wield us, you must provide for us, strengthen us.'

<Do you create *strength* by dragging rotting hulks of wood far from the Waste they were built to traverse? Does leading a train of invalids and children make you *strong*?> There is new, unsettling fury in the Skyfather's words. An audience with a god ought to be unsettling, she knows, yet this is more than the peals of thunder and crash of lightning behind her eyes. <You would ask for my favours when you might harden yourselves, cast aside your weaknesses, and become the weapon I need. There will be a time for children, and a time to mourn those left behind, after the dawn of the new world.>

The words needle Ral as she rides back towards the main column. The windships still scrape over the grassy plain to either side of the imperial road, which would break them on its cobbles. They creak as their runners rattle and drag over the hard earth. She has hoped they would lend her storm speed and ferocity, but they have become little more than berths for those too weak to ride or walk day after day, and consume time with their constant need for repair. A war should be fought by warriors. In a world not given over to madness, her war band would have left their families and elders in the Skyfather's Hall.

She imagines twisted beasts stalking its streets now and terrible, hook-taloned raptors circling its walls.

When the war band left the Skyfather's Hall, necessity demanded that all the Girzan ride forth, not just the warriors. Now, necessity might demand that those who cannot sit a saddle or draw a bow stay behind. The notion disgusts her even as she sees the truth in it.

Returning to her place in the column, she orders stock to be taken of their food supplies, both those borne by the herds and those in the stores aboard the windships: dried meats, barrels of brined olives, and hard biscuits. While she voices these orders to her adjutants, not telling them of the dark path she contemplates, Elsol Url Tabr and a guard of hunters from the Red Bull band approach, reining in at a respectful distance to observe. Their presence rankles Ral, particularly that of the old herbmistress, who combs her fingers through her braided beard and watches with a steady, weighing gaze.

Here would be a solution – a callous one, but justified: the Red Bull could be sent away, their herds confiscated. If there is any weakness in the Skyfather's spear, it is in them. How can she trust that they will hold their place in a charge if they refuse to acknowledge her leadership? The time for battle draws near, and with it an end to her tolerance for doubt.

The adjutants set off and Ral turns to meet Elsol. 'Have you decided at last to swear fealty to the storm, or do you yet hold yourselves above and apart?'

Elsol chuckles dryly, rolling back her shoulders, making her necklace of small bones and looted silver clatter. 'An old conversation, Stormrider. No. You have been to the imperial outpost. It was empty, I gather, in that I heard no sounds of battle.'

'Undefended, not empty,' Ral corrects. 'What was there to be taken has been, and as your riders were not with us, they have no claim to the spoils.'

'A few arrows and suits of old armour. Alas, to what use we might have put such riches.'

It would be a simple enough order to seize their herds. If they try to resist, Ral will burn them to ash with lightning.

Elsol waves a gnarled hand as though wafting away an offensive smell. 'Apologies, Stormrider. I did not intend to bicker with you. We should speak, and plainly. We are truly in Sienese lands now. Unfamiliar terrain and territory.'

'Do you think I am unaware?' Ral snaps.

Elsol's smile is tight. 'No, Stormrider. But it would be wise to hold a council of war, would it not? To prepare the bands for our first battles? That *is* why you have led us south.'

'The Sienese are in retreat,' Ral says. 'You would know this if you had sent warriors to the outpost.'

'Even so.'

'I am sending scouts. They will find the enemy legions, and we will hunt them down like the frightened hares they are. There is no need for discussion. All but the Red Bull have sworn to follow my orders without question.'

Elsol nods slowly and breathes deeply, bracing her sagging body as though for a blow. 'Yet there are other things to discuss, are there not? You have sent riders to count the herds – not only yours but *our* herds as well.'

'Would you deny an ally that right?' Ral asks.

'No. I only wonder at your reasoning. Though I suspect I know it already.'

'Then enough with careful words. I am not some skittish doe you must stalk and encircle. What do you want, Elder?'

Elsol sweeps her gaze over the column, then to the rolling hills, dotted with stands of trees, beyond. Save the conjured wind that fills the sails of the ships, the air is calm as it rarely is upon the plain.

'How long, do you think, until we run out of food?' Elsol

asks. 'Before or after we meet the Sienese in battle? And will that meeting be on a field or at the walls of a city, where we must lay siege – against our custom – hoping that our supplies outlast our enemy's?'

'I am a Stormrider, not an augur.' Ral holds her voice level, though her anger whirls and flashes with lightning.

'And you are young, and can be forgiven, perhaps, for not thinking of these things.'

'I have thought of them. A thought is not knowledge, Elsol. Our supplies run thin, yes, but as I said, I have sent scouts—'

'Scouts, yes,' Elsol cuts in. 'If there were game to be had, they might bring some of it back along with whatever word they hear of Sienese movements and fortifications. But there is no game, as you and I both know. We can only rely on the herds, and you push them too hard.'

Ral fights down the urge to call wind or conjure lightning to make some display of power, to remind the elder why she ought not be interrupted. Her voice grates as she speaks. 'We eat only the young males and females past rearing age.'

'As is wise. But that will not replenish the herd. It is spring, Ral Ans Urrera. Our days should be filled with the grunting of bulls and lowing of sows. There should be mares with heavy bellies already.'

'It is the chaos.' Ral points to the sky. 'Do you expect horses and cattle to know the season when the weather itself turns mad?'

'It is the march,' Elsol says.

'Bands move about in spring every year.'

'Not at this pace. You exhaust us all with this southward drive, the herds included. If you give them no time to rest and be at ease, they will not mate.'

Ral bursts out laughing. 'You would have me do what, then? Baulk at the dawn of battle? Slow our pace when we are already running low on food?'

‘I would have us return to the steppe.’ The words are a chill wind in Ral’s bones. Elsol pushes on. ‘To save our people, you must lead them back to lands they know.’

‘There are no lands they know anymore,’ Ral seethes. ‘The emperor has seen to that.’

‘You cannot argue that we have better chances of finding game and forage in the southlands than in our own.’

‘We have little hope in either place.’

‘Then let us die in our own lands!’ The elder’s voice is a thunderclap, leaving Ral stunned. ‘You won them back, and for that we thank you, but now you lead us off to starve and devour ourselves, or else be broken against imperial walls.’

‘You doubt the Skyfather?’ Ral canters Falling Star a step closer to the elder and rises in her saddle like a looming stormcloud. ‘His blessing alone has shielded us from the destruction that tears apart our world.’

‘Will he not offer it if we do not ride to war?’

Ral only stares down at the elder, who does not cower.

‘Then it is no blessing,’ Elsol says. ‘It is an exchange.’

‘Without it, you will surely die.’

Elsol chews her lip. ‘Then bargain on our behalf, Stormrider. Slow our pace, only long enough for the herds to get with calf and foal. Give us a chance at a future. Do not only spend us in a charge towards vengeance.’

‘I could cast you out.’ The words come out cold, like a blade. ‘You have always been free to leave the war band, Elsol. Now you must leave behind your herds as tribute to the Skyfather and the storm. Return to those lands you love and die there as you will.’

Elsol’s laugh is brittle and mocking, which only stirs the rage in Ral’s heart. ‘We are dead either way, here or there, Stormrider,’ Elsol says. ‘The An-Zabati have long believed that the Skyfather is cruel and capricious, not worthy of worship. Now I am convinced.’

'So be it.' Ral says, her blood thundering in her ears. 'Without your bellies to fill, this war band will have more than enough to reach Centre Fortress. And when your people ask why you have been cast out and destroyed, tell them the Skyfather is cruel.'

Ral turns to a remaining adjutant. 'See that it is done,' she says, wheeling Falling Star around and digging in her heels. She expects a shout of rage or a plea for mercy but hears only the pounding of her own blood and the churning of hooves beneath her.

<You would do better to send the invalids and weak away,> the Skyfather chides her. <The Red Bull have warriors who will now be wasted.>

She grits her teeth and wills him to silence, though she knows it does not matter. He is a god. 'I have done what I have done. The war band will survive to trample the emperor's bones to dust. That is enough for me.'

She rides to the top of a hill at the edge of the Skyfather's protection, breathing hard. Her father would look on her with shame. Even when two bands go to war, unless there is reason for one to destroy the other utterly, no raider takes so much that their enemy cannot endure, cannot rebuild their herds. She has taken everything from the Red Bull, killed a band that should have followed her.

The memory of the *Dunecleaver* in the distance, listing on its shattered runner, taunts her.

The Red Bull should have sworn to her. If they had, and if Elsol had not challenged her constantly, she could have found another way. But it is too late now. Any show of remorse or weakness would only give the reins to Elsol and see the war band delayed longer than it can afford, if not turned back.

Already, Elsol and her escort ride towards the contingent of Red Bull. They will try to steal their herds and flee, yet she can see also that her adjutant has spread word of Ral's orders.

There may be fighting soon. She should return to the line. It will sicken her to hurl lightning against Girzan, but the Red Bull have rejected her – rejected their people's purpose. If a few must burn to cow the rest, so be it.

'Stormrider!' A voice breaks through the dark cloud of her thoughts. A rider, whipping his horse to a froth. 'Stormrider! There is something you must see!'

Falling Star leaps to a gallop at her urging. Have the scouts spotted the retreating garrison of the watchtower? Her war band may yet draw blood this day, which would be balm to her doubts and an answer to those who question her.

The approaching rider wheels about and points to the south-eastern sky, where the rolling hills rise into a low mountain range, near enough that the ridges and slopes stand out in jagged detail.

What Ral at first takes for a second peak, trailing a long ridge line, shifts. A scree of boulders heaves up, swings across the face of the mountain, and crashes down, sending a cascade of billowing snow to batter the treeline below. The nearest face of the ridge turns, like the head of a serpent.

'What is it?' Ral breathes.

'One of the beasts of chaos, like the twisted hounds?' the rider speculates, believing she speaks to him.

<It is an ancient weapon,> the Skyfather answers. <A tool of war crafted in an elder age, before anyone now alive walked the world. Twisted, now, to terrible purpose.>

The weapon – a many-limbed beast, lithe as a serpent, its body seemingly built of stone – takes another step, sparking another avalanche that tears down the face of the mountain. Falling Star screams and dances sideways, though the weapon is too far for him to have seen.

'How long until it reaches us?'

The rider cocks his head. 'It has drawn nearer since I spotted it. Without knowing its size, it is difficult to say.'

<This is a distraction! Tenet has sent it against you as a delaying tactic. He knows we are coming and knows he cannot stand against us. He hopes to frighten you off or buy himself time.>

The beast takes another juddering step. It seems as a bird perched on the back of a horse – save that the horse is, in fact, a mountain range. Weakness grips Ral's heart. She is prepared for legions, for Hands and Voices in force, for the emperor himself. For what is he but a witch like her, without the blessing of a god? But this … The scale of it wakes something small and weak in her: a mouse scurrying from the shadow of a hawk; a deer bolting at the glimpse of a lion's stalking eye.

'I want reports at the end of every watch,' she says, forcing her eyes away from the mountainside. 'The sun does not shift in the sky without my hearing how much nearer that thing has drawn. Do you understand?'

'Stormrider, you may—'

A rolling clap of thunder pulses out from the mountainside. The ground leaps, sending Falling Star tumbling, his legs kicking at the air. The shouts of men and screams of horses are but muted, half-voiced notes beneath the constant hammering, as though the earth itself is a drum. Ral scrambles to her feet, ignoring the flailing horse behind her. Where the stone beast stood, the mountainside is bare. Below, at the treeline, old-growth forest comes apart like paper, trees exploding upwards in a rippling line that surges towards Ral at impossible speed.

'Back to the column!' Ral roars. Falling Star is on his feet. She calls wind to lend her speed and leaps into his saddle, sawing his reins to bring him under control. 'All of you, back to the column! Form a defensive line!'

Little good it will do them. Whatever that thing is – weapon or monster – it will shatter what windships remain and trample men and horses alike to a paste of blood and bone.

'Can you stop it?' she prays.

<Yes,> the Skyfather says. <But not without risk.>

'If you don't, it will break your spear.'

<The Girzan? They would distract the empire's armies, yes. Give you some cover in your assault. But you and I together are enough. They are not worth the risk.>

Ral tears her eyes away from the roiling cloud of dust, foliage, and broken earth. 'I will not abandon my people.'

A long moment of hesitation holds. The silence of the god is as vast as the horizon.

In an eruption of foliage and earth, the stone beast splits one of the mountain foothills, travelling not over it but through it. Soil and torn vegetation tumble from its black, angular carapace. It has doubled in size. In moments it will be upon her.

'Skyfather!' Ral cries.

<Flee now.> The command burns in her mind. <Before it is too late.>

The beast opens its maw, showing teeth like spears made for killing mountains, longer and wider than any man's body. Its eyes are pits that burn with unearthly fire. The earth no longer quakes – its footfalls are too near and too heavy; all the world trembles like a plucked string with its tread. It is terror brought to life, something against which no mortal could ever stand.

Ral sets her jaw and drives her heels into Falling Star. The horse screams but charges over the thrumming ground. She gathers lightning to hand, forms it into a flashing spear. Then more, drawing as deep from the well of her power as she ever has. The air bursts to hissing steam down the length of the weapon she has made. The heat of it burns Ral's face like the summer sun.

The beast lowers its head. A pressure wave of air races before it, whipping Ral's clothes like flags in a whirlwind. Its footfall breaks the earth, casting out fissures. One slices open the earth beneath Falling Star's feet, and Ral calls a wind and hurls herself into the air, towards that gaping maw. Her mount plummets, his scream breaking as the earth swallows him.

An enemy against which no mortal could stand. But Ral Ans Urrera has never been mortal. She is the storm.

She opens her hand. A single arc of lightning lances out, so bright it darkens the noon sky, and strikes the stone beast between its glowing eyes. Obsidian cracks, splinters. The beast rears back, its mad charge halted. The wall of dust and debris following in its wake surges past, battering Ral to the ground. She lands hard, hears ribs and collarbone crack, yet feels nothing but triumph as she rolls to a ragged stop.

Dust surges over her, then settles. She lifts her head, hoping – believing – the beast lies dead.

It stands erect, mouth agape, eyes still burning. A scar of splintered glass carves a narrow, bright line across its face. It studies her for a moment, its eye like a star in the distant sky above, piercing through her, breaking her heart.

A dozen aching, tearing breaths later, it lowers itself. Begins to walk again, then to run, its strange, serpentine limbs thundering into the earth, jostling Ral. Each of the monster's steps is a fresh bloom of agony.

<Stupid girl.>

She wails at the sky. 'You need us! You promised to protect us!'

<What good is a spear that resists its wielder?>

'Do this for me and I will do all that you command!' The stone beast gathers speed. Below the hilltop, the column breaks and scatters. One of the An-Zabati ships begins to wheel about, sails straining against the masts. If not for the constant thunder of gargantuan footsteps, Ral would hear a chorus of thousands screaming. 'I will send away the weak! All who are of no use to you! Only save the rest!'

In a matter of breaths the stone beast will be upon them.

A thunderclap, loud enough to pierce through the rumble of the beast's charge, peals across the sky. The strange billowing clouds overhead split and are scattered by a flare of lightning. From the heart of the flare, the Skyfather steps into the world.

The smell of a rainstorm and wet earth roils from him. His flesh is the crystalline blue of a clear mountain sky, his mane of black cloud alive with sparks and rumbling thunder. His robes shine as white and pure as the full moon. Eyes that flash like the sun settle on Ral Ans Urrera, the storm – his spear.

Though he walks the world, his voice still burns within her mind.

<I accept your oath.>

Like a diving eagle he falls, arm drawn back like a taut bow, his fist its arrow. The stone beast turns, slows its stride, rears back to face his assault. A mantle of blazing winds wreathes him, glinting like flame. The beast extends one of its snaking limbs, its many joints compressing and surging outwards. Winds howl. The sky shudders. The earth rumbles and splits as the Skyfather strikes.

The stone beast's limb shatters. Shards of smoking stone rain down, carving divots in the earth, as the beast reels backwards, maw open wide. Ral watches, transfixed, astonished, and ashamed that she had thought to bargain with a being of such power.

The Skyfather draws back his arm once more. Winds churn. Lightning bursts between his knuckles. A blow to flatten mountains, primed to crush the stone beast to ash and dust.

In the silence before it falls, another thunderclap sounds – low and nauseating, as though tearing at something deep in Ral's chest. A figure, tall and dressed in Sienese armour of black lacquer edged in red, appears in the air, held aloft on wings of pearlescent light. Ral blinks, her mind reeling, unable to believe what she sees. The figure gestures and four more thunderclaps sound. Four more wakes scream through the world. Four more armoured figures appear on the ground, forming a square with the Skyfather and the stone beast at its centre.

The Skyfather's sun-bright eyes grow wide. He tries to change direction in the air, but the momentum of his attack carries him down, like a lightning bolt flashing to earth. Only his head turns, in that moment, to face the figure with golden wings.

<NO!>

The word rocks Ral, sends her sprawling, even as five deadening wakes of magic roil out from the armoured figures – the four on the ground, the one in the air – each carving out a sphere from the pattern of the world surrounding himself. The spheres shimmer like thick glass and feel, to Ral's sixth sense, like the edge of the Skyfather's protection, dividing up the pattern of the world. But there is a difference. Within the sphere that surrounds her, her grip on her power fades. She clutches for it, means to strike out at these Sienese who have appeared from nowhere, but it is as insubstantial as morning fog.

In that instant, she is no longer the storm.

And she watches, terror-struck, as the spheres overlap where the Skyfather hangs in the sky, suspended in his moment of astonishment and death for a single heartbeat before he vanishes, in all his power and glory, like mist.

The figure in the air falls, briefly, without his wings. Now they catch him – the spheres having faded, their work complete – and flutter, as though made of feathers instead of light, as they lower him to the ground, paces from where Ral lies paralysed by fear and awe.

The figure takes a slow, considered step towards the stone beast, which stands motionless, its shattered limb extended, maw agape. The fire in its eyes is dead.

'An unfortunate loss,' the winged figure murmurs in the trading tongue, accented by rich Sienese. 'And not even a necessary one, if you had simply let yourself be brought at my first summons. How much death and destruction might have been avoided if you had simply come when I called. But all has turned out well enough, I suppose. An old friend used to say, "Every missed turning in life's path is an opportunity to seek greater, unexpected sights."'

The figure removes his helm, letting hair as black as ink and shimmering as silk flow free. He fixes her with deep, piercing eyes full of cold calculation. 'Well then, Ral Ans Urrera, shall we return to Centre Fortress? We've a great deal more to do.'

15
The Way Beneath

Koro Ha

'We've been doing this for a good while on our own,' said Tuo Pon, a crewman of the *Swiftness* whose wiry, corded arms bore dozens of pale scars. Claws had torn fresh wounds on his left thigh, but he limped only slightly, as though the pain were little more than an annoyance. He had come stumbling into the safe house that morning, along with a jittery young deckhand called Ina Kal. Both were survivors of the violence at the city gate, and both had refused healing for their numerous injuries. 'A good bandage and a mouthful of painkilling herbs will do for us, tutor.'

Ina Kal nodded solemnly in agreement, then winced as Goa Eln rubbed an acrid-smelling ointment onto his bruise-mottled shoulder.

Others joined them as the day wore on. Men and women who had worked for Orna Sin inside the city, some keeping the pulse of other criminal organisations – both allies and rivals – and others with low positions in Sienese households that let them eavesdrop or catch glimpses of the papers on a magistrate's desk. As they filtered through, each delivering a fragment of the current condition of the city, Koro Ha realised how little the wealthy and powerful thought of those who worked for them. Things meant to be kept secret might find a servant's ear through no particular subterfuge, simply because the servant had come to be considered little more than a mobile, functional piece of furniture.

The thought gave him pause. How often had he bothered to get to know the servants in the many, many wealthy households in which he had lived during his years as a tutor? Perhaps the steward, or the mistress of the kitchens, but only those ranking highest had ever warranted his attention. It was an unfortunate aspect of Sienese society, though one that now worked to his advantage.

Few were allowed to pass through the Voice's Wall, but among these were the Toa Aloni porters and labourers upon whose work the Sienese still depended, even in this time of crisis. A few such brought word to Yin Ila and told of the strange nature of the Wall – of hours or even days seeming to slip by as they moved through it. Some reported a strange tingle down the spine, and all spoke of the odd mirage that marked its boundary, seeming to bend parallel lines apart in eye-watering ways.

Yin Ila kept careful notes of these reports. Any attempt to rescue Orna Sin would mean traversing the Wall. Unfortunately, none of her spies could say for certain where he was being kept, although they carried plenty of news of the condition of Sienese society in Sor Cala. The merchants and lesser civil servants who had built their estates on the hills at the city's edge had fled inwards, begging shelter from friends or acquaintances with dwellings nearer the governor's hall. They were overcrowded and afraid. Whispered rumours among the Sienese told that contact with the rest of the empire had been severed, that the Voice no longer received the gift of sorcery from the emperor.

'Then how's he holding up that magical wall?' Yin Ila snapped after the third spy reported that same rumour. 'I'd be tickled to learn the Sienese have lost their magic, and with it their biggest bloody advantage, but I'll not believe it on a snatched fragment of overheard fearmongering, even one repeated a dozen times.'

Word that the Sienese had fled the outlying garden districts bolstered Koro Ha's spirits. Even Yin Ila had to admit that panic among the Sienese created opportunities. Orna Sin had dreamed only of creating a vestige of Toa Alon, a generation of Toa Aloni scholars who might preserve their culture in a future of imperial dominion. Sien's rule in Sor Cala had been a tightly closed fist, allowing little room for dissent, let alone organised opposition. If their control of the city began to loosen, however, there might be a chance for something more: a union of those who opposed the empire – political rebels such as Orna Sin, yes, but also proud artisans and others who chafed at Sienese oppression, and even opportunistic criminals, as Orna Sin had once been.

For the first time in living memory, the possibility of freedom had been kindled in Toa Alon. All it needed was the right leader to stoke it – a leader like Orna Sin, perhaps – and the right moment to throw fuel on the fire. A moment, Koro Ha hoped, like the discovery of whatever secrets Uon Elia had left buried in the ancient city.

Ancient lore, the old stonespeaker had described it in his dying breaths, passed down from one generation of stonespeakers to the next. Whatever it was, Koro Ha could only hope it might serve as a symbol to spur the Toa Aloni into unity and action. Even if not, he was the last stonespeaker, the last to bear the burden of that secret. It was not a duty he had sought but was one he had nonetheless accepted and would see through to its end.

The first task lay beyond Koro Ha for the moment. The second, however, might prove simpler to pursue than he had feared. Orna Sin's estate had been in one of the outlying, now abandoned districts, and might not even be under guard if Yin Ila's spies told true. They sent agents to the estate to confirm, and a week after their arrival in the city learned that, indeed, Orna Sin's garden stood empty, its gate ajar.

'They must not have found the tunnels, then,' Koro Ha observed.

'Or they filled them in,' Yin Ila pointed out. She rolled her shoulder and winced, though seemed to be recovering her range of motion. 'We'll take a look for ourselves once this bloody arm stops gnawing at me whenever I try to use it.'

Still, he clung to what hope he could.

The better half of Yin Ila's agents reported not on the Sienese but on the Toa Aloni. As expected, the underworld had risen up to fill the void left by the withdrawal of Sienese power and influence. A cavalcade of names, of individual leaders and their organisations, washed over Koro Ha, leaving him little to latch on to, though Yin Ila and Goa Eln took studious note of which gangs controlled which territory and which underworld bosses might prove allies or enemies.

Koro Ha had only one question of import for these informants, though so far none had recognised his family by their descriptions or names, which disappointed him but did not surprise him. He had no reason to think that Yan Hra, Eln Se, or his father – and certainly not young Rea Ab – had any association with Sor Cala's criminal element. He nearly abandoned the question but went on asking it, the descriptions becoming rote recitations. Filial duty demanded that he leave no thread unpulled, no matter how unlikely.

At last, on the eighth day, an interview with a grizzled, one-armed smuggler yielded fruit.

'I knew Yan Hra, years ago,' the man said, scratching at the stump just below his left elbow. 'We worked the quarry together, until a block crushed my hand. Hard to find work as a one-armed stone-cutter. Turned to my … ah … current line o' work after that. Still saw Yan Hra from time to time around the taverns, though. I'll put the word out that you're looking for him. Koro Ha, was it?'

Koro Ha fought the urge to seize the man's hand in gratitude. 'Yes! Yes, please. He can find me here or leave a message about where his family is staying.'

Yin Ila frowned. 'Are you sure that's wise, tutor? Of all of us, you're the name the Sienese might leave the shelter of their wall to hunt. Might not want to spread it all over the city.'

The smuggler shrugged. 'I can be discreet, Captain. I'll use no names, just put it out that Yan Hra's got family looking for him.'

Yin Ila grimaced but agreed, and for the first time since his arrival in Sor Cala, Koro Ha felt his spirits lift and his burden of fear grow lighter. Any day now, surely, a message would arrive telling him that everything was all right, that the family he had twice abandoned was safe and waiting for him, or Eln Se herself would come, wrap him in a tight hug, and tell him they'd all been so worried and were so glad he'd made it back. Such news would not be of much import to the broader effort of uniting the Toa Aloni factions and liberating the city – certainly not as much as rescuing Orna Sin – but it would do a great deal to ease his mind. But days passed without word, each sunset dampening Koro Ha's spirits till that first blaze of hope had faded to a guttering candle flame.

On their twelfth morning after arriving in the city, Yin Ila rolled her shoulder, took a few practice swipes with a knife, and announced herself well enough to venture out to Orna Sin's garden. Much as he wanted to stay and wait for any word of his family, his parallel duty to Uon Elia and the burgeoning possibility of real rebellion in Toa Alon drew Koro Ha back out into the streets with her. He followed her, Tuo Pon, and Ina Kal on their meandering route through alleyways towards the garden district while Goa Eln stayed behind to keep an eye on the safe house.

Orna Sin's estate, like the garden estates of many lesser Sienese merchants and bureaucrats and nearly every Toa Aloni with wealth to their name, lay along the rolling hills at the city's north-western edge. The division between the Runoff and the merchant estates was stark, marked by an archway of smoothed stone carved with Sienese forms: plum trees in bloom with lion serpents entwined with their roots. In the Runoff, as in the Tanneries, shopfronts and doorways faced the street with slate tiles bearing trade sigils hanging from the lintels. On the far side of that stone arch, guarded by Toa Aloni men wearing blue armbands – Koro Ha still struggled to remember which colours matched which gangs and what leaders – the street was lined by high walls of whitewashed brick, an oppressive sameness broken only by entryways through those walls and the alleyways where one garden ended and the next began.

The gardens nearest the Runoff were guarded by more men and women with blue armbands. Some flanked the gates while others lingered in alleyways, playing at dice, gathering around water barrels, or otherwise lounging while they waited for orders. Yin Ila kept her face shadowed by her hood. Orna Sin and his organisation had largely stayed aloof from the power struggles of the underground, but lingering resentments might have festered, particularly now that the old hierarchy of power within the city had collapsed. The chaos that offered the opportunity to throw off Sienese rule also posed a more immediate and pressing danger.

Before long, however, they passed empty alleys and boarded-up gates. As with the Tanneries, scattered detritus spoke to the haste with which the Sienese had fled their homes: here a cart with a broken axle stood still laden with a matching set of tables and chairs; there a few scraps of mud-spattered silk lay draped in an alley. An unsettling silence descended, quieter even than the Tanneries had been. There, the quietness had at least been broken by rats and the distant howls of dogs.

'I'm surprised they've bothered to hold onto the city gates,' Koro Ha observed. 'They seem to have abandoned everything else.'

Yin Ila scoffed. 'You didn't think that entry tax was to feed the poor and desperate, did you? A Hand might use cultivation to keep the granaries full, but even if the rumours that they've lost their magic are false I suspect the Sienese can find a better use for their sorcerers.' She shook her head with a wry chuckle. 'Sometimes I forget you spent the last few decades as little better than one of them, tutor.'

Her comment rankled Koro Ha, but he could not argue with it. Their own resources – mostly dry goods of the sort sailors ate aboard ship, stashed in the safe house – were dwindling and difficult to replenish. Soon enough, he suspected Yin Ila would ask him to supplement their stores with his magic, a thought that made him shudder. Of course, the monsters from the forest had not attacked *because* of his wielding cultivation – nearness in time did not indicate causality; any half-educated student knew that much – but still.

They walked in the eerie silence a while longer, peering deep into shadowed alleys, until at last they came to the familiar entrance to Orna Sin's garden. The gate hung open, unlatched, lacking the protective barricade of boards and nails common to the other estates. The hinges creaked as Tuo Pon eased his way inside, a knife in his hand, his eyes darting and alert. After a moment, he waved them through.

One of two hanging scrolls depicting wondrous landscapes still hung beside the entrance, only a bare, pale patch marking where the other had once covered the wall. Herons still waded in the lily pond – now choked with overgrowth – though they cocked their heads cautiously, their comfort in the presence of human beings common to garden animals long eroded.

Yin Ila sent Tuo Pon and Ina Kal to sweep the main buildings of the estate. First, to be sure they were truly alone – the Sienese and the gangs may have abandoned this area, but there was no guarantee that desperate folk had not decided to risk squatting in luxury far from the centre of the city. Second, to search for anything of use that had been left behind – not gold or silver, of course, but the kitchens might have dried meat, and there might be tools or weapons abandoned in some forgotten corner.

'Well then, tutor,' Yin Ila said when they had gone, setting off towards the secluded teak grove in the far corner of the garden. 'Let's see if Uon Elia left anything at all to help us unravel his riddle.'

The trap door itself was undisturbed, at least. Fallen leaves and a covering of woven grass and scattered earth hid it from all but a knowing eye. Koro Ha retrieved the brass tool – like a rake but tipped with only a single, hooked prong – slotted it into the small hole at one end of the stone door, and levered it open.

'It's no darker or danker than the belly of a ship,' Yin Ila muttered to herself as she swung onto the ladder cut into the wall. Koro Ha waited until she had faded into the darkness below, then followed her, his slight amusement at her obvious reluctance bubbling up from beneath his own simmering anxieties.

Yin Ila's feet thumped onto the floor of the tunnel. A rattling sound echoed up, then the snap of flint and steel before the warm, steady glow of an oil lamp pushed back the gloom. Koro Ha eased himself off the ladder and followed Yin Ila down the familiar corridor, covered floor to ceiling in looping knotwork that spelled out Orna Sin's dream of a Toa Alon preserved and eventually – after decades, if not centuries – reborn.

Koro Ha wondered how Orna Sin would have felt to have seen armed Toa Aloni patrolling the city streets, wearing the armbands of rival gangs – not, he was certain, the rebirth the old smuggler had hoped for.

The tunnel opened out into the dome of what once had been a temple, tilted at a dizzying angle yet holding firm. A weighty face watched them from the centre of that dome, its sculpted features shrouded in deep shadow. Tightness gripped Koro Ha throat as the lantern revealed the vine mats, neatly stacked, that had once served as seats for Uon Elia's students. He could almost hear the old stonespeaker's voice echoing in the vaulted space, weaving tales of Sor Cala's founding, still strong after more than a century of life and the wasting sickness that would, in a year's time, claim him. But whatever secret Uon Elia meant for Koro Ha to find, he doubted it would be lying out in the open in what had once been his classroom.

They pressed on deeper into the tunnels, the home that the stonespeakers who had survived the burial of the ancient city had built in the ruins, following passageways lined with delicate stonework of intricate knots, some in the form of leafy vines or roots, others stylised in a more angular, abstract fashion. They passed facades of ancient buildings, carefully excavated by the stonespeakers and stone-cutters in Orna Sin's employ. The tunnels reached only a few handspans above Koro Ha's head, but he could imagine the wonder and beauty of the city's towers and soaring domes, the sun glittering on marble carved into forms as delicate as lace, all still buried in the earth above his head.

Most intersections were marked only by a plane of earth and stone, carved with nothing more than a few words in Toa Aloni script indicating what lay beyond. Koro Ha had only begun learning to read Toa Aloni, but he picked out the words for *bath* and *gathering* on one such wall and the word for *market* on another. Clearly, the stonespeakers had known the layout of the city and had prioritised certain areas over others. Perhaps a clue to what Uon Elia meant for him to seek lay in those priorities.

Many smaller buildings had collapsed or caved in beneath the weight of the mountain overhead, leaving only broken remnants of their facades and doorways filled with rubble, but a surprising number seemed whole, or at least only partially damaged. Of these, most of the buildings they passed appeared unexplored. Carefully excavated windows revealed most floors to be littered with detritus and dust, but a few had been cleaned out and used as living spaces by the stonespeakers. One featured the withered remnant of a garden, a few dozen sickly, pale plants growing in pots and beds of soil – mostly beans, mushrooms, and gourds. Only the magic of cultivation had allowed the stonespeakers to feed themselves during their decades buried beneath the earth.

At last, they reached the second domed structure, where Uon Elia had made his home and where Orna Sin had first brought Koro Ha to meet him. The space it contained was smaller than that of the first dome, though it was in somewhat better repair. Its tall columns bore only small, hair-thin cracks, and none showed signs of crumbling. The dome overhead stood sure and high enough that the light of Yin Ila's lantern only brushed it, leaving the vast face feathered by a golden glow. More lanterns hung from the columns and a stoppered ewer of oil stood against the wall. Soon, Koro Ha held a lit lantern of his own, and Yin Ila set about setting flame to the rest, filling the space with light that made Koro Ha blink after so long in the gloom.

'Well,' Yin Ila said, putting her flint and knife away. 'I suppose we should start our search here, eh? What exactly are we looking for?'

Koro Ha swept his gaze around the space, divided by ropes strung between the columns, from which mats of vines hung to create the impression of rooms. 'I've no idea,' he said, grimacing, and stepped towards the makeshift chambers. 'I can only hope I'll know it when I see it.'

Yin Ila looked askance at the nearest column, dubious of the hair-thin cracks. 'Best get to it, tutor. I know this place has stood like this for near a hundred years, but I can't help feeling it's a gentle nudge away from crushing us to bloody paste.'

It quickly became clear that the place had once been home to a small community. Only one of the spaces still boasted a bed – a surprisingly large one, sturdily constructed, presumably hauled from a surviving house elsewhere in the city – yet there were tables and wooden chairs enough for a dozen people. Koro Ha wondered why Uon Elia had bade his students sit on mats rather than the chairs, and presumed it had something to do with the Toa Aloni equivalent of Sienese propriety – another fragment of his culture suppressed by the conquerors and likely lost for ever now that death had taken those who carried it in memory.

That melancholy thought set the tone for his perusal of the stonespeakers' gathered artefacts, most of which were practical objects speaking less of ancient secrets than of ordinary lives maintained under extreme circumstances. There were the necessities, of course: blankets and baskets, chamber pots – Koro Ha winced, imagining the unfortunate place where those had been emptied for the last century – combs, brushes, chisels, and hammers. A barrel held picks and shovels, well maintained – the tools necessary for the ongoing project of unearthing the buried city.

But there were also simple comforts. A stone carving in the shape of a tortoise. A brass incense burner, though Koro Ha thought this temple's supply of incense must have long ago run out. A woven mat, hung up to form one of the walls, painted with a scene of blue sky, drifting clouds, and distant mountains. This last twisted Koro Ha's heart. The stonespeakers had spent so long alone, so long denied even the simplest pleasures of human life, yet they had endured, and these small luxuries had been the cornerstone of that endurance. A few months of isolation upon the Black Maw had nearly broken Koro Ha until he had found new purpose in learning Uon Elia's magic, preserving Toa Aloni culture for the future. It was a purpose, he decided, not unlike that which had buoyed these stonespeakers throughout the dark, uncertain decades.

'Oy there, what's this?' Yin Ila's voice echoed. She held up a pair of objects, one a book of rough paper bound in slats of weathered wood, the other a nearly perfect sphere of green stone that glimmered in the lantern light, hair-fine carvings of intricate knotwork covering its surface. Gingerly, Koro Ha took the book, his fingers trembling, yet his hopes of an easy clue were soon dashed.

'You don't happen to read ancient Toa Aloni, do you?' he muttered.

'Never was particularly literate,' Yin Ila replied. 'Just enough to keep the ship's accounts and pass the occasional message we didn't want the Sienese deciphering.'

'They would have a truly difficult time deciphering *this*.' Koro Ha was able to pick out the occasional word, or at least a familiar stem or word shape, but the writing was in a fluid hand, one loop and knot bleeding into the next. There was no telling how long it would take him to decipher the book, and he doubted there were any in Sor Cala who could read it easily.

'It's something, at least,' Yin Ila said. She held the stone sphere up to the lantern light. 'And what a bauble this is! Never seen anything like it. You think one of them made it or found it down here?'

‘I couldn’t hazard a guess,’ said Koro Ha, turning a few more pages in the hope that the text became more coherent further into the book. He recognised a handful of words, and could nearly understand snatched fragments – something about a garden deep in the city, perhaps? Or was it *under* a garden? Not since his first days as a child in Teacher Zhen’s school, memorising Sienese logograms by rote, had he felt so lost in a page of text.

He could only hope that this was, indeed, what Uon Elia had intended for him to find, else he might waste weeks trying to decipher it only to discover it was no more than the journal of one of the stonespeakers. Whatever Uon Elia had sent him after related in some way to the stone beast the Black Maw had become and, in all likelihood, to the terrible hounds that had attacked the gates of Sor Cala. A notebook of historical interest would not help him solve those problems no matter how much it proved a wealth of Toa Aloni culture and history.

‘You know, I’ve had a thought,’ Yin Ila said, surveying the temple. ‘Uon Elia and his lot lived down here for decades, yes? This place seems secure enough, what with having only the one entrance. Might make for a decent shelter for those folk with nowhere else to go. Safer, maybe, than living in those empty garden estates, even if you have to worry about the ceiling falling in. You could even turn Orna Sin’s garden into a farm. Pop your head up to tend it, scurry back down in case any of those freakish wolves come sniffing around. What d’you think?’

‘I suppose you could,’ Koro Ha muttered, not paying close mind to Yin Ila’s words. He turned another page and nearly dropped the book. There, in a rough but recognisable sketch, was the glass sphere Yin Ila had found.

‘Bleed me, tutor, you look like another bloody island’s reared up before your eyes,’ Yin Ila said. She peered over his shoulder and whistled. ‘How about that. What’s it say?’

Koro Ha answered with a glare, then turned back to the page, desperate to glean anything at all. The sphere must be important. The author of the book had not bothered to sketch anything else, after all. Yet effort and need alone did not make the looping script any more comprehensible.

'Come on,' Yin Ila said. 'I've other business today, and you can dredge through that book back at the safe house as easily as here. More, even. We might even be able to scrounge a dictionary from somewhere, if that'll help.'

Reluctantly, Koro Ha stowed the book and sphere in his satchel, then hefted his lamp. Of course Toa Aloni secrets would be written in Toa Aloni. If only Uon Elia were still alive, or had lived a few months longer, even, just long enough to explain these mysteries. If only he had, at the very least, brought Koro Ha further along the path towards literacy in the language. In the wake of conquest and brutal suppression, the future of a people and the continuation of a culture had come to rest on such a thin foundation, and Koro Ha had become its cornerstone, albeit a crumbling, terribly inadequate one.

No matter. He would bear that burden as best he could and do everything in his power not to let that future collapse. He touched the rough lump of the book in his satchel and whispered a prayer to the silent gods, looking down from the domed ceiling, that he would be enough.

16

Planning

Foolish Cur

From the parapet of the governor's estate, I watched dawn break over the mountains, washing Eastern Fortress in sharp, brisk light. I sat cross-legged on the cold stone, dressed in a common tunic and trousers to replace those Burning Dog had burned away, the broken hilt of her sword in my lap. The sunlight, as it brushed my face, felt cold and distant, and I wondered if my every experience of warmth from this day on would feel a pale shadow when compared to the searing heat of Burning Dog's flame.

Perhaps Clear-River was right. Perhaps she could never have been convinced. Perhaps all my gestures of contrition had been only fuel for her rage. Of the two of us, he had always been the better politician.

What could I have done differently? Was there a moment when we had first met at Iron Town, years ago, or sometime during the march to Eastern Fortress, when I might have said one thing rather than another, taken a different turn on some half-perceived path that led into a future where Burning Dog survived? Where Frothing Wolf, even, survived? Or my uncle? Or were we all little more than strands in the vast, inscrutable weave of the pattern, threads pushed and pulled according to a design far beyond the capacity of our understanding? If all the world was but an interchange of energies, did that not mean that even we, despite our seeming capacity to choose, to pursue goals, to dream of better futures, were but a product of that interchange? Our lives little more than sparks rising from an ever-burning fire, carried by winds beyond our comprehension?

A comforting thought. A balm for my guilt. If all I had done was little more than an expression of the pattern's vast, eternal dance, then I could no more be blamed than a single thread in a tapestry for marring a masterpiece, or a wave for swamping a floundering ship on a stormy sea.

Yet it was a thought I knew to be false, for I had reached out with my will and reshaped that pattern, added steps to its dance, twisted the threads of its weaving. I had made the world other than what it would have been without my interference. There could be no retreat into blameless fatalism for me. Which meant I had to act.

My hand curled tightly around the canon I had made, my fingers brushing down the carved pact marks. The fetish bore the key to wielding magic within the dome of Hissing Cat's seal – an impossibility, the seed of a mystery I had only just begun to solve, clinging to life by a strand of healing sorcery while Burning Dog's flames tore me apart. If it proved correct, the solution might yield the means to force the gods to stalemate and to stitching the frayed pattern of the world back together.

Hissing Cat's seal did not prevent *magic*, after all. Not precisely. Rather, it carved out a smaller, simpler version of the pattern, then asserted it – as I had once asserted the pattern against the emperor's canon in my duel with Voice Usher – preserving the simplified pattern's natural flow. Hissing Cat's will, reinforcing that simplified pattern, could easily overwhelm any other witch or sorcerer's attempt to change it, stifling their magic.

I held up the strip of bone. What a strange thing I had made. A construct built to unify all three layers of the pattern. Mental walls raised in the layer of the soul – that layer of the pattern where the will dwells, where magic is done – and anchored to a bit of dead, old bone. Not tied to a single living being, as a pact mark ought to be, but existing in the pattern on its own, able to affect any mind at the touch of a finger. When Hissing Cat had created her seal, it seemed that the canons of witchcraft, as well as any magic done with them, had become part of the simplified pattern she had asserted rather than separate from it. Precisely why this was, I did not know, but I could see a use for it. To force the gods to a stalemate, we needed to create countless seals throughout the world, yet there were too few witches of the old sort left for this mammoth task. The emperor had meant to supplement his own power through his canon of sorcery, using his Hands and Voices as a conduit to expand his reach and seal the entire world himself. I could do something similar, perhaps something even more potent, more effective. Perhaps something that would not even require a witch, a sorcerer, nor anyone at all to create and maintain the seal.

Naphena had etched her will in silver onto the obelisks of An-Zabat, filling her oasis with water drawn by magic from deep beneath the earth. In theory, my canons of witchcraft were not so different.

I felt the spark of an old fire in me, the light of curiosity that had first kindled in childhood and had been fed steadily throughout my life, until mistake after world-shattering mistake had thrown soil and water on the flame, dousing it. My fist tightened around the canon until the edges of the bone bit into my flesh. As swiftly as that fire had flared, it faded.

If I had learned anything in my life, it was the importance of caution, particularly when playing with half-understood forces able to reshape the world. As eager as I was to set things right,

I would not dash foolishly into the darkness again. I needed time to think and to experiment, which would mean spending time outside Hissing Cat's seal. First, though, I owed her a long-needed respite.

She was slouching against the trunk of Oriole's scarred tree, breathing slowly, wrapped in her furs. At the sound of my footsteps her eyes snapped open, red and sagging for want of sleep.

'It's done,' I said and knelt on the other side of the arc of shoulder blades she had arranged at her knees, each carved with her strange runes but not yet cracked by the white-hot tip of her needle. 'The Army of the Wolf will join with us. We've bought a little more time.'

'Clear-River already told me.' Despite her weariness, her eyes held a piercing intensity as she searched my face. An unspoken question burned behind them, yet she did not ask it, perhaps too exhausted to hear the answer, or afraid of what it might be. I felt too numb to wonder long. 'A shame about the girl. We all told you she would never listen.'

I nodded even as my mind flinched away from the topic. 'It's done, anyway,' I said again. 'I promised you rest, and you'll take it. No arguments!' I snapped as she gathered herself, like a storm about to spit lightning. 'If you pass out and the seal collapses, the whole city will fall to ruin.'

'In the last war with the gods, I held a seal on a system of caves for thirty days straight,' she snarled.

'That's as may be, but you were quite a bit younger then, and at the prime of your strength. Let me do this for a while. Sleep. Attend to your other needs. When you're ready again, I will gladly pass the burden back, but just as I'll never restore the world alone, you cannot protect the city alone.'

Her mouth worked, formulating some rebuttal, but finally she harrumphed and planted her hand on Oriole's tree. 'Well then, I'd better get on my feet. If I let the spell go while sitting down I'll likely pass out, piss myself, or both.' With a grunt she heaved herself upwards, then slumped back down. I moved to lend a supportive arm, but she flapped her hand at me and growled, then tried again. On the third attempt, with one arm pushing against the earth and the other pulling on a low-hanging branch, she managed to reach her knees and then her feet, with only the slightest hint of a drunken sway.

'Be ready,' she said. 'Open yourself to the pattern.'

I did so, and felt the flow of the garden around us: the growth of what plants remained, the slow settling of earth disturbed by battle, the distant heartbeats of the guards atop the pavilions. I felt a powerful urge – as a man addicted to drink might feel at the smell of his favourite wine – to reach out, to do something as simple as conjure a flame on my own without the aid of the canon of witchcraft in my hand. With a shuddering breath I gave in, twisting the threads of the pattern in that old, most familiar way, expecting a burst of cinnamon scent and the play of fire across my fingertips.

'No use in that, boy,' Hissing Cat snarled. 'Not unless you mean to pit your will against mine and see if you can overwhelm my seal.'

Ashamed, I released the half-formed, impotent spell. 'I'm ready,' I said.

Her lip twitched. 'No,' she said. 'No, I don't think so.'

It is an easy thing to turn one's shame into anger. I hurled mine at her. 'Don't be stubborn! You need a rest. You agreed. What was that a minute ago about pissing yourself?'

'If you take over the seal, you'll be able to let it fade on a whim. You could gain access to magic again, Cur, at the mere risk of a hundred thousand lives or so.'

'I am not as selfish as that,' I protested, 'nor such a fool.'

'Oh?' She cocked her head. 'If you had succeeded just now and torn through the seal, it would have collapsed. You confessed to me yourself, when you first stumbled half-frozen into my cave, that your first and only obsession has always been magic. Holding a seal offers no profound sense of oneness with the universe, no deeper understanding of the pattern. Quite the bloody opposite.'

I felt as I imagined Oriole's tree must feel: charred and battered, clinging to stability with what few fibres of strength I had left. Hissing Cat's accusations were a frigid wind, heavy with ice, threatening to overwhelm me and leave me broken and collapsed.

'Do you not trust me?' I asked.

Again she worked her mouth, chewing over her response. Perhaps I was not hiding my fragility as well as I imagined.

'Clear-River told me what you did for Burning Dog,' she said at last. 'If not for that, I would say no. After it . . . I believe you are trying, at least, to make good on the trail of bloody wreckage you've left in your wake. Fine. As I said, open yourself to the pattern.'

I did so, and at once that nagging urge surged within me to reach for magic, to slake my thirst for its texture, for the feeling of holding the power to bend the very fabric of the world to my will. My teeth creaked together in my desperate need to quench that thirst, but I did all I could to give no outward sign of the struggle within me.

'All right then,' Hissing Cat murmured.

Pressure built within my skull as her mind reached into mine. Her presence carried a heavy weight that radiated outwards, reaching to the distant edges of the city, like a vast wheel of iron with my neck for its axle. The weight gradually settled on me, filling me with the first creeping tendrils of bone-deep exhaustion.

Hissing Cat breathed a low, rattling sigh and slumped against Oriole's tree. The bags under her eyes seemed deeper than before, but she moved more easily now that she was unburdened by the seal.

'Hold it tightly,' she said, heaving herself back to her feet. I nodded and reached out, tracing the contours of the seal, locking my attention upon it and the effort to hold it in place – a far more difficult task than holding a seal against only the emperor had been. That seal had encircled only our bodies and had to resist only his effort to shatter it from within. Now, I held at bay the chaos rippling through the world beyond the seal, battering at it from without, a thousand god-wrought spells like a thousand crossbow bolts slamming into the same plate of armour.

Hissing Cat's mind retreated from mine, relieving some of the pressure but none of the burden. I looked at her exhausted face with a new sense of appreciation. For weeks she had devoted every ounce of herself to maintaining the mortar and stone of these vast, besieged walls, and the prospect of holding the seal for even a few hours while she took her much-needed rest felt a monumental task. She grunted by way of thanks, then slumped off towards the inner dwelling of the estate, where presumably a bed would be quickly found for her, perhaps Golden-Finch's own.

I settled myself in her place at the base of the tree, behind the arc of oracle bones she had laid out. The runes on them were fresh, ready for her fire-heated needle to pierce and crack them, revealing to her eye some secret of the pattern. I had never really understood what she read in the oracle bones. She claimed they offered warnings from the pattern, but she and I both knew the pattern to be a force without will, not a mind interested in her fate. Further, she worked no actual magic when reading them. They must be little more than some vestige of the life she had led and the beliefs she had held before becoming a witch and glimpsing deeper truths, the last remnant of an ancient religion, long forgotten by all but the lone woman still practising its rites of fire and bone after millennia.

I hefted one of the shoulder blades, running my fingers along the runes. The insect-like scratches were meaningless to me but were able to hold any meaning I might attribute to them, not unlike the marks I had carved in the canon of witchcraft. I might easily have reached into the pattern, into the layer of the soul, and anchored the seal to the bone – not to create a canon permitting some other to wield the magic that maintained the seal, but a far simpler thing, the very same thing Naphena had done to anchor her conjured oasis to the obelisks of An-Zabat: the bones themselves might hold up the seal, sparing Hissing Cat's and my own attention for the larger problem of repairing the shattered world.

Such a simple act, and one I so profoundly longed for, not only for its practical usefulness but also to feel once again a certain dominion over reality. All my life I had longed to master magic, and here was an opportunity to demonstrate that mastery, to make something to rival the feats of the greatest ancients. All I had to do was reach out, let the seal fade for but a moment, and rebuild it while binding it to the shoulder blade.

A moment's hesitation spared the world whatever terrible consequence might have followed such an indulgence. I did not know with any certainty that I could truly do what I envisioned. The envisioning itself captivated me, and the desire to test myself, to impose a vision upon the world, nearly pulled me into ruin – yet I had learned. The world and all the uncountable souls within it had suffered unfathomably when last I had plunged blindly, wielding uncertain magic. I would not do so again.

And so I hesitated, long enough for a servant to arrive with an evening meal. I set down the shoulder blade and accepted the bowl of simple gruel he offered, flavoured with a slice of melon and a few grains of salted pork – rare luxuries from the estate's dwindling supply. I sat leaning against Oriole's tree, ate, and wondered if I would ever again have the confidence to leap, as I had so often leapt, into the unknown.

'You want to *what?*' Clear-River stood across the arc of shoulder blades from me, the dawn sun catching in his wild curls. 'Alder, the negotiations with the Sienese are just beginning. I need your help. You're the only other person on our side who understands the way they think, how to argue with them, how to convince them that we all stand a damned sight better chance of surviving together than we do at each other's throats.'

Two days of holding the seal had left me bent backed. Every muscle in my body sagged beneath that invisible, vital weight. Hissing Cat had woken only briefly the previous evening, after sleeping an entire day, to eat a meal and send a runner to check and make sure I was not yet on the verge of collapse. I had sent the boy back with every assurance that I could hold the seal as long as Hissing Cat needed to regain her strength – words I was beginning to regret.

Yet as Traveller-on-the-Narrow-Way wrote, long before he assumed the guise of Doctor Sho, 'Every injury is a lesson and every boon bears its own undoing' – assuming, that is, that the aphorism was not contrived at some later date by the emperor, or some scholar, and misattributed, as Doctor Sho claimed so many had been. Regardless, two days of holding the seal had left me deeply fatigued, but had also afforded me plenty of time to think through my next steps with a rare, careful thoroughness. No simple impulse, this plan, nor the first solution to come to mind, but something deeply considered, weighed against a dozen options and selected with a sober if sleep-deprived mind.

'There is too much to do and not enough time to do it. I cannot be everywhere at once, Clear-River. Seek Pinion's aid in the negotiations if you need it,' I said, clipping the words carefully to avoid slurring them in my fatigue. Clear-River wore open incredulity, but I pressed on. 'Besides, if I succeed, I might return with not only an argument but an edict from the emperor insisting upon their cooperation.'

'Won't he be behind one of these seals?' Clear-River waved an arm, as though to encircle the city. 'Even if he were willing to talk, you won't be able to reach him.'

'Do you think the emperor is cowering, doing nothing?' I asked. 'If I take him at his word, his life's work has been building the empire into a weapon to prevent another divine war. Now that one is here, he will be doing all he can to end it.'

'If he has not given in to despair,' Clear-River snapped. 'You ruined his plans, Alder. You nearly killed him. Maybe he's sprawled out in his palace, drinking his way through the riches of the imperial cellars, occupying his hours with his concubines and servant girls behind the walls of his seal, sucking as much pleasure from the marrow of the world as he can before the end.'

I blinked up at Clear-River, astonished by his outburst. 'Is that what you would be doing in his place?' I asked.

'No!' Clear-River growled. 'I would be doing what I'm doing now! Whatever I can to keep people alive, buying time for the people who can fix this to find a way to do so. But I am not the emperor, and neither of us knows him well enough to speculate about how he might be spending his last days before the end of the world.'

'True enough,' I admitted, then beckoned over a passing soldier coming off her shift atop one of the pavilions and instructed her to fetch Doctor Sho.

Clear-River scowled at the soldier's back. 'All right, let's say Sho agrees with you. Do you intend to go out into the forest on your own? As far as we can tell, those monsters out there are drawn to magic. Your transmission will draw them like iron to a lodestone. You'll need guards, which we can't spare right now. The Sienese know the armies of the Wolf and Fox are reintegrating. They know there are those among us still who would rather storm their fortifications and put them all to the sword than negotiate, no matter what I say. It stands to reason they might decide to attack first.'

'As a certain someone may or may not have written a long time ago, "When the people are deprived and desperate, they hammer their sickles into swords." Surely you can spare a few bows and spears? There are still hunting parties venturing out, are there not?'

Clear-River worked his jaw. Something visibly nagged at him, pushing tight the corners of his eyes and mouth, telling of a feeling desperate to be expressed yet held back. At last, in a rolling sentence full of fragments, it burst from him. 'After everything, we go crawling back? Beg his help? After Setting Sun Fortress? He deserves to die, Alder. I don't give a damn that we need him.'

I let his words hang in the air a moment, for they deserved to be given the honour due to truth, to be heard without rebuttal, to linger with finality. Yet in our broken world, other terrible truths overwhelmed them.

'But we do need him, Clear-River,' I said simply. 'We need his knowledge as much as his power. Hissing Cat has been isolated in a cave, and I would wager even in her prime she was never much of a mind for complex problems. I'll not risk breaking the world further by trying to fix it in ignorance.'

'Wise of you,' Doctor Sho's voice floated up from the base of the hill. He always looked odd to me without his medicine chest, like a tortoise lacking its shell. Clear-River regarded him with curious fascination. He had been slow to believe the old doctor was, indeed, Traveller-on-the-Narrow-Way, and still held doubts. 'Deeper wisdom would remind you that the emperor already made you an offer of cooperation – one you answered with a sword through the lung, as I recall. Asking for his aid now will be an admission of weakness, and Tenet has always been keenly aware of where he stands in relationships of power. If he agrees to work with you, it will be an agreement to let *you* work for *him* to pursue whatever solution he deems best.'

Doctor Sho had climbed the hill while he spoke and now stood between Clear-River and me, his gaze sweeping between us. 'If I know Tenet well – and I did, once, and might still – that solution will return the world to the way it was, with him atop it and his empire encircling all. *Protecting it*, he might say, though in the same way a wire cage protects a songbird.'

Better that than this, I wanted to argue, but swallowed the words. Doctor Sho and I had been back and forth over his vision of a better world – one without magic, without the gods. Until he came to me with an actual proposal for how such a thing might be accomplished, it was equally futile and absurd to contemplate the notion, let alone argue against him.

'Fair enough,' I said. 'But will I be able to reach him, do you think? Or is Clear-River's vision of fatal hedonism more likely?'

'Tenet is a deeply, deeply flawed man,' Doctor Sho said after a moment's consideration. 'He is not, however, a coward, nor would he abandon his subjects – nor, I might add, was he ever particularly interested in hedonism. A bit of a poet, but beyond that he wields finery like a weapon. A projection of wealth is a projection of power, after all. Suffice to say he will not be hiding *within* a seal. I would wager he has fortified his palace against the unwoven and from there transmits his canon, and with it the power to *make* seals, to his Hands and Voices throughout the empire, using them as proxies to protect as many of his people as he can.'

The notion puzzled me. 'How could he, though? The moment

a Voice raised a seal, he would be cut off from the emperor's transmission, wouldn't he? And then the seal would fail.'

Doctor Sho glared at me. 'I don't know. I've never used magic before, let alone toyed with it as you and he have. That said, while I don't know *how* he would accomplish such a thing, it seems like something he would do, and I have every confidence in his ability to determine the means. Don't forget, using the Hands and Voices in precisely this way would have been central to any plan of his to finally destroy the gods.'

Something about the notion still troubled me, like a knot in the string of ideas Doctor Sho had expressed. Perhaps when I was less exhausted, I might tease it out. For the moment, though, I had the answer I needed.

'You see, Clear-River?' I said. 'If there is a chance to negotiate, I have to take it.'

Clear-River's gaze was steady and unwavering. For all his desire for peace and his willingness to forgive old crimes for the sake of a better world, first at Burrow and now here in what remained of Eastern Fortress, that goodwill fell short of forgiving the emperor. I could little blame him for his outrage, but neither did I have any choice.

'Hunting parties go out every three days,' he said. 'I'll send someone to wake Hissing Cat. You won't want to go into this as tired as you look.'

I dipped my head. 'Thank you,' I said.

He smiled thinly, turned on his heel, and set off to shoulder another of the hundreds of burdens that had fallen on him, none of them as weighty as the seal I held but in combination just as vital to the survival of the city.

'Will that be all?' Doctor Sho said just as thinly, with a flat, veiled expression. I ached to share some joke, to ask how the clinic was faring, or to inquire after Running Doe's health. We had seen each other little since our reunion, busy as she was in the clinic, which was gradually filling with patients suffering exhaustion and malnutrition even as the wounded from the attack on the city recovered. She had come to examine me briefly after learning of what I had suffered in my confrontation with Burning Dog – unsatisfied, apparently, by Doctor Sho's assurance that I was as hale as ever – but had been called away to tend to her patients almost as suddenly as she had appeared. I could conjure the words in my mind, and the desire to express them, but they died against my teeth.

'Yes,' I said, surprised not to hear anguish in my voice, crying out to repair our broken camaraderie. 'That will be all.'

He grunted and left me. Alone, fixed in my purpose, clear of mind for the first time in memory, I watched him go.

A better world . . .

A beautiful notion – albeit one I could little imagine how to achieve – from a man whose beautiful notions had formed the foundation of a violent, oppressive empire. Yet somehow he had managed to lose neither his hope nor his faith that the next world he envisioned would not be twisted beyond recognition, his words and ideas put to terrible purpose. That no matter how catastrophic his failure, next time he might succeed.

If I lived a thousand years, I might never learn such strength.

17
Ultimatum

Ral Ans Urrera

The grey, roiling clouds drift, covering the expanse of blue sky where the Skyfather appeared. Fat drops of rain burst to steam as they strike the corpse of the stone beast. Even dead, it holds the heat of its furious charge.

Ral kneels in its shadow, staring at the sky. The clouds rove senselessly, devoid of any shepherding hand. The rain falls when and where it will, with no mind to need. The warmth of the sun, shrouded by clouds, is neither cruel nor comforting.

Her voice is raw, her prayers shouted and wailed and screamed until she can only croak. The emperor stands over her, dressed in armour lacquered black and red, his hair flowing freely beneath a golden circlet.

He gives orders in clipped Sienese. One of the four soldiers who appeared with him – Hands, Ral presumes, though she has never seen Hands of the emperor so heavily armoured – seizes her by the elbow and hauls her to her feet, then down the hillside. The earth is churned and shattered, like a savaged corpse – scars of the stone beast's brief battle with the Skyfather. She stumbles over a fragment of smoking black stone that scrapes and burns her shin.

A god is dead. She watched him die.

The other Sienese approach the column of Girzan and An-Zabati with all the confidence of men at the heads of legions rather than lone warriors. None so much as draws the sword at his belt.

Monstrous howls reverberate across the plain, sending a lance of fear down Ral's spine. Dazed she might be, but instinct and terror give her the presence of mind to sweep her gaze over the horizon. The shimmering silver line of the Skyfather's protection has vanished, leaving her people vulnerable to the twisted monsters that now stalk the world. Dark shadows swoop against the churning clouds and slink between the hills. She sees movement in the column below – hunters leaping to horseback, stringing bows, readying to fight.

She knows, in the bleeding pit of her heart, that it is hopeless. A wave of the monsters might be repelled, but another will come, and another, until the Girzan are reduced to gristle and bone. The world is ending, and with the Skyfather's death the only hope her people have is lost. Despair digs at her, hollowing her out, leaving her only a stumbling shell propelled by no more than the Sienese warrior who pulls her along by the elbow.

A party detaches from the column: Garam, leading warriors, at the head of a group of elders representing the bands. Elsol is among them.

Terrible, sickening laughter bubbles in Ral. If Elsol and her kin had already departed in exile, there might have been some chance of the Girzan way of life surviving. A poor chance, without the Skyfather to protect them, but better than they face now.

The emperor killed a god. How ridiculous she had been to imagine herself the storm that could break him.

The riders rein in. Bows rise with nocked arrows.

'Stormrider!' Garam calls. 'What is this? What has happened?

I thought … Where has the Skyfather gone? His protection has vanished and the beasts are massing to attack!'

How can she tell them? After all her promises, all her posturing, all the hope she offered – after they swore to her and followed her to war – how can she tell them that their god is dead?

'You are now under the personal protection of the emperor of Sien,' one of the Sienese warriors says, 'who slew the beast that threatened your column and the god who brought chaos to your lands. He is due all deference! All honour! All loyalty!'

The Girzan elders murmur, their eyes flitting from the speaker, to the emperor, to Ral. The emperor steps forward and extends his hands to either side with a broad, gracious smile. His eyes are still as cold as the winter sky.

'You have strayed, children of the steppe.' His voice booms over the plain, cresting the heads of the elders to reach the ears of the column. Ral distantly feels a new wake from him, something akin to calling the wind, but she cannot summon the will to comprehend it. 'You have been led astray by the god of your ancestors, the Skyfather, most cruel and capricious of his kind. You need no longer fear him. He is banished for ever from the world. Yet the horrors he unleashed, the unwoven dogs he sent to drive you like cattle to fight his war – spilling mortal blood, the blood of your brothers and sisters! – will outlive him. But do not let terror seize your hearts!' He gestures. The pearlescent feathers that sprout from his back sweep like the vast sleeves of an imperial robe. 'My Fist will escort you safely to Centre Fortress, which is true to its name: a sanctuary against the gods and the chaos they have unleashed. A haven to shelter you while your Stormrider and I defend the world from the Skyfather's ilk.'

His words are a babbling madness. Why would she ever fight beside him? He, whose servants slaughtered her family? He, who killed her god? She ought to stand, to drive a spear of wind and lightning through his heart, to let him choke on his hubris and his blood. *That* is what the storm, the spear of the Skyfather, would do.

Terror binds her to the earth and births a gnawing question. There is no longer a Skyfather, and he no longer wields any spear. What, then, is she? Why has she suffered? Why was she born?

'Stormrider, have you agreed to this?' Elsol's voice cuts through whirling thoughts. 'Have you knelt to the empire?'

'Her agreement is inevitable,' the emperor declares. 'You have known cruelty at the hands of my servants. I will not apologise for this. It was necessary. To win freedom and safety, humanity had to be forged into a single pillar, strong and firm enough in its foundation to hold aloft the sky. What we did, we did to that end, to secure a new dawn and a new world free of divine meddling and menace.

'You were deceived, I know. Your minds reel at these revelations. Yet I tell you, the Skyfather only ever meant to use you to avenge himself upon me, to settle a grudge born thousands of years ago when I and my kind first dared to challenge the gods.'

'Free?' The word bursts from Ral. 'Free to be carved apart, our bodies stacked like cordwood? Free to have our herds stolen and our sacred city occupied? The gods never did worse to us than you.'

'They do worse now.' The emperor gestures to the horizon, to the gathering shadows of twisted monsters drawing nearer by the word, their howls echoing. He expects the beasts to come and feels not a twinge of fear. 'All of this is a product of their ancient war. Your lives were lived – as your fathers and your grandfathers, for generations, lived their lives – in a peace that I and my kind forged with our struggle and blood. In the eye of the storm. But the eye has passed and the storm rages again, as it was always destined to. The gods cannot help it. It is their nature.

'They were conjured by terrified minds desperate for something greater than themselves to protect against the beasts of the field, against the terrors of the night, against the spears and envy of their neighbours. But the gods outgrew their creators, and when they found their cousins among neighbouring tribes, their battle broke the pattern of the world – and breaks it now, for they defy it by their very existence. Their every act sends unpredictable, unalterable ripples that twist the pattern out of its natural flow. The unwoven, the contortions of time and space, the fragmented weather – these are only the beginning. I have seen rivers burn and forests turn to dust, mountains birthed and swallowed up by the infinite abyss. We leashed them, long ago, with our pacts, to save the pattern before the chaos extinguished all human life. This time, I would end them.'

His gaze sweeps across the assembled elders, then settles again, cold and unyielding as steel, on Ral. 'Who but the most selfish of hearts would sacrifice the world to save a loved one, or a way of life? Would you rather the world be frayed to nothing?'

Never has she heard words spoken with such confidence, as though his words themselves are spells that solidify reality, define what *is* and what *is not*. Perhaps they are. What, after all, is a culture but an enduring collection of such weighty words, passed from generation to generation?

Ral has no such confidence. No sense of how the world is or ought to be. Only a bleeding hollowness within her, and the memory of her father's face atop the pile of her tribe's severed heads.

Another party approaches on foot: the An-Zabati – Atar, the winddancer, and her ship's captain, Katiz. They stop a dozen paces behind the elders.

'We will soon join battle with the twisted ones,' Atar calls out. 'Whatever has happened here, and whatever you discuss, none of us will survive if we do not defend ourselves.'

The emperor smiles. 'True enough, girl.' He gestures sharply to two of the Sienese soldiers – his Fists, sorcerers like his Hands and Voices. One positions himself nearby, facing towards the hills, the heap of the stone beast's corpse, and the distant mountains. The other vanishes with a clap of thunder – magic which leaves a wake that makes Ral's stomach fall and nearly brings her to her knees. He reappears on the far side of the column, prompting a chorus of startled shouts.

While the Fists do this, the emperor's face takes on a faraway look, as though his mind is fixated elsewhere. The constant weight of transmission that roils from him seems to deepen. Garam locks eyes with Ral, drops from his saddle, and slowly and silently draws a knife. She ought to warn him away, she knows – nothing can harm this emperor, who has slain a god – yet his brazenness kindles her hope.

An unsettling tension runs through Ral's body. The air, from the earth to the sky, shimmers in great sheets rising from the two Fists who stand to either side of the column, sheets that extend in an arch, meeting above the column, enfolding it like a parcel wrapped in cloth. It is the same sort of shimmering that filled the five spheres that killed the Skyfather.

'There. Sufficient protection,' the emperor says. 'Not a true seal, but any twisted one that passes through those barriers will be ripped apart.'

'How is it done?' Ral asks. Her curiosity is genuine, in part, but the question also draws the emperor's attention away from the elders, and from Garam, who takes slow, careful steps. Two Fists are occupied with the barriers, two with watching the column. If he can draw near enough and strike before the emperor can react, perhaps the storm will not have ended after all.

The emperor answers with a wry smile. 'You would have me share knowledge before you kneel? You, who have resisted my every overture?'

What *overture*? His servants offered her no alliance before they slaughtered her tribe. The Voice of the Skyfather's Hall spoke of such a thing only after she had fought her way through the city, and he threatened to torture her into compliance if she refused him. Ral seethes but forces her eyes to fix on the emperor. In the periphery, Garam takes slow, careful steps.

She realises, now, how to create an opportunity. 'If you will not give me the means to protect my people, I will take them,' she says.

The emperor bursts out laughing, and Ral strikes. A terrible magic, but one she knows well, for she traced its every tortuous contour while she lay in the belly of a windship, and later while the corpses of her people burned around her. Ribbons of light unfurl from her splayed hands, reaching for the emperor to enfold him in their grasp. She will bind his magic, as hers was bound, and *take*—

The emperor's laughter ends in a snarl. With a flick of his wrist he works a spell with a wake that fill her limbs with twitching agony. Her ribbons of binding light shatter.

Garam's dagger glints as he lunges, his face a mask of rage.

Another wake, harsh enough to freeze Ral's bones.

The dagger falls to the earth, spattered with a mist of blood. The frayed wreckage that remains of Garam staggers backwards a single step, then collapses in a wet heap.

'Are your ears stoppered?' the emperor seethes. He turns his hand and ribbons of light lance out, wrap around Ral's body, and close her mind. She sobs, ripping and tearing at the blinding aurora that fills her thoughts, but it only redoubles in strength.

The emperor rounds on the Girzan elders. 'What of you? You have been led by this deluded, vengeful fool. Will *you* hear sense? I would save what I can of humanity, even the barbarous dregs of the world's far-flung corners. Submit and be saved, or wait for the gods to trample you in their warring.'

Murmurs rise from the elders, yet Elsol's voice cuts through confusion and fear. 'The Red Bull will return to our lands,' she declares. 'The rest of you may do as you will.' She turns her back on the emperor, on the promise of safety. The other elders of the Red Bull follow, along with a few from other bands, falling into a ragged line of defiance.

'Your protection is nothing but enslavement by another name,' Atar sneers. 'We sacrificed our city for freedom. We would sooner die.'

The emperor watches the An-Zabati, the Red Bull, and those who have chosen death. With a wave of his hand, he might scour them from the world. Ral knows this and braces for the feverish wake, the crack of thunder, the stink of burning flesh.

'A pointless waste,' he declares, then fixes his gaze on Ral, never acknowledging the obeisance of those who have knelt to him, as though their submission were as natural and common as the rising of the sun. 'They will be devoured by the chaos, and all they hope to preserve with them. Unity is our only strength now. You must see that.'

Ral scoffs at him, even as his power binds her, even as her heart tears itself to pieces. 'What is the point of trying to convince me? You have already won.'

A frown splits the placid calm of his expression. He turns to one of his Fists, issues orders in hurried Sienese, then stands over her. 'Cooperation would be much easier for the both of us,' he says. 'There is a power I would have you wield to save the world. Teaching you to use it will be far easier if you do not fight me at every turn.'

Ral, at last, finds the strength to spit. Only on his booted feet, for she lies bound and tortured, but it is enough to stir a wind of courage, however slight, however incapable of breaking the granite weight of his power.

The emperor scowls at her, then works a magic that twists her gut into knots and hurls them both halfway across the world.

18

A Question of Doctrine

Pinion

'We could leave a scar, if you want,' Running Doe murmured.

Pinion shook his head, sending another twinge beneath the bandages and liniments that wrapped the right side of his face.

Running Doe sagged. 'I understand,' she said, though she did not sound at all pleased with his decision.

He had accepted the old wiry-haired doctor's medicines and bandages as a defence against the threat of infection, but would accept nothing more. Alder – Foolish Cur, he corrected himself – still refused to restore his severed hand. Pinion would bear his own reminder, the physical manifestation of his mistakes and those parts of himself he must leave behind if he were to have any hope for a future.

For two days he had flitted between waking and sleeping. He lingered, now, in that liminal space at the end of healing, ready to rise and take action but uncertain of what action to take. His life's every goal, every driving force, had been stripped away from him. Yet in that raw nakedness he had begun to understand deep, difficult things, captured more in undercurrents of emotion than in any coherent argument. Things that had been veiled by the doctrine that had defined his world. An uneasy feeling that threatened to blossom into anger at the emperor, at his father, at everyone who had played a part in weaving and maintaining that veil. At himself, most of all, for having glimpsed behind it and yet refused to tear it away.

Running Doe left him to attend to her other patients. Another of the infirmary nurses brought him a bowl of thin congee, which he ate gratefully before rising from his bed, wincing at the flicker of pain beneath his bandages. Lying about only exacerbated his sense of aimlessness and reminded him too much of time spent dazed and stupefied on his back in a palanquin, borne away from the horror of Setting Sun Fortress. He had spent enough of his life wallowing in guilt, shame, and regret.

The warmth of the afternoon sun eased some of the tension in his wounds. A few of the Nayeni fighters scattered about the courtyard in groups eyed him warily. His own hackles rose at being surrounded by so many people he would have counted enemies not long ago, but he offered cordial nods and smiles. They were allies now in the struggle to survive the chaos that gripped the world. Still, he sought solitude and mounted the parapet walk, where he needed only to shrug off the occasional sideways glance of the archer keeping watch.

The city of Eastern Fortress sprawled out below him. Here and there people travelled through the streets, moving openly but quickly. The renewed alliance between the two Nayeni factions had restored something like peace to the embattled city. Pinion traced the maze of its streets and alleys, wondering what had become of Captain Huo. He had heard nothing of his fate while Burning Dog had held him prisoner, which gave him some hope that he had managed to escape. Yet the man had been badly injured. How long could he survive in a starving city gripped by war, in districts controlled by those who would count him an enemy?

Pinion found himself hoping the captain had managed to

find shelter somewhere, a place to hole up and heal. Of course, when he did, he would surely become a fresh thorn in the side of the Nayeni cause – which was of course now Pinion's cause, too, strange as that was.

'Good to see you on your feet.'

Clear-River crested the top of the parapet ladder. It was still difficult to believe that he was the same man as the deferential if argumentative magistrate of Burrow, whose challenge may well have been the first crack in Pinion's sense of the empire's righteousness. Now he seemed older, suffused with a dignity and wisdom that belied his plain clothes and dishevelled hair.

'When I am well enough, I would like to be put to use,' Pinion said. 'Whatever use you can find for me. My skills may not be well suited—'

'Are you well enough now?' Clear-River interrupted.

A wind curled over the city, stirring Clear-River's hair. Fallen leaves swirled across the battlements and down to the garrison courtyard. For much of his life, Pinion had let himself be carried and tossed about in much the same way – by his father, by the pressures and expectations of imperial doctrine and hierarchy.

'Yes,' he said firmly, despite the ache from his missing eye. 'What do you need?'

Clear-River leaned against the battlement. 'The Sienese still control a third of the city, including the garrison granaries, meant to feed the city in the case of a siege. They'll know by now that we are no longer at one another's throats. They may even know that Burning Dog is dead. With the rebellion unified, we are enough of a threat to put real pressure on them, but we only have enough food to survive another two weeks, at most, on half rations – or else stop feeding the commoners. But I for one didn't join a rebellion to watch people starve.'

Clear-River straightened, his expression grave. 'I have been negotiating for some time with the Sienese leaders – a few surviving Hands and other influential men. I've arranged to meet with them tomorrow. We have to convince them to lay down arms, unify the city, and give us access to those granaries *now*, before our people get desperate enough to attack and plunge the city back into war.'

'They won't be easily convinced,' Pinion said flatly.

A wry laugh shook Clear-River's shoulders. 'Indeed, they likely won't. Which is why I need you.'

Pinion nearly pointed out that, of the two of them, Clear-River had managed to convince *him* to spare a man's life. Why should Clear-River need any help constructing an argument? But a moment of introspection yielded the answer. He opened his hand and looked down at the silver lines still branded there, a mark of authority he now wore with shame. 'My capitulation will undercut my arguments as thoroughly as your bloodline,' he said.

'It might,' Clear-River agreed. 'Then again, to some of them it might reinforce your conviction.'

Terrified and cornered as the Sienese were, and dependent upon their enemies for protection from a threat they did not understand, Pinion doubted they would perceive his willingness to work with the Nayeni as anything but cowardice. They might even take his wounds for evidence that he had been tortured into compliance. At the very least, his capitulation was a stark violation of propriety, of profound ingratitude for all that the emperor and his empire had provided.

Simple enough, then, to anticipate their arguments. Now, he thought wryly, what might serve to counter them?

They sequestered themselves for the rest of the day in a suite of rooms that had once served as Pinion's father's study, rooms he had never before been permitted to enter. A few decorations had been left in place – landscape paintings, a jade bust of one of his father's favourite sages – but the dust on the tables and shelves and marks on the floor spoke of a great deal of rearranging in the few weeks since the battle. The library of Sienese classics and commentary remained, however. These Pinion and Clear-River attacked, spurred on by a dozen pots of dark tea, sifting through volumes in search of any angle of argument that might convince the Sienese leaders to perceive cooperation not as weakness or betrayal of their values but as proper fulfilment of their role within the foundational relationships of Sienese society and moral thinking.

Gradually, they compiled an arsenal of quotations and references – arrows in their argumentative quiver. Enough, Pinion mused, to convince any examination proctor of their case. Yet he feared it would be far too little to break down the barriers of fear, mistrust, and confusion in the aftermath of the battle, in the wake of the chaos that gripped the world. While they ate a scanty meal of stewed greens and millet gruel, he turned his mind to other arguments less anchored to reason than to the vagaries and currents of the heart.

Once, what felt a lifetime ago though in fact was only a matter of months, he had convinced the emperor to change the course of his war in Nayen with a half-considered plan, built upon his own fears and dredged from the subconscious layers of his mind. Now, he would go armed and well prepared, every nuance of his case considered, mulled over, and honed to a precise point. The first argument had drowned Nayen in bloodshed. He could only hope the second would return naked blades to their sheaths.

Only when they doused their lantern for the night and collapsed to their blankets amid the piles of books and the notes they had taken did Pinion realise that not once, all the while he mulled over the problem, had he wondered how Oriole might have approached it, or what he might have done. The realisation saddened him, strangely, though it ought not have. He wanted to believe – as he was sure Foolish Cur wanted to believe – that Oriole would have perceived the cruelty of the empire long ago, that he would have prevented the horror at Setting Sun Fortress at the very least. But however Pinion wished to imagine him, Oriole had imagined himself a hero out of the ancient romances. Would Su White-Knife, master of devious traps and cunning stratagems that cut the heart out of enemy armies, have seen Setting Sun Fortress as a horror, or only as a clever manoeuvre, however distasteful?

Pinion's father had served the empire loyally to the end, never questioning, never reckoning with the hypocrisy and horror at its heart. Would Oriole have been any different? Would the child who stood at their father's knee, offended by an injustice meted out to his servant playmate, have let his heart break for the people of Nayen? Or would he have hardened himself, casting aside childish frustration to embrace the cold, brutal logic of empire?

Pinion dreamed that night of Yul Pekora, of the riding field in his father's garden, as it had been, where Nayeni now practised their archery. Of Oriole on the back of his favourite stallion, its grey hair glistening in the sun as he rode, revelling in the pulse of muscles beneath him, in the rush of wind. Who could say what the dead might have done in our place, what horror or heroism they might have worked upon the world, had their lives matched ours in length?

Pinion woke and resolved to put these questions behind him for ever. He would remember Oriole, but as he had been, in all his boyish enthusiasm, untroubled yet by the vagaries that had haunted Pinion's adulthood. It was a nostalgic image but an honest one, he decided as he rose, dressed himself in scholar's robes, and followed Clear-River and their honour guard out into the city.

*

Soldiers in scarred armour stood behind piled stone reinforced with broken furniture, their heavy crossbows braced. Rows of spears protruded like the spines of a porcupine from the ranks behind them. Clear-River approached the barricade alone, holding aloft a flag bearing the logogram for peace. The captain of the barricade met him, his hand never leaving the hilt of his sword, eyeing the honour guard at Clear-River's back.

Despite all the horror and stress of the last year, anxiety still bubbled in Pinion's chest. Would any of these soldiers recognise him as a Hand of the emperor? Or worse, as the governor's son? He told himself again that he had betrayed nothing by allying with Clear-River – at least, nothing that had not already betrayed his trust and his sense of justice. Not that these common soldiers would sympathise. The thought of explaining himself to Captain Huo, for whom obeisance to the hierarchy of empire had been everything, was enough to transform the tension within him into a dark bemusement.

Still, he found himself wishing they had brought canons of witchcraft with them, the carved strips of bone that somehow granted the power to wield magic despite the seal over the city. The hilt of Burning Dog's sword remained unclaimed. They had left it, and Clear-River's canon, in the safekeeping of the strange witch Torn Leaf and the healer Running Doe. If the Sienese did indeed plan treachery, the Nayeni could ill afford the canons falling into enemy hands.

The Sienese captain shouted the order to let them through. Soldiers dragged away an overturned bookshelf and Clear-River waved for Pinion and the honour guard to follow.

Pinion steeled himself, rehearsing the layered arguments he had prepared as he followed Clear-River into what would once have been his sanctuary within this embattled city, and which now felt like the den of some hungry, agitated beast.

The captain led them to an empty house just beyond the barricade. Two of their honour guard followed inside while the rest arranged themselves near the doorway, as though the ten of them would be able to storm their way into the house in the event of any treachery and escape to the Nayeni partition of the city.

'It's all right,' Clear-River whispered. 'We've held negotiations here before.'

'Yes, *you* have,' Pinion replied, trying to keep from fidgeting. 'They don't have much reason to hate *you*.'

'A turncoat magistrate may not represent such a severe insult to propriety as a severed Hand,' Clear-River said, bristling. 'But it *is* an insult.'

The barricade captain left them in the main room of the house, which had been arranged to suit their purposes. The walls were bare, with pale stains showing where some decorations had once hung – landscape paintings, to mark it a Sienese house, or some Nayeni tapestries? The long table and the six chairs, arranged in two sets of three, facing each other, showed no adornment, and their simple style might have fit a common merchant's household as well as a minor official's. Every fleck of character had been scrubbed away. Only the room's location behind the Sienese barricade ruined the illusion of truly neutral ground.

'Take a breath, Pinion,' Clear-River said as he rearranged the chairs, moving one from their side into the corner of the room, then spreading the other two out and moving them a pace back from the table. Satisfied, he positioned himself behind the right-side chair – the place of an advisor – and gestured for Pinion to take the other, deferring to him as though their imperial ranks still mattered. 'I already have a rapport with them. Let me guide the conversation into the argument you intend to make. No need to worry. The worst that can happen is they kill us and spare us a slow, lingering death while the world falls to pieces.'

The stable arch of the chair's back beneath his palms helped to settle Pinion. He managed to smile at Clear-River's quip, and was about to rejoin with his own when the door opened to admit the Sienese delegation.

The first delegate was a man he did not recognise, a minor official or a wealthy merchant, by his dress, with the haughty eyes and upturned chin of a man recently come to power and savouring the novelty. The second was Hand Jadestone, who had long served as the magistrate of this quarter and had been a frequent guest in Voice Golden-Finch's home. At the sight of his face, familiar even after hardship had stripped it of fat and its knowing smile, Pinion felt a twinge of fear. But it was the third delegate who filled his mouth with ash.

Captain Huo seemed an entirely different man from the filthy, beaten, bedraggled prisoner who had escaped, wounded, from Burning Dog's warriors. He walked with a limp and one arm in a sling, but he wore armour of black enamel and silver filigree. A silk headband bearing a repeating pattern of the emperor's never-changing name in golden thread wrapped his forehead above a face mottled with still-healing bruises. At the sight of Pinion, his eyes lit first with surprise, then with burning fury, and his good hand fell to the hilt of his sword.

'Traitor,' he growled.

Pinion stumbled backwards, toppling his chair and falling against the wall. Huo rounded the table, his sword bright in the lamplight.

'Sheathe your blade, Marshal!' Hand Jadestone snapped.

Every line of Huo's body tensed. Slowly, the blade rasped back into its sheath and he bowed to Hand Jadestone. 'I apologise for my outburst, Your Excellency, but that this severed Hand now sits across from us as a representative of the rebellion reveals the treason I have long suspected. Allow me to execute him as doctrine and propriety demand.'

'You will do no such thing. Comport yourself as your rank demands or have it stripped from you, and with it your right to attend this meeting.'

Huo – now the marshal of Eastern Fortress, by some twist of military succession – ground his teeth but fell into another deep bow. 'Of course, Your Excellency. I apologise—'

'Sit down or leave, Marshal.' Hand Jadestone dipped his head to Clear-River. 'You must forgive the marshal, Master Lu. He has suffered recently at Nayeni hands, as I am sure you know.'

'As did I, for a time,' Clear-River cut back. 'As did Hand Pinion, more brutally than either me or your marshal.'

Pinion regained his feet, a fresh throb in his missing eye and the embarrassment of having fallen only a whisper beneath the roaring need to escape the room and Huo's hateful, cutting glare.

'Yes, I can see that,' Hand Jadestone said, 'which makes me wonder how he has come to sit *beside* you, Master Lu. Are your torturers so skilled that a few days in their care can make a son forget the murder of his brother and father, to say nothing of his duty to the empire?'

'I am here of my own will,' Pinion said firmly. 'Burning Dog tortured me, not Clear-River, nor Hissing Cat, nor anyone in their camp. Now she is dead. And I mourn my brother and my father, but I would honour them by preventing old grudges and misapplications of doctrine from drowning this already wounded city in blood.'

'Enough preamble, then,' the Sienese delegate Pinion did not yet know cut in. 'Let us hear what the barbarian and the traitor have to say, Your Excellency, Marshal.'

Clear-River gestured to the chairs. Hand Jadestone fixed Pinion with a long, appraising stare, then took his seat. 'I agree,

Master Fan,' Hand Jadestone said as the others settled into their places. 'It would be impolite not to hear them out before sending them back to their witch queen. What do you propose, Master Lu? You want to bargain for our grain again, I presume?'

Clear-River leaned back in his chair as though lounging. 'As Hand Pinion said, Burning Dog is dead. Her faction has accepted Hissing Cat as their leader. The Nayeni in Eastern Fortress are united. In days, they will be ready to storm your barricades.'

'You may outnumber us,' Huo snarled, 'but you will bleed a river for every city block you take. We have stolen your barbarian bone magic. We have soldiers while you have only farmers with hunting bows and mangled ploughs.'

'And sickles, and boar spears, and ancestral swords,' Clear-River counted off on three fingers, then let his hand fall and shrugged. 'But I would prefer it not come to that, and I would like to believe you feel the same. Enough people have died in this city, and the world outside its walls would devour us if we tried to leave. While we might all find the fact distasteful, we are indeed trapped here together, forced into a relationship. I propose only that it need not be an antagonistic one. "When all things align to their proper place, there is harmony," as the famous quote describes. It falls to us only to determine what those proper places are.'

'It does not *fall to us*.' Huo leaned across the table. 'The emperor stands above all and ordains our places. It falls to *you* to accept, not to demand.'

Clear-River looked to the far corners of the room, as though searching for something. 'Where is the emperor, then, to help us resolve this dispute? He was in Eastern Fortress not long ago. I saw him myself. Gone elsewhere, I suppose, to solve grander problems than ours. And he left us without a Voice to transmit his guidance.' Clear-River clicked his tongue and shook his head. 'Alas, we are on our own, Marshal.'

'We would not be, if not for your rebellion,' said Master Fan. 'Your witches very cleverly killed our Voices – including this one's father.' He gestured to Pinion with a sad smile.

'Even if a Voice survived, this city is cut off from the wider world and from your canon of sorcery,' Clear-River said. 'Not to disadvantage you but to preserve us all from destruction. Something only Hissing Cat and Foolish Cur – only we Nayeni – can achieve.'

'A boon you grant as much to hold the threat of its loss over our heads as from the goodness of your hearts, I'm sure,' Hand Jadestone said.

Clear-River shifted his relaxed, commanding affect into one of exasperation. 'From the beginning, my goal has been to save as many lives as possible. The Nayeni share that goal but are rightly unwilling to submit to imperial rule – which has been *far* from beneficent – to achieve it. It falls to you, then, to accept or to force our hand.'

'But you do not speak for all of them.' Now Master Fan leaned back, his arms crossed, drumming his fingers on his sleeve. 'Yes, Burning Dog's faction may have aligned with Hissing Cat's – by the sages, such distasteful names – yet it is not factions that concern us. There may well be those lofty souls among you who will take no vengeance for Setting Sun Fortress, or for perceived slights suffered under these decades of imperial rule, but I suspect there will be just as many unable to forgive, unable to forget. I am only a merchant, Master Lu, but a very successful one, and that success has come as much from caution as from clever boldness.'

'To put a sharper edge on Master Fan's point,' Hand Jadestone said, 'can you guarantee that the moment we lay down arms and agree to cooperate, we will not be cut down in the street by a vengeful mob?'

They've let me live, and I was as responsible for Setting Sun Fortress as anyone. Pinion swallowed the words. Best not to draw too much attention to his treatment at Nayeni hands.

'I can no more guarantee that than you could promise me every minister in the empire truly abides by imperial doctrine,' Clear-River said. 'Particularly those aphorisms about gently guiding and nurturing the common people, or that rebellion and war follow as the natural consequence of cruelty.'

'Then how can we negotiate?' Hand Jadestone countered. 'Even if we agree in good faith to an armistice, you cannot promise to control your people, and I cannot guarantee that whatever promises I make will not be overridden by my superiors.'

'If, that is, you ever make contact with them again,' Pinion pointed out. 'I was aboard the emperor's own ship when the gods descended. A whole fleet, each ship with a Hand or a Voice aboard, destroyed in moments. The world is not what it was, Hand Jadestone.'

Silence held for a moment, until Huo hammered the table with his fist. 'It will be again. The emperor's name is never changing. We may suffer and die, but order will be restored.'

'Yes, well. Until then, it behoves us to find a way to live together.' Clear-River leaned forwards. 'If you do not open your granaries to the Nayeni, it is only a matter of time before hunger drives them to storm your barricades. If you *do* open them, you will earn some good will with the people here, and they may begin to forgive, or at least to forgo vengeance. More, it is your *duty* to ensure these people do not starve. They are your younger siblings in the great family of the empire, are they not? Perhaps not those who rejected imperial rule by taking up arms, but that is a fraction of the population of this city.'

'We are all in this predicament *because* of the Nayeni rebels.'

Master Fan jabbed a finger at Clear-River. 'You speak as though their starving is *our* fault, but it is *yours.*'

Hand Jadestone nodded in agreement. 'Whatever warning aphorisms you invoke, whatever guidance a magistrate ought or ought not follow, rebellion cannot be forgiven. It is the most fundamental offence against propriety, against all that we owe the emperor, whose will alone defines right and wrong, and whose will, in this, seems clear. If not for the ... occurrence ... which young Pinion has invoked, the people of this city would have suffered far worse than hunger when the storm of the emperor's wrath fell upon this island, as once it fell upon Sor Cala for an offence of *fractional* severity.'

'In my last conversation with my father, he invoked that same idea,' Pinion murmured.

Clear-River shot him a sideways glance. This line of argument fell outside the scope of their plans, which called for a gradual undermining of the rebellion's culpability via repeated use of aphorisms concerning the responsibilities of the empire's leaders to their subjects, coupled with evidence of the degradation and suffering of the Nayeni under Sienese rule culminating in the massacre at Setting Sun Fortress. Yet Hand Jadestone's words had stirred something in Pinion, breathing life into an ember of outrage that burned bright now, searing away his fear of Huo's hatred, stoked by the echo of his father's voice insisting upon the sanctity of a bit of *calligraphy* when only days before thousands of innocents had died at the hands of his subordinates.

'What idea?' Master Fan looked from Hand Jadestone to Pinion and back. 'Which, that is to say, of the dozen or so ideas to which the esteemed Hand has just given voice?'

'The notion that right and wrong are but emanations from the emperor's will, like the canon of sorcery,' Pinion said, too heated to give a second thought to Clear-River's warning glare. 'It is a notion I have heard countless times, often to justify the most terrible of the empire's actions. Which is odd, considering there is no aphorism or quotation from the sages to support it.'

'Of course there is!' Hand Jadestone blurted.

Pinion shook his head firmly. 'There is not. It may be a point of doctrine, repeated often and so assumed to exist within the classics, but Master Clear-River and I spent the last day sifting through every one of the classics, even through many of the early commentaries. There is no such quotation. No aphorism. Wherever this idea came from, it was not from Traveller-on-the-Narrow-Way or any of the other sages. In fact, I suspect that if an examination candidate invoked this notion in an essay, a proctor would only be doing his due diligence by issuing a failing score.'

Now it was his turn to lean forwards, folding his hands and planting them on the table in front of him, his gaze locked on Hand Jadestone's narrowing, furious eyes. 'According to the Sienese canon, the emperor did not define good and evil. Quite the opposite, in fact. He is as bound by the requirements of propriety and morality as anyone. And I maintain that here in Nayen, if not all throughout the empire, *he* violated those requirements long ago. Certainly long before the fall of Eastern Fortress.'

'The emperor is father to us all!' Hand Jadestone snapped. 'Traveller-on-the-Narrow-Way himself wrote, "As both the elder brother and the younger owe obedience to their father, so the myriad subjects of the empire, magistrate and commoner alike, owe the emperor their loyalty." There is your aphorism!'

'The Classic of Streams and Valleys.' Pinion nodded. 'Where not a page later the sage writes, "As a father's duty is to guide, protect, and provide for his children, so is the emperor's duty to all he rules." How, I ask you, does massacring a city provide its people with guidance? With protection?'

'An end to rebellion,' Master Fan said flatly. 'Stability for the province and the good, law-abiding citizenry.'

Pinion smiled warmly, as though addressing a child, though his heart still pounded in fear. 'A rebellion that doctrine would hold – as we have already established – resulted from the empire's failure to fulfil its duties in Nayen. If it is, indeed, the purpose of the empire to bring stability and civilisation, does it not seem odd that it provokes such violence and instability wherever it conquers? In Toa Alón, An-Zabat, here in Nayen—'

'Resistance by ungrateful barbarians,' Huo sneered. 'Too small-minded to recognise the gifts of the empire.'

Huo's was a common attitude among the soldiery, Pinion had come to understand during his brief tenure leading an imperial legion. Not always an honest one, though. It was often an idea held in self-defence, reducing the colonised to something less than human: barbarians, animals that could be brutalised without remorse. Huo's reddening face and burning eyes seemed to speak to his conviction, yet they might just as well have revealed a deep guilt left to fester in some dark, isolated corner of his heart.

Pinion knew all too well how rage and hatred could serve to mask such guilt.

Clear-River planted his palms on the table, seizing control once more of the conversation. 'Again, a notion not found in doctrine. They are subjects of the empire. Their discontent reflects the failure of the empire to meet its duties. As Master Pinion has so eloquently pointed out, imperial doctrine is on *our* side, not yours. It is not only practical for you to do as we advise and avoid drowning this city in blood, but by any measure, save fanatical loyalty to what you *assume* to be the emperor's will, it is also *correct*.'

Hand Jadestone shifted in his seat. His eyes darted away from Clear-River's gaze. A wash of relief swept through Pinion. The argument had found a gap in Hand Jadestone's defences. Of course, celebration was premature; he knew all too well how easy it was to give in to the temptation of doing what came easily rather than what felt right.

'Is there *nothing* you Nayeni will not stoop to?' Huo snarled. 'Even twisting the words of our own sages against us, confounding good sense with all this *talk*.' He turned to Hand Jadestone and bowed deeply, nearly touching his forehead to the table. 'I know this severed Hand well, Your Excellency. These men are duplicitous. Weak minded. These words are only smoke to obscure the certain truth. If you embrace them, they will plant a dagger in your back.'

'Marshal.' Pinion kept his voice low but honed its edge. 'Why were you summoned to the *Ocean Throne*?'

Huo slowly unfolded from his bow. 'To receive the commendation of the emperor. The highest of honours, one I could never have dreamed of—'

'For your role in the retreat from Greyfrost, yes?' Pinion cut him off, fighting the urge to rub his wounded, throbbing, itching eye. 'A retreat you resisted and questioned at nearly every step.'

A quiver of outrage tugged at Huo's lip. He opened his mouth to speak but Pinion pressed on, bowling over him, not in the least ashamed to trample the proprieties of conversation. If these men would not hear reason, calmly and respectfully voiced, let them hear his rage.

'Do you know why *I* was summoned? Like you, it was to receive a commendation, but with it an invitation to serve as the emperor's advisor. The retreat from Greyfrost, the massacre at Setting Sun Fortress – these horrors, these acts of such *praiseworthy tactical brilliance* ...' He sneered and tapped the side of his head. 'They were *mine*, Huo. If not for my planning, the emperor would have bade us stay in Burrow, to slow the rebellion there, perhaps to be torn apart by Foolish Cur. Of the two of us, I, not you, have served the emperor to the very hilt.

I, not you, earned his trust and respect as no other Hand has in generations. Even then, I doubted the good of what we did. I saw, again and again, skulls shattered and the bodies of *children* torn apart. Yet still he offered me the world. A commendation for you, perhaps a place in his Fist … but I was to be Traveller-on-the-Narrow-Way come again. And do you know what my role was to be, in the emperor's words? *To see what he could not. To protect the empire from his own blindness.*'

Pinion hammered his fist on the table. '*That* is what I am doing here. Protecting the empire – the world – from the blindness of fools like you.'

Huo's good hand flexed into a trembling, vicious claw. Hand Jadestone touched his arm in a gesture of restraint as he stood slowly, his expression incredulous. 'You can hardly expect me to continue these negotiations, Master Clear-River. It seems young Pinion's mind has given way to the stresses of his last days of imperial service and the treatment he suffered at Nayeni hands. I am willing to reopen our discussion, perhaps tomorrow, but only if *you* will participate in good faith, in the genuine interest of restoring peace to the city, not to press such *ludicrous* interpretations of imperial doctrine.'

Huo nearly knocked over his chair in his haste to follow Hand Jadestone from the room. Master Fan was more deliberate, pausing at the doorway.

'We will none of us survive if we spend our effort in fighting,' the merchant said quietly, lingering on the far side of the open door. 'Yet it is difficult to forget the loss of blood and prestige, is it not?' He shut the door without waiting for an answer.

Pinion leaned on the table, his forehead cupped gingerly in his hands, gritting his teeth against the mounting throb of pain behind his missing eye. 'I'm sorry,' he murmured. 'That wasn't the plan. I let myself get heated. I should have kept my mouth shut and let you make our case.'

'No.' Clear-River squeezed Pinion's shoulder and smiled. 'Hand Jadestone would sooner throw himself on his sword than compromise, I think. The man is deluded. He seems to believe the emperor will return to Nayen at the head of another fleet any day now. Marshal Huo ... well, I don't know him well, but I don't think there is *any* argument that might budge him. But of the three, Fan is the one we needed to reach.'

'He is a merchant,' Pinion scoffed. 'Whatever power in the empire the merchant class has, it is given begrudgingly. Jadestone and Huo will never be swayed by him.'

Clear-River tapped the side of his nose. 'I was a magistrate, Pinion. I know things a Hand does not – like, for instance, the way currents of power flow through towns and cities rather than through audience halls. Fan is not a man without compassion, and unlike a soldier or a bureaucrat a merchant is rarely willing to die to protect imperial prestige. More, the other merchants, who actually *own* most of the grain at stake, will listen to him. They chose him as their representative, after all. But that is enough talk for now.' He stood and motioned for Pinion to lead the way from the room.

Relief washed through their honour guard at their re-emergence from the house. Clear-River apologised for the delay and fell into step. All the way back to the governor's estate, Pinion nursed confusion, disappointment, and a slow-burning coal of outrage. How could men close their minds so thoroughly to the truth? To the very texts that formed the foundation of all they served and all they claimed to believe?

Showing them their errors would never be enough, though the fact rankled. There were deeper reasons, less coherent than doctrine, that motivated men like Huo and Jadestone – that dwelt within, he suspected, nearly all who held power in the empire. Fear and ambition. Willing blindness to the horror of their own deeds.

How much of the world's pain could be laid at the feet of such half-considered impulses? How many lives, throughout history, had been shattered to salve the bruises on the souls of small, powerful men?

19

Labyrinth

Ral Ans Urrera

The wake of the emperor's magic wrenches every joint in Ral's body, threatening to rip her apart. One moment she lies bound upon the steppe in the shadow of the stone serpent, watching the An-Zabati and the Red Bull reject the offer of imperial protection while the rest of her people are herded southwards like cattle. The next she is sprawled in a vast, windowless chamber beneath a vaulted ceiling of interlocking brackets and heaves vomit onto the tiled floor. The emperor issues terse commands in Sienese and a pair of soldiers with his brand upon their fists seize her by the armpits and drag her from the room.

At the doorway, they pass through a shimmering haze, like the heat mirage that clings to the horizon in summer on the steppe. A fiery pain lances through her, and with it another wave of nausea and disorientation that nearly strips her of consciousness.

When she regains her senses, she realises that the searing aurora, the terrible spell that bound her magic, is gone, yet the phantom limb of her power can only grope impotently for the wind and lightning.

The guards drag her down a staircase, through shadow-thick catacombs, and hurl her into a cell. The door slams shut and a lock clicks. Two weeks pass – she knows this, assuming they feed her once a day, for she carves a line into the brick wall each time the shutter in the door slides open to admit a loaf of dry bread and a cup of thin, tasteless porridge and to retrieve her chamber pot.

Two weeks spent first paralysed, a heap of inanimate flesh on the floor of her cell, empty of everything, even self-hatred and sadness. Her stillness is broken first by racking sobs that seat a deep ache in her ribs and skull and strip her throat raw. No anger rises in her, only a deadening of feeling to match her deadened sense of the world, all magic locked away by whatever strange spell grips the catacombs. Two weeks of silence, for to admit a sound, to admit a thought, would carry her back to the moment of her god's death, to the moment of her failure and her world's ending.

The passage of time commands her attention – punctuated by the mechanical repetition of eating, sleeping, eliminating waste. It is the longest stretch of time she has spent without seeing the sky.

The squeal of hinges – so much louder than the sounds of the sliding shutter, the bread and the cup shoved across the floor, the footsteps approaching, passing, and fading into nothingness – draws her up, for a moment, from the depths.

The emperor stands over her, dressed in a robe of red silk and silver thread. Something within her stirs to life. If she lunges and closes her hands around his throat, will she be able to squeeze the life from him before his guards cut her away or he burns her to ash?

Only a gust stirring dry, brittle leaves.

'It would be better if I could convince you.' There is weariness in his voice, in the bags beneath his ancient eyes. He seems to consider for a moment, then squats beside her. It is an astonishing posture, unsettling in its humanity. 'You know the chaos that grips this world will destroy it. Even if the balance can be restored to what it was, a hundred years from now, or a thousand, another like you will arise and shatter it again. As long as the gods are allowed to live, the world will weave its way closer and closer to its final end. The end of humanity. The end of meaning. You and I, however, have a chance to destroy that cycle, to remove the thread of divine caprice, cruelty, and manipulation from the pattern.'

He shakes his head slowly and searches her eyes. 'What is the worth of one life against the fate of the world? The worth of a thousand? A million? A leader must make choices. Sacrifices. The true, moral good must allow for tremendous suffering for the few, if it means the survival and comfort of the greater whole. That is something Traveller never understood. But you have begun to understand it, have you not, riding at the head of your people?'

He waits, as though expecting an answer. Ral can conjure none. Her mind is stripped bare by this unexpected conversation. She has never imagined the emperor a man who would bother to explain himself.

When she says nothing, he sighs. 'My plans have fallen to ruin. I gave other minds too much credit, assumed that the logic of what I did would be obvious to anyone able to discern it. And so chaos grips the world, a chaos that must be comprehensively eradicated. Fortunately, there is another way.' He leans towards her. She can see the flecks of amber in his dark irises. She might have crushed his throat in her hands, but he transfixes her, like a serpent making ready to swallow its prey. 'There is a weapon, Ral Ans Urrera. One that could be bent to my purpose – our purpose. The annihilation of the gods. Yet, loath as I am to admit this, not even I can wield it alone. The effort to simultaneously reshape its power to our ends and put it to use would destroy anyone, even me.

'But *you* . . .' He chuckles softly. 'You show promise. A depth of unusual skill in manipulating magic and unusual resilience in the face of enormous pain, enough to break conventional binding sorcery through sheer force of will. Something no one, not even a witch of the old sort, ought to be able to do. It is a talent in need of honing, true, but given time and training you could reforge the weapon even as I wield it, and together we could save the world. Do you understand?'

At last, she finds the strength to lunge, her hands curling like claws. A burst of air hammers her against the wall before her arms have left her sides. He stands, looming over her. The cracks in the facade of his authority have sealed. He stares down with all the cruelty of the empire.

'Of course you would not listen,' he snarls. 'Not even to save your own people. A weakness in barbarian character, one I was too slow to scrub out. Very well. Know that I do this only to save every life in the world.'

For a single heartbeat, magic returns, like light breaking through a stormcloud, warming the dead, frigid earth. A sharp breath fills Ral's lungs, and then a weight as heavy as the moon falls on her shoulders. A wake of sorcery burns into her mind, as bright as the aurora, encircling her, carving paths into which the weight falls and accretes, becoming walls as unyielding as iron.

The emperor heaves another sigh. Ral feels a twinge of worry. At first her concern feels unnatural, like ill-fitting clothes forced upon her, but she sees in him the echo of her father, returned to the camp after a long, unsuccessful hunt, all exhaustion and disappointment. A part of her, buried somewhere deep in the labyrinth he has made of her mind, screams hatred, would hold tight to the sight of her father's severed, rotting head atop a pile of corpses. But the sound rebounds from the walls his sorcery has made, loses itself, fades.

'It may be unsettling at first,' the emperor says, 'but you will become accustomed in time, and then we will talk again.'

He leaves her there, in the silence, with her worry for him and her desire to lend whatever help she can, and beneath it all, buried in the labyrinth, a fragment that can only howl.

She ceases to count the days.

Her meals come more frequently and feature richer fare: a weakened wine instead of water; rice flavoured with quails' eggs, vegetables, and meat instead of porridge. Hunger no longer gnaws at her, nor does the infinite emptiness that gripped her. Over time, she grows content, save for the occasional, piercing fear rising from her depths – at waking, or in the moment sleep takes her – that her thoughts are not her own, that her mind has been made a maze, as much a prison as her cell.

The emperor comes to visit her, still haggard, still demanding her pity and her admiration. He fights to save the world, she understands without being told. His struggle is holy and just. An unquestionable good. Any tragedy in its wake – a family massacred, a father butchered, a god destroyed – is but the cost to be paid for a better world.

He refines her command of magic, explaining to her intricacies and secrets that she grasps immediately. During these visits, the oppressive silence that radiates from the walls is lessened. She is allowed to feel the world truly again and given free rein to reach out, to wield her power, guided by his gentle hand. Her mind is fertile, tilled soil, ready to receive these seeds of wisdom and power, needing only his words and presence to put down roots.

Soon – it feels soon, although everything but his lessons and her gratitude slips through her like water through a sieve – a Fist releases her from her cell and escorts her out of the catacombs to an upper level of the structure – a palace, as it turns out, windowless but richly decorated. Wonders like she has never before seen hang from the walls: tapestries of gold and silver, suspended chains of glass set with gems of every imaginable colour, landscape paintings that capture every corner of the world. Upon them all, on hanging scrolls or inscribed on the paintings themselves, elegant calligraphy. Comprehension of the emperor's language is among his many gifts. As much as the meaning of the words, she is moved by the sweep of the lines, the emotion captured by the movement of a brush. At times, even a hint of some abstracted depiction – a horse, a diving fish, a pavilion, a lion serpent, a soaring hawk – stirs her heart like nothing else she has seen.

For a moment, she remembers seeing such things – simpler, less grand in scope – decorating the Skyfather's Hall and remembers thinking them garish, a defilement of her people's sacred city. It is a moment that stirs the howling in her heart, only for the walls that shape her mind to shift and tighten and leave her, again, basking in the glory and artistry around her, admiring the emperor's curation and refinement, and above all the grace and beauty captured in his written words.

Her new rooms are austere but comfortable. She has a bed now and a rug upon the floor instead of scattered rushes. A single candle. A ewer kept filled with water, and with it a pair of clay cups – no more need to worry that thirst will rise before her appointed meal. The Fist still locks the door behind him as he leaves her, but she knows now that she is not a prisoner but a precious treasure that, after proper training – after the emperor has taught her all he means to teach – will become a weapon to save the world.

It is what she wanted. What she dreamed of, leading her people in their mad death march across the steppe and into the Sienese heartland. Then, she understood so little. She had recognised the horror of the world but had misplaced blame and anger, attributing guilt not to those responsible but to the painful means by which a better world might truly be made, like a child who hates a dose of bitter medicine more than the illness it is meant to cure.

She sits on the rug and recalls her most recent lesson. Her magic is bound, but she does not mind. It is enough to repeat the exercises, to prepare herself for the emperor's next visit. She will delight him with her diligence and her progress, she decides, and smiles to herself.

She wishes only that the landscape paintings on her walls were windows, that she might catch a glimpse of the sky.

20

A City Beneath the City

Koro Ha

'Orna Sin is alive,' Yin Ila said, leaning in the doorway of Koro Ha's small apartment, one of dozens of rooms excavated in the two weeks since they had opened the tunnels beneath Orna Sin's garden, inviting the desperate and unsheltered to take refuge in the ruins of the ancient city. The ringing of picks and hammers filled the tunnels as out-of-work stone-cutters unearthed more living space and, in the process, searched for anything that might point Koro Ha towards the deep lore Uon Elia had charged him to uncover.

For two weeks Koro Ha had painstakingly sifted through the journal found among Uon Elia's belongings, making extensive use of a dictionary Goa Eln had secured from Orna Sin's abandoned library. Yet he still had only a scattered handful of comprehensible pages, most little more than accounts of the stonespeakers' daily lives: charts detailing the progress of their sunless gardens; accounts of the illnesses and ageing that took them, one by one.

Now, he looked up from the journal and his pages of notes. 'I'm sorry?' he said, certain that he had misheard Yin Ila.

'One of our people brought word,' she went on. 'A rumour,

really, but more than we've had to go on. It puts Orna Sin in a dungeon under the governor's estate. Alive.'

Koro Ha's spectacles rattled between his trembling fingers as he set them on the table. *Orna Sin. Alive. Languishing in an imperial dungeon.* 'Is this rumour enough to act on?'

'On its own? No,' Yin Ila said. 'If true, it only confirms what I had assumed, but the lad who brought it also carries word for the Obsidian Blade, the black sashes. They're the closest thing to a power centre in the Runoff, these days. My informant tells me they've planned a raid on the imperial food stores behind the Voice's Wall, to take back some of the grain the Sienese stole with their gate tax. Tonight.'

She crossed to the table, planted her hands on the rough wood, and leaned towards him. 'It's a chance, Koro Ha. We can get a team into the estate dungeons and out again while the Obsidian Blade hold Sienese attention. You promised me on the deck of the *Swiftness* that you would do anything in your power to help save him. Well, the time's come to deliver.'

Koro Ha scrubbed a hand through the unruly curls of his hair. His mind conjured images of Yin Ila, Tuo Pon, and the other sailors from the *Swiftness* scrambling over walls, cutting throats, hunting through mould-eaten dungeons for Orna Sin's cell. 'What can I do?' he asked. 'I am no fighting man.'

'You stonespeakers have a knack for finding things, right? If he is in that dungeon, your magic will lead us right to him. More, he's likely been tortured near to death. He might need healing.'

'And my use of magic in the heart of Sienese territory will be a beacon to every Voice and Hand still in the city,' Koro Ha pointed out. 'If I were to dowse for his location or heal him, we would become the distraction for your friends in the Obsidian Blade rather than the other way around.' Besides, he had no true skill in healing, nor anything that might serve to focus his dowsing sorcery on Orna Sin. And an unspoken worry hung over him, despite his knowing how foolish the thought was, that his use of magic at the city gates had drawn the terrible monsters from the forest.

'If I could be of use to you, I would,' Koro Ha went on, as though he might argue away the guilt stirred up by Yin Ila's long, considered stare. 'But I would be only a hindrance. My time is better spent here, with this journal, seeking whatever it is Uon Elia meant for us to find.'

Yin Ila rapped her knuckles on the table. 'After everything Orna Sin did for you? For Toa Alon?' Yin Ila She jabbed a finger at the glass sphere on the table. 'You wouldn't have ever *met* Uon Elia if not for him. This place would still lie buried. The stonespeakers would have died off. Surely he deserves your taking some measure of risk?'

Koro Ha tried to picture himself sneaking through the governor's estate, a knife in his hand, following at Yin Ila's heels, cutting their way into the dungeons. He shuddered.

'I'm sorry,' he said. 'I can only wish you luck.'

Yin Ila nodded slowly. Without another word she left him there, alone with what few clues Uon Elia had left behind.

The rest of the day passed slowly. Koro Ha was well skilled in the art of focused reading, well practised in spending days alone in a candlelit room with no company but a book. Such a situation usually offered him comfort, yet that day his mind wandered like a hound without its leash, drifting away from the journal, the dictionary, and the intractable problem of translation, conjuring again and again images of Yin Ila and her fighters, of flashing knives, of Orna Sin's bloodied, emaciated face.

Agitated, he rose from his desk. Stretching his legs had always helped his mind to refocus, and as the last stonespeaker – inheritor of magic, yes, but also an elevated role in Toa Aloni society that fit him about as well as a suit of armour – he felt a responsibility to keep an eye on how the refugees were adjusting to their new home in the buried city.

To a continuous drumbeat of pickaxes and shovels, he wandered the ever-growing network of tunnels. The stone-cutters worked diligently at all hours, but even at their frantic pace, slowed only by consideration for safety and cave-ins, they struggled to keep ahead of the swelling population. New arrivals to the buried city were housed in the two temples, beneath the gaze of the stone-faced gods, trading privacy for the uncertain promise of safety.

As he passed one of the freshly excavated homes, Koro Ha glimpsed through a window a family huddled around a sickly child. Many of those who had sought shelter in the buried city had brought illness with them, a low fever that had as yet claimed no lives but proved resistant to conventional treatments and herbal medicines. The sight of the child redoubled Koro Ha's nagging guilt. With a touch of his hand and a simple spell, he might have healed any of the sick among them – assuming, of course, he wielded the spell correctly with his limited skill and experience.

More troubling, food stores were running low, not only in the buried city but in all of Sor Cala. Plans to convert Orna Sin's pleasure garden into a farm had been made but not yet acted upon, and in any case would not produce for the better part of a year – unless, of course, Koro Ha sped up the process with the magic of cultivation. The thought transported him back to the city gate, to the memory of howling, inhuman voices and monstrous jaws.

As yet, no one had suggested that he use magic to solve either of these problems, and so he kept the notion that he ought to do so to himself. One thing at a time, he reasoned. If anyone seemed soon to succumb to illness, or if Yin Ila came to him with word that people had begun to starve, he would do what he could regardless of his fears. Yet he found no relief in walking the tunnels, and so returned to his room, determined to make one last effort with the journal before sleep took him.

Clues elsewhere in the text had given him the context he needed to begin making sense – albeit with a low degree of confidence – of the page that accompanied the sketch of the strange glass sphere. The text on the sphere itself remained entirely enigmatic, but he had determined that references to *garden below* did indeed refer to a space below the city – not within the buried city itself, but *beneath* it. In truth, the word *garden* seemed a placeholder, an oblique reference to another, prominently appearing word he had yet to translate. More, it was almost always paired with a name he did not recognise, *Ambal Ora*, which might have been the name of the garden itself, or of its creator, but in either case meant nothing to Koro Ha nor to anyone he asked.

All day he had been muddling over a persistent, irritatingly half-formed notion that this *garden* might in fact be one of the caves where the Toa Aloni had gone to worship the stone-faced gods long before building their temples. Koro Ha's mother had taken him to such a cave in the foothills of the Pillars of the Gods several times in childhood, until his Sienese education made him uncomfortable with the risk of participating in such an illicit, forbidden practice. If this notion proved correct, it stood to reason that whatever secret Uon Elia meant for him to find would be found beneath a place of worship, though the two temples already excavated had been thoroughly explored and yielded no hidden passageways or further hints. If only he had a map of the old city, he could plan a project of excavating whatever temples remained buried.

Defeated for another day, he went to his pallet, trying desperately to shunt fears for Yin Ila and the others away from the forefront of his thoughts. He should be with them, he knew. He had promised his aid. Yet what could he do? Fear and reticence stayed his hand even from so simple a thing as healing a fever or growing a handful of crops.

'It ought never have been me,' he murmured into the darkness, regretting, far from the first time, the twisting turns of fate that had led him into Uon Elia's company, and thence into power he had never wanted and lacked the courage to use.

Shouts and thundering footsteps dragged Koro Ha from sleep. Lantern light swept the tunnels, spilling through his open doorway, casting a figure in silhouette.

'Hurry, tutor!' Goa Eln said, voice tight and pleading. 'There's no time!'

Terror burned away the drowsy fog behind his eyes as he threw on his robe and followed her. Frightened, angry voices echoed from the temple ahead. Faces peered from windows and doorways, and with them drifted whispered questions. Was it an attack? Had the Sienese found this place at last? Or worse, had the monsters that stalked the edges of the city clawed their way into the tunnels?

'What's happened?' he asked Goa Eln.

The young sailor grimaced. 'We found Orna Sin, is what. You'll see, tutor. We're nearly there.'

At first, Koro Ha could not believe the body sprawled on the blood-stained table was his friend and employer, the burly smuggler with the flashing smile and heavy arms. Leathery, scarred skin stretched taut over withered muscle and joints like gnarled roots. More scars layered his torso like the scales of fish, each marking a piece of flesh sliced away. His breaths came in low rasps, like air from a tattered bellows. His remaining eye wheeled in his head, unseeing.

'His pulse is like a frayed thread, stonespeaker.' Yin Ila's voice cut through Koro Ha's shock. 'You have to hurry.'

Koro Ha's hands trembled as he reached for Orna Sin. Until now, he had closed cuts on an old man's finger, nothing more, and those lessons had come with dire warnings. Teetering on the edge of death as he was, Orna Sin's heart might give out before healing magic could stabilise him.

More chilling still, Koro Ha recalled the monsters at the gate, come howling from the forest in the wake of his magic. *Now is no time for foolishness!* He chided himself. *One thing happening after another is no sure sign of causality. A dozen aphorisms ought to remind you so, and any student would know them all.*

'What are you waiting for?' Yin Ila urged.

Would he let fear stay his hand while he watched his friend die? Was he that much a coward?

Koro Ha gritted his teeth, touched Orna Sin's quivering shoulder – it was like touching a bundle of twigs wrapped in shreds of threadbare cloth – and poured magic into him. Calm descended, dulling the horror, quietening his nagging fear. Orna Sin stared up at him, his eye bulging, showing a yellowed edge of sclera.

'You're all right now, Orna Sin,' Koro Ha whispered. 'Things will be all right. Give it time.'

The eye bulged further still. A low rattle sounded from Orna Sin's throat.

'Something isn't right,' Goa Eln muttered.

Orna Sin's arm shuddered upwards, clutching at his chest. His mouth opened in a wordless scream. He spasmed, his elbows and the back of his head slamming into the table, drawing fresh trickles of blood, and then again.

'Hold him down!' Yin Ila shouted. Koro Ha baulked but Yin Ila caught his arm.

'He could die!' he protested. 'Please, Yin Ila.'

'If you stop, he dies for certain,' she growled, her other hand touching the hilt of her knife. 'So I'm not going to let you.'

'It will only make things worse!' Koro Ha moaned. 'Please, Yin Ila! We can stabilise him with bandages and medicine. When he is stronger—'

'You *promised*, tutor.' The fine bones of his wrist twisted in her grip. 'This is *your* end of the bargain.'

Orna Sin's back arched like a drawn bow, heaving upwards on shaking heels and shoulder blades. A breath hitched in his emaciated throat. Even the calming wake of healing could not dull the edge of this nightmare, yet Koro Ha pressed on. He had promised.

'Keep your shit together, Orna Sin!' Yin Ila howled. 'I can't bloody well do this without you, you old bastard!'

If he dies, I will have killed him. The thought rebounded within Koro Ha's skull. He recognised it as madness but could not shed it from his mind. *If he dies, I will have killed him and caused him all this pain for no good reason.*

A breath rattled through Orna Sin's ribs and he collapsed back to the table. His eye rolled lazily.

'Bloody god-fucking dammit!' Yin Ila spat. Her grip tightened until Koro Ha feared his hand would shatter, then released. She pressed it to the side of Orna Sin's neck, digging for a pulse. 'Come on, you old goat. *Come on.*'

That eye, for the space of a breath, fixed on Koro Ha, meeting his gaze. A lingering, glazed stare, clouded by pain and madness. The old smuggler's mouth opened, his lips twisting to form words, but he lacked the tongue or the breath to voice them.

One last, shuddering breath.

'You can't do this!' Yin Ila pounded on Orna Sin's chest, as though shattering his ribs might spur him back to life. 'You can't do this! Fuck! FUCK!'

'He's gone, Yin Ila,' Koro Ha said, his voice seeming to echo, as though rebounding from another room. 'I'm sorry. I did all I could.'

She rounded on him, her eyes burning and bleary. 'No you *fucking* did not. You could have been with us. We carried him for *hours* through the streets.' She pulled herself from Orna Sin's corpse and dug her fingers into Koro Ha's robe, pulling until his collar squeezed his airway shut. 'If you'd been there, you might have saved him. Those hours might have made all the difference. Did all you could? You cowered here while your friend *died*, tutor.'

'Yin Ila, that's enough,' Goa Eln snapped, pushing herself between them. 'Get some air. Killing the stonespeaker won't bring Orna Sin back, and then where would we be?'

'Exactly where we are now,' Yin Ila snarled, not taking her red-rimmed eyes from Koro Ha. 'Fucking lost.' She stormed from the temple, her boot heels ringing.

'I'm sorry,' Koro Ha said. 'She's right.'

Goa Eln shook her head. 'Maybe. Maybe not. It was a close thing, getting in and out of that dungeon, tutor. With you along, maybe we never would have reached Orna Sin. Things happen the way they do. There's no reweaving the pattern.'

She was right, of course. Any student prepared for the imperial examinations knew as much. Yet guilt gnawed at him as he stood over Orna Sin, watching Goa Eln and the others cover his body with one of Uon Elia's woven mats. He touched the old smuggler's face through the sheet of vines. What had he been trying to say, Koro Ha wondered? Might those words have offered him any solace, were Orna Sin able to hear them?

'We'll bury him in his garden,' Goa Eln suggested. 'By the pond, and with a hefty sack of tobacco. He'd like—'

A scream split the air, echoing from deeper in the tunnels, from the direction Yin Ila had gone. Goa Eln's knives flashed into her hands. Koro Ha followed after her, his heart thundering. *Proximity in time does not indicate causality*, he told himself again and again as he and Goa Eln waded through the river of bodies fleeing the rebounding screams. The sound led to the house Koro Ha had passed earlier, where, through an open window, he had glimpsed a family caring for its sickly child. Blood now spattered the edges of that window. A body lay crumpled in the tunnel just outside it, one arm ending in a ragged stump. Ceramic shattered with a crash, followed by a howl of pain. Something dark and lumbering lurched just out of sight.

Goa Eln was through the doorway before Koro Ha could stop her. By the light of a toppled lantern he followed her, though with every step his legs shook and his throat convulsed. Yin Ila, a stone-cutter with a pickaxe, and a man cradling a broken arm huddled in the far corner of the room, facing down a creature woven from the fabric of nightmares.

Almost human. Pale, sickly flesh. A claw protruding from the thick toe-band of a sandal. Shoulders hunched too far backwards. The arm bent strangely, as though jointed in the middle of the bicep. The horrific shape shuddered, then turned its child's face, dribbling snot, weeping desperately.

'Mother?' it sobbed, its arm probing about the room; closing around the leg of a woman slumped lifeless in a pool of blood, squeezing it with a sickening crackle. 'What's … happening … to me?'

Koro Ha recoiled, tripped over his own feet, and scrambled to the far side of the tunnel. His thoughts were shredded, like a cast-off draft of an essay. He stared at the window, refusing to believe what he was seeing.

A determined shout and a meaty *thump* sounded from beyond the door. A sickening scream followed, then silence.

As though watching the scene from a distance, Koro Ha

stood. His body moved without conscious purpose, dragged forwards by the pull of necessity, as though some unnatural force carried him. Four slow, measured steps across the tunnel. With the last, his sandals brushed the pool of blood that crawled from the open door.

He became aware, suddenly, of the stink of emptied bowels beneath the bright copper scent of blood. The stone-cutter bent with his arms braced upon his knees over the child-faced corpse. His pickaxe protruded from its back. Lying still, and seen clearly, the creature was all the more terrible. Its face seemed the only feature unchanged. Its limbs were too long and folded back upon themselves, like an insect's, and still twitched, spreading streaks of ichor across the soiled floor. The body itself, now split by the stone-cutter's blow, arched strangely, its spine no longer human.

Yin Ila stared at the monster, favouring one leg. Blood poured down the other from a gash below her hip. Koro Ha nearly crossed the room, drawn by guilt and the pain on her face. But healing magic had caused this, somehow, as cultivation had drawn the twisted wolves from the forest to the gates of Sor Cala.

Goa Eln looked to Koro Ha, as though a mark upon his mouth and a year of education in magic had made him an expert in the nightmare that had come to grip the world. Soon the tunnel filled with a rumbling, fearful speculation as people peered through the open doorway and the window. Yin Ila rounded on the crowd, shouting with the stern authority of a ship's captain in a storm, 'Lurking about here won't bring answers any faster! Back to your homes! You'll have word when there's word to be had.'

The crowd dispersed, grumbling and with backward glances, but soon the tunnel and the bloodied home were clear, save Goa

Eln, Yin Ila, Koro Ha, and the stone-cutter who had felled the creature. Goa Eln put a hand on the stone-cutter's shoulder. 'It wasn't a child anymore. You did right.'

The man, still bent double, his face roiling with nausea, blinked up at the words. 'Not *anymore*? What the hell was it? You know, don't you?'

'As do you,' Yin Ila said flatly. 'You've heard the rumours of what stalks the far corners of the city and the wood beyond the walls.'

The stone-cutter groaned and vomited, then stood, gagging and hugging his chest. 'I thought we were safe here. I thought that was the point.'

'Safe from some things,' Yin Ila answered, with a long, searching stare at Koro Ha. 'Not from others, it seems.'

In time, the stone-cutter left the house. Goa Eln crossed her arms, as though to shield himself from the gruesome scene, the twisted child, the slaughtered parents.

'The boy had the fever,' Yin Ila said, keeping her voice low and pointing with her chin. 'That's what it is, isn't it? The start of this … change.'

Koro Ha could hardly manage to nod, let alone speak an answer.

'How long until the others start to change?' Yin Ila asked.

If I wield no more magic? Who can say? The moment I touch it … The trembling in his legs threatened to buckle his knees and leave him sprawled in the ruin and gore. He said only, 'I don't know.'

'And there's no way to prevent it?'

'No,' Koro Ha said, 'save behind the Voice's shield. That is its purpose, I imagine. To protect the Sienese from this horror.'

Goa Eln sucked air through her teeth. 'So, what? We send anyone who starts getting sick to the Sienese?'

'No,' Yin Ila said. 'Gather the sick. Take them to the far temple. Set guards over them, people willing to do what's needed if any start to change.'

A sob broke from Koro Ha as the last of his strength gave way. Goa Eln caught him and kept him from collapsing into the bloody mess he had made.

'Easy, stonespeaker,' Goa Eln said. 'Come on, let's get you back to your room. I'll have folk sent to prepare the dead and … well, make the place liveable again.'

Koro Ha let himself be carried from that place, his mind still distant, floating above the world, alienated by the horror, by the pain, by the double-edged nature of the world made so much sharper by the absurd twisting of reality. What was the point in carrying such power if to wield it inevitably birthed such horror?

The mark above his teeth had long felt a burden, but now it began to claw at him, not only weighing on his shoulders but sending poison through his blood. It was not, as he had previously believed, a momentous blessing that carried with it great responsibility.

It was a terrible curse.

Sleep took him, creeping in from the dazed edges of his awareness. He awoke, stiff and startled, to the creak of his door and a familiar, squat silhouette with her arm in a sling.

'We need to talk.' Yin Ila crossed to his blankets and lowered herself to lean against the wall. A flat weariness sagged the lines of her face, though the corners of her mouth were still tight with long-simmering anger. 'It wasn't your fault, tutor. None of it.'

'Of course it was.' The last fog of sleep faded, burned away by the twin torches of guilt and anger. 'At the gate and here. Magic makes those things, Yin Ila. Twice now—'

'There's no one else in the city who can use magic, is there?' she cut him off. 'Except the Sienese, but they're cowering behind that wall of theirs. As awful as it's getting down here, it's worse up there.'

'You say that as a kindness,' Koro Ha said.

She frowned at him, her eyes as sharp as any knife. 'Do I have good reason to be *kind* to you? Those twisted wolves and all manner of other things stalk the city streets. The Runoff is fractured – people cowering in their homes, venturing out only when starvation and thirst drive them to. The gangs have spilled rivers of blood, mostly each other's. Sor Cala – at least the Sor Cala above ground – is unravelling. That we've had only one poor child twist into a monster I attribute to either fortune or some blessing of whatever gods are left in the world. It wasn't your fault.' There was a pause, something left unsaid. A reminder, Koro Ha imagined, that while Yin Ila might not lay the twisted child's death at his feet, she had not forgiven him for everything. 'Anyway, I can't have you thinking that it was. I can't let that paralyse you.'

Relief welled up, but doubt held it back. Yin Ila did not truly know what she was talking about. None of them understood what the twisted creatures were, nor why one thing – child, creature – might be affected and not another. He wanted to believe her, to let her words soothe the ache in his chest and the hateful fires in his mind, but that desire made him flinch back. What was worse, to accept responsibility falsely or to feel relief – gratitude, even – that the world was more broken than he had known?

'But Orna Sin ...' He shook his head. Easier to speak plainly than to let the wound fester. 'I should have gone with you. He might have been saved.'

Yin Ila took a slow breath. 'Could be. Could also be you would have tripped over your own feet and alerted the dungeon guard, seeing us all cut to pieces before we could reach him. Don't carry that guilt, tutor. All we can do is keep moving. Keep struggling. Keep trying to make a future for our people, no matter how fucked up the world gets. That's what Orna Sin would want. Speaking of which, did that journal yield anything yet?'

He gestured to the writing desk, where the journal lay open on his scattered pages of notes. 'Bits and pieces. Nothing useful.'

With a grunt, Yin Ila loomed over the desk. The pages rustled as she sifted through his notes. 'What's that mean? That knot swirling back on itself?'

'I read it as *garden*,' Koro Ha said, still nursing guilt but happy to speak of a failure that did not cut quite so sharply. 'Called Ambal Ora, or perhaps made by someone by that name. It features prominently in the journal, and obviously in relation to the glass sphere, but I can't make sense of it. At times it suggests there may be another layer of Sor Cala somehow buried beneath this one. A twice-buried city, if you will, that the stonespeakers were searching for.'

'Isn't that what Uon Elia said, though?' Yin Ila asked. 'Secrets buried beneath the city, in the roots of the Pillars of the Gods?'

'Indeed, which gives me all the more reason to think this is what he wanted us to find. Only I can't find anything that points the way to this garden.'

Yin Ila tapped the journal. 'I've seen that symbol before. Quite bloody often, in fact.'

An eddy of astonishment made Koro Ha sit up straighter. 'Where?'

'Don't get too excited, tutor,' Yin Ila said. 'I know it from decades back, when I was but an ankle-biter running the streets. Street kids leave messages for one another, marks to tell which kindly old woman's offer of a bed comes with strings attached – the sort I'll not sully your ears with – or which old hard-eyed but soft-hearted butcher will look the other way while you pick through leavings for scraps. This,' she tapped the journal again, 'marked places of safety. Secluded alleys outside the usual patrols – gangs and Sienese alike. Inns that might offer a crust or some thin soup to a waif. Stables where you could sleep a night or two before they chased you out with pitchforks. That kind of thing.'

Koro Ha slumped back against the wall. 'I doubt the stonespeakers composed their journal with the signs and signals of street urchins.'

'True enough, but symbols have a way of trickling down, don't they? There were plenty of stone-carvers in Toa Alon still able to work in the old writing. Plenty to decorate Orna Sin's garden and the tunnel down here. Most, I'd wager, couldn't properly read a word of it, but they knew the forms. Could be the street urchins remembered something the rest of you forgot.' With the tip of her finger, she drew the symbol in the air with practised ease. 'Sanctuary, Koro Ha. That's what it means.'

Koro Ha nodded. 'Even so, that knowledge does little to help me find whatever – or wherever – they sought.'

'I'll send you some maps,' Yin Ila said, hefting the glass sphere. 'Orna Sin had a collection. Must be a few left in his estate. In the meantime, pull yourself together. We need your mind, and we may have need of your magic. At the very least we need what you represent.'

Koro Ha searched her face, his confusion plain.

'Food when it was scarce, healing what no herb or surgeon could, a means to find lost treasures and lost people,' Yin Ila said, a gentle smile showing her golden teeth. 'In the old stories, the stonespeakers always represented hope.'

She tossed him the sphere. His heart leapt into this throat, but he managed to catch the thing in his lap. When he looked up, Yin Ila had gone, her words lingering, haunting him like a beneficent spirit. He turned the glass sphere in his hand, studying the swirling markings carved with such precise care into its face. Four of the marks seemed to him like a more complex rendition of the *sanctuary* symbol, with an additional knot within the central swirl. It was the only thing he recognised, as all the script seemed an even older form than the archaic writing in Uon Elia's journal.

Despair clawed at him again. Even these tunnels, which he had imagined safe, had been touched by the chaos that now tore through Sor Cala. He thought of Eln Se, of Rea Ab, of his father. There had yet been no word of them, nor of Yan Hra, his brother-in-law. A reasonable man would have accepted their deaths. Something barbed and writhing lodged in his chest, though, at the memory of Rea Ab – a bright girl who could have become so much, done such great things, if not for the constraints of the empire and her upbringing – revelling in the beauty of Orna Sin's garden.

The twisted child's face rose in his mind, as though reflected by the surface of the sphere, and he shuddered. Perhaps Rea Ab's death was a blessing, if dead she was. Better that she had not lived to see the world unravelling.

How much worse would things get, he wondered? And how soon? A matter of days? Weeks? Surely not years. Already food supplies ran low, and the only hope of replenishing them lay in the magic of cultivation, which would only speed the end.

The stonespeakers always represented hope.

A laugh broke from him, almost a sob. Uon Elia might have brought hope, but what did Koro Ha, the Sienese tutor, truly know? What could he do? All his education lay in the interpretation and language of imperial doctrine, not archaic Toa Aloni nor the secrets of old Sor Cala.

His fingers ached from clutching the sphere tighter and tighter as his thoughts descended deeper and deeper into darkness. Magic might speed the unravelling, possibly causing greater suffering in the short term but a quicker end. Yet if death and failure were inevitable, why *not* speed them along? There was one stonespeaker's trick left to him, after all, the simplest and the first he had learned.

He shut his eyes and held in the centre of his mind an impression of the glass sphere – not only what it looked like but its texture too, both the oily smoothness between the markings and the fine roughness of the marks themselves. The soft *clink* it made when he set it on his wooden desk. The strange internal appendage by which he worked all his magic reached out, filling the air with a faint cinnamon scent as it probed into the sphere in his hands, capturing the essence of it, reaching out into the world for its match. This was dowsing magic, used by stonespeakers in ancient days to reveal the secrets of the earth – iron, jewels, veins of marble – and if there was any mercy left in the world, it would lead him now to the most precious of all buried secrets.

At first he felt nothing – no distant echo to guide him to the sphere's match. There had been little reason to think that it would, of course, and if his dowsing *did* lead him towards anything, it might only be to some other artefact of carved glass, to just another sphere, and no closer to understanding the importance Uon Elia had placed in them.

The cinnamon scent grew stronger. Each moment he held the spell added to the chaos that tore through the world, stripping years from the lives of children, driving those already touched by the twisting a step closer to their terrible fates.

Guilt gnawed at him, but he held firm. None of it truly mattered, he knew. Anything he did only delayed the inevitable, except for this. Stonespeakers represented hope, and that hope lay in the glass sphere and whatever Uon Elia had sent him beneath the earth to find.

A pulse rippled through the world, like a hook, affixed to some distant anchor, tugging at his heart. His breath stuttered but he held his magic, found his feet, and followed the pull out into the tunnel. It led him only a few hundred paces, in fact, to the end of the tunnel the stonespeakers had first dug – the very same temple where he and Yin Ila had found the sphere, and where even then Goa Eln was organising an infirmary for those touched by the twisting fever.

Strung ropes hung with woven mats divided the temple into dozens of sections. Curious faces – children, their caregivers – peered out from between the mats, watching Koro Ha cross the temple, following the pull of his dowsing. It grew deeper, as though he were the chamber of a spike fiddle and the bow were drawn more firmly across the strings, till his bones shook with the resonance. A stronger, more powerful note with every step. Above, peering down from the flickering shadows of the ceiling, stared the eyes of a stone-faced god.

The source of the resonance, the object of his dowsing: the twin of the glass sphere.

It had been here all along, just above the heads of the stonespeakers, in the temple where they had made their home. Had they known? If Koro Ha had been better able to understand Uon Elia's journal, would this secret have been revealed weeks ago, before Sor Cala fell to chaos and horror?

'What now?' he whispered, searching the dark angles of the face above him. He hugged the glass sphere to his chest. The resonance pulled so strongly he feared it might drag him off his feet. An urge filled him to reunite the sphere with the face in the stone, as though their separation was a mortal wound in desperate need of healing and the resonance between them but an echo of deep pain.

An absurdity. Stone was not flesh.

Yet he had watched stone walk across the sea.

Perhaps the world held more absurdities, more strangeness than his Sienese education could admit.

Still, he hesitated. Caution bade him release the dowsing. Perhaps Yin Ila could arrange for a scaffold to be built, for stone-carvers to better examine the face above. Perhaps find a setting on its surface somewhere, as in a piece of jewellery, where the glass sphere might be affixed.

Stone eyes stared down at him. Waiting. Pleading. The resonant pulse of pain through the world shook him. He saw Orna Sin, his body broken, and the twisted child, its innocent face full of fear.

It was not a rational act, not a reasoned thing, no product of doctrine or argument or careful thought, yet it seemed the sort of thing Orna Sin or Uon Elia would have done. A great risk, a leap into the unknown to save his people.

Holding the dowsing link between glass sphere and stone face, he introduced another layer of magic – healing, flailing in the dark, that brought with it a wash of sudden calm.

He tasted salt. There were tears, he realised, in the curls of his beard.

The earth heaved beneath him. Shouts of alarm rang out as cracked pillars groaned and coughed a shower of dust. He sprawled backwards, thrown from his feet. The sphere of glass slipped through his fingers. A spike of panic cut through the deep, tranquil ocean of healing sorcery, fear that it might fall to the ground and shatter, and with it the last of Sor Cala's hope.

Yet it hung, like a fixture of the heavens, in the air.

Slowly, the sphere drifted upwards, its carved surface glinting in the lantern light. Feet that had scrambled in panic only a moment before paused, and turned. A child gasped. A last flicker seemed to fill the sphere before it touched the forehead of the stone face and, as though glass were water, flowed onto it.

The pounding reverberation rose to a climax, then burst. It tore through the world like the explosion of a chemical grenade, rolling outwards in a single cresting wave, weakening as it spread from its epicentre but never vanishing. Koro Ha knelt, awe holding him to the earth, crowding out every thought, every possible explanation for what he had witnessed.

A crack sounded somewhere below him, and then a grinding that shattered the calm in the temple and sent people again scrambling for safety.

Koro Ha only knelt, overwhelmed, and watched as the earth split beneath his knees and opened, stone sliding like oil.

This was no magic Uon Elia had prepared him for, like nothing he had ever imagined. When the earth ceased to quake, the floor of the temple had reshaped itself. He knelt now at the top of a staircase that spiralled downwards into the roots of the Pillars of the Gods, vanishing after a dozen steps into shadows.

He released his healing spell, yet the profound serenity that gripped him still held. His every emotion had been overwhelmed. In time, perhaps, confusion, wonder, even terror would bring him again to his knees. But not yet. For the first time in his life, there was no room within him for fear.

He stood and took a lantern from one of the pillars, then mounted the stair, holding the lantern ahead of him to cut through the dark and ward against the unknown.

21

The Emperor and the Cur

Foolish Cur

'It's sort of a moot question, isn't it, Vole?' Darting Buck's voice echoed through the tunnel that led from the western garrison into the world beyond Hissing Cat's seal. 'If there *is* game to be had, we'd like to have it, and if there *isn't*, there's not much else useful you or I could do, is there?'

The young hunter glowered in the lantern light. 'I'm just saying, is all. If whatever's twisting animals into monsters keeps at it long enough, there won't be anything left in the world but monsters, right?'

She addressed the question to me. The other five members of our party – men and women armed with bows and boar spears – seemed determined to look anywhere and everywhere else, as though by ignoring my presence they might pretend this were only another outing to dredge the forest for what little game remained. Only Vole attempted to engage me in conversation.

'I don't know,' I answered honestly, trying not to show how much the notion troubled me. 'Hissing Cat might. She's lived through this before.'

Vole nodded but scrunched up her face. 'Don't think she'd

spare me a moment to answer questions, though. Frankly, she scares the shit out of me.'

'Rightly so,' I observed, and hoped she would leave things at that.

'The way I figure is this: whatever's happening out there can't make the world too unliveable, right? It can't kill *everything* or it would kill the gods too, and if they're the cause of it, they'll stop before things get too far.'

'How do you figure that, Vole?' Darting Buck growled. 'They don't much need to eat, as I understand things.'

'Well, we're supposed to burn incense to 'em, and leave out food and things,' Vole pointed out. 'Why'd we ever bother doing that if they had no use for it? If we all die, who'll do that sort of thing?'

'Maybe they don't *need* it, just like it,' Darting Buck argued. 'Like a king or the emperor. If you don't bow and kiss the ground, they don't *die*. They just cut your head off for insulting 'em. Gods could be the same. Burn incense, give sacrifices, so they don't do … well, what they're doing now.'

Vole grumbled under her breath, mustering her next argument. One had sprung into my mind while Darting Buck was speaking – even after everything, this sort of dialogue was what I had been most thoroughly trained for. We were only speculating, of course, not unravelling the complexities of doctrine, but the argument was a pleasant enough diversion to keep my thoughts from gnawing on harder, more uncomfortable questions.

'I'm not so sure about that,' I said. 'Kings and emperors might not starve to death without the adulation of their subjects, but ponder this: without it, would they remain kings and emperors? The man might survive, but the office will wither if it goes unrecognised.'

Sienese propriety was, indeed, founded upon that very notion.

A governor was not a governor if the people of his province paid him neither mind nor honour, and just so for all the institutions of the empire: fathers and sons, Hands and Voices, the emperor himself. Perhaps deference to the gods was much the same.

'There you have it!' Vole shouted triumphantly, her voice ringing through the tunnel. A few of our silent fellows covered their ears and glared at her, but she ignored them. 'The gods can't kill *everything*! If they're all that's left in the world, they wouldn't be gods anymore.'

It was an interesting idea, and one I had not considered before, but simply because an argument had led to such a conclusion did not make it true. I knew too well the ways in which logic and deduction could distort reality, bending it around useful premises to fit the needs of institutions – or, perhaps just as often, the needs of troubled minds seeking justification for the seemingly arbitrary trajectory of their lives. Still, it was worth tucking away in a corner of my thoughts. Yet I had no time to give it due consideration, nor to tease out its implications, for as the echo of Vole's shouts faded, we emerged through an open gateway into the denuded field between Eastern Fortress and the surrounding woodlands.

We held just outside the tunnel, still within the sphere of Hissing Cat's seal. Its edge showed itself in blades of grass seeming to bend at sharp angles and in the strange curve of the horizon, as though the geometries that defined horizontal and vertical had been shifted out of alignment.

'How far out d'you need to go?' Darting Buck asked.

'Only a few paces,' I said. Already I itched for the rush of power, the return of that special awareness of the world that had been with me since childhood. Touching the canon of witchcraft – left behind in Hissing Cat's care, for I would have no need of it on this outing – had offered only a shadow of true freedom, of true power. For the first time since I had broken the world, I would feel it again in all its fullness. 'And only for a few moments,' I said, as much to myself as to them. I would reach out to Tenet, and if he heard me, we would converse. When our parlay was done, or if my attempt was met with silence, we would return to the safety of the seal and the walls.

Darting Buck wheeled his hand and the company of hunters formed a circle around me, with Buck leading and Vole at my back. 'Slow and steady,' Buck said. 'Anything so much as brushes a fern or snaps a twig, you shoot.'

Tension to rival the hunters' bowstrings held as we crossed the barren field, our feet swiping through cropped grass beginning to grow wild again. As we neared the eerie, half-perceived line, Darting Buck put up his fist and crouched, his ear close to the ground and his eyes slowly sweeping the forest, only a few paces beyond us.

'We all cross, but we don't go into the woods,' he said. 'If we're to be attacked, I'd like to see the bastards coming. Understood?'

A chorus of affirmations answered him. He straightened, nocked an arrow to his bowstring, and crossed the edge of the seal.

Watching him turned my stomach. As his leg passed through, it seemed to topple. His foot found purchase on what to me looked like an expanse of sod somehow propped cockeyed to the plane of the earth around it. The others followed him, either so accustomed to the sight not to be bothered or preferring to join him and put the unsettling mirage behind them. They herded me forwards. Recalling my arrival in the city, I braced myself for churning nausea and flickers of phantom pain.

As though thrust from a cave into the glaring sun of the Batir Waste, or doused repeatedly with boiling and then freezing water, the sudden awakening of sensation overwhelmed me. The sixth sense by which I felt the pattern of the world had been not dulled but isolated, given only the occasional taste of a wake of witchcraft or the weight of Hissing Cat's seal. A tongue fed only bland paste will recoil on first tasting pungency or spice, or will find the mild sweetness of honey cloying and sickly. Just so, I found my awareness of the pattern not a glorious return to freedom but overwhelming.

My knees buckled. I hugged my chest, my teeth chattering, as I felt the slow growth of every blade of grass, every tree. Distant sounds reverberated infinitely and churned the subtle currents of the air. Sunlight and shadow traded heat and cold along their borders.

Vole caught my arm, but I waved her off. 'I'm all right,' I said, taking slow breaths, gathering in my awareness. I stared at a blade of grass, focusing on perceiving it only by sight, letting the pattern drift into the background. When the sizzling sensation faded from my nerves and the nausea from my stomach, I stood. The rest of the hunting party had crossed the barrier and formed an awkward, oblong ring around me, keeping as far away from the edge of the forest as possible, per Darting Buck's command. A few sideways glances sized me up, worried at my strange reaction, which had been so much more extreme than theirs.

Darting Buck put a hand on my shoulder and searched my eyes. 'You steady?'

I nodded and braced myself. Already my passage through the barrier seemed a distant memory. My old desire for magic and mastery, born when I had first felt my grandmother conjure flame, had clawed it down. My heart raced in anticipation, in fear.

'If anything seems off, or if I tell you to, drag me back over that line,' I told Darting Buck, recalling the last time the emperor's mind and mine had been joined. There was no sense in telling the hunters that if I succeeded in reaching out to Tenet, he might simply seize control of my mind and body, as he had so nearly done before. I was wagering that he needed me as much as I needed him, that he would recognise that neither of us could hope to win against the gods alone.

I dug deep into memory, conjuring up every strong image of the emperor I held – his seat upon the Thousand-Armed Throne, the crushing weight of his presence, his descent from the smoke-stained sky of Eastern Fortress on wings of light, his chest weeping blood while he lay in Voice Golden-Finch's garden – and reached out. If he were within a seal, shielding himself from the wake of the gods' war, my transmission would find no recipient and would only flail in emptiness. Either way, the heavy weight of my magic descended, settling on my shoulders.

'I've begun,' I said.

Darting Buck chewed his moustache and checked his bow-string. Vole rolled her shoulders back, stretching her slight frame to its fullest height. Whatever my magic drew, I could only trust them to defend me. If I fought back with fire, wind, and lightning, it would only call down more twisted creatures. I shut my eyes and held my memories of the emperor – and trepidation, regret, and terror with them – firmly in mind.

A low, throaty rumble sounded from the forest, then a scream, terribly human but full of a wildcat's rage.

'Only a few moments, you said,' Darting Buck muttered.

I tried to ignore him, to become as a sphere of jade attending to nothing but the pattern and my place within it – an unsettling exercise, for the flow of the pattern was not as it had been. It had once been a river, full of motion but directed by a single flow. Now it roiled and churned as though boiling. The ripples of the war between the gods, their struggle occurring unseen in the deepest layers of the pattern, in what Hissing Cat had called the layer of the soul. The contortions in the world were but the bubbles of that boiling rising to the surface, bursting, bending and battering the material world. If the tales Hissing Cat and the emperor had told proved true, the twisted beasts and the fracturing of time would be only the beginning. Soon the bedrock of the world itself would heave and shake, the air would fill with fire, and all beyond the boundaries of seals like Hissing Cat's would be destroyed.

I had to put an end to it, by any means, before that happened. For that, I needed Tenet's knowledge and the power of every witch of the old sort in the world. I poured that need into my search for his mind, refocusing my attention, waiting for the pull of transmission towards the heart of Sien.

My focus was broken by another yowl, this one closer, and the creak of a tree brushed by some monstrous form. Bowstrings sang around me. Arrows whipped through the undergrowth. There was a yelp of pain, then the crashing of a body in its death throes.

'Fuck! What the fuck is that? A bear?' I heard Vole yell.

'Shut up! It doesn't matter. Keep shooting!' snapped Darting Buck, each phrase punctuated with a bowshot.

I breathed deeply, returned to the sphere of jade. I would not fail here. I had endured fear and danger; they would not chase us back into the seal. I would reach the emperor, link our needs, and find common purpose in saving what lives could be saved.

Stranger, more terrible voices rose in hunger and pain from the forest, answered by rhythmic volleys. Just how many arrows, I wondered, had Darting Buck and his hunters brought?

<Well, well,> said another voice, silent to my ears but thundering against the walls of my skull. <I suppose I ought not be surprised, and yet I am. A brash thing, to reach out in this way after our last meeting. I thought you were intelligent, boy.>

I recoiled, nearly severing the connection between us. Fear would accomplish nothing. We could only survive by pressing forwards, even into terrible danger.

<We need to talk,> I said, trying to hide my need and desperation. <Help me put an end—>

<Help *you?*> The emperor did not laugh, but I felt his bleak amusement. <Oh no, boy. Much as you need it, I've better things to do than teach an idiot child, let along bargain with one.>

His presence surged, like a mountain lunging. Weight and structure flowed into my mind, forming the foundation of myriad labyrinthine walls that began to grow, threatening to seal my consciousness in a prison not unlike the canon of sorcery. I had anticipated such an attack, though it nonetheless sent a spike of panic through me. I was by no means the emperor's equal in skill with transmission, but I had learned that *preventing* a spell from taking hold was far simpler than casting one, upon either the pattern of the world or another mind.

With a thought, I severed our connection. The labyrinth collapsed and I reached out again, following the still-fresh memory of that brief interaction through the pattern.

<So you're no longer the idiot you were.> I felt the emperor's amusement, like that of a cat that has watched a mouse scurry into its burrow. <I should have assumed so. By all accounts you have always been a quick study.>

<We don't have time to bandy words,> I snapped. <Listen to reason, Tenet. We must work together if we are to restore the world.>

<Ha! Imagine calling one who stands above you as a god by his *name*. And demanding his *cooperation*. Amusing. Absurd, but amusing. *You*, of course, are always welcome to help *me*, as I was saying before you shattered a thousand-year peace and stabbed me through the heart.>

<You nearly killed two people dear to me.> I ground my teeth, remembering Running Doe sprawled in the garden, struck down by the emperor's lightning. Arguing would accomplish

nothing. <Believe that I lend you aid and not the reverse if the distinction matters to you. Either way, we need one another.>

<I offered you this chance already, Wen Alder,> the emperor said. <You rejected it. Though perhaps now, after witnessing the suffering I spent *lifetimes* building a bulwark against, you have changed your mind.>

<About your empire and its cruelty? No,> I said. <About the need to overthrow the gods? Yes.>

<The one is but the means to achieve the other.>

A tree cracked and crashed to the earth, borne down by some huge howling body. Darting Buck shouted orders, the words muffled by the symphony of bowstrings and monstrous screams.

I bristled at his flippancy, which ran counter to all the bombast and ritualised elegance of the Sienese culture he had created and enforced. <Could the gods be sealed away in the deeper reaches of the pattern? In the layer of the soul?> I considered revealing that the idea had come from Doctor Sho – from Traveller-on-the-Narrow-Way – but doubted he would appreciate my revealing his presence to the emperor. <Could such a thing be done?>

A pause held, as though I had caught the emperor off balance – if that were even possible. <An old notion. Was this Hissing Cat's idea? No matter, I suppose. Can it be done? Who knows? If it could, I would not do it, and neither would you.>

<If it would spare the world from the gods and from the ambitions of men like you, I would.>

<Oh?> A skein of wry mirth coated his words. <And what of *your* ambitions, Alder? You forget, I know your mind well. Would you give up your dream of achieving true understanding, true mastery? You have fallen far if you now think it better to lock away secrets and power than rein them to your will. A shame.>

I bristled again, remembering my horror at waking after the

battle at Eastern Fortress to find myself drugged with witch's eye, my power temporarily held at bay, though Doctor Sho had only dosed me to protect us both from the attention of the twisted ones – the very same beasts whose snarls and gnashing teeth now filled the air around me. Darting Buck, Vole, and the others could little afford my indulging in this argument any longer.

<Will you agree to work together with me or not?> I demanded. <We must put aside the grudge between our peoples long enough to win this war with the gods.>

<No. We will not *work together*, Foolish Cur. I have made my terms clear enough. Agree to serve me and you may play a part in repairing the damage you have done before I kill you.>

<Hardly a reasonable offer.>

<I am an emperor, boy,> Tenet seethed, <not a merchant to be bargained with. And while I would gladly make use of you, as I have made use of others, I have no *need* of you. Accept my rule, as you rightly should, or—>

A piercing wake rippled through the pattern of the world, making my body feel at once weightless and shaken by some unseen force. It shattered my thoughts into countless fragments, and with them the link I had forged between myself and the emperor. I gasped, pitching forwards onto my hands and knees, my palms scraping against a fallen branch. The sounds of battle around me faded to nothing more than a few distant howls and the sound of limbs churning through the undergrowth.

'What the hell?' blurted Vole between heaving breaths. Her quiver hung empty on her hip and her twin swords were coated in thick black blood. She stared toward the south, where a few saplings swayed in the wake of the retreating twisted ones. 'What d'you make of that, Buck?' She turned when he did not answer. 'Buck?'

He lay a few paces behind her, wide jaws filled with too-human teeth closed tight around his chest, crushing ribs and splitting his lung. A bloody mess and the shaft of an arrow, still clutched in Darting Buck's white knuckles, filled the socket of the creature's eye.

Three of the other hunters also lay dead, their bodies broken, slowly weeping the last of their blood. One of the survivors heaved a sob and knelt beside a fallen comrade.

Vole's red-rimmed eyes found mine. 'You're done here, I take it?'

'I am,' I said. 'Thank you.'

She nodded sharply and wiped her swords on her trousers. 'Was it worth it?'

It was a question I could not answer honestly, for I did not know. That strange wake through the world – like a tidal bore surging upstream, running against the pattern, passing through me, disrupting the flow of both nature and magic – consumed my thoughts. Not only the wake itself, either, but the emperor's reaction to it, which I felt in our last moment of contact before my transmission was severed.

Vole shouted orders. The five surviving hunters stowed their weapons and gathered up their dead. I followed them, trying to make sense of what I had felt, nursing a thousand questions.

Only one thing was certain, and it at once terrified me and buoyed my hope. The emperor, for the briefest of moments while the pattern shook with that strange, distant wake from the south, had been deathly afraid.

22

An Echo from the Heart of the World

Foolish Cur

'I felt it,' Hissing Cat said as she prodded at the pad of each finger in sequence with the tip of her iron needle. It was the sort of fidgeting I might have expected from a nervous examination candidate, not from one of the most powerful women in the world. 'It hammered at the walls of the seal, like a god had finally decided to try and tear it down. Not that they could …' She trailed off and shook her head sharply, rattling the skulls in her hair. 'No, Cur. I have no idea what it was. But I can tell you where it came from.'

I perked up. A cloud had clung to me since my conversation with the emperor, so suddenly interrupted by a rolling wake through the pattern of the world. Three Nayeni warriors had died to facilitate that conversation, which had accomplished nothing. Imagining that the emperor might cooperate with me had been the height of foolishness – another mistake, another three lives marked down on the ledger of my life.

'Somewhere beneath the Pillars of the Gods,' Hissing Cat went on. 'A few witches of the old sort retreated there. Built a stronghold. I thought Tenet destroyed it, but …' Again, she shook her head. That twinge of fear I had felt from the emperor took on another, ominous meaning. 'None but those who built it would know what this was, Cur, and I fear they are long lost to us.'

'It is a long voyage to Toa Alon,' Clear-River observed. He stood a few paces behind Hissing Cat, his arms crossed, his hair stirred by the breeze that sent leaves swirling down from Oriole's tree. Pinion stood beside him, his one good eye seeming to peer into the retreating distance. Running Doe and the Raven – representing the two ever-so-gradually integrating halves of our forces – stood at the edge of the gathering, completing our council. Doctor Sho should have been there too, but he had refrained from joining us, claiming his patients needed him. Besides, he had said pointedly, he had made his position *blisteringly* clear already.

'There are quicker ways to travel,' Hissing Cat said. 'Tenet has made abundant use of them these last few weeks, I suspect. Difficult to teach, though, and impossible to reach an unfamiliar destination. Of course, I've been to Toa Alon before, and it's only a bit more complicated to take someone with you or send them ahead.'

'So you propose … what? Abandoning us and chasing after this wake from nowhere?' The Raven scoffed. 'Leaving us without the seal on the city? Our *one* bit of leverage over the Sienese, as I have been made to understand?'

'The negotiations were not wholly ineffective,' Clear-River pointed out. 'There are fissures in the Sienese leadership. With enough time, we could bring them around.'

'How much time do we have?' I asked Running Doe.

She grimaced. 'Ten days at current rations. Maybe twice that if we stretch things to the limit. But we're already feeding people far less than we should. Most of the patients in the clinic are too malnourished to heal well. They linger as much from hunger as sickness or injury.'

'If our fighters are starving,' the Raven said, 'and we can't hold the seal over the heads of the Sienese, they will sweep through us like a scythe through a wheat field. We should strike now. It will be a bloodbath, but no less than the Sienese deserve, and then it will be over.'

'You sound like Burning Dog,' Pinion murmured.

The Raven leaned towards him. 'She was far from wrong about everything.'

'Enough.' They turned towards me, the Raven's posture relaxing, but only a little. 'We won't abandon the seal. We can't. But neither can we ignore this wake from the south. It frightened the emperor. He will make a move – send a proxy, or go himself to investigate it, and without delay. Whatever it is, we do not want him to reach it first. Is that fair to say, Hissing Cat?'

She grunted. The shoulder blades that lay before her, fanned out in an arc, drew my eye.

'There is a way to leave the seal in place while Hissing Cat and I go to Toa Alon,' I said. 'It will take a bit of time, but—'

Hissing Cat's eyes looked over my shoulder and narrowed. I followed the line of her gaze to see my grandmother standing at the bottom of the hill, dressed in her armour and wearing a sword, as though she intended to assault the Sienese quarter alone despite her age and withered arm. 'I would speak to my grandson,' she said firmly.

'You are welcome to join our council,' I said.

She laughed deep in her chest and shook her head. 'My advice wouldn't be heeded. No. Only with you, Foolish Cur, before I go.'

Go? At that, I stood. 'We'll continue in a moment,' I told the gathered council. Running Doe watched me with a worried smile. 'I'm sure it's nothing,' I reassured her, then joined my grandmother at the base of the hill.

'What is this?' I asked. 'What do you mean, *go*?'

'My son is dead,' she answered. Her shoulders slumped and her withered arm twitched. 'I'm tired, Cur. What little I could offer this war has been stripped away – and it hardly seems a war, any longer. Whatever's left to do, I leave to others. It's time I went home, or at least back to the nearest thing I have to one.'

A pang shot through me. She spoke of my father's estate, in the countryside to the south of the city. It was far enough away and isolated enough, I hoped, not to have been affected by the chaos of the gods' war, yet a part of me knew that nowhere in the world would be untouched. That I had abandoned my parents to almost certain death, if not at the claws of the unwoven, then from starvation or – a sickening thought – twisted into monstrous beasts themselves, left to roam our island, hunting those dwindling, rare places yet untouched by horror.

Another mark against me in the ledger.

'You can't know if there will be anything left,' I said softly. 'Mother might—'

'You think I don't *know that*?' she snapped, her voice thick with fear and rage. 'Boy, I have watched everyone else I have ever loved either destroyed, twisted, or ... well, whatever has become of you. My daughter might yet live. If she does, I should be with her. If she does not, then I would know for certain and mourn her as I mourn her brother and her father, for however many days I have left. I tell you this only as a courtesy, so that next time a whim seizes you and you feel some guilty urge to seek me out, you will know where I have gone.'

Misguided arguments darted through my mind, followed by an urge to threaten her or to send runners to bar the gates and prevent her from leaving. A rift had grown between us, true, but I still loved her, perhaps as I had loved no one else in the world. My mother and father were distant shadows, illuminated only by occasional flashes of clear memory. As fraught as my relationship with my grandmother had always been, it stood at the core of me, as central to who I had become as my friendship with Oriole or my education in Sienese doctrine.

'Please, wait a while,' I said. 'If the unwoven come, or some ripple of the gods' war brings destruction down on her house, you can little hope to protect her. Let me put an end to this and we will find her together, if she yet lives.'

'You are right,' she said. 'I can't protect her. In truth, I have never been able to. But *you* could.' She searched my face a moment longer, but whatever she saw there soured her expression. She huffed, turned on her heel, and walked away. I watched her until she vanished behind a standing stone, one of the few ornaments of Voice Golden-Finch's garden yet untouched by the effort to remake it into a fortress.

A tear threatened the corner of my eye. I scrubbed it away, took a steadying breath and rejoined the council atop the hill.

Words passed between Clear-River, Pinion, Hissing Cat, Running Doe, and the Raven. I attended as best I could, though my mind wandered far. It seemed that no matter how we wove our way through the many threats and obligations at play, some point of failure would draw too taut and snap, unravelling it all. Each problem had a solution, but each solution would worsen another problem. More, all solutions were only temporary. The city would run out of food eventually. If I took on the task of holding the seal, Hissing Cat might use the magic of cultivation – which I had yet to learn – to foster a garden around its edges, but with both of us occupied there would be no witch of the old sort to oppose the emperor or deal with any unforeseen problems that might arise.

Humanity had survived the last war between the gods by the strength of the witches of the old sort, but now a millennium of pact magic and the emperor's canon had culled our ranks. As I had been drawn into the trap of learning these simplified forms of power, so too had every potential witch been snared. There might be others in the world like the Girzan witch in Atar's company who had so troubled Okara, but how to find them? How to train them up in time to end this apocalypse, before it left the world too shattered ever to be repaired?

Tenet, at least, had found a way around this problem, a way to make witches of the old sort – or, at least, a way to extend his own power as such through bodies marked with his tetragram. He had watched the world end once already. I could understand, as I never had before, why he would be willing to wield such terror and brutality to prevent its ending again.

The Raven and Clear-River stood across from one another beyond the arc of Hissing Cat's shoulder blades, their voices rising as they went back and forth over the question of a final battle against the Sienese, a last bloodletting to unify the city. To me, it was a question that had become like some abstract morality tale on the imperial examinations. Perhaps there was a right answer, and perhaps writing it well, with impeccable calligraphy, had some value, but what would it matter a month from now? A year? What would it matter when Hissing Cat's strength at last gave way and the unwoven tore through the streets of Eastern Fortress?

I shook my head. Questions of morality, of survival, of tactics and strategy … All were little more than dust, to me. In the deepest chambers of my heart, only one thing conjured any feeling.

My hand found Running Doe's arm. 'I'm going after her,' I murmured, and stood.

Silence fell on the council. Clear-River muttered the trailing end of some argument, then fixed me with a confused glare.

'You all understand these problems as well as I do,' I said. 'I trust you to come to the correct decisions. There is somewhere else I need to be.'

Clear-River opened his mouth, no doubt to try to convince me to stay and help them cut through the impossible knot that bound us, but a sharp gesture from Pinion quietened him. I told them to factor me into their plans as they saw fit and set off across the garden.

'Wait!' Running Doe called, running up behind me. 'Where are you going?'

It would have been easier to smooth away the worry in her face with a gentle lie, but I had spun enough lies in my short life, nearly hanging myself by them many times. 'To follow my grandmother. She goes to find my mother, if she yet lives.'

'It's death beyond the seal, Foolish Cur.' Running Doe shook her head firmly. 'You've seen for yourself. And it only gets worse further from the walls. If you go, you might not come back, and if you *do* it might be only to die a few days later from whatever the world out there does to you.'

'All the more reason to find my mother, and my father,' I said. 'I can't abandon them to that fate, Running Doe. They can't hope to defend themselves, and my grandmother is little better equipped. Nayeni magic alone won't save them. I have to go. They're the only family I have.'

She winced slightly, as though my words needled her, and stepped towards me. 'You were dead, Foolish Cur. After the battle. I thought we had lost you – I thought *I* had lost you – and there hasn't been enough time, with the clinic and everything else ...' A tear rolled from the corner of her eye, over the ridged scars that lined her face.

I reached out, my chest aching as though it would rip apart, and brushed it away. 'During the battle, I thought the emperor had struck you down. I thought I had lost *you*. I'm sorry. It wasn't my intent to make you—'

She pulled my face down to hers and kissed me. For that moment, my fear, my guilt, the burden of undoing all the damage I had done, faded to little more than the babbling of a brook – until she loosened her embrace and I felt again the urgency of my grandmother's words and my parents' fate.

'I'll come back,' I said. 'There's too much to do for me not to, anyway.'

She smiled, brushing away another tear. 'Then go.'

I felt the urge to kiss her again but hesitated, still feeling her scars and my neglect of her since returning to the city as a rift between us. It was a moment of indecision I felt keenly. The longer I waited, the harder it would be to catch up with my grandmother. Finally, I turned to follow her, first walking, then running through the streets of Eastern Fortress, imagining I might catch her before she left the protection of the city.

My heart sank when I reached the garrison gate. Torn Leaf, still in command there, told me he had seen my grandmother and had at first barred her from leaving, until she had touched her sword hilt and made it *pointedly* clear that she meant to be on her way whether she left clean or soaked in blood.

She could not have travelled far. I passed through the tunnel, once more emerging into the world beyond the city walls. The unwoven would harry her if she veered and travelled on the wing. She would be on foot, surely, and still within sight of the gate.

Such hope was dashed as I passed the edge of Hissing Cat's seal. Again, the sudden reawakening of my sixth sense sent pain and nausea rippling through me, leaving behind pulsing cramps as it faded down the lines of my limbs. A wake of veering, somewhere over the forest to the south.

I spat a curse. How long before that wake drew the unwoven? Just as worrying, how long before time and space began to twist around my grandmother? Doctor Sho had said that the fraying of the pattern seemed somehow constrained by perception. In that case, as long as we remained together, near enough to perceive one another – even if, I had to hope, only by the wakes of our magic – our sense of time and location would remain the same. If I followed on the wing, I stood a chance of maintaining that connection. But veering would only draw more of the unwoven, as would any attempt to fight them off. Death at their tearing claws and ripping beaks would soon follow.

The cramps diminished, which meant, at least, that my grandmother still moved southwards. They had not killed her yet. But as soon as I ceased to feel that wake, the unravelling of the world would complicate any attempt to reach her. I might follow only to arrive at my father's estate days too late, or hours before her.

The wise thing, I decided, once more drowning the desires of my heart in the deep waters of responsibility, treating myself not as a human being but as a piece upon a Stones board, would be to return to the council, abandoning Broken Limb to her chosen fate. Her survival would turn no tide in the war against the gods or the Sienese. She was no great and powerful witch of the old sort, nor a skilled politician. She was only my grandmother.

I veered and took to the sky.

I felt the unwoven at once, their sickening wakes like oil on my skin, drawing closer and closer. A conjured wind lent me speed and I readied myself to hurl fire and lightning, to carve a path through them to reach my grandmother, who would surely be lying bloodied and broken before long. Half-human shrieks and howls rose from the forest beneath me. The canopy exploded in a rain of broken branches and scattered leaves as a dozen winged beasts burst forth, each utterly unique but all gnarled and contorted, their joints following impossible angles, their distended bodies defying all logic of natural biology. I cut them down, burned them to ash, yet felt the oily wake deepen and thicken as more and more rose to replace those I killed.

My only hope was to reach my grandmother and make a seal around us before I was overwhelmed.

An unwoven with a body like a serpent carried by wings as wide as an eagle hawk's darted past me, turned in the air, and dived down, curving around the blade of lightning I hurled towards it. Teeth like a saw blade tore through my wing. A burst of flame turned the serpent to a falling clump of ash, and a pulse of healing repaired the wound, but the effort of defending myself on the wing slowed me. The more time I wasted fighting off my attackers, the more likely I was to lose the wake of my grandmother's magic, or to arrive too late to save her if she, too, found herself embattled by the unwoven.

I thought of crafting a whirling shield of wind and fire around myself, a smaller recreation of the dome of magic I had conjured at Greyfrost Keep. But the more I fought back, and the more furiously, the deeper the wake of sorcery I would leave in the fraying pattern of the world and the more unwoven I would draw. It was a cycle without end. The only solution was to craft a seal. Doctor Sho and Hissing Cat had told me it was possible to walk while holding a seal, but I would never reach my grandmother in time on foot.

Unless . . .

If I were human, I would have burst out laughing. The notion was an absurd one yet, however strange, did not defy the laws of magic as I understood them. The complexity of it would be draining, but less so than fighting off a horde of unwoven all the way to my father's estate.

I reached deep into the pattern and traced a sphere, as I had traced one around myself and the emperor while we had battled in Voice Golden-Finch's garden, but I held back from fixing the seal in place. Within that first sphere I traced another, just big enough for my eagle hawk's body, and inverted it, defining a space between the inner surface of the first sphere and the outer surface of the second, crafting a shell with myself at its core.

For a dozen heartbeats, I held the shape in my mind, to be sure I could maintain focus in flight, all the while continuing to hurl waves of fire and lightning at the unwoven that pursued me. With every wing-beat I recalibrated the spell, keeping the shell fixed in relative position to me even as it travelled through the pattern. It was a tricky mental exercise and I lost my grip twice, each time scrambling to recreate the space I had defined.

The horde of unwoven grew thicker and thicker, and I was forced to fight harder and harder to maintain my grip on the spell I meant to weave. Either it would work and I would be safe within the shell or it would fail, but I could not experiment any longer without risking death.

With a deep breath and a moment of mental preparation, in case I suddenly found myself forced back into a human body while hurtling at incredible speed over the forest canopy, I carved the seal.

Not silence but a sudden quietness descended. Rather than a thousand wakes through the world, foremost the sickening, oily feeling of the unwoven, I felt only two: the cramps of my veering and a dragging weight like transmission, but muted, like a beast's howl through a stand of bamboo. My sixth sense probed the contours of the shell I had made and found them as impenetrable as Hissing Cat's seal, though paradoxically I was aware of the origin of that wake within my own mind. I held it, yet it contained and bound me. A bizarre sensation.

More importantly, it had worked. For a time the unwoven circled around me, diving close but never touching the edge of the seal. At first I feared that they still sensed my presence and would continue to gather, trailing me as I pursued my grandmother. I might reach her, but I would bring a nightmare in my wake. Gradually, one by one, they peeled off like dogs that have lost a promising trail and, confused and disappointed, go in search of another.

A celebratory shriek tore itself from me as my mind chased the implications of what I had done, considering ways this shell might be used to solve all manner of the problems we faced. There was only one downside, which quickly sobered me: in cutting myself off from the broader pattern of the world, I had also cut myself off from the wake of my grandmother's veering. I could no longer track her. For a panicked moment, I worried that my loss of her wake meant that our shared perception had been severed and that the unravelling of the pattern would pull us into separate labyrinths of fractured time and space. But of course she likely felt the wake of the magic I had wrought, even if I no longer felt hers.

In any case, I knew her destination. I would fly straight as an arrow towards my father's house. With luck, I would intercept her on the way, or find her there harried but alive. Then I could enfold her in my shell and heal her wounds, and together we would discover my mother's fate. Perhaps we would bring her back with us, and my father and their household with her.

My discovery had filled me with a rare optimism. She would fight them off, at least long enough for me to reach her and enfold her within my protection. In the back of my mind, I knew I was as likely to pass by her ravaged corpse, if not more so, but in that moment anything felt possible. I rode the feeling all the way to the familiar hills and valleys of my childhood, over the very walls of my father's garden.

23
A Return

Foolish Cur

As I landed, I extended the shell as wide as I could. It had been difficult, but not impossible, to hold a seal over the entirety of Eastern Fortress. Maintaining the two matched, inverted seals more than doubled the effort required, and I found it a challenge to enfold my father's modest estate.

'Grandmother!' I called. The pond that had served as a backdrop to so many of Koro Ha's lessons, where once ducks and carp had swum and turtles had bathed in the sun, had become a brackish pool choked with lily pads. Even the songbirds that my father had loved to watch flitting from tree to tree had vanished. An eerie silence held, more mundane and more unsettling than the magical silence created by my protective shell, broken only when I called out, 'Mother! Father!'

As I drew near the house, a chill gripped me. The oiled-paper screen on one the windows had been torn to tatters. A rust-red stain marred the wooden stairs to my father's reception hall.

'Grandmother!' I called again, quickening my pace. I had seen a great deal of death. None of it, I found, had prepared me for the thought of opening a door to find my mother's corpse.

Three bodies sprawled across the floor of my father's reception hall, amid pools and spattered arcs of dried blood. All three wore servants' dress, though one seemed hardly human. Its sinuous limbs ended in hooked claws and its legs folded backwards, like the hind limbs of a dog. A number of shallow wounds lined its arms and face, but a deep gash down the length of its neck, as from a sword or a heavy knife, had spilled its life's blood. It coated the floor around it in brown-black smears that spoke of a long, flailing death.

Footprints in dried blood fled the scene. I followed them, past toppled furniture and a broken lacquer screen, into the women's apartments. Bloodstained clothes littered the floor of my mother's room. Such disarray had not touched that place since the Sienese soldiers had come hunting my uncle. The survivor – my mother, I dared to hope – had tried to clean herself, it seemed. A small smear of blood on a wall, and another, left a trail that led out of the women's apartments and back into the garden, towards the gate.

There, in a crumpled heap, lay my grandmother.

Each heaving breath sent blood pulsing from deep gouges that lined her flanks. Her good arm lay beneath her at a contorted angle. I reached for healing magic, and realised to my horror that the shell I had woven around the estate must have stripped her of her magic, forcing her back to human form, leaving her to plummet to the ground with all the momentum of an eagle hawk in flight.

'You'll be all right,' I whispered, half to reassure myself, and began to knit her wounds. The calming wake of healing magic did little to settle my racing pulse. Her broken bone knitted and the wounds in her sides began to seal, but there was always the chance that her heart would give out from the strain as my magic drew on her strength.

Relief came at last when she coughed, rolled over, and glared up at me, her face full of fury. 'What the hell are you doing here?' she demanded in a hoarse whisper.

'I couldn't leave you to be torn to pieces,' I said. 'And you were right – we cannot abandon Mother. I should have come to find her the moment the world fell to chaos.'

She grunted and, leaning on my arm, hoisted herself to a sitting position. 'Did you find her?'

I shook my head and told her of the terrible scene in my father's reception hall. She scowled and stood, wavering for a moment, then finding her strength and rolling back her shoulders. 'If she's still alive, she'll have gone to the temple.'

'Would she?' My mother had always opposed my grandmother's lessons at the Temple of the Flame. She had lived as a Sienese wife should and hated my uncle for waging his war.

Gingerly, my grandmother patted down her flanks and frowned at the tears in her armour and the tunic beneath it. The wounds in her sides had healed, leaving only faint pinkish scars. 'You're getting better at that,' she remarked, flexing her withered arm. She took in my father's estate with a disgusted glare. 'Long before she was … this … she was the daughter of a temple priest and the keeper of a common house. She knows where the Temple of the Flame is. Whatever else she's become, the little girl at the heart of her will think of it as a place of safety.'

She set off into the forest, as though she had not lain on the edge of death only moments ago, and I followed, dragging the sealing shell around the estate with us. I understood her urgency, though I dared not give voice to the fears that churned in me. If my mother was not at the temple, we would have nowhere else to look. We might search the island and never find her – particularly now, as the wake of the gods' war loosened time and space. She would be lost to us, whether she lived or died. The thought threatened to kill what little hope I still held.

There was no telling how much time had passed for her here.

Like the garden, the path to the temple was overgrown, no longer kept trampled down by our night-time journeys. We heard no skittering creatures in the undergrowth nor birds calling down from the canopy overhead. The stone wolves greeted us as they had that first night, though now their menace was less abstract, evoking less a child's fear of an unknown power than presenting the ferocious visage of an enemy. Okara's bared snarl was no warning but a threat. I found it absurd, in that moment, that I had ever compared the genial mountain dog who had been my companion to this statue. Only the net of scars that crossed its muzzle and eye were the same.

'Bright Jay!' my grandmother called – and I realised, with a start, that that was my mother's Nayeni name. It had never before been spoken in my presence, its panel in the book of wooden slats that recorded our lineage scored into illegibility. A powerful longing swirled up within me, an echo of scents and feelings pressed deep in the core of me in earliest childhood, before my first conscious memories were made: the need a child has for its mother's presence, for safety from the unknown, for a well of love and comfort of infinite depth and purity.

Not all are so blessed to have such a mother, and indeed I was not. Our relationship, from my first memory, had always been strained by the tensions of our household, of empire, of my father's ambition. My childhood held only glimpses of the ideal that we all, from the moment of our birth, deserve. The ideal for which I found myself yearning with paralysing depth at the sound of her name.

My grandmother and I mounted the steps to the Temple of the Flame, so familiar from our countless night-time lessons. The same tiled roof, broken in places. The smell of guano was lessened, and no bright eyes peered down at us from the rafters. The window, once torn by fallen bamboo, had been repaired, the paper screen replaced with wooden boards. The floors had been swept free of dust and detritus.

'Bright Jay!' my grandmother called again, and I joined my voice to hers.

A shadow fell across the floor, heralding a figure who emerged from behind the altar, a kitchen knife in one hand and a curved, rust-bitten sword in the other, dressed in the simple homespun clothes my grandmother and I had once worn to visit this sacred place. She stood there a moment, lit by a blade of light falling from the broken ceiling, her eyes slowly widening in disbelief.

'Mother?' The word fell from her lips in a disbelieving whisper. The knife, and then the sword, clattered to the water-stained floor. She crossed the distance in three strides. My grandmother met her, arms flung wide.

Words passed between them, half heard, stripped of meaning by my dizzying relief. *She was alive.* Through everything, somehow, she was alive. Some gentle grace in the pattern of the world had preserved her, despite all my failure, despite all the destruction I had wrought, the mothers and children dead or for ever separated because of me. There was no justice in it, but she was alive. Gratitude nearly buckled my knees.

'Alder?' my mother said, her tear-filled eyes finding mine while she clung to my grandmother, as though she were a child again and *her* mother's presence had finally made everything safe. 'Come here, son. Gods, you're alive! I thought ...' A sob silenced her. Two steps brought them within the reach of my arms, and as I touched her I began to weep, blubbering incoherent apologies and reassurances that everything would be all right. Reassurances I uttered even as I feared in that moment, however absurdly, that she was not in fact my mother, whom I thought surely dead, and that the woman standing before me, cradled in my arms, was an impostor.

'Where is Father?' I asked when I had regained some control

and we sat together on the floor. My mother wore a tear-stained smile and gripped my hand as though anchoring herself to the reality of this moment, reassuring herself that my grandmother and I were no illusion.

She shook her head. 'He was away on the mainland when … I have not had word of him. Or of anything. Only a few panicked visitors from Ashen Clearing in the first days, shouting what we took at the time for madness. Steward Lo sent them away. Only days later, he … Well, you saw for yourself, in the reception hall.'

My grandmother took in the temple around us and the small repairs made here and there. 'You are here alone?'

'Orchid and Sapphire, two of the serving girls, were here with me at first. After … I thought we would be safer here, as though these old gods would chase away the curse that had taken Ashen Clearing and made poor Lo into that monster.' She rubbed at her eyes and a quiver shook her smile. 'We took what we could from the house – food stores, mostly – and made repairs. We had thought to plant a garden, but I woke one morning to find the girls gone. Orchid had been talking nonsense about walking to Eastern Fortress.' She searched our faces. 'Is it better there? Do you know?'

'Safer from the curse,' I said, and did not mention the brimming tensions, nor the dwindling food supplies. 'If they made it, I'm sure they're all right.'

She nodded slowly, accepting my grim reassurance. 'I've been alone since then. Two or three weeks, I think? It's been difficult to say. Sometimes the days seem to stretch on and on. Other days are over as soon as they begin, it seems.'

I shuddered. Despite her long exposure, the chaos that rippled through the world had not yet twisted her into one of the unwoven. Why it would have taken the steward so early and left her and the servant girls alone, I could not begin to guess.

I could only, once again, thank the random nature of whatever strange forces shaped this new, terrifying world.

Our reunion settled into silence. My mother leaned against my grandmother, who stroked her hair until she fell into a quiet sleep.

'I'm going to stay here, with her,' my grandmother said. 'You've no need for me anymore in Eastern Fortress.'

'We could bring her back with us.' I made a sweeping gesture. 'This is hardly a safe place. I can hold the protective shell, or even a simple seal, and escort you back to the city.'

'No, Foolish Cur. We could, I suppose, but back when distances made sense it was a three-day journey. Can you afford to spend three days walking an old woman and her daughter through the countryside? You've bigger problems to solve. Problems *only* you can solve, however ridiculous that seems. No. We'll stay here.'

'She's survived this long, but it will only be a matter of time until the unwoven find you,' I said, and did not give voice to the more terrible possibility, evidenced by the carnage in the reception hall.

She answered my worry with a wry smile. 'I suppose you'll just have to put things right before that happens.'

I glared at her and stood. I would not abandon them without protection. While I had held Hissing Cat's seal around the city, a notion had occurred to me, recalling Naphena's obelisks in An-Zabat, which, though only silver and sandstone, had called water from beneath the Waste for generations after their creator's demise. I could little risk the entire city to test such a method, however, not when Hissing Cat was there and able to maintain the seal, but my grandmother was stubborn. Worse, she was correct: it made more sense for them to stay here. But I would make it safe before I left.

My first thought was the book of names, rich with meaning

and portable, like the canons of witchcraft. If my mother and grandmother changed their minds, they might carry it with them and journey without me to Eastern Fortress. The destruction of the obelisks, and with them the spell they had anchored, hung too heavy in my mind, and the book of wooden slats was too fragile, too much a risk.

Instead, I stood before the three wolf gods – statues of wrought stone; durable, little weathered through centuries of neglect. I touched the scars that lined Okara's snout. They would serve, I decided, though the thought of offering protection by way of the same god who had plunged the world into chaos and horror turned my stomach. However distasteful, there was no better option, and I would not leave my mother and my grandmother – my last family in the world – vulnerable.

I prepared myself, structuring the spell in my mind before I released the shell to weave it. It needed to be anchored to the wider pattern of the world, after all, rather than the minuscule, isolated pattern around us.

With a turn of thought, I released the shell. Sensation rushed in as the smaller pattern collided with the broader world, disorienting me for a moment before I reached out, tracing the contours of the anchored seal I would leave behind and the marks in stone that would hold it fast. Though urgency prodded me, I took my time. If there were any flaw in what I would make, I would be abandoning my mother and grandmother to certain death.

<Foolish Cur,> a voice echoed in my mind, and with it a heavy, thundering wake. It was a voice I knew far too well, and my attention turned at once from weaving the seal to defending my own mind, ready to put up walls to seal myself from the pattern. I stared into the eyes of the stone wolf before me. As a child, I had felt them watching me – an illusion, I had presumed. But why, after I had tried so desperately to reach him,

would Okara speak to me only now, when I stood before his likeness in stone?

<Because there is reason for it now,> he said, answering my thoughts. I threw up barriers, a maze within my own mind, isolating his voice within one barren corner. He would hear only the words I conveyed to him.

<You should have answered me when this all began,> I said. <But then, you had no reason to. I had done what you wanted: shattered the pacts. Released you all to wage your war and crush the world and its people like so many insects underfoot.>

<It is not in my nature to apologise.> The snarling stone seemed to scoff at me.

<I only mean to establish where we stand.>

<You've no reason to trust me, but you never really did, did you?> Though the words might have been mocking, there was no such texture to Okara's presence in my mind. It was only an observation, such as one a scholar might make while considering the strange behaviour of an insect. <And I, for my part, have done only what was in my nature. We cannot choose our natures, can we, Foolish Cur? I found a weapon and I used the means I had – the means I was given: guile, wit, clever obfuscation – to turn that weapon to my ends. In my position, you would have done the same, and in the same manner.>

<You could have been honest with me.>

<I was. Whatever you think, it is true that all I did was secure my own survival and the survival of my people.>

<At the cost of how many innocents?> I seethed. My hand curled into a fist and the stump of my right wrist seized as though my missing hand might grip a sword.

<I did not break the world, Foolish Cur. You did that as much as I, to kill the emperor and free your people. That you failed to achieve your ends does not absolve you of guilt nor pile more upon my head.>

<What do you want, wolf?>

<Only to share information. I think, in some limited fashion, our interests still align. It is not my intent, after all, to see the Nayeni people scoured from the world. Far from it. My deepest, most central aim has always been your preservation. What more would you ask of your god?>

<I don't have time to listen to this. Say what you mean to say or I'll cast you from my mind.>

Something like a chuckle resonated through the weight of his voice. <Ah, I've missed your arrogance, Foolish Cur. The Skyfather is dead. Tenet lured him out. The idiot made himself vulnerable.>

I remembered the myths and legends of An-Zabat, which Atar had shared with me while we had sat on the sands beneath the moonlight, our bodies salty with sweat from dancing, her eyes bright as the stars. The Skyfather was cruel in those tales, little interested in the people of the Waste. It hardly seemed a tragedy that he had been slain.

<The gods are my enemies now,> I pointed out. <Why should I care about this death, other than to celebrate it?>

<Because the balance of power is shifting. There are few factions among us left. The Sienese gods have long since lost themselves, stripped of identity and purpose by Tenet's wily erosion of their worship. They only rage, directionless, unthinking. Tollu, Ateri, and I will bring them to heel before long, and then this will all be over.>

His words stunned me. The notion that the war between the gods might already be nearing its resolution seemed impossible.

<You are surprised,> Okara observed, gloating. <Do you think I could not have done all of this centuries ago? There have been young witches of the old sort before you, Foolish Cur. Plenty of dull swords lying about, ready to be hefted and sharpened. But the timing was never right until now.

<It was a balance, you see. The longer we let Tenet expand his empire, eroding the power of our rivals one abandoned temple at a time, the more the odds would fall in our favour when the war resumed. Waiting too long, of course, meant risking that our own power would be too diminished to act. To our excellent fortune, he put off invading Nayen until last. Only the Skyfather and the stone-faced gods of Toa Alon remained whole, and the former was a bone-headed fool while the latter had all the initiative of glaciers. Now it is only a matter of ridding the world of the shrieking, mindless husks of neglected gods and the war will finally be won.>

I put my hand on the statue's head to steady myself. <Why are you telling me all of this? Why now? Why not from the beginning?>

<None of it would have convinced you then,> Okara said. <Certainly not so well as the promise of aid liberating your people from the clutches of the empire. As for why I tell you now, I know you well, Foolish Cur. You are true to your name, and certain to do something very foolish. There is no need for you to act. Only stay in Eastern Fortress, preserve as many lives as you can, and wait for the war to end.>

My mind reeled, struggling to integrate this revelation into my understanding of the world. Of course, that assumed it was, indeed, a revelation. Okara had made me his puppet through trickery and half-truth once already. I would not be so easily used again.

Why was he telling me this? What *something very foolish* did he hope to dissuade me from doing? Two developments stood out as possible answers. First was the shell I had made. Might it threaten the gods somehow in a way that sealing magic did not? A possibility, but not one I had time to explore. Second was the strange pulse through the pattern of the world, emanating from the south – from the Pillars of the Gods, in Toa Alon, Hissing

Cat had said. Yet the pulse had frightened the emperor, who stood against the gods. Why should these ancient enemies be troubled by the same event?

Curiosity dug at me, but I had left myself, my mother, and my grandmother unprotected too long already.

<This is all very fascinating,> I told the god, <yet sadly my foolishness is boundless, as you should know, and will not be curtailed by the warnings of a traitor.>

<Come now, Foolish Cur—>

Whatever else he had meant to say vanished with the weight of his presence in my mind as I carved deep into the pattern of the world, crafting a shell with Okara's statue at its heart and anchoring it to the web of scars across that stone muzzle. Once more, the eerie silence of the smaller pattern filled the world around me.

My mother had fallen asleep, her head in my grandmother's lap. Grandmother nodded on the edge of joining her, her back against the brass door of the altar, where she had conjured a flame so many years ago and, in a small act that would echo through history, awakened my fascination with magic. She stirred as I sat beside them, her eyes fluttering open.

'I felt something,' she said.

'I made a seal,' I said. 'Well ... it doesn't matter. There's a hole in the seal, by the statues of the wolf gods. If you have any cause to use magic, you will be able to there, in a limited capacity. Just know that passing through the seal will undo any spell you happen to be weaving at the time.'

She smirked. 'I know that well enough.'

I felt my cheeks redden. 'I'm sorry about that.' Yet another wound dealt by my thoughtlessness.

She offered neither reassurance nor condemnation, and so I pressed on through the awkwardness, which needled me like a bramble. 'You'll be safe here, at least as long as you have food, and as long as no one breaks the statue of Okara. I thought to anchor the seal to something portable, so you could follow me back to Eastern Fortress if you decided—'

'Thank you,' my grandmother said. 'What you've done is more than enough.'

I nodded, swallowing a knot in my throat. 'I'll sit with you a while longer,' I said, 'but I'll have to go soon. They need me. More, everything that's happened is my fault. I have to put it right.'

She swept her gaze around the room. 'I remember when you begged me to teach you magic. Over and over again, I put you off – until, in your usual bone-headed fashion, you figured it out for yourself. Do you know why?'

'Because I wasn't ready.'

She shook her head. 'No, Foolish Cur. Because I was afraid. Because a part of me agreed with your mother, and understood why she would marry that man, why she would become Sienese, at least as well as she could. I hoped to plant the treasures of our culture in your heart, stories and memories – the Iron Dance, our gods – and then to send you off to live the life your mother wanted for you. A safer life, but carrying the seed of Nayen, in case – and it seemed a certainty, then – the rebellion failed and the last embers of resistance were stamped out. I knew if I carved the witch marks into your hand, it would shape the path of your life, and largely for the worse.'

'If you hadn't, I might have fought you at Greyfrost,' I said. 'It could have been me leading that army at Usher and Cinder's side instead of Pinion.'

'You're missing my point.'

My mother murmured. We sat quietly for a time while grandmother stroked her hair, easing her back to sleep.

'We make our choices, boy. We do what seems right to us. What makes sense. We can't know what the consequences will be. Torturing yourself because an act that seemed right at the time turned out to be a mistake is stupidity itself. You have to learn from your mistakes and move on, not dwell on them, else guilt will devour you, close you off from yourself, drive you away from the things that matter most.' She brushed a tear from her leathery cheek and smiled. 'Ask me how I know.'

My mother's eyes fluttered open. Bright Jay. A name scoured from the records of our family, its erasure a scar in her heart and, I was sure, in my grandmother's. How many nights of my childhood had resounded with their arguments? When – a question that wrenched my heart – had they last shared a moment like this, of comfort and kindness?

'My boy,' my mother murmured. She reached for me and I held her hand. Once, it had been as delicate as a songbird, permitted no labour. She had been a woman kept as a trophy, as part of my father's prestige. Now, thick callouses lined those fingers, and below them, across her palm, her old naming scar. 'You've grown so much, even since I last saw you. What was it, only a year ago? You've suffered so much. I see it in your face.' Her gaze flitted to the stump of my right wrist, then back to my face with a sorrowful smile. 'You're going again, aren't you?'

I could only nod. Any word would have shattered into a sob. She squeezed my hand. 'I understand. There is so much I would say to you. There always is, and always will be. You are my son, Wen Alder, Foolish Cur. Wherever you go, whatever you do, whatever you must endure, remember: you are my son, and you have my love.'

'And you have mine,' I managed, the words escaping me in a gasp. Tears blurred my vision as I kissed her hand, and stood, and left them there. I had done all I could. Much as I wished for my journey's end, to lay my head down and rest and worry no more, the world was still broken, and no matter Okara's reassurances, I could little trust the gods.

24

Ancient Lore

Koro Ha

The stairs wound downwards for what felt like leagues. Koro Ha's sense of time began to slip as he descended step after step, his lantern casting thick shadows, illuminating only the next dozen paces ahead and the smooth walls of uncarved stone.

No hammer and chisel nor tunneller's pickaxe had shaped this space. The deeper it led, the more Koro Ha's heart thundered, his pulse racing in the silence. Uon Elia had spoken of ancient lore buried beneath the city, in the very roots of the Pillars of the Gods. Had he traversed these impossible stairs, hidden by magical means Koro Ha could hardly begin to understand? He hoped so. It made him feel less alone, less like an ant wandering the abandoned halls of a palace.

From time to time, he paused to sit on the steps and rest his weary legs. The downward-spiralling stair was far less treacherous than the slick, glassy rock of the Black Maw, but he was no less an ageing man and poorly fit for such exertion. Eventually he would have to turn back – the upward climb would require far more effort than the downward, after all – yet something pulled him on, a pull like dowsing magic, though he cast no spell.

The stairs levelled out and became a tunnel, its walls so high that the light of his lantern only brushed the arched ceiling. Here, at least, there were decorations, reaching from floor to ceiling. A repeating pattern of recursive loops that wound in and out of one another, similar to Toa Aloni writing but suggesting no meaning that Koro Ha could discern. The repeating nature of the inscrutable pattern and the deep darkness of the tunnel made him feel as though his steps carried him nowhere at all, as though he traversed the same stretch of hallway again and again – a panic-inducing thought that nearly chased him back to the stairwell, back to the temple. He felt an absurd but nonetheless terrifying fear that he might become lost in the endless tunnel. Dozens of people had observed the bizarre, wondrous spectacle of the stairwell's opening. Surely by now someone had gathered a party and followed after him? It would be prudent to turn back, to meet them, and to face this alien, subterranean world together, wouldn't it?

His thoughts cut off as the tunnel at last came to an end. The light of his lantern revealed what at first seemed to be a convex wall, like the surface of a stone egg, lined with that same looping pattern. Only a hair-thin division revealed it as a doorway, albeit one without any latch or handle.

The means to open it, then, would be magical, like the stairwell. Yet now he had no glass sphere to serve as a key, nor any idea where another like it might be found. Feeling childish, he set down his lantern and tried to slide his fingernails into the hair-thin crack, as though he might, with the strength of his calligrapher's hands, pry it open. He took a step back, rubbing his abused fingertips, and muttered, 'They couldn't just put a handle on the thing, could they? Had to make it a puzzle.'

He sat against the wall, the raised pattern pressing uncomfortably against his spine. Perhaps Uon Elia could have deduced the means to open the door, but Koro Ha found himself once more without the Toa Aloni frame of reference that might have yielded an answer. Dejected, he resigned himself to resting until the ache in his hips and his old bones subsided, then returned to the stairwell. There were stone-carvers who might be able to deduce something of the pattern on the walls, or of the manufacture of the door itself.

His lantern flame began to gutter for want of oil, and his legs began to shake with the effort of the upwards climb. An ache settled into his lungs and throat, and dizzying pain pulsed behind his eyes for want of water. Every dozen steps, he sat and waited for the pain to subside. A long climb, but one he could manage, he tried to reassure himself, though he recognised this thought for what it was: a paltry effort to stave off looming panic. What a fool he was, to venture into the unknown without water, without any supplies to speak of beyond a half-empty lantern.

At last, the flame of his lantern died and the darkness closed in, swallowing everything but the sound of his breath, the firmness of the stone. He waited, hoping his eyes would adjust, but no sliver of light could ever pierce the layers of stone and earth that surrounded him. He would have to climb the hundreds of steps back to the tunnels above on his hands and knees if he hoped to survive.

He braced himself for miserable hours, for the terror he could already feel burning in the base of his skull, just as a feather of lantern light fell from the steps above him.

'There he is!' someone shouted.

Footsteps and jangling harness heralded the arrival of a half-dozen burly men and women, led by Goa Eln, all wearing heavy packs laden with tools, supplies, and weapons.

'Gods, tutor, do you have any sense of self-preservation at all?' Goa Eln said, her voice ringing with laughter and relief. 'Imagine opening an ancient magical passageway leading who the hell knows where and just *heading off to explore it on your own!*'

The others laughed nervously, shaking their heads. One of them handed him a water skin and he shivered at the touch of moisture on his tongue. Almost at once, the aching in his muscles seemed to ease. He handed back the water skin, which hung empty in his hand.

Goa Eln stared, all her mirth evaporated. 'You are lucky as *shit* that we came looking for you.'

'I've never been much of a spelunker,' Koro Ha muttered, extending a hand. Goa Eln helped him to his feet. 'Though I did manage to find something of interest.'

Two of Goa Eln's party, a man and a woman with a variety of differently shaped chisels hanging from their belts, huddled together, examining the egg-shaped door, tapping it with their hammers and prying at the thin line that marked its opening. Despite himself, Koro Ha thought of Yan Hra, his brother-in-law, which stirred up the not-quite-settled pain of his family's disappearance. The woman of the pair managed to seat a thin chisel between the two halves of the door, but a dozen ringing hammer blows accomplished little – only a few flecks of stone knocked free and a pulsing pain between Koro Ha's ears.

'If it is a door, I've no bloody idea how it opens,' the woman said eventually. 'Not just in terms of how *we're* supposed to open it but, on a mechanical level, how it even *would* open. Do you see runners? Any evidence of hinges? The thing's seated in the wall like a gem in a socket, to my eye.'

'Was there any evidence of a staircase in the floor of that temple?' Goa Eln planted her hands on her hips, as though a defiant stance might convince the door to open. 'Any thoughts, tutor? How'd you conjure up this tunnel, anyway? The folks who came running – screaming, really – after they saw what you did weren't exactly coherent in their explanations. Something about a glowing rock and a face in the ceiling?'

Koro Ha did his best to explain the process of his discovery, beginning with the impulsive decision to use dowsing magic on the sphere. While she listened, Goa Eln tapped her chin. When the account reached its end, she shot him an impish grin.

'When I was a little girl, my grandfather used to tell me this story,' she said, 'always out of earshot of my parents, and usually late at night. The myth, so he claimed, of Sor Cala's founding. There were three important characters.' She counted them off, raising a finger for each. 'A stone-cutter, a healer, and a gardener.'

'I know the story,' Koro Ha said, somewhat astonished. He had thought the myth, which Uon Elia had shared with their students, otherwise lost to Toa Alon. 'Assuming that dowsing correlates to stone-cutting . . .'

His voice trailed off. He placed a hand on the door – a convex surface entwined in looping forms. An egg, he had thought at first, but just as easily a taproot bulb, or the bud of a flower in early spring.

For the second time, he put magic to what seemed far from its intended use. Yet, like healing, cultivation could be directed outwards, into another body, and that body might be formed of stone as easily as vegetation. Only that stone ought not grow, no matter how it was stimulated and encouraged by a pulse of magic. The invigorating wake coursed through him like a surge of adrenaline, then out through his hand and into the unliving stone.

His magic was answered by a sudden, savage thirst, desperate as desert sand at the touch of water, drinking in the power, pulling it from him. The wake redoubled, careering through his body till he feared his heart and lungs would burst. Still the stone door seized upon his magic, drawing in more and more, until at last it began to move.

There should have been a creak of grinding stone, a cascade of dust tumbling from ancient mechanisms in desperate need of maintenance.

First, the looping forms began to turn, spiralling into themselves, shrinking until the convex surface stood bare. Then the structure began to move, splitting down the hairline crack, each half rotating into the wall of the tunnel, utterly silent save for a gentle sigh like an indrawn breath as the door at last opened. Only memory and a gap in the looping decoration on the walls testified to the door ever having existed.

'Bloody eerie,' Goa Eln observed, then stepped through the gap. 'We might as well see what it was hiding, eh?'

Koro Ha's knees buckled. He collapsed against the wall, each breath like a wind scouring his lungs. He had never known exhaustion so profound, not even during the deepest rigours of his preparation for the imperial examinations. Every muscle felt like the pulp left behind after fruit has been pressed for its juices.

Ran Sa caught him before he fell to the floor. 'Oy! Are you all right, stonespeaker? Gods, he's pale as a mole rat, and his eyes are wheeling. Get him some water!'

Absently, he felt the press of metal against his lips and the biting cold of water against his teeth. He had a vague awareness of people moving around him, which was odd. Where was he? Where was his pupil? The boy had run off again, likely distracted by a flitting bird. Gods, he was too old for all of this exertion. He should have never agreed to this assignment. No student had ever taken so much out of him, not even Wen Alder. This boy Bo Spring-Happiness was just a lost cause, as far as he was concerned.

'Hey, tutor, focus on me, eh?'

Faces swam above him. For a moment he picked out Goa Eln's, her usual grin broken into a jagged frown, and returned, hazily, to the present moment. Why was she so upset? Had something happened?

'What's wrong with him?'

'Bleed me if I know. None of us knows a damn thing about all this magic shit, do we?'

'We should carry him back up. Get him to a proper doctor.'

'Can't he heal himself?'

'Not with his eyes rolling in his head and his arms all jelly like they are, can he? Idiot.'

It's all right, he tried to say. *I just need another little nap. Just a few minutes of sleep. Enough to recover.* But some little voice, screaming at the back of his skull, told him otherwise. Told him that this had been a step too far, that an old body could endure only so much, even with the support of magic. Uon Elia might have lived three hundred years, but he'd carried that power from his youth, and Koro Ha had been an old man when he'd shouldered the burden. This was a task for a younger man, for a proper successor to the stonespeakers, not the cast-off dregs chosen only out of pure necessity.

<Be easy, child.> Another voice. Not his own. Rumbling in his bones, drowning out the fear, the pain, the exhaustion, the concerned chattering of Goa Eln and the others – who, he realised suddenly, no longer searched his face but looked down the tunnel, their mouths open and eyes wide as coins. <That portal was never meant to be opened by a single soul. Has so much been forgotten?>

The rumbling grew louder. It sounded not only within his mind, he realised, but echoed through the tunnel around him. Though it felt like a ball of iron, and his neck as flimsy as a strand of seaweed, he managed to lift his head and follow Goa Eln's gaze.

Had he enough energy for his heart to seize and give out, it would have. Instead, he felt only a distant bafflement. Then again, what was one more impossibility in a day so full of them?

A myth come to life stood over him, its stone face as placid as that which had peered down from the temple ceiling, set in a head as jagged and sharp as a mountain peak. Slow, gentle arms reached out and enfolded him, lifting him from the floor. An easy warmth flowed from them and into him, rolling in and out like the tides. With each pulse his mind began to clear and the weight, like wet sand, that filled his limbs began to fade.

<You have no cause for fear,> the stone-faced god said. Its mouth was unmoving, yet it turned its eyes on Goa Eln and the others. Somehow – he could never begin to explain how – Koro Ha knew that they too heard its strange, soundless voice. <We are your servants, and we have served dutifully. In truth, we had begun to wonder that you never came.> Its gaze turned upwards, as though to pierce through layers of stone and earth to seek the sky. <I see, now, what has changed.>

Gently, it set Koro Ha on his feet. All his exhaustion, both the mundane and the magical, had been soothed away.

<Come,> the god said, and turned back to the open doorway, its footsteps ringing in the stunned silence. <There is much, we fear, to explain, and much to do if your kind are to be saved.>

It paused after a dozen paces and turned back towards them, like a patient hound leading its master onwards. Muttering a curse, Goa Eln walked after the stone-faced god, followed by the rest of her party.

'Spelunking, my ass,' she whispered as she passed Koro Ha. 'Did you know we would find this here?'

He could only shake his head. Since he and Uon Elia had fled Toa Alon for the Black Maw – perhaps earlier, he now realised; perhaps as long ago as his first meeting with Orna Sin, or Wen Alder mounting the dais to receive the imperial tetragram – his life had been like a fisherman's skiff on the open sea, tossed in the dark by wind and waves lashing out from deep below and beyond his comprehension. In that light, it ought not surprise him that those waves would carry him into the presence of ancient gods long thought silent, if not dead. Yet something very like fear trembled within him – terror, and a dizzying awe.

<You will want light, of course,> the god's voice thundered silently. A warm glow filled the tunnel, soon as bright as dawn, seeming to emanate from between the walls themselves. After a moment, Koro Ha realised that, in fact, a layer of yellow moss that glowed with an inner light had burst suddenly to life in the hollows between the twining decorations.

'Well, burn me to a crisp,' Goa Eln murmured as the tunnel opened up, leading out onto a ledge overlooking a vast, soaring chamber. The scale of it struck Koro Ha's mind blank as a fresh sheet of paper. The glowing moss clung to every stone surface, evidenced only by the constancy of its yellow light. A mist, gathering into tufts of cloud, obscured the ceiling of the chamber, swirling around stalactites, giving the impression of curving paths on the faces of inverted mountains. Water dripped from their mist-wreathed tips into deep pools in the rock floor, one of which churned with the slow current of an unseen stream. Below, stalagmites had been shaped and carved into dozens of smooth-walled structures. Windows showed through to their hollowed interiors. Each could house dozens of people, if not more. And in the spaces between them lay dark, fertile soil ready for planting.

<It is to your liking, stonespeaker?> the god said, studying Koro Ha. He thought he felt an echo of anxiety in the words, as though anyone could bear witness to such a marvel and be anything but impressed.

'Very much so,' Koro Ha breathed, barely able to summon his voice for sheer awe. Safe housing for hundreds, if not thousands. More than enough clean water. Plentiful land for farms and gardens, though of course want of sun would mean only certain crops would grow, like the gourds, mushrooms, and beans Uon Elia and the other stonespeakers had cultivated in the ruins of the old city. 'But what is it? Why is it here?'

The stone-faced god tilted its head. <This was our purpose.> Its words carried a hint of confusion. <Was this not known to you, stonespeaker?>

'No. Far from it.'

The god paused before speaking again. This time, Koro Ha felt its worry and confusion clearly. <You must forgive us. Until the calamitous wakes of war began to churn the pattern of the world, we did not think anything was wrong. Even so, we could have done nothing. The seal on the portal to this place could be opened only by mortal power.>

While it spoke, Goa Eln and the stone-carvers had fanned out across the ledge, gaping at the scene that sprawled before them. Now, Goa Eln turned back towards the stone-faced god.

'You've been trapped down here?' Goa Eln said. 'For how long?'

<Lifetimes upon lifetimes, child,> the god answered. <Though *trapped* is not the word. We chose to lock ourselves away. After the last war, when the pacts were made, we sought to preserve our original purpose. We were never warriors, you understand. Our makers were builders, cultivators, healers. Our ways mirror theirs, as all gods are but manifestations of the dreams of their creators. Here we have safeguarded the means for your survival, though I fear it may not be enough.>

'Looks like plenty to me,' one of the stone-carvers muttered. She peered through the space between her extended thumb and forefinger. 'By quick reckoning, nearly the size of Sor Cala!'

<Indeed,> the god said. <This place was built in the aftermath of war, as a safeguard against its return. Yet there is more. There is a power hidden here, should the need for it arise.>

It gestured with one slender, stone arm towards the heart of the chamber. At the centre of the strange, welcoming landscape stood a stalagmite larger than the rest.

<A tool, forged by one who worked magic without a wake before he left and sealed this place. A weapon that only one of his kind might use.>

25
Right and Wrong

Pinion

Following Foolish Cur's sudden departure, the council disbanded, each member returning to their duties. Pinion, who had no task of his own after the unravelling of negotiations with the Sienese, felt strange trailing behind Clear-River, as though he were a lonely child desperate for a friend – which was to say nothing of his awkwardness whenever memories of their tense encounter at Burrow arose like sulphurous bubbles in a mountain spring.

Left alone and unoccupied, Pinion's mind returned again to memories of brutality. Images of pain and anguish that ever drew his thoughts like iron to a lodestone. Questions that had smouldered in him like coals since Setting Sun Fortress burned brightly anew, stoked by the strange trajectory his life had taken in the last few days.

Burning Dog's death, the bladed fist of wind he had inadvertently conjured, the spray of blood and crack of her bones, ought not trouble him. The throbbing darkness where his right eye should have been testified to that truth. Yet Wen Alder had tried to bridge the hatred between them, enduring agony to give her as much of the vengeance she craved as he could – an effort wasted when Pinion killed her. A strange guilt needled him, as Setting Sun Fortress needled him, and drove him back to his father's library.

Several of the writing desks in the library were missing – appropriated for kindling or building material, he supposed – but the stands and shelves had been left alone, and the scrolls in their wooden cases and the books in their bindings of cloth or silk remained. He and Clear-River had spent the day before their ill-fated negotiation with Hand Jadestone, Master Fan, and Marshal Huo combing these tomes for any argument or aphorism that might make the Sienese pliable. Now Pinion returned, seeking his own far less pragmatic, far more vital answers.

Pinion had always been drawn more to poetry than to scholarship. A clever verse that rang with meaning, as the rich tone of a bronze bell demanded a pause to linger and attend, might offer a pleasant tingling down the spine and a new, heightened perception of the world's beauty. Reading volumes of dry, dense commentary on the sages and the classics – seemingly composed for impenetrability, like puzzle boxes made of words – had only ever been an obligation. In his perusal he lingered over a few well-loved poems, like old friends offering some new insight evoked by the recent twisting and turning of his life. Yet his answers would not be found in a clever turn of verse but in the volumes with titles such as *The Third Discussion on the Classic of Upright Belief* or *Reconsideration of Streams and Valleys: A Commentary on the Colonial Peasantry.*

For a thousand years, theories of justice outlined in the classics and clarified by these commentaries had shaped the moral feelings of millions of souls. Ideas that had driven sons to self-hatred whenever they doubted the wisdom of their fathers. Ideas that had strengthened the arms and stomachs of men who not only swallowed their bile as they did their bloody work but felt a satisfaction in service as their blades carved apart the innocent. Ideas that had allowed the empire to wreak horror upon the world and congratulate itself for so doing.

It was a nightmare that Pinion refused to accept – not without struggling to make some sense of it, at least. There must have been a point of deviation, some trend in the commentaries away from the original intent of the classics and towards some new orthodoxy, contorting truth and wisdom into a weapon and a balm to salve the souls of the usefully wicked. If he could find it, if he could write a commentary of his own – a commentary on the commentaries, tracing their history from good roots to twisted, rotten fruit – he might …

He wanted to laugh. He had nearly thought the words *redeem the empire*. But no, that was impossible. Yet he had to believe that these ideas, these structures, had not been built entirely to serve the emperor's ambition.

Pinion selected a volume from a shelf cataloguing the earliest treatises: *The Ranks of the Bureaucracy: Definitions of Hierarchy According to the Foundational Familial Dichotomies.* A dry, convoluted, bizarre tome, if memory served, yet one central to an applied understanding of imperial doctrine. He set the book on top of the shelf, where it fell open to a page marked with a single peacock feather, dulled by dust and age.

With trembling fingers he touched the feather, wondering at its origin. The page held part of a discourse examining the relationship between a governor and the Hands of his province as analogous to that of a father to his sons. Had his own father marked this page? And if so, why? What doubts or questions had led him to re-examine his role as governor? Or, if Pinion dared to hope, his role as a father?

The library door creaked open. Grateful for a distraction, Pinion looked up. Doctor Sho stood over a rack of scrolls, sifting through their titles, seemingly unaware of Pinion's presence in the room. Pinion cleared his throat and the old doctor started, then smiled thinly at him, pausing only for a moment before returning to his search.

'The medical texts are on that shelf, by the door,' Pinion said.

The doctor answered with a pointed sniff. 'I've little use for them.'

'What are you looking for?' Pinion asked, feeling slightly abashed. Of course the old man would be well learned, and likely familiar with this library anyway. The Nayeni had held the estate for some weeks now. 'This used to be my father's, and I spent quite a bit of time here in my youth.'

'Too late.' The doctor plucked a scroll case from a rack of classical poetry, ran his finger down the inlaid logograms of its title, and tucked it under his arm. 'What are *you* looking for, boy? Not worried someone will find you here and think it a bit odd that a son of Sienese nobility, despite ostensibly joining the rebel cause, spends his days reading through the esoterica of doctrine?'

Pinion cringed at that. It was not something he had considered, and a new guilt bubbled up at the thought. Here he was, reading dusty tomes to try to salve his angst, while everyone he hoped to count as a friend struggled to save lives. Even if he found the point where Sienese doctrine had gone awry, how would that avert the next disaster? How would it chase the gods back into their hiding places? Recent experience told him there was little chance it would even convince the Sienese leadership of their wrongheadedness.

'And reading drivel at that,' the doctor muttered under his breath, peering down his nose at the book in Pinion's hands. 'What is this? Nostalgia for your days as a student?'

It felt absurd to explain himself to the doctor, yet no less absurd to invent an excuse.

'Something more foolish than that, I fear. I thought … Well, the empire is cruel and unjust – clearly – but there must have been something pure there once. I was searching for … I don't know, something to show that the sages themselves, at least, were genuine in their attempt to describe right and wrong. That those who earnestly believe in these ideas were drawn by something of real value rather than some trick.' He paused, clearing the lump in his throat and smiling apologetically at the doctor. 'It must be more than the flickering, ever-shifting masks of a face-changer. Mustn't it?'

Doctor Sho stared up at him, his eyes filling with anger.

'I'm sorry,' Pinion said. 'You don't want to hear this. You are Sienese, but clearly you decided some time ago that the Nayeni cause was just. I ought not burden you with my confusion, which I am sure will work itself out in time.'

'Switching sides in a conflict this deep can be difficult,' the doctor said eventually. 'A bit like breaking a badly healed bone to reset it properly.'

'Yes,' Pinion smiled again, glad that his words seemed to have diffused the doctor's anger. 'I suppose I'll have to limp about for a while until the bone knits true. Morally speaking.'

The doctor harrumphed and turned to leave yet hesitated at the doorway, his fingers drumming on the scroll case he had taken from the rack. The awkwardness of the moment broke when footsteps sounded in the hallway outside, heralding the arrival of a messenger bearing word that Foolish Cur had returned and the council would resume upon the hour.

The news surprised Pinion, given that the council had broken up only a few hours earlier. He had little notion of where the Wen family estate was, but he had imagined it at least a day's journey there and back, even on an eagle hawk's wings. But of course beyond Hissing Cat's seal, time and distance flouted expectations. At least in this case it had been to the rebellion's advantage.

Pinion thanked the messenger and returned the volume he had been reading to its place on the shelf, musing as he did so at Alder – no, Foolish Cur; he had to be careful not to slip into old patterns of thought, even about as simple a thing as a name – at Foolish Cur's strange departure and sudden return. A brief errand on behalf of his grandmother, nonetheless treated with the utmost urgency and importance. Was that due to a lingering vestige of Sienese propriety, or a parallel virtue of Nayeni culture pointing backwards to some first doctrine, crafted in the caves and forests before language, before tradition, before volumes of commentary? The same moral truth, perhaps, that had led Foolish Cur to accept Burning Dog's vengeance, up to the very edge of his own death?

The memory of that truth still burned in Pinion's heart. It had flared so bright, in so much grief and rage, at Setting Sun Fortress. With a fragment of Foolish Cur's strength, of his willingness to suffer for what was right, might Pinion have found it within himself to stand against the empire's brutality?

'They were genuine,' the doctor said.

Pinion blinked at him, embarrassed at having drifted off into the murky waters of his thoughts yet again. 'I'm sorry, I should be going,' he said, yet the doctor's stare fixed him in place.

'Let that be a crutch while you hobble about on that broken moral leg,' Doctor Sho said, his voice a strained rasp, though his eyes were as hard as ever. 'The sages were genuinely trying. And they tortured themselves in the effort to get it right.' He left Pinion in the doorway to his father's library, puzzled by words with obvious meaning yet which seemed to carry hidden weight.

Pinion lingered a moment more, then tucked the peacock feather into his sleeve. He toyed with its downy end and wondered at the doctor's conviction, and at his apparent pain, while he crossed the garden towards Oriole's hill, the scarred tree, and the silhouette of Hissing Cat – a woman out of those ancient days before humanity had cloaked the lamp of moral feeling in their hunger for a clearer, brighter light.

'It's not that I don't believe you,' Hissing Cat was saying as Pinion reached the base of the tree, where Foolish Cur had already begun to address the rest of the reconvened council. 'I'm just having a bloody hard time wrapping my head around how it works.'

'You draw the outer edge first, and then the inner, and hold the space between them in your mind,' Foolish Cur said. 'The seal is ultimately shaped like a ring, not a sphere, so you can still wield magic – at least of the old sort – within the inner area.'

'What about pact magic?' the Raven pressed, rubbing a thumb down the scars on his right hand.

Foolish Cur nodded, though the others looked to Hissing Cat. She shrugged and the ravens' skulls in her hair jangled, seeming like a dead flock all shaking their heads. 'I've never tried anything like this, so I couldn't say. In theory, the pacts are just a narrowing of what the old magic could do.'

'But not imperial sorcery,' Clear-River pointed out, cutting to the point.

'No,' Foolish Cur confirmed. 'The emperor's transmission can no more penetrate the sealed ring than the unwoven can.'

Clear-River fixed Foolish Cur with a long, steady stare. 'If we do this, we will have our full complement of witches, and the Sienese will have only their handful of canons of witchcraft.'

'If we strike fast, we could cut them down before they can guess what happened,' the Raven said, a smile creasing the corners of his mouth.

'If they ever could,' Hissing Cat observed with a grunt.

Pinion swallowed against a thickness in his throat. At least the others wore distaste – Clear-River a bitter twisting of his mouth, Running Doe a bracing before plunging back into cold waters, Foolish Cur a sorrowful cast to his eyes. They were all Nayeni, Foolish Cur's mingled blood and Clear-River's training notwithstanding, and he could not fault them for seizing this opportunity to finally win freedom for their island home.

More, he was Sienese, and had joined the cause of Nayen only days ago. As Huo had judged his every word as the lies of a traitor, Foolish Cur and the others might perceive his concerns as sentimentality for his own blood and culture. They might forgive him, but they would not heed him, he was sure.

Nevertheless.

'We sued for peace less than a day ago,' Pinion pointed out, surprised that his voice held no hint of a quaver. 'Can we attack them now, in good conscience, without giving them a chance to consider our terms?'

'Terms they rejected outright, as I understand,' the Raven said. 'I'm not so bloodthirsty as Burning Dog. If they wanted peace, I'd give it to them, but our people will starve without their stores, and they don't seem inclined to make a deal. Every soul in the rebellion would kill a Sienese to save a Nayeni, and that's a fact.'

Running Doe put her hands to her hips, where swords would once have hung, as though ready to challenge him to a duel. 'I say Pinion is right. If there is a chance they'll come around, we shouldn't butcher them. I've seen enough open throats.'

'Is there such a chance, Clear-River?' Foolish Cur asked. A strange satisfaction lit his eyes, as though some deep, troubling question had at last been answered.

'Master Fan, the merchants' representative, might come around,' Clear-River answered. 'I don't think Hand Jadestone or this fool Marshal Huo ever will.'

'Not even if they understood, completely, that they stood no fighting chance?' Foolish Cur asked. 'Do you think they would rather die for the emperor than live, shamed and defeated?'

This last question felt aimed at Pinion, yet he could summon no answer.

'What was it Su White-Knife was fond of saying, in the romances?' Clear-River mused. 'Something like, "A rat will run until the end of the alley, where, if it finds no way of escape, it will bite and claw to the bitter end."'

'We're offering a way of escape,' the Raven snarled. 'They're the dumb bastards who refuse to take it.'

'We grew up among them, as part of them,' Foolish Cur said, taking in Clear-River and Pinion with a gesture. 'Though none of us, I think, ever felt doctrine so deep in our bones as this marshal and Hand Jadestone do. To them, disobeying a command of the emperor will be a worse crime than killing an infant. Setting Sun Fortress proved that, didn't it? Tell me, Raven, would you slaughter an infant to save your own life?'

The Raven scowled. 'What, then? This stalemate can't last much longer. Either they cooperate or it comes to fighting, whether we attack now or when our people start to starve.'

Foolish Cur tilted his head back, staring upwards as though the answer might be written in the white calligraphy of the clouds. 'There isn't enough time,' he said at last, still gazing at the sky. 'The emperor is moving. I should have gone to Toa Alon already.'

Pinion lowered his head. Again, he wished that the world did not so often pose puzzles whose every answer promised terrible pain. Was this feeling, he wondered, the root of all the convolutions of imperial doctrine? Was it nothing more than centuries of men trying to reason away their guilt when faced with no acceptable path?

'This will not be another Setting Sun Fortress, Pinion,' Foolish Cur said, smiling. 'I promise.'

A promise which, despite his own inability to imagine a

way through this maze that did not end in either starvation or bloodshed, Pinion found that he believed.

26
Battle's End

Pinion

Messengers were sent to arrange a parlay at dawn in a last attempt, so Clear-River explained in his fine calligraphy, to resolve their differences and avoid unnecessary bloodshed.

Under cover of night, moving in clusters of threes and fours, avoiding the rare Sienese patrol and hiding their battle harness beneath threadbare cloaks, the bulk of the Nayeni army occupied the buildings nearest the territory claimed by Hand Jadestone. Pinion stood at the battlements of his father's estate and watched one such party vanish into the night-time dark.

There would be bloodshed. The Nayeni wanted it. *Needed* it. The outpouring at the city's fall, interrupted by the gods' arrival in the world, had not slaked a thirst built up by decades of suffering. He could only hope that Foolish Cur's plan would prevent a surging flood.

He ought to have slept, yet, as on the night before his imperial examinations, he found that when he set his head down, it only filled with flitting thoughts. And so he paced the halls and walked the battlements, tracing familiar paths rendered strange by the presence of the Nayeni, by their tents and bivouacs in the field where he had learned to ride, their watch platform built atop his mother's favourite pavilion, and the constant murmur of their language, still strange to his ear even though he had grown up in a city where it was more commonly spoken than his own tongue.

This was their city. Their palace, too. Soon, it would all be theirs – the whole of the island – not only by right but in truth. He had been raised to find the regression of civilisation back into barbarism horrifying, yet despite the part of him that nursed such feelings as it skulked in nostalgic, childhood memories, cloaked in little doubts and fears he could no more expel from his mind than the shreds of love and grief he still felt for his father, he found the notion a comfort. The world might be crumbling toward its end, but the Nayeni would be free of the empire and all its cruelty in these last days.

If only that freedom could be won by a less bloodstained path.

The chill of night began to fade as Pinion retraced his long, circuitous route through the estate for a third time, following the walkway atop the southernmost stretch of wall. Dawn splashed blue and orange across the wispy clouds like a wash of watercolour paint, a scene that drew his eye until his gaze fixed on the strange, still-churning mass of black smoke that hovered over the harbour. It had held there since the gods' emergence, though Pinion had noticed it less and less in recent days, just as one comes to ignore, after long exposure, a familiar stain on a stretch of wallpaper.

'There you are,' Running Doe called up from the courtyard behind him, her voice sharp in the crisp air of early morning. She wore her battle harness, though instead of swords she carried only her canon of witchcraft. 'It's past time to muster. Clear-River is waiting by the palace gates.' She looked him up and down, frowning. 'I don't know much about Sienese fashion or propriety or whatever, but I get the sense a rumpled, slept-in robe isn't the right gear for this meeting.'

'Unless my intent is to offend Hand Jadestone into apoplexy,' Pinion mused, hearing his distraction in his own voice. Now that he had noticed the black cloud again, its presence behind him needled the back of his neck like the gaze of a predator. 'I'm sorry. I was lost in thought.'

She nodded solemnly. 'It won't be like a normal battle, will it?'

'No. Not only that, though.' He gave in, turning towards the horizon. The sphere still hung there, unmoving after all this time, like the egg of some terrible creature out of ancient myth suspended by a magic beyond his knowledge.

'Whatever's got you transfixed, it'll still be there when this is through,' she said. 'If you were one of my soldiers back in the day, I'd have yelled at you to get moving by now. I can't promise I won't, either.'

'Running Doe,' he said, lifting a finger. 'What do you see over there? Just above the harbour?'

'Can't see it very well from down here, can I? And I'm not about to jog all the way up there just to answer a strange question when we're supposed to be on our way—'

'Like a cloud,' he said, his voice quavering. 'A dark cloud in the shape of the moon. It's been there since the fall of the city.'

'I don't …' She paused, as though aware that her answer might shatter him like glass. 'I try not to look at it, Pinion. I asked Hissing Cat. She said it's part of the wakes of the gods' war. Like the way time and distance are all twisted up. Our minds don't know how to make sense of the damage dealt to the pattern.' She grimaced up at him. 'I'm sorry. I don't really understand it myself.'

'It's all right,' Pinion said. There was comfort in the fact that the black cloud represented something *true* about the world, however terrible, and not some brokenness in his mind. Dozens of questions unfurled from her explanation, like a loose thread pulled that soon undoes the warp and weft of a garment.

Questions he locked away. There would be time for them later, and to pose them to those who might offer answers, when that day's terrible work was done.

Two hundred Nayeni soldiers approached the Sienese barricade openly, arranged in formation behind Foolish Cur and his party. Hand Jadestone stood at the head of his own forces – a full legion strong, comprising the vast majority of Sienese soldiers left in the city, if Pinion had to guess – flanked by Master Fan and Marshal Huo. The skittish merchant wore a heavy frown while Huo's eyes shone brightly, almost gleefully, his expression a stark contrast to that of the Raven, who stood frowning between Pinion and Running Doe, his fingers drumming on the hilts of his swords.

Pinion fought the urge to peer through the windows of the buildings around them, many of them two or even three storeys high, looming over the open street like guard towers.

'A show of force, this time?' Hand Jadestone called across the plaza, his gaze fixed on Clear-River. 'We are not intimidated. We have the might of the empire behind us.'

'Do you?' Foolish Cur answered.

Jadestone cocked his head. Slowly, as he studied Foolish Cur's face, realisation struck. 'I had wondered at your absence,' he said in formal Sienese. 'The Severed Hand. A traitor twice over. The cause, as I am led to understand, of a great deal of this island's suffering.'

'We are offering you one more chance to surrender,' Foolish Cur said, brushing aside the barbs in Jadestone's words. 'If you refuse, we will fall upon you and take what is ours by right.'

'Yes, I had heard that you claim to be one of them.' Hand Jadestone twisted his mouth like a disappointed tutor. 'The trailblazer, I suppose, of the misguided thinking that has led young Pinion so far astray. You threaten us, yet the little army behind you is a bare fifth of the legion I bring to bear.'

'Numbers are not everything,' Foolish Cur answered.

'Ah, will there now be some nonsense about the fire in rebel hearts that makes each of your untrained thugs worth a dozen imperial legionnaires? Or no. You refer to your notorious prowess with magic, do you not? Well …' He gestured wide to the walls of the city. 'There is no magic in Eastern Fortress.' With a smile, his hand darted up one sleeve, retrieving a strip of pale bone. 'Save for that granted by these strange devices. Weapons you created, I am given to understand. Fortunately, half a dozen or so fell into our hands during the fighting.'

At such a distance, the pact marks were indistinguishable from the natural cracks of the bone, but the sight of that weapon in Sienese hands made Foolish Cur's posture stiffen and his eyes narrow in outrage.

Pinion's heart thundered behind his ribs. Foolish Cur had promised them a chance. One last negotiation. He had promised that this would not be another Setting Sun Fortress. Yet in that moment, the heat of his anger seemed fierce enough to burn away good sense.

'So, as you see, severed Hand,' Jadestone said, 'you have no advantage here.'

As the last word fell from his mouth, a wake as heavy and thunderous as the emperor's presence pulsed through the world. Behind it, an awareness of all things, of life and death, of light and dark, heat and cold, all moving from one body to another, shifting and dancing in a timeless, eternal exchange overwhelmed Pinion as sudden torchlight blinds the eyes on a cloud-darkened night. He blinked against the onrush, resisted the urge to cover his ears, shivered through the flurry of needlings and cramps that surged up and down the lines of his limbs.

Jadestone retreated a single tremulous step as the Raven and a cadre of six Nayeni witches showed empty hands and conjured fire.

'What is this?' Jadestone demanded, his voice a quivering shriek. Pinion could almost see his phantom limb reaching blindly into the pattern and finding it empty of the emperor's canon.

'Our advantage,' Clear-River said, badly suppressing a smirk. 'You were warned, Hand Jadestone, that you would lose our protection if you refused to cooperate. And you have lost it. Though we are not so cruel as to expose the common folk under your rule to the dangers beyond the seal.'

Jadestone stared at him, uncomprehending.

'Throw down your arms,' Foolish Cur demanded, weariness weighing his voice. 'Return the canons of witchcraft you have stolen. Agree to share resources and relinquish rule of this city and this island to its people.'

'To its people?' Master Fan brushed at the front of his robe, clearly unsettled by Jadestone's reaction. 'I am given to understand the matter of leadership led to division among your people. Who will rule?'

Foolish Cur grimaced. The question had yet to be decided. Those who had claimed the Sun Throne lay dead. Hissing Cat had assumed leadership of Harrow Fox's forces, though seemingly due only to the deference she naturally demanded. Pinion looked to the Raven, but if he aspired to Frothing Wolf and Burning Dog's claim, it did not show behind his furious excitement.

It would be Foolish Cur, Pinion knew. No one else could rival his authority or his provenance as Harrow Fox's nephew. Then again, he little understood Nayeni culture, let alone its seemingly arbitrary rules of succession.

'For now, to our military leadership,' Clear-River said. 'There will be a king soon enough. This crisis has left little time for the pageantry of a coronation.'

Master Fan licked his lips and nodded. 'I say we agree, Jadestone. We can't hope to—'

In a single motion, smooth and empty of hesitation, Huo drew his sword and slashed the merchant's throat. Master Fan's blood drowned whatever else he meant to say. A curtain of red flowed between his fingers as he grasped the wound and collapsed.

Jadestone, rebounding from one shock into another, could only gawp at his marshal in disbelief.

'To surrender to barbarians is treason,' Huo snarled. His gaze fixed on Pinion. In his eyes, Pinion saw the countless times on the long march from Burrow to Eastern Fortress when the line of tension between them had nearly snapped – a line drawn taut by his nearly commanding Huo to behead Burrow's garrison commander for refusing an order. Though Huo had baulked at the order, he had stood ready to follow it. 'By imperial doctrine, the penalty for treason is death.'

Huo turned to his legion and waved the bloodstained sword. A roar went up, a thousand voices thundering with pent-up fear, with the terror of the world's unravelling. Voices that resounded with a need to strike out, as though by unleashing violence they might hammer the world back into some sensible shape. As though only the might of empire and the edge of a blade could restore peace and hope where it had all but faded to nothing.

Pinion had felt the same things in that wordless roar, an echo of his worst impulses, of everything that had led him from Greyfrost to Setting Sun Fortress, to the falling sword, the levelled spear, and the spray of innocent blood.

The Sienese, still roaring, surged past their own barricades. The Raven stepped forwards, his teeth gleaming in the light of the flames he had called, and hurled them. The other witches of his cadre followed, some veering into beasts that answered with their own howls and bared teeth, others drawing swords that flickered with hungry fire.

'No!' Pinion cried.

Too late.

A sword had been drawn and blood had been spilled. Little matter that it had been both Sienese sword and Sienese blood. Now the dam would break.

A hand caught his arm and pulled him back. 'Get down!' Running Doe shouted.

Pinion fell to the street as a volley of crossbow bolts shattered against a whirling dome of wind, its lung-freezing ache roiling out from Clear-River, who stood with the Nayeni witches with a strip of bone in his hand.

A volley arced up from the two hundred Nayeni assembled in the street. Another wave rained from the windows above, sowing death and confusion. Panicking Sienese turned their shields towards the windows just as the witches hurled a wall of flame into their ranks. Roars of battle fury bled into screams and death rattles.

Pinion tried to stand, though his wounds ached and his ruined eye throbbed. Fear would have him flee, but something deeper – something that reacted not with terror but with horror, coupled with a profound demand that this carnage go on no longer – carried him towards the line of battle. He was a Hand of the emperor. He wore the tetragram on his palm. An empty authority, true, but perhaps he might still be able to put it to some use.

Running Doe's fingers bit into his arm. 'You aren't armed!' she shouted in his ear. 'Get inside!'

He pulled away, slipping free of her grasp as a grenade burst against Clear-River's shield. Chemicals spun away in flaming droplets. The fighting had yet to come to close quarters. The Nayeni poured arrow after arrow, cutting down the front rank of Sienese soldiers as quickly as they could be replaced. Yet still the Sienese charged, leaping over charred bodies, only to be met by arrows, gouts of fire, and blades of wind that made themselves known only as explosions of blood and severed limbs.

A blow to the shoulder knocked Pinion to his knees. A bolt sprouted there from a slowly deepening stain, only a handspan from his throat. He stared at the blood, still not feeling the wound beyond that initial, stunning impact, until a flash of sunlight on steel drew his gaze. A Sienese soldier, his face marred by a blackened wound, loomed over him. Pinion felt a jolt in his chest at the sudden certainty of his own impending death, though by now it was a familiar sensation.

A chill seized Pinion's lungs. Blood spurted from a hole between the soldier's eyes and he collapsed.

'What are you *doing?*' Clear-River roared in Pinion's ear. 'You can't fight! Get back with the auxiliaries!'

'I can put a stop to this!' Pinion answered, astonished by the calmness in his own voice. He tried to stand but a pulse of pain from his shoulder sent him back to his knees.

'You were here to help negotiate terms!' Clear-River stepped around Pinion, his face a hard mask as he sent another dart of wind through a charging soldier's throat. 'Too late for that, now!'

'You can't endure this any more than I can,' Pinion argued. 'Give me a chance to talk them down!'

Clear-River's eyes never left the line of battle as he offered Pinion a hand up. 'There comes a moment when the time for talking is past. Now find Running Doe and have that wound treated. This will be over soon enough.'

'I can't,' Pinion said, and pulled away from Clear-River. He held his wounded shoulder, wincing at every jostling step. A few dozen Nayeni had closed with the front line of Sienese, among them a veered wolf and a witch wielding flaming swords. The melee was no less one-sided; only one of the Nayeni regulars took a spear to the gut or a sword to the arm for every five or six Sienese who fell.

Lightning flashed up from the Sienese ranks, blasting apart the facade of one of the buildings from which Nayeni arrows poured in an unending torrent. A scream sounded, and a corpse trailed smoke as it plummeted from a shattered window. Evidently Hand Jadestone, or one of the others he had trusted with the stolen canons of witchcraft, had joined the fighting at last. The Nayeni still had their advantage, but the battle would only become more brutal now as both sides brought magic to bear.

Pinion gritted his teeth and raised his right hand high, splaying his fingers and flexing his palm, doing anything he could to make the tetragram branded there as visible as possible.

'Stop this!' he screamed, hoping the light would catch the glimmering lines of the emperor's name on his palm – a mark that shamed him now, but one that might save lives. 'Throw down your arms, in the emperor's never-changing name!'

He heard only a sound like the crunch of ceramic, which echoed, reverberating for a single, distended moment, before pain swallowed everything.

27

To Save a Life

Foolish Cur

I was beginning to wonder if some cosmic force – beyond the gods themselves, for in that moment I stood beyond their influence – were aware of my every plan, my every fear, my every dream. Had followed me with perfect closeness and clarity from the first childish plan I ever devised and determined to amuse itself by thwarting me. The occasional success allowed my hope to go on burning – though it guttered like a dying candle flame – but always at those moments of greatest importance, when the stakes were highest, that force stood in my way, cut me down, and twisted the knife, taunting me with my own complicity.

Oriole's death. My accidental betrayal of the An-Zabati. The shattering of the world in my failed attempt to kill the emperor.

Huo's sword flashing through the throat of his own ally and with that spray of blood shattering the fetters that had held back the hatred between Nayeni and Sienese simmering in Eastern Fortress.

A thousand curses broke against my clenched teeth, holding the shell that now protected the city. If Hissing Cat had not collapsed from exhaustion as I took the weight from her, she would have felt the wakes of this absurd battle – a massacre, truly, to answer Setting Sun Fortress. Her arrival would end things. As it was, I could do little while I held the shell, which demanded twice the attention and effort of an ordinary seal and was far more vast than the protection I had created around my father's estate.

A part of me wanted to release it, to restore the seal, as though doing so might return the flow of time to that moment before Huo drew his sword, or as if depriving the Nayeni of their advantage might end the fighting. Both were impossible. Just so, this outpouring of Nayen's rage and Sien's fear and hatred could not be dammed.

I did what I could, deflecting arrows, answering a bolt of lightning from the Sienese ranks with a shield of light, healing those felled by crossbow bolts. The battle had surged past me, and what little strength I could spare while holding the shell would hardly match a witch of the Raven's strength. Better, I reasoned, to hang back, provide support, and ensure that a stray bolt did not punch through my eye.

I will admit, looking back, to cowardice. I would save those around me, but I had dealt enough death and wanted no more lives – not even the lives of my enemies – to weigh on my conscience.

Above the clamour of battle, I heard Clear-River's shout, turning just as Pinion rushed forwards, his left hand clutching his wounded shoulder, the other held aloft as though it could extinguish the bonfire of hatred. Had he both his eyes, he might have seen the grenade arcing towards him, might have thrown himself behind the cover of Clear-River's whirling defence.

Ceramic broke against the street tiles. Flame burst upwards, carrying Pinion with it.

He landed in a crumpled heap, torn and bloody.

I had pursued him the length of our island, hoping all the while that some moral feeling to mirror my own might kindle in him. Setting Sun Fortress had dashed that hope – or so I had believed. Yet that light had shone in his eye these last days since Burning Dog's death. Dozens of times I had seen him crossing the garden and felt a longing to speak with him, to share memories of Oriole, and to ease his burdens of guilt and shame, which must have been so similar to my own.

His wide, unfocused eye rolled in its socket, overwhelmed by pain, beneath his remaining fluttering eyelid. Red froth filled his mouth with each slow, rattling breath.

'Pinion!' I called, trying to draw his attention, to anchor him before his consciousness slipped away.

'A … Ald … Foolish Cur.' The words were wet and thick in his throat. 'You … have to …'

A spasm rolled through him. His mouth twisted into a wordless groan.

Grenades burst overhead. Lightning and fire flashed as I knelt over him. All the attention I could spare I focused on the bloody rents in his robe, on the flesh beneath, and on the trickle of healing I could muster to seal those ragged tears and punctures, full of shattered clay and scraps of cloth.

There were dozens. To simply pour healing magic into him, forcing his body to restore itself, would tax him to the point of death. Had there been two or three grievous wounds, I might have knit them one by one with that spare trickle of power. I could slacken my grip on the shell around the city, risking that my concentration might shatter, and with it our protection from the chaos that seethed through the world – and the unwoven, who would surely descend on this magic-rich battle in an instant.

Here was a second chance. I had failed to save Oriole, but I had the power and the skill to save his brother. Only circumstance prevented me. Were I willing to risk the city, I could have. Except that strange, cackling force beyond the gods had once more seen fit to taunt me, conjuring my deepest wounds and denying me the chance to heal them.

His eye, at last, fixed on mine. So like Oriole's eyes.

'It's too much,' I rasped, swallowing against a sob, my hands trembling. 'I …' The words refused to form. How could I tell him that I had to let him die?

He blinked, opened his mouth, but his response was lost in another well of red froth. One of his hands pawed at me, down my arm. His fingers, weak as a child's, closed around mine. Blood poured form his slow, measured smile.

He understood. There was some comfort in that, at least.

'I'm sorry,' I stammered, and then again: 'I'm sorry.' I would have gone on, apology after apology, until his last breath left him.

But, of course, I was not alone.

A hand pulled me back. I whirled, teeth bared, to find Running Doe's eyes full of a hard-edged sympathy.

'Let me, Cur,' she said. 'It is why I am here.'

She gently but firmly pulled me away, then knelt and put her hand to Pinion's brow. Slowly, steadily, his breathing began to ease. The seeping wounds that showed through his tattered robe began to close.

I was not alone.

I had read the battle wrong.

In the buildings above me, in the ranks behind me, Nayeni fought not only from hatred, not only from fear for their lives. As an infected body burns with fever, so a suffering people burns with rage, which builds and builds until it can be contained no longer and must burn out the oppressors like the sickness they are – a terrible thing to witness, a painful thing to do, but necessary if the body is to survive.

The innocence of the Nayeni had been stolen, a prize seized in conquest. Yet Clear-River had offered peace at every turn.

Even when we held the power to slice through the Sienese like a blade through paper, we had offered peace.

They had rejected it.

Pinion clung to hope. He was still young to the rebellion. The fever did not yet burn brightly enough within him. The pain of the infection did not yet demand the finality of a surgeon's blade. I, too, had once been so young.

Too many had died. Too many had suffered. If the Sienese wanted this to end not in cooperation but in a river of blood, then let it end so.

I stepped to the edge of the whirling shield of wind, pushed my hand through to the open air, and released my hold on the shell, hurling all my focus, all my rage, into a single act. A final, pointed brush stroke to end this hideous logogram. A final word to brook no further argument.

A wake rolled out from me, as searing as the desert, filling my lungs with ice and my bones with fever. Light to rival the sun burned at my fingertips, so bright it darkened the morning sky. Lightning, fire, and wind compressed into a single line, a white-hot bar the width of my arm. At its touch, the air screamed. Steel boiled in its passing. Armor shattered. Bodies came apart like dead, rotten trees.

As I rebuilt the shell – my shoulders heaving, my limbs shaking – I blinked away the black after-image seared into the back of my eyes and swallowed against my rising gorge. The front line of Sienese soldiers had been reduced to a smear of ash. A furrow had been ploughed through the ranks behind them, as though the legion itself was nothing more than churned earth, the broken remains of corpses forming heaps of blackened bone and flesh. There, among the char and ruin, I saw a corpse adorned in the filigreed armour of a Sienese marshal, heat-cracked and smoking. A few paces behind it I glimpsed the face – pale and slack in death – of Hand Jadestone, who had once welcomed me into the heights of Sienese society at the banquet after my examinations.

Hundreds of Sienese eyes fixed on me. Dozens had already collapsed to their knees, their weapons fallen from shaking hands. They were leaderless, terrified, moments from panicked retreat. *A scalpel leaves ruin in its wake*, I told myself. *Only when the sickness is expunged can wounds be knitted and the body begin to heal.*

'Will you hurl yourselves again and again into the fire,' I called out to them, 'or will you let that be the end?'

A silent stillness held. The Nayeni, too, stared in horror and disbelief.

A ripple moved through the Sienese. Some threw down their weapons and knelt to join those already brought to their knees in terror. Some turned and ran, pushing their way through the ranks around them in animal desperation. Shouts went up, a dozen conflicting orders – calls to retreat, to surrender, to counter-attack.

'Enough!' a booming voice called out. A soldier in ordinary armour, decorated only with a sergeant's logogram on his pouldron, stepped into the furrow of ash and broken bodies. He swept battle-hardened eyes over the ranks behind him, then met my gaze. 'That is enough. We cannot stand against this. We surrender.'

Behind him, the last of those who still held their weapons battle ready began to throw them down in a clattering rain of steel on stone. I let my hand fall to my side. Clear-River shouted orders to our soldiers to collect the discarded weapons, then called out to the Sienese: 'Those who leave their armour and weapons behind are free to return to their homes!'

Soon the blood-slick street lay buried under discarded armour, that bearing the logograms and sigils of officers beside the unadorned, scarred mail of peasant conscripts. Gradually the force dispersed, men dressed in simple tunics glancing over hunched shoulders as though expecting a volley of arrows to rise and cut them down.

'You truly mean to let us go?' the sergeant, still wearing his armour, asked Clear-River.

'We came here not for vengeance but for peace,' Clear-River said.

The sergeant turned to watch the dissolving legion. 'It will not be as easy as this.'

Clear-River grunted agreement. 'No. But it is a beginning.'

I left them to that beginning, to negotiate the new order that would shape the city, now that Nayen was free. Running Doe still knelt over Pinion. The ragged holes in his robe showed pink, healthy flesh beneath the bloodstains.

He would live. They all would live. But only for so long.

The war in Nayen was over. It was time, now, to put an end to the war with the gods.

PART 3

The World

28

City in Shadow

Ral Ans Urrera

It is a slow process, like learning to walk again. Part of her feels as though she ought to be quicker, as though her mind wades through a thick, dragging fog whenever she tries to work magic. Another part accepts the truth: before, her power was wild and uncivilised; now, it must become accustomed to the constraints of the emperor's will. One day in five, the emperor himself attends her practice rather than the unnamed Fist who serves as her tutor. His disappointment at her slow progress gnaws at her and kindles an inward-burning hatred.

'I'm sorry,' she says, kneeling before him after failing, yet again, to weave magic as he demands. She can manage the simpler shapes, the spheres and walls, that the Fists demonstrated on the steppe – a feat unworthy of her, she knows, and unworthy of the emperor's need. Anyone with a modicum of talent might be put to such a use. She is different. A witch of the old sort, he calls her, his equal in potential and his superior in resilience, if not in understanding or in power.

'For every day we waste in this, tens of thousands die,' he says, a seething anger seeping through his carefully controlled expression.

Her own anger burns to match his, rising from the deepest corner of the labyrinth he has built in her mind. It charges through the corridors, which shift, vanish, and rebuild themselves, always driving her back into the shadowed depths. It flares and fades, like a light in the corner of her eye.

If not for that burning anger, that barbarian hatred, there would be no need for the labyrinth, for the constraints that make her slower than she ought to be. She would have mastered the forms by now, ready to move on to the next step in her training, to the heights of skill required to stand at his side against the gods. She hates herself for bearing such a fire within her.

She furrows her brow against a sudden, pulsing agony between her eyes. The world around her seems to come alive with light, an aurora outlining her bed, the chamber pot, the paintings on the walls, even the emperor himself. Her teeth grind together as she tries to bite back the pain.

'Not enough!' He roars, toppling his chair as he rises, hands curled into trembling fists. Ral shirks back, ashamed. 'Do you think our enemies – the gods, the rebels – waste time like this? The world ends around us, and your sloth and weakness stand in the way of its salvation!' He turns to leave, pausing in the doorway, his fingers drumming on the wooden frame. 'I expect more of you. You are little better than a Fist, as you are. I will return in five days' time. Fifty thousand more lives, Ral, will rest on your shoulders when I do. Do not waste those deaths.'

The door slides shut and the lock clicks into place. A low moan boils in her throat. One of her fists rises, unbidden, crashes into the side of her head with all the fury she feels and cannot face.

She will beat this hateful anger out of herself if she must. She *will* become useful. She *will* make good on all the crimes of her past, overcome this resistance that still burns within her, and help him save the world.

When the pain within her skull has faded, replaced by the ache of slow-blossoming bruises on her forehead and knuckles, she turns her mind again to the task the emperor has set for her. She takes slow, methodical breaths, turning her attention inwards, towards the heart of the labyrinth. Without its obstructing, distracting walls – she cannot help herself; the thought rises unbidden, sweeping through her like a wind – this would all be so much easier. A growl silences that hateful notion. Slowly, dragging herself every step of the way, she finds the peace at her core, the stillness at the eye of the storm. The energies of the world whirl around her. She reaches into them, feels their currents, their flow, and breathes them into her.

It is a simple thing, now, to trace the walls of her room, or the contours of the hallway outside, and fill that space with those energies, carrying away any magic that would disrupt their natural flow. This is the power the emperor would have her master and then transcend, to reshape the hidden weapon he means to turn to his own purpose – a weapon, he has told her, that would strip all the wonder and beauty from the world, one made by fools and cowards willing to sacrifice anything to be rid of the gods. Too weak, too lacking in vision, too unwilling to bear the cost of saving all that is worthy of salvation.

Words that stir her. She can see in the cracked mask of his expression an admirable unwillingness to bend, and she too would save what beauty and wonder can be saved. Yet the part of her that remains, buried in the labyrinth, sees through his facade.

That part of her, a distant whisper, reminds her of Atar, the flash of her scarves in her mourning dance for her people after the wreck of the *Dunecleaver*. There was beauty in An-Zabat. Beauty that the empire crushed to nothing and scattered on windships, doomed to die on broken runners. Just as, before Ral's birth, there was beauty and wonder among the Girzan.

Stormcallers, with their secrets and rituals, preserved now only as a kernel among far-flung tribes like the Red Bull. Otherwise scoured from the earth by the empire.

Such thoughts prompt the labyrinth to reshape itself in a painful, shuddering transformation, constricting her mind with new patterns that crush that voice at its heart to silence, that force her to think only of how far she is from the mastery the emperor demands.

Our enemy is guileful, he told her. *Clever. Unlikely to face us in open battle, as the Skyfather did, and will not so foolishly fall for bait or a trick. They must be driven from hiding.*

To that end, she reaches deeper, below the churning, into something like the tension between heat and cold that births every storm. A layer below even her own thoughts, which become as slippery as the metaphors she needs to make sense of what she feels grows elusive. There was something of this in the elders' stories, she thinks. When they told a tale, it presented one meaning on its surface – a hero's wanderings or a warrior's bravery – but carried its true message beneath it. Some lesson to be learned, better communicated in this obscured, elided way than stated directly.

It is here, the emperor has told her, that the gods make their home and their fortress. It is here that she must strike at them, if she is to be of any use.

She reaches deep, takes in the tension, the interplay of fundamental forces that give rise to all things. It surges through her, filling her veins with fire, making her teeth groan to the point of cracking. Her thoughts blur to incoherence, becoming only a low, howling pain and a single-minded purpose. Even the walls of the emperor's labyrinth shudder. They cannot break, she knows, but their shuddering reverberates with her own pain and terror at the power she holds, which will surely tear her soul apart.

Always, before, this was the point of failure. The bridge that she could not force herself to cross for fear that it will not hold, that she will plunge into a void too terrible to imagine.

Not yet.

She will not give in.

She is Ral Ans Urrera.

The storm of a people's rage, their pain, their need for vengeance once burned through her. She was the spear of a wrathful god. She has endured worse than this.

Such thoughts turn her stomach even as they lend her strength. She seizes the divine power that fills her, threatens her, and makes ready to invert it, hurling it inwards, twisting the pattern back on itself in a storm that will scour away any power, any spell, any god it touches. It may destroy her, for her mind is a kind of magic, is it not, transcending the eternal laws of interchange that define the world and determine its flow? Still, she wrestles with the power, bending it into the contorted, annihilating shape the emperor demands.

Her bones creak. Pain blossoms behind her eyes. Blood trickles into her mouth. A howling fills her ears, and then a percussive blow like the snapping membrane of an over-tightened drum.

Vertigo hurls her down.

Silence envelops her.

Nausea boils up. Her eyes wheel until they are blind to all but a blur of meaningless, shimmering colour, and then blind to all.

She wakes in darkness. A hacking cough seizes her. She rolls onto her side, her head throbbing and ears ringing. *So close.* A little more and she would have remade herself into the tool the labyrinth insists that she must become.

A sob racks her already aching lungs. She weeps, her tears sluicing dried blood into her mouth. If she had the strength, she would rise and try again, but two failures in one day have left her body broken and her mind as fragile as cracked porcelain.

Sleep takes her again, carries her down into dreams of the open sky and the sway of grass, of the thunder of horses' hooves and the flash of summer lightning.

Three days later, the emperor returns.

She is awake, already practising her breathing exercises, awaiting the Fist, who will guide her through the forms. These last days she has not come so close to success again, always shying back from the agony that tore through her. But that is acceptable. It is the emperor's presence, his disappointment, that makes her failure ache until she would gladly hurl herself into fire to make it end. In his absence, she can perform the exercises, strengthening herself as she once did under the guidance of the Girzan elders when she first learned to call the lightning.

Yet it is the emperor, not the unnamed Fist, who enters her room when the lock clicks open. Terror surges within her. Not of him – he is radiance itself, deserving only of worship – but of her own weakness, her inevitable failure. Her body is not ready yet to endure again the agony of her fullest effort.

A Fist she does not recognise follows behind him and thrusts an undertunic and a robe of green silk and silver thread into her arms.

'Dress yourself,' the emperor says. A savage, desperate anticipation fills his eyes. If she did not know him well by now, she might believe that it is fear. 'We are leaving, whether you are ready or not. Already we have dallied too long.'

Ral obeys, wondering all the while where he will take her, and to what end. Is this a consequence of her failure? Has she proven unworthy, unable to serve her purpose? Or have the gods made headway in their war, forcing the emperor to act before she is ready?

If it is the last, she will destroy herself to serve his purpose. It is not a decision but a truth that radiates through her, though that screaming voice in the depths of the labyrinth rails against it.

The emperor leads her from her cell, back to the central domed space where they first arrived when he brought her from the steppe. A dozen Fists await them, all dressed in battle harness and armour of black scale. They salute, though the emperor gives no sign of recognition. He only walks to the centre of their loose formation and reaches out with magic. The weight of his attention traces a line around the gathering, enfolding them all, and then strikes at the world itself.

Light and sound distort and swirl around her. Her joints scream and her stomach roils as the emperor hurls them all through the rent he has made. They emerge in an instant that stretches infinitely. A scar in her memory to match that of his carrying her away, unwilling – before the labyrinth, before she understood – from the steppe.

The air itself smells strange, full of foliage and water, though they stand in an empty city square. A tiled street, scarred in places by gouges that look made by giant claws and blackened by bloodstains. Around them loom stone buildings carved with elaborate ornamentation. The sight stuns Ral – the Skyfather's Hall is the only city she has known, and its construction was all of wood or wattle and daub. This must be a city of magic, she decides, for no human hands could move and shape so much stone.

The Fists fan out and Ral perceives the feverish wake of battle sorcery held ready. The emperor mutters under his breath, takes his bearings, and sets off down a street that leads uphill, away from the plaza, towards a vast stone gate. Ral follows, still uncertain of their purpose here. Worry gnaws at her until her thoughts collide with the walls of the labyrinth and are shunted away. It is not hers to wonder anymore, not hers to fret and plan, but only to obey and serve.

Voices rumble from the alleyways. Faces watch from windows overhead. A cluster of young men with knives tucked in their black sashes and fresh scars on their arms eye them, considering a challenge. One of the Fists calls lightning and scours the tiles at their feet to runny, molten slag and they retreat, shouting curses.

'I haven't been paying enough attention. They could be hiding anywhere in this mess,' the emperor mutters as they approach the gateway. Crossbowmen dressed in Sienese armour stand the walls. They raise their weapons and shout challenges. The emperor glares up at them. 'Open the gate,' he orders, conjuring a blast of wind to make his words boom and rumble, shaking dust from the ramparts. Heartbeats later, the gate rolls open.

'Bring me to Voice Sprouting-Elm!' the emperor roars.

A succession of whingeing, terrified officials usher them deeper into the city – a guard captain, then his commander, then a balding magistrate who quivers all the while he leads them and insists again and again that if they will only wait the governor will send an honour guard and palanquins to bear them the rest of the way, and that it is shameful to all his servants in Sor Cala that the emperor walks openly through the streets. His babbling elicits only a scornful glare from the emperor, which finally seals the magistrate's mouth and redoubles the shaking in his limbs.

Another gate stands between them and the inner city. Before traversing it, the emperor reaches deep into the world and weaves a lattice that envelops him and the tendrils of his transmission. A slight shiver works through Ral as they pass beneath the gate, and the labyrinth within her fades for a moment, as though during that heartbeat of time it were utterly insubstantial, a wall of fog rather than of stone. The moment passes even as she observes it. The part of her that rages within the labyrinth can only scream and wail and pound its fists on walls that were, moments ago, no more than mist.

Messengers and stewards scramble ahead of them, throwing open the doors to the governor's estate, shouting a babbling string of Sienese to herald their arrival, racing ahead of them – presumably to warn the governor and the rest of the household of the emperor's arrival. Ral watches it all with disdain. This is no time for pageantry. While the war against the gods rages, urgency, not attention to propriety, defines the emperor's every act.

Yet though she finds these cringing, scurrying people unctuous, she cannot help but marvel at the garden around her. Plants she cannot hope to recognise grow in rich, sculpted stands. Vast decorative stones stand stark and uncarved, shot through with the grainy, glimmering decorations bestowed by nature. Bronzes replicate all manner of wonders: lion serpents, rearing horses, fantastical birds with their wings flung wide. There are living creatures, too: cranes that wade in lily ponds, songbirds that leap between the branches of a cypress tree, a young doe that pauses in her grazing to watch them pass.

Such ostentation at once astonishes and enrages her. Does the keeper of this garden not know that people starve throughout the empire? That the world shatters and tears and grows more and more unliveable by the day? That before long the unravelling will come for them and their garden, too, rending it all to nothing?

Her rage is only inflamed as she follows the emperor through a low circular gateway and into a segment of the garden defined by a wide pavilion with a slow stream trickling through the centre of its floor. Three men dressed in flowing silks – one wearing the tetragram upon his brow, the others carrying it on their palms – stand smoothing their clothes and hissing hasty orders to their servants, who gather up a collection of small cups and paper boats. One of the Hands goes rigid as he notes their approach. Soon all three face them and prostrate themselves, the high colour of embarrassment overwhelming the pink flush of alcohol on their cheeks.

'Your Majesty,' the Voice says, forehead pressed to the tiles of the path. 'Welcome to Sor Cala and your province of Toa Alon. My sincerest, most ashamed apologies that you were not properly received. This comes as a surprise—'

'Of course it does.' The emperor's voice crackles through the air. 'Who but I could have warned you that I was coming, Voice Sprouting-Elm? You need not apologise for the reception, such as it was, though you have a great deal else to be ashamed of.'

The Voice sags. 'Your Majesty, the Toa Aloni were rebuffed from our granaries and dozens of the thieves killed, with dozens more rounded up. The few who—'

'What do I care for mouthfuls of grain?' The emperor steps forward. 'You shame yourself by cowering behind this shield, abandoning the city to the barbarians, when its keeping was your *only* task. That failure I cannot forgive.'

Voice Sprouting-Elm has time only to look up in terror before a dart of blinding fire bores through him, burning a channel from his forehead to the small of his back. The corpse collapses, steam and a foul stench rising from the ruin. The emperor makes a sharp gesture for one of the Hands to rise. He stands, his knees visibly shaking beneath his robe.

The emperor touches the Hand's forehead, making a series of quick strokes. The Hand winces in pain, then his eyes widen in astonishment. He touches the glimmering scar the emperor has dealt – a tetragram, but drawn in flowing calligraphy rather than the blocky logograms that adorn every other sorcerer in the empire.

'You are Voice here now, Tan,' the emperor says. 'It falls to you to bring this province under control, as well as can be done given the circumstances. To that end, your first task will be to scour the city for a barbarian witch. A stonespeaker. One who has been, in all likelihood, hiding here undetected for decades. One my servants here have allowed to escape notice, and who now readies a weapon that should have been buried. Find them.'

Voice Tan opens his mouth, a question in his eyes and furrowed brow.

'If you prove insufficient to the task,' the emperor says, clipping each word short, 'you will face a far worse death than your fool of a predecessor.'

In answer, Voice Tan once more falls prostrate, and only when the emperor has turned his back to follow a steward towards the deceased governor's living quarters does the Voice rise and begin shouting orders. Soon, Ral imagines, the empty streets of the city will flood with soldiers. The people who peered out of their scarred homes will be dragged into the open and put to the question. Wherever this Toa Aloni witch is hiding, the empire will root them out.

She wonders at the importance of finding this person. The emperor, after all, might have delivered these same orders by transmission from across the world.

She remembers the way his eyes appeared not an hour ago as he loomed in her doorway: wide and burning with some inner light. She had not thought it possible then – and even now, as soon as her mind settles, the labyrinth leads her thoughts away, yet they circle back, again and again, to a truth that the walls in her mind refuse to allow. And though her thoughts cannot dwell long enough for that truth to breed a matching terror within her, the part of her that knows it rejoices and repeats it again and again until the walls of the labyrinth echo and shudder.

Absurd as it seems, the emperor is afraid.

29
Farewells

Foolish Cur

Too often, those who shoulder the greatest burdens rarely survive to enjoy the better worlds they strive to create, a lesson I should have learned first from Naphena's tale. Burning Dog, Frothing Wolf, and my uncle had fought longer than anyone for Nayen's day of liberation, and all died long before its dawn. Only my grandmother would ever know the freedom they had fought for, and how many years did she have left?

Now, as I prepared to leave Eastern Fortress, these thoughts made me wonder if this was not the emperor's most significant mistake: an unwillingness to sacrifice without the promise of reward. An attempt to remake the world for the better, perhaps, but only as long as he still stood atop it, preserved and dominant.

With these weighty thoughts, I put my hands to the array of shoulder blades set amid the roots of Oriole's tree. As when I had anchored the shell of protection around the temple of the flame, I reached through the markings in the bone into the deepest layers of the pattern, where souls and gods dwelt. Fatigue swept through me as I anchored the shell around the city in place, compounding the exhaustion I already suffered in the aftermath of the last battle for Nayen.

I leaned against the tree, feeling the rough, blackened bark of its scar. Hissing Cat swept her gaze from horizon to horizon, as though she could see the spell I had wrought.

'Impressive,' she said. 'With enough time, we could make a few thousand of these to really threaten the gods. Or even a few of your little bone canons with sealing spells.'

'With enough time,' I repeated. 'Which is the thing we lack most. The Sienese granaries will feed the city for a few extra weeks, but then we will face all the same problems again. There is an enforced peace, for now, but it will erupt into new violence the moment enough people have to watch their children go hungry, knowing the millet that feeds an old enemy might fill their bowl instead.'

'So you'd rather we go bolting off to Toa Alon, chasing some strange wake through the world just because it spooked Tenet? How will that feed a starving child?'

'I don't know,' I answered. 'But something momentous shook the pattern to its foundations. We should know what it is, whether it bodes good or ill.'

In truth, I could not answer her honestly. Yes, Eastern Fortress would run out of food in a matter of weeks, but that was not the certain eventuality I feared. I had shouldered too much, caused too many deaths, made too many mistakes. A new desire gripped me more powerfully than any I had known since my first taste of magic left me in its thrall.

We can only do so much harm before the need for atonement overwhelms us. We either pursue it to the hilt or abandon ourselves to guilt, shame, and hatred. I stood balanced on that knife edge, uncertain of where I would fall but believing, however foolishly, that to act might be a balm for my soul.

'When I was outside of the city, I spoke with Okara,' I said.

Hissing Cat's tired eyes burned with sudden fury. 'Well? What the hell did the dog want?'

'To gloat.' I briefly recounted my conversation with the god. '"Only the stone-faced gods of Toa Alon remain," he said. Whatever this sudden wake of power was, it came from Toa Alon, and it drew Tenet's attention. It made him *afraid*.'

Hissing Cat grunted. 'The gods of Toa Alon are hardly warriors, Cur. They gave their people many powers with their pact, but none of much use for violence. If there are any of those bastards I can imagine being on our side, it's them.'

I had not considered this possibility, and it filled me with a sudden, burning hope. I knew very little of Toa Alon – only what I had gleaned from my tutor, Koro Ha, and Jhin, my steward, in An-Zabat – but what I did know encouraged me. Their gods, far from the warlike wolves of Nayen, were worshipped principally for their wisdom. I recalled, too, when I had lain on the edge of death after restoring my grandmother's arm from Usher's torture and the gods had gathered, ready to condemn me. Okara had rushed to my defence – a ploy, I now understood, to win my loyalty – but it had been the strange gods with bodies of stone and heads like the peaks of mountains who had adjudicated my fate.

'Then we have delayed too long already,' I said.

Hissing Cat rubbed her eyes. 'If we appear in the middle of Sor Cala and find ourselves surrounded by a few dozen Hands and Fists, will you be able to defend yourself? If the emperor attacked your mind, could you fend him off?'

I wanted to insist that I was strong enough. Waiting felt more dangerous than plunging ahead, despite my exhaustion. The emperor might uncover what he sought and turn the tide of the war while we slept.

'Tomorrow, Cur,' Hissing Cat said, an unusual softness in her voice. 'We both have a chance to sleep, finally. Let's take advantage of it. One night of hard-won peace before plunging back into war.'

'Tomorrow,' I agreed, suppressing my desperation. I could see that I would not convince her, and I had learned through hard experience that a lack of caution, even in the face of urgency, more often yields sorrow than success.

Leaden limbs and sagging eyelids testified to my need for rest, yet though I could accept a delay, I could not overcome the fear that inactivity would give me too much time to dwell on the memory of Sienese soldiers mown down like grass before a scythe. The furrow through the bodies. The smear of ash on paving stones.

The final cost of peace, I told myself. A part of me, at least, finally understood Harrow Fox, my uncle. Like him, and like Frothing Wolf and Burning Dog, the war had eroded my moral objections, like teeth worn to nubs by constant gnashing. But the roots still ached.

As evening fell on the city, I went to visit the infirmary, as though the sight of our wounded might assuage my guilt. More, I hoped to see Running Doe and Doctor Sho before my departure. There was no telling whether Hissing Cat and I would return from Toa Alon, nor any way of knowing if our adventure would yield the end of the war with the gods that I hoped for. Whatever the outcome, there was a very real chance we would never see one another again, and I ached at the thought. Doctor Sho and I had had our differences, but he had been steadfast, despite his secrets, and Running Doe ...

It felt as arrogant as any notion that had ever entered my mind to believe that my death would hurt her in the way hers would hurt me – the sight of her on the edge of death had stripped all strength from me. Yet I did believe it, and I feared my death as much to spare her the pain of it as for any other reason. The last thing in the world I wanted was to cause her more suffering than I already had.

A deeper, harder emotion drew me as well, one I could face only at a slant rather than head-on. It was cousin to the guilt I felt for the slaughter of the Sienese, only for the one who had thrown his body between warring armies, who had nearly died in one last desperate plea for peace.

The guest house where Usher and I had stayed during our residency in the estate had been filled to bursting with cots and medicines. The myriad smells of a sick house greeted me – the pungency of medicines, the copper-and-iron smell of blood. Nurses moved among the wounded, changing bandages. I caught sight of Clear-River among them, canon in hand, knitting a ragged spear wound in a Sienese soldier's flank. Torn Leaf had been conscripted to aid the healers as well, and I felt a calming wake pulsing from him as he ran his hands over a patch of blackened flesh on a young woman's arm. He looked up from his work, spotted me, and stood, raising an arm to wave me over just as a nurse caught him by the elbow and led him to his next patient.

I wandered among them, wincing at each blistered face or stained bandage. In time, when all this suffering was forgotten and the world had been made whole again, the descendants of Nayen might remember our battles with pride. Might even lionise us, chronicling our struggles and triumphs in romances, as though we were Brittle Owl and the other heroes of Nayeni legend.

The prospect disgusted me. Even if the world were put right, even if the empire were destroyed, ambition, greed, and hatred would draw people into war again and again. The only thing that might dissuade them was the memory of its cost. A cost too easily forgotten, scrubbed away by those who preferred to remember glory without the blood and offal, without the horror that settles in the bones even of those whose cause is righteous. It is vital that any record of war captures the horror that twists the hearts of all who fight, and the naivete, arrogance, and foolishness that breeds those horrors. I can only hope I have honoured the truth in crafting my own account, with all its foolishness and fumbling.

Raised voices drew me into an adjoining room, which I realised on crossing the threshold had once been my own small apartment when I was an apprentice Hand. A half-dozen cots lined the walls, each bearing a gravely wounded Sienese soldier, one of whom wore bandages from the bridge of his nose to the crown of his forehead, his left arm ending at the elbow in a stump. He writhed, tossing his head from side to side, shouting incoherent snippets of outraged Sienese. Running Doe knelt over him with a teacup full of pungent brown liquid balanced in her hand. The sight of her sent a happy, fretful jolt through me.

'It will ease the pain,' she urged the soldier. 'Would you rather go on in agony than sip some bitter liquid?'

'No!' the man blurted in broken Nayeni. 'Hands away, filth! Hands away!'

'Let me try,' I said, joining Running Doe at the man's bedside.

She stood, startled by my sudden appearance, but her shock soon faded to a greeting smile, and then a frustrated glare down at her patient. 'We've done all we can with magic,' she said. 'Any more and his heart will give out, Sho says. This will help revitalise him. If he refuses it much longer, the scars on his eyes will set and make it *much* more difficult to fix them.'

I stifled a laugh at her stubbornness. No soldier, no matter how hardened, would be able to long resist the young woman who had hammered at me until I agreed to take her into battle at my side. Still, things would go more smoothly if the poor soul could understand what she was saying. I took the cup of medicine and knelt over the patient.

'If you would like your eyes back, drink this,' I said, holding the cup to his lips. 'It is medicine that will make you strong and able to withstand the healing you need.'

'Why should I accept it?' the soldier snarled. 'Filthy barbarian trickery.'

'The fighting is over,' I said. 'If they wanted to kill you, they would put a knife to your throat not poison in your medicine.'

He barked a laugh. 'Not the medicine. The healing. Stole our magic, didn't they? Battle sorcery, healing, all of it. Turned it against us. Disgraceful to accept that help. But what would you know of disgrace? You speak like a magistrate, but you serve them. Get away from me. Let me die with my dignity.'

I nearly threw the medicine in his face. Running Doe put a hand on my shoulder and pulled me away. 'I take it from your expression that that didn't go as planned.'

I gave her back the medicine. 'It's good of you,' I said. 'To heal them.'

'Clear-River insisted.' She furrowed her brow, then shrugged. 'He's right, though. They wouldn't do this for us. By doing it for them, we might be able to lay the foundations of the world he wants to build here. Even if they refuse our help, at least we tried. It's the right thing to do.'

Her words stirred a warmth in me. The night we had spent together had been a product as much of our mutual need for comfort on the eve of likely death as our desire – and yes, the freckles around her dimples still caught my eye and stirred a flurry in my middle. Yet there had been friendship there first. Not an uncomplicated one – my every relationship, it seemed, had been complicated by some accident of my birth or station – but one I would cherish nonetheless. And if we survived, there was perhaps the possibility of something more.

'Did you want to see Pinion?' she asked, and doused all my warm feelings in chill water.

I nodded and she led me away from the eyeless Sienese

soldier's grumbling shouts, back through the crowded main room, and into a small chamber that would once have housed a servant or minor steward. There, alone, Pinion lay on his cot, his remaining eye rimmed red with fever, gazing up at the narrow window. Bandages showing spots of blood encircled his chest and right thigh.

'He'll live,' Running Doe whispered, 'but he refused healing magic beyond what was needed to stave off death.'

Slowly, he turned his face towards us, wincing. 'Foolish Cur,' he murmured, and relaxed. 'You have more important things to do than visit me.'

I could think of no fitting response to that. Running Doe excused herself to attend to her other patients, though I suspected her concern was as much for our privacy. I bade her farewell, wondering if it would be the last time we spoke, then went to Pinion's side and gingerly laid a hand on his shoulder. A smile twitched at the corners of his mouth.

'You still haven't restored it,' he said, his eye drifting to the stump of my right wrist.

'Is that why you've refused healing? For your eye and for … this?'

He nodded weakly. I held up my severed limb, feeling – as I did whenever I put my mind to it, though less and less often now – the absence of that hand like an echo. An urge to curl fingers that no longer existed.

'Do you think the world would be any different if it wasn't so easy to put our wounds right?' he asked. 'If things were more difficult, if we felt the pain and suffering more sharply, if our broken bones needed time and agony to knit, would we more often hesitate before lashing out?' His eye searched mine, as though it were a question I, or anyone, could truly answer.

'The Nayeni fought one another, yet they held no healing sorcery until I joined them,' I pointed out.

He nodded slowly, the flicker of a smile creasing into a frown. 'But their wars did not span the world. The empire thinks so little of life, so little of the suffering it causes. I wonder if that is because those who lead it have never reckoned with the real cost of what they do. They write tomes and scrolls full of arguments to justify it all, but none of it beyond the earliest classics offers more than a glancing recognition of a dying child's pain. They stand apart from that suffering.'

I thought of my years of education, of my apprenticeship with Usher, dedicated to the mastery of magic and imperial bureaucracy, the twin levers of power. Both had the effect Pinion described, of distancing actor from action – magic by manipulating the world at a whim, bureaucracy by separating cause from effect with layers of paperwork and subordinates. Bridging that separation had been what ultimately turned me away from service to the empire. So too, it seemed, for Pinion.

And magic, I know far too well, had much the same effect. A wave of battle sorcery or a gout of flame or razor wind could kill dozens in a moment, a feat that, if undertaken by the sword, would exhaust one's arm and soak one in blood. The piles of charred and broken bodies in the aftermath would hold its own horror, but less, I had to imagine, than the rhythmic crunch of blade into bone, the spattering of gore. Even the empire's preference for chemical grenades and crossbows served to reduce the common soldier's exposure to the nightmare of their work.

The chain of thought burned through me like a bolt of lightning.

'We have to reckon with the cost,' Pinion whispered, straining to sit up, as though bringing our faces closer together might bridge the gap from his thoughts to mine.

I choked back a sob. 'I understand,' I managed, and eased him back down to his cot. 'Just don't go to join Oriole quite yet. You can't reckon with anything from the grave.'

His laughter broke into coughing, and when it had settled he said, 'That would be too easy, wouldn't it?'

'It would,' I agreed, and clasped his hand. 'Rest well, Pinion. We will need you on your feet to guide the rest of us through the reckoning to come.'

His expression faltered at that, but he nodded solemnly. 'We will need you too, Foolish Cur.'

I was not so certain of that, but I left him with my assurances.

In the hallway, Doctor Sho stood waiting, wiping his hands on a scrap of linen. 'Saying your goodbyes, then?' he asked.

'Setting things as right as I can,' I answered, hesitated for a moment, and then told him what Hissing Cat and I planned. The rift between us remained, made all the more complex and painful by the knowledge that he, as Traveller-on-the-Narrow-Way, held perhaps as much responsibility as the emperor himself for all the suffering Sien had caused. Yet Doctor Sho had been a friend to me, even if reconciling the old, eccentric man who had walked the length of Nayen in my company with the ancient sage whose writings had reshaped the world proved all but impossible.

He combed a hand through the wisps of his beard, grunted to himself, and fixed me with a challenging stare. 'I'm going with you.'

'That's madness!' I spluttered. 'You don't fight, and they need you here besides!'

'Running Doe has the clinic in hand,' he said. 'I planted the seeds of all of this, boy. I should be there when it ends.'

'Even if it doesn't end the way you hope?' I recalled his strange plan: a separation of the layers of the pattern, isolating us from the gods, and from magic – an impossible task, I thought, or at least not one I could imagine how to achieve.

He only grunted. 'I should make sure Running Doe has all

the medicines she might need,' he said, turning away. 'Until tomorrow, Cur. Don't dare to leave without me.'

We couldn't have done so if we'd tried. After a few hours of fitful sleep, I woke to join Hissing Cat beneath Oriole's tree and found Doctor Sho already there. Instead of his medicine chest, he carried a small satchel of provisions and a walking stick, and had dressed in the same baggy trousers and tunic he had worn on our trek across Nayen. I had prepared similarly, though could not bring myself to take any food from the city's dwindling provisions beyond a few strips of dried meat and a pouch of dates, and on my belt I wore a knife. In our travels together, I had learned the value of having such a tool, and magic might prove elusive in Toa Alon if the emperor, or one of his Voices, had raised a seal against the chaos that gripped the world.

At last Hissing Cat arrived, carrying nothing but the rattling skulls in her hair. The last of her oracle bones had gone to the array now planted amid the roots of Oriole's tree, anchoring the shell I had woven around the city.

'He's coming, then?' Hissing Cat said on seeing Doctor Sho. She jabbed her chin at his staff. 'Taking the opportunity to thump Tenet over the head before the world ends, I take it?'

He shifted uneasily. 'You should know, when the spell takes hold, it may … reverberate … strangely.'

She cocked her head. 'What the hell are you talking about?'

Doctor Sho looked from Hissing Cat to me, then back again, pulling at his beard. 'The emperor … did something to me. Ages ago. We had a falling out, shall we say. He threatened to keep me alive long enough to see his plans succeed. I don't know what he did – I've never understood this magic business – but it stopped me from ageing.'

My mind, as though of its own volition, immediately began to puzzle through how the emperor might have done such a thing.

Hissing Cat barked a laugh. 'What a bastard. So, what? You're afraid that whatever he did to you will interfere with our little jaunt to Toa Alon?'

Doctor Sho's face reddened with embarrassment. 'As I said, I don't know how any of this works.'

'What he did to you can't be much different from how he and I kept ourselves alive, can it? He ripped his way back to Sien without a moment's hesitation. You're worrying for nothing.'

Doctor Sho grumbled but nodded agreement.

'All right, then.' Hissing Cat drew us in with a gesture. 'Get close, now. No sense in exhausting myself tearing a bigger hole in the pattern than is needed.'

I took a deep breath, preparing myself for that stomach-wrenching wake that had radiated from the emperor when he had fled the garden, not far from this very spot.

'Wait!' Clear-River called from the base of the hill. He hitched up the hem of his robe and ran the rest of the way of up the slope.

Hissing Cat rolled her eyes. 'Another bloody delay …'

Clear-River glared at her. 'You can't just disappear without saying anything! The Sienese have surrendered, but the peace is fragile. You and Alder are the sword hanging over their heads. If they learn you're no longer in the city—'

'Then don't let them learn,' Hissing Cat snapped.

'There are dozens of them here in the infirmary,' Clear-River pointed out. 'Word will spread.'

'You don't need us,' I said.

Clear-River ran his hands through the wild tangles of his hair. 'I'm sorry, Alder, but as much as you wish we didn't, we do.'

'Weren't you the one nipping at my heels, wanting to race off to Sor Cala last night?' Hissing Cat glowered at me, the skulls in her hair rattling. 'If we're all through with our farewells, it's time we were on our way.'

'Goodbye, Clear-River,' I said, and wished, not for the first time, that he had surpassed me in the imperial examinations. From our first meeting, he had shown himself to be much shrewder and more savvy than I, recognising the revelation of my magic for the opportunity it was. He had been willing to exploit it to his advantage, but had stepped back from crossing the line into revealing it and plunging us both into danger. If he and not I had been Hand Usher's apprentice – more, if he had been born with the talents of a witch of the old sort – then perhaps the story of our world would have been written differently. Perhaps Okara would have found him less easy to manipulate, and Nayeni liberation might have come without the shattering of the world. Or perhaps power would have corrupted the seed of goodness in him that had first taken root at Burrow and now blossomed here in Eastern Fortress. In any case, I had faith in him. If we failed, he would find the way forwards, if anyone could.

Or so I told myself, to calm my racing heart and subdue my fears. Fear of the unknown we were about to plunge into. Fear, too, of the danger still looming here. Of the chaos tearing through the world, and of the hatred between Nayeni and Sienese, quieted now, but simmering and ready to boil over at the slightest agitation.

'You'll do well by them,' I said, as much for my sake as for his. 'By all of them. Better than I ever could.'

He only stared at me, speechless, as Hissing Cat reached deep into the pattern and tore it like a paper screen, hurling us through the gap and to the other side of the world.

30

All That Our Ancestors Left Behind

Koro Ha

A pillar filled the centre of the hollow stalagmite, so wide that a dozen men linking arms could not embrace it. It soared upwards, tapering until it joined the ceiling. Carvings lined every span of its surface, curling and interweaving, a lattice of unimaginable complexity. It would have taken decades to carve by ordinary means, meaning that it – and all the rest of the wonders hidden here, in this chamber deep beneath Sor Cala, buried at the roots of the Pillars of the Gods – must have been made by magic. *What* magic, though, Koro Ha could not begin to guess. Certainly no stonespeaker had wielded powers equal to those behind the creation of these marvels.

<You are not wrong,> the stone-faced god answered when he asked, awestruck in the shadow of these secrets. <No stonespeaker crafted these but your predecessor, Ambal Ora, who forged your pact. These were his works.> The stone-faced god gestured to the pillar, its expressionless face – itself like a carving in living rock – sweeping upwards to take in its vastness. <He and his fellows parlayed with the gods and put an end to the war, but Ambal Ora knew that in the long march of time, war would come again. He prepared this place, and this weapon, for that eventuality.>

There was the solution to one puzzle, at least: not the name of the sanctuary itself, but its maker.

'What happened to him?' Koro Ha asked, trying to tamp down the flaring candle of hope. If this Ambal Ora were still alive … But no. If he were, the stone-faced god would have brought them to him, surely.

<A mortal body, no matter how gifted with divine will and power, can only be pushed so far before it breaks. We warned him that what he intended would exhaust him. He insisted that the future was worth his every effort, his every sacrifice. His bones are buried here, in the stone.> The god's ghostly voice carried an echo of regret and sadness. <He had faith that Naphena, if none of the others of his kind, would return here and turn this weapon to his envisioned purpose, should it prove necessary.>

With his finger, Koro Ha traced the carvings, depicting a version of Toa Aloni script older and more intricate even than the carvings on the glass sphere. This, perhaps, was the oldest example of his written language in all the world. With time, perhaps decades, perhaps centuries of scholarly attention, some sense might be made of it.

The stone-faced god watched him with unblinking eyes at once lifelessly flat and filled with infinite depth, and Koro Ha felt a fool. Of course there could be no secrets older than a god. 'What does it say?' he asked.

<It is a prayer,> the god said, <or perhaps a wish, for it is not directed at us, nor at any god, but only at the nebulous, infinite expanse of the future. A wish for the world to come, that it might be worth the cost of its birth. I could read it to you, if you desire, though it would take several hours.>

'The cost …' It was prudent to know, he decided, before they brought the refugees currently living in Uon Elia's tunnels down to this secret, ancient garden. 'You say it is a weapon. Is it dangerous? What does it do?'

<It is no danger to you, nor to any mortal,> the god answered. <It is designed for a single purpose, layered with magics that defy even my understanding. A masterwork, woven into the stone itself. To call it a weapon is, perhaps, too simple. It is a tool. An artist's brush. A stone-carver's chisel. A means to transform the world into something other than it is.>

'Yes, but how?'

The stone-faced god seemed hesitant to explain; Koro Ha felt an undercurrent to the thoughts it sent into his mind, like a rip tide pulling back from the shore. <We do not wield magic as mortals do. When Ambal Ora created this weapon, we struggled to trace the continuity of what he did. It was like trying to read meaning in the scattered field of stars, or the whirling patterns the wind writes in sand, or the fissures in ancient stone. It is difficult for me to understand, let alone to explain. There are things, perhaps, that even we gods cannot fully comprehend. Yet I can say this: it will carve apart the pattern of the world and weave it anew.>

Koro Ha rubbed the pads of his fingers with his thumb, still feeling the rough surface of the carvings. How could he help but fear such a violent, destructive notion? The world he knew was far from perfect. It was a world of empires, of poverty and the suffering of children, of humiliation and regret – yet there was beauty there too, in the light of understanding in a student's eyes, in the composition of a stirring verse. The world already frayed around the edges. If it could not be stitched back together, perhaps it ought to be rent and remade. Though the question naturally arose: what sort of world had Ambal Ora intended to make from the tattered remnant of this one?

Koro Ha shook his head. There was little point in worrying over Ambal Ora's weapon, whatever it did. By the stone-faced god's explanation, Koro Ha could not wield it. Nor, in all likelihood, could anyone alive. Better to put his mind to problems that lay within his power to solve.

The stone-faced god followed him from the hollow chamber. As it had done when they'd entered, it swept its hand along the stone. The smooth edges of the opening flowed together as though the stone of the pillar were alive. Koro Ha shuddered. How long, he wondered, before he finally grew accustomed to the world twisting and contorting around him?

Goa Eln's effort to begin settling Ambal Ora's cavern had begun to transform it. A cluster of young women moved though one of the loamy fields, planting seeds which, though long reserved for the next year's crop – whenever it proved safe to farm again – had been destined for a cookpot only a day ago. Small green shoots already pushed their way up from the earth, while a plum pit buried in a neighbouring field had already produced a juvenile, twiggy tree. Koro Ha paused to observe it for a moment, as he did whenever he walked past it, transfixed by another nascent branch pushing its way out of the narrow trunk, by the unfurling of its delicate, waxy leaves – perhaps the greatest miracle the cavern had to offer. The magic of cultivation flowed through every field, as though the earth itself worked the spell.

Gratitude like water through a breaking dam threatened to overcome Koro Ha, yet he continued on his way. There was work yet to be done. He could fall to his knees and weep thankful tears when the people of Sor Cala were safe, fed, and housed.

A few of the people working the fields looked up at the passage of the stone-faced god, covering their faces and dipping their heads in awe and worship, muttering prayers of thanks. The god did not react, though it must have understood. In truth, it had been Ambal Ora, not the god, who had prepared all of this, leaving for his legacy the shelter his people would need, as though he had peered into the future and seen the very tragedy that would befall them. Preparations kept secret to preserve them in the face of history's shifting, dangerous tides.

Thinking of how close the empire had come to eradicating the stonespeakers, and with them the key to Sor Cala's salvation, filled Koro Ha with a burning rage like nothing he had ever known. Had the emperor known of this place? Had he intended to destroy it when he had called the mountain down and buried Sor Cala? Koro Ha struggled to decide whether he found that possibility more or less outrageous than the notion that the emperor had wrought such destruction in ignorance. Once, when he had still been enthralled by the logic and potency of imperial doctrine, he would have believed the former. Now, he was far from certain.

The hollowed stalagmite nearest the tunnel, and thence to the buried city and Orna Sin's garden, had become something of a command centre. There, Goa Eln and a team of surveyors worked to map the enormous cavern and organised the distribution of living and work space. As Koro Ha arrived there, she was in the midst of welcoming a fresh group of refugees – two women of middle age, a younger man, and a dozen children. None shared any common features, yet they were a family nonetheless, the sort forged by need rather than blood. A guide led them down into the cavern and the children nearly stumbled over themselves, unable to tear their gaze from the wonders that surrounded them.

'Master Koro Ha?'

A young boy's voice. One he knew, and which shook him to his core. He searched the faces of the children. Only one, a tall boy with sharp features and bristly, unkempt hair, had no eyes for the cavern.

'Lon Sa.'

Koro Ha met the boy's stare, a storm of emotions building

within him. Surprise to see one of his former students. Joy that the boy was still alive. Horror at the thick scar that traced his cheek and at the deep hollows around his eyes. Sorrow that he was here, alone, as a member of this family Koro Ha did not recognise. The question *Where are your parents, my boy?* broke against his teeth. A dozen others darted through him. All would only stir up whatever suffering Lon Sa had endured since Koro Ha had seen him last. Instead, he took a step forwards. Haltingly, his body shaking, the boy matched that step, then buried his face in his teacher's chest, shuddering with tears.

'You know him?' the older of the two women asked, though all the while she stared at the stone giant in Koro Ha's company.

Koro Ha nodded and held Lon Sa closer. 'He was my student.'

'After Mister Mah, you just disappeared,' the boy sobbed, then scrubbed at his eyes with the back of his hand and collected himself. Koro Ha could not help but smile at his brave face, even as it broke his heart anew. 'We thought you were dead! What happened?'

'More than I can explain just now,' Koro Ha answered. 'A great deal has changed for me since I was your teacher.'

Lon Sa looked over his shoulder at his adoptive family. 'Me too. Too much.'

'Tutor!' Goa Eln waved him over. 'You're needed!'

Koro Ha gave the boy another squeeze. 'I'm sorry, Lon Sa, but I have to go,' he said, though he wanted nothing more than to stay with the boy. He had long since given up hope of finding Eln Se or Rea Ab or his father, though he still carried the comb of carved horn he had found in the ruins of their home. At least one of his students had survived. Not everyone he had known and loved was lost.

'Come find me later,' Lon Sa said, pulling away, collecting his dignity with an outpouring of words. 'Or I'll come and find you. We should have tea – if they have tea down here, anyway.

I'm so glad you're alive, Master Koro Ha. It's honestly hard to believe.'

Lon Sa ran back to his family, already spinning tales of his time as a student in Orna Sin's garden, studying the Sienese classics by day and – in secret, in the very tunnels that led to this cavern – Toa Aloni culture by night. By rights, he or one of his classmates should have carried on the legacy of the stone-speakers as Uon Elia's successor, not Koro Ha, although that future might still come to pass. It would be good to teach again. Perhaps a room in one of the stalagmites might be reserved for a school—

'When I said *you're needed*, I didn't mean in some kind of hypothetical, future sense,' Goa Eln chided, grabbing him by the elbow. She paused to dip a quick bow to the stone-faced god – who only cocked its head in an oddly human gesture of confusion, or perhaps amusement; it was difficult to tell, given the immobile nature of its eyes and mouth – before dragging Koro Ha away. 'Yin Ila sent for you, and she's already in a bad enough mood to chew rocks.'

'Goa Eln, do you think one of the rooms—'

'Sure, fine, whatever. Just go talk to Yin Ila before she bites someone's head off.'

True to Goa Eln's warning, Yin Ila paced the length of the room, her right hand squeezed into a fist, rising to rap at the planks balanced on wooden stools which served, for the time being, as a table. Scrolls covered in sketches and figures made by Goa Eln's surveyors, describing the dimensions and contents of the cavern, lay scattered about the floor along with a spilled pot of ink and a half-dozen brushes. Whoever had been busy at work before Yin Ila's arrival had fled the thunderstorm that roiled around her. Only Tuo Pon remained, his arms crossed, the fingers of his right hand toying with the pommel of his fighting knife.

'There you are,' Yin Ila barked, rounding on Koro Ha as Goa Eln all but tossed him into the room. 'Tell me, tutor. This weapon the god spoke of. How quickly can we make use of it?'

Her agitation made Koro Ha's skin crawl, infecting him like a breath of plague. His stomach turned as a memory arose: the image of a child's face, mounted like a blood-spattered trophy atop a monstrous, bestial body, looming over a pair of savaged corpses. Yin Ila's expression made him fear that a dozen such beasts rampaged above their heads even as they spoke.

'What's happened?' he asked, fighting to keep a level voice.

'The Sienese have taken to the streets, that's what,' Yin Ila snarled. 'Not content to cower in their quarter any longer, it seems. Things were bad enough with the bloody wolves and birds and whatever else, and the gangs still clinging to scraps of power, but we could move people through that mess and into the tunnels. Now we don't dare, else risk the Sienese following us here and fucking massacring us all like a weasel in a rats' nest.'

'It's worse than just that,' Tuo Pon muttered. 'Rumour has it that the emperor himself is in Toa Alon.'

Koro Ha reeled. 'What reason could he have to come here?'

'Can't say for sure, but at this point, given that a literal *god* is walking around on the other side of that door, I'm far more willing to believe wild stories of his immortality.' Yin Ila jabbed her finger towards the column at the heart of the cavern that housed Ambal Ora's weapon. 'I wager he knows what that thing is and wants it for himself.'

'Could it help us?' Goa Eln asked.

'The weapon?'

'The god.'

All three of them fixed Koro Ha with long, searching stares. Since their first meeting, when Goa Eln and the stone-cutters in her company had heard its voice as well, it had spoken to no one but Koro Ha. 'Stonespeaker', it turned out, was more than just a title; beyond his ability with magic, his role was to serve as the intermediary between the gods of Toa Alon and their people.

With a pass of the stone-faced god's hand, rock flowed like water. By its power, trees grew to maturity in a matter of days. The deep, draining wound Koro Ha had suffered when overextending himself to open the doorway to this cavern had healed in a heartbeat at its touch.

None of the legends and tales Koro Ha knew – neither those snatched fragments he recalled of his father's tales, nor the stories Uon Elia had told Lon Sa and the other children – portrayed the stone-faced gods as warriors. They were builders, gardeners.

The god held the power to resist the emperor. Of that, Koro Ha had little doubt. Asking it to wield that power in violence, however, felt like sacrilege.

'The weapon might,' Koro Ha said, 'if we could use it. It requires greater magics than I can wield.'

'Then the god, Koro Ha!' Yin Ila's fist splintered the makeshift table. She glowered, rubbing the scraped heel of her hand. 'The world is crumbling around us. The god offers us sanctuary, and I will gladly take it, but I will *not* be satisfied to see it house a few hundred when it might shelter thousands.'

And who are we to make demands of a god? The thought sprang unbidden and was deeply entangled with Sienese doctrine. The stone-faced god was not the emperor. He had no reason to think of its will as absolute and unquestionable. Yet he did. Its power placed it over him, and a mind accustomed to hierarchy for five decades did not forget its habits in a single year.

'I will ask,' Koro Ha said. 'But I can promise nothing.'

'Regardless, we need to move more people into this place as soon as possible,' Tuo Pon said. He gathered up the papers on the floor and laid them out on the broken table. 'How many can we accommodate, Goa Eln?'

While they set to discussing the logistics of moving thousands of people through the tunnel and into the cavern's hundreds of rooms – and the likely need to build shelters on some of the fields, and how much of that land they could afford to put to any use but food production – Koro Ha excused himself. The stone-faced god remained where he had left it on the path nearby, its empty gaze surveying the cavern. It seemed to Koro Ha like a statue of a shepherd: still and silent, watching the horizon for any threat to its flock.

'Eerie bastard, isn't he?' Yin Ila whispered, following him from the room.

Koro Ha gave her a withering stare, as though she were a student and might be cowed into respect with a look.

She glared back, her eyes blunt as cudgels. 'I didn't grow up with much use for gods, Koro Ha. No statue or face in a stone wall ever put food in my mouth or shelter over my head.'

'Nor mine,' he replied. 'Yet this one does now.'

She grunted. 'By your own account, it sounds like this Ambal Ora person made all this. The god only keeps watch over it for him, like a jumped-up steward. Well, it's been watched over – stewarded quite well, thank you – and passed on to those of us who need it. Lot of good it will do if the emperor finds us.'

'Must this miracle solve all of our problems for it to be worth our gratitude and awe?' Koro Ha felt his anger rising and quickly tamped it down. He was far too old to let himself be sucked into an argument that could have no winner. It would crack the facade of his wisdom. 'I am certain it will do all that it can to help us, Yin Ila.'

She crossed her arms and left to return to the tunnels, muttering that if the stone-faced god would not defend her people then she at least would throw her body between them and the empire.

'Well?' Koro Ha asked the stone-faced god when she had gone. 'You surely heard our conversation. What do you make of it? Will you fight for us? *Can* you?'

The god turned its head – an eerie motion, its smoothness hinting at muscles that could not be there, lying beneath the stone. <Is that what you would have us be?>

'The emperor of Sien, a powerful sorcerer, has come to Sor Cala,' Koro Ha said. 'If he finds this place, he will destroy it. He will try to destroy *you*, if he can.'

<We could oppose him.> The god's thoughts were like the movements of a glacier, crawling across eons of time: slow, methodical, but gradually changing. <It is not within our nature, but it is possible. We were not conceived as protectors.>

Confusion swept through Koro Ha. 'Not conceived …' The god spoke as though it were not eternal, as though it had been created, or even born. More, that it had been created to serve a *purpose*. No legend he knew spoke of this. The gods were eternal, weren't they? As ancient as the roots of the mountains.

It occurred to him that he stood now in just such roots, beneath the Pillars of the Gods, in a place that was far from natural. A place overflowing with artifice and magic, watched over by this god, at the behest of a man who, however powerful, had been a mortal.

'Who … *What* conceived you?'

<Your need, stonespeaker.> The god flexed its hands, as though feeling their strength for the first time. <And your need, it seems, has changed.>

31
Into the Mountain

Foolish Cur

One moment we were all standing on the hill below Oriole's tree. The next, with a sickening dizziness and a blurring at the corners of my eyes, the architecture of an unfamiliar city rose around us. Towering structures of stone reached towards the heavens, carved with all manner of elaborate decorations, most formed of looping, interwoven lines. They put me in mind of An-Zabat, though while those structures had been of sandstone, many of these were of marble shot through with veins that glittered in the sun.

Doctor Sho went to his knees, green with nausea. A small parcel wrapped in red cloth tumbled from his sleeve and rolled a few paces across the paving stones. I bent to retrieve it for him, but before I could he snatched it up and tucked it back in place, then retched. 'You couldn't have made that any smoother, I take it?' he grumbled, wiping the wisps of his beard on his sleeve.

Hissing Cat's mind was elsewhere. She stared to the south, towards a barren, rocky mound that rose from the centre of the city, not far from where we had appeared. Outrage burned in her eyes. 'What would terrify Tenet more than knowing something he tried to destroy has survived?' She gestured at the mound with her chin. 'Whatever made the wake that left Tenet pissing himself, it's under there.'

I remembered a tale my steward, Jhin, had told me in An-Zabat, of the garden city of Sor Cala, which the emperor had destroyed by hurling down the peak of a mountain. The tale supported her conclusion, yet my mind drifted elsewhere, towards a crushing wake that emanated from the north: a hole in the pattern, a seal woven of interlocking strands, one even more complex than the hollow shell I had anchored around Eastern Fortress.

'He's here,' I said.

'Of course he fucking is, Cur,' Hissing Cat snarled. She shook her head and muttered under her breath as she set off towards the rocky hill.

'Wait,' I called after her. 'That's his wake, isn't it? Why would it be over *there* if what he's looking for is under the hill?'

'Overconfidence? How the hell should I know?' she shouted back, her voice echoing between the stone facades. 'But now that we're here, he won't drag his feet any longer. Get a move on!' She had already plunged down a side street and would soon be out of sight.

We started after her, Doctor Sho keeping pace with me despite his nausea. Our footsteps echoed down the empty streets. Eastern Fortress had felt eerie and empty while its people huddled for shelter from the factions warring in its streets, but this was worse. Marble facades showed brutal damage. Sculptures had been shattered by grenades or magic, stone marred with deep, parallel gouges. A lupine howl rose nearby, its distance difficult to gauge as it echoed through the streets.

In my father's house, I had glimpsed what the chaotic wakes of the divine war could make of a person. Imagining that horror wrought on the scale of a city such as this – as vast, at first impression, as the great oasis city of An-Zabat – sent an aching shudder through me. Yet we had seen no corpses, no blood, no signs of fighting but this material damage. I could make no sense of such absence, though I was grateful for it.

'Is she planning on walking straight into the hillside?' Doctor Sho muttered.

A low wall encircled the hill, cutting it off from the rest of the city. Hissing Cat stood before it, fists digging into her hips, glaring as though her disdain for the wall itself could tear it break from brick. She reached out a hand and I felt the stirrings of a wake of magic, a burning coal in my chest.

'Wait!' I shouted. 'He'll feel the wake of it!'

'He already felt our arrival in the city!' Hissing Cat shouted back. 'We don't have time to waste. And get behind something!'

Before I had a moment to heed her advice, a roar shook the street and the coal in my chest burst to flame. Dust cascaded from the buildings around us. A light as searing as the sun poured from her hand, through the wall, and into the hillside. Earth and stone burst apart and scattered like a pile of dry leaves tossed by a gust of wind.

The light vanished as suddenly as it had appeared. I knelt in the street, my chest heaving for want of breath.

'What, a little magic's enough to bring you to your knees?' Hissing Cat shouted, her voice echoing from the still-glowing depths of the tunnel she had carved into the hillside. 'What happened to that smug bastard who planned on killing Tenet? Pull yourself together, Cur, and try to keep up.'

The walls of the tunnel groaned and cracked around us, the surface of the stone turning black and glassy as it released the heat of Hissing Cat's flame. A haze hung in the air, though Hissing Cat had somehow cooled the floor of the tunnel, leaving it smooth save for the occasional jagged fissure.

The knowledge that Tenet would not be far behind us hounded me throughout that downward climb, each step treacherous, the walls still seething with heat, the ceiling holding a greater and greater weight of piled earth and stone above our heads. I wondered how long the walls of the tunnel would hold. The mine shafts near Iron Town had collapsed not long after Usher and I had ordered our soldiers to destroy their supports, and they had been far shallower than this.

As terrible as the depth was, the darkness that enveloped us, as the latent glow in the cooling walls faded, was even more oppressive. I conjured a candle-flame, but it did little against the gloom, which pressed in from ahead and behind. Hissing Cat plunged on, just beyond the small circle of light, heedless of the darkness, until she stopped suddenly, almost mid-stride, gazing at the floor before her and muttering under her breath.

'Do you feel that, Cur?' she asked. 'Below us?'

I reached into the pattern, through the layers of earth and stone beneath our feet. Strange structures – unnatural, built by human hands and not yet adhering to the flow of the pattern – testified to the presence of an ancient city buried here, destroyed by the emperor's magic. Then my awareness brushed against something stranger still, like the edge of a shield against magic only less confounding. Not a void in the pattern – I could almost glimpse a shape beyond it, vast and cavernous – but a barrier my awareness could not penetrate no matter how I tried.

'Like the shell around Eastern Fortress,' I murmured, then looked to Hissing Cat in horror.

'It isn't him,' she said. 'I'd know the wake of Tenet's will anywhere.'

A tremor rippled through the earth around us and my shoulder slammed into the wall as the floor leapt beneath me. Doctor Sho dropped to his hands and knees. A crack sounded overhead and glittering dust rained down.

'What did you do?' Doctor Sho shouted over a second rumbling in the earth.

'Nothing!' Hissing Cat yelled back, then hauled me to my feet and pushed me down the tunnel. 'Now *run!*'

Shards of glass as broad and sharp as knives shattered against the floor. Doctor Sho slammed into my back – propelled by his own shove from Hissing Cat – as we sprinted downwards, all fear of losing our footing swallowed up by our panic, kindled by the rumbling earth and falling rock. My heart thundered and my lungs heaved in my chest as I reached into the pattern and called a whirlwind to hold back the rain of debris.

Something heavy cut through my attempt at protection and slammed into my left shoulder, sending me sprawling. The stump of my right wrist reached to cradle the wound and felt a jagged, blood-slick edge. A hand caught the back of my robe and hauled me to my feet, sending a judder of pain down my back and the length of my injured arm.

'Just run!' Hissing Cat roared.

I found my feet and ran, though she did not take her own advice. A wake of magic burst from her, listless and leaden like exhausted muscles, fanning out across the walls of the tunnel. I had never felt its like before, but I could feel it working in the pattern, stilling the quake around us and shoring up the walls.

'Fuck!' she screamed, and the magic she had been weaving came apart like unravelling thread.

I whirled to face her, swallowing my own scream at the lancing pain from my shoulder, fearing that Hissing Cat had been felled by a similar piece of debris. She knelt, her face veiled by her hair so that she resembled a gnarled bush in which a family of skull-faced ravens nested.

'What happened?' I went to her side, but she shrugged off my attempt at aid.

'What did I say?' she snarled, hauling herself to her feet, her breath coming in gasps. She shoved me down the tunnel. 'Just run, Cur!'

She ran after me, and this time made no attempt at magic. The earth roared and shook around us. Glass split and shattered, biting into our hands and faces, and blood soaked my robe. While I could heal my wound, I could ill afford the time it would take, nor the calming effect the ensuing wake would have on me, subsuming the adrenaline-soaked terror that kept me running through the pain, heedless of the shattering tunnel.

'It's blocked!' Doctor Sho's voice echoed back, piercing like the final note of an opera. He was leaning against a pile of rubble, his legs shaking, his lungs heaving. I flailed out with my sixth sense, probing into the mass of fallen stone and earth. If it were only a few paces wide … but no. The tunnel ahead of us had collapsed, giving way to the pressure of the mountain piled overhead and the quaking of the earth. Hissing Cat might be able to break through the blockage, but not, I feared, before the rest of the tunnel fell and buried us.

Desperate, I let my awareness fan out. There had been a chamber below us, an open space, one that had resisted our magic and where the source of the wake we sought would surely be found. How far downwards had we journeyed in our flight? Deep enough almost to reach that cavern? My sixth sense sought the strange resistance that had marked the edge of the cavern. Instead, I felt a current of wind through open air.

'Out of the way, Sho, unless you'd rather be burnt to ash than buried alive!' Hissing Cat shouted.

'There!' I pointed to the right-hand wall. 'Carve a tunnel there! There's a cavern not a dozen paces beyond this wall!'

Light burned from Hissing Cat's hand even as she raised it. The wall caved inwards, stone burning to acrid steam even as she plunged ahead, calling a magic of mixed wind and water as chilling as anything I had ever felt to cool the floor beneath her feet. Doctor Sho and I ran after her, the heat singeing our hair and aching lungs, and I could feel the prickling of fresh burns on my face. Every step jostled the stone shard wedged in my shoulder, sending a flare of agony down the length of my arm. Still the earth shook around us, seeming to redouble its efforts, as though intent on burying us before we emerged into the cavern ahead.

Cool air swept in past Hissing Cat and the light at her hand went out. In its absence, the residual glowing of the walls seemed dim and the strange cavern ahead dimmer still, despite globes of flickering lamplight. I went to my knees, gulping to fill and soothe my lungs. Hissing Cat dragged me a few paces further, away from the tunnel and the threat of its collapse. But as quickly as the quaking had begun, it had ended. The ground no longer leapt beneath us, as though the earthquake had been localised entirely to the tunnel, or had been *trying* to trap us and ceased the moment we emerged and its opportunity came to an end.

Gasping for cool air to soothe my lungs, I reached for healing magic. Gently, I probed the edges of my wound, pushing out the intruding shard of stone, which fell to the floor and shattered. The shoulder rolled easily enough in its socket and I stood, pulling my bloodstained tunic away from my chest.

'Well, bleed me dry,' Hissing Cat murmured, her voice raw and her breath ragged. She walked a few paces into the vast, columned space. A dome hung over our heads, bathed in shadow that resisted the feathery fingers of light that reached up from hanging lamps. I could only just make out the contours of a stone face carved into the apex of the dome. 'Tenet thought he'd crushed this place to dust.'

Doctor Sho gazed up from where he stood, doubled over to catch his breath. 'To think this temple could stand for so long beneath such a weight.'

Hissing Cat grunted in amusement. 'Never underestimate Toa Aloni architecture.'

'There's a door,' I said, pointing to a mat of woven rushes that hung in a doorway. We all stared at it. Our minds had been perhaps too exhausted – and stunned by our survival – to register the implications of the burning lamps, but here was certain proof that someone had been living in this cavern.

'More of those mats over here,' Doctor Sho observed. 'Sleeping mats?' He knelt and scraped some dust from the floor with his finger. 'These look like herbs. And there, an old bandage. Was this a sickroom?'

Hissing Cat shushed him, then eased the door of rushes aside. She whistled, then stepped through. 'Someone's been busy down here, and not that long ago by the look of things.'

The doorway led into another tunnel, one which seemed a terrible mirror of the streets above our heads. Stone facades as intricate and ornate as any we had seen in the streets – and many much more so, despite time and weathering – had been lovingly excavated from the earth. Some of the structures had even been hollowed out, their interiors made liveable again, and the occasional scrap of clothing or refuse we came across reinforced Hissing Cat's conclusion that these spaces had been quite recently occupied.

'Were there people living down here all this time?' I wondered aloud.

'Unlikely,' Doctor Sho said. 'Perhaps there are tunnels other than the one we made leading up to the city. We may have unearthed a parallel Toa Alon, one persisting beneath the empire's feet for a generation or more.'

Whoever had dwelt here, and for however long, it was clear that they had stirred up the wake we were chasing. That they had seemingly vanished from their homes layered anxiety atop the fatigue I carried after our mad dash and my injury. Just as unsettling, we had yet to pass through any kind of seal or barrier. This tunnel, though underground, was just as exposed as the city above to the chaotic wakes of the divine war that tore through the pattern and made men and beasts into monsters. The earthquake might, in fact, have been such a wake.

The terrible possibility that all the inhabitants of this place had suffered the same fate as my father's steward clung to my mind like a cobweb as we passed empty doorways and abandoned artefacts, though not – I noted hopefully – any that looked particularly useful. If all the people in this place had been either twisted into monstrosities or been slaughtered by their neighbours, they would surely have left cutlery and tools behind.

We passed several intersections. At each, one road had been only partially unearthed. Following the main street led us to another domed chamber. Here, the stone face in the ceiling seemed gilded with shimmering green glass or translucent jade bearing swirling carvings that looked almost like some strange form of writing. Beneath the face, in the centre of the floor, a stairwell spiralled downwards.

'It's right below us,' Hissing Cat murmured, and I noticed the subtle wake of her attention reaching down into the depths of the earth, towards the strange barrier.

We hesitated at the top of the stairwell. There could be no certainty of what we would find at the bottom. All we knew was that it was something of vast, world-shaking power. Something that had terrified the emperor. And it was that thought of him, and of the certainty that he even now pursued us into this place, that compelled me take one of the lanterns from the wall and begin our final descent.

A thick layer of dust on the steps had been disturbed by footprints and the jagged tracks of carts. At times, the passage of hundreds if not thousands of people who had preceded us had all but swept the ancient steps clean, leaving only scant piles of dust along the walls.

'That answers one question,' I observed. 'But why excavate the old city before descending these steps?'

'Ask them when we reach the bottom,' Hissing Cat said, 'if they're inclined to talk.'

A sobering point. The people of this place had wielded incredible magic. It stood to reason that they opposed the emperor, but we could not guess how they would react to our arrival, nor whether our ultimate goals aligned.

Yet even the three of us – Doctor Sho, Hissing Cat, and I – did not necessarily share the same goal. I knew Doctor Sho's purpose well enough, though I still had little idea how to achieve his dream of a world stripped of magic. Perhaps he believed that he would find the means of doing so in this buried city, or perhaps he knew more of what we might find than he admitted. It was difficult to trust him after he had kept so many secrets.

For my part, I intended first to discover what had so troubled the emperor, and then to oppose his reaching it, either to destroy it or bend it to my will. To my mind, anything that threatened him was a boon, and anything he might turn to his own ends was a threat. Nayen had been free for less than a day. I would sooner Doctor Sho achieve his aim and scour the world of its wonder and mystery than allow the emperor to restore his rule.

At last the stairwell ended in another tunnel. Its ceiling soared overhead, far beyond the reach of my torch, above walls carved with intricate latticework that seemed a distant ancestor to the decorative facades that had lined the excavated buildings of the buried city – which had, in turn, seemed the progenitor of the city's current architecture. I marvelled at the age of those designs, which recalled to me the carvings in the catacombs beneath An-Zabat that Atar and I had traversed dozens of times in our journeys out onto the dunes, or the paintings upon the walls of Hissing Cat's cave. The forms were different – these were far less representational – but they held the same sublime potency of age and obscurity.

'Quit gawking and get your head together, Cur,' Hissing Cat whispered. 'Not much further now.'

A presence filled my mind, rumbling and inevitable as an earthquake. <Turn back,> its voice thundered, sharp as cracking stone. <You are unwelcome here.>

Hissing Cat peeled back her lips, her teeth gleaming like blunted knives. 'Did you two hear that?'

Doctor Sho pulled at his beard, peering into the shadows ahead of us. 'We are no threat to this place!' he called. 'We oppose the one who buried your city!'

<This is the last refuge of Toa Alon.> The words held the unbreakable certainty of bedrock. <You are not of Toa Alon. You are unwelcome.>

I reached out towards the voice, meaning to communicate our intent and our friendship, wondering if the speaker was perhaps a witch of the old sort, one who had dwelt here below Sor Cala as Hissing Cat had dwelt in her cave. But even the wake of the emperor's mind, though weighty and powerful, was not as strange as this. Its thoughts held no current, no flow, as though fixed in place in ages past.

No. That was wrong. They moved, but like the movement of stone, subtle and imperceptible, shifting across generations upon generations of time. Only Okara's thoughts had been so strange, though his had been different, flighty and inconstant as flame.

<We come to warn you,> I said, walling off my fears of the gods and my hatred for their war. <The emperor of Sien, who means to destroy your kind, knows of your presence here. He means to kill you. We would offer an alliance against him.>

A slow shifting, like the bones of the earth grinding against one another, a mountain range plunging upwards over eons, gave rise to an answer.

<We are your ancient enemy,> the voice rumbled. <Yours and the woman with you. Why would you defend us?>

<Thousand-year-old battle lines need not define the present,> I answered, thinking of Clear-River and Pinion, even of Atar, all of whom had been my enemies before they became my closest allies. I hoped that the memories would lend a weight of truth to my words. <The emperor is the greater threat, as are the gods who still war for dominance. If you take no part in that conflict, we have no quarrel with you.>

I had become too accustomed to intractable negotiations, first with my uncle, then with Burning Dog and the Sienese at Eastern Fortress. The voice was slow in answering. It belonged, I was sure, to one of the stone-faced gods of Toa Alon, which my steward Jhin had told me of in An-Zabat. My stomach churned and my body tensed with fear of rejection and the duel that would follow. Hissing Cat shifted beside me, and I could feel the iron spar of her will held ready to carve into the pattern. Of the two of us, only she had killed gods before.

At last, the glacier moved. <It is for the people of Toa Alon to decide, and they would meet with you.>

'A god bowing to the will of its people?' Hissing Cat said with a wry grin. 'I'd have sooner expected a river to run uphill.'

'Could it be a trick?' Doctor Sho asked.

'It doesn't matter,' I answered. 'Whatever Tenet's after here, it lies beyond this tunnel. We go through either as guests or by force.'

Doctor Sho tugged at his beard again, then slid behind Hissing Cat, hunching slightly, as though ducking for cover. 'On we go, then,' he muttered.

The echoes of our footsteps took on an eerie ring as we proceeded, the lantern held high, as though by glimpsing the stone-faced god in the distant reaches of its light we might discern its true intentions before it had a chance to strike.

Soon enough the flickering lantern light was drowned out by a strange, greenish-yellow glow that emanated from the carvings in the walls. Doctor Sho, his fear forgotten for a moment, ran his finger along one of the carvings, then scraped off a piece of luminescent moss, touching it with his tongue and breathing in its scent.

'Like nothing I've ever seen,' he murmured, then looked to Hissing Cat, who only shook her head.

We snuffed the lantern and continued on our way. The patterns on the walls were soon filled with the glowing moss, which reached all the way to the vaulted ceiling, giving us our first glimpse of the tunnel's enormity, which was vast enough to enclose any structure I had ever seen, even the obelisks of An-Zabat. No human hands equipped with ordinary tools could have accomplished such a feat.

'Tenet isn't the only bastard who's been busy,' Hissing Cat murmured.

A joke at her expense bubbled up, nearly spilling from my mouth. One could only wonder, after all, what she might have accomplished if she had not spent the time since the end of the last divine war hiding in her cave, poring over countless carved and cracked bones. Naphena had built her oasis, Tenet had built his empire, and here in Toa Alon another of her kind – for after the truce and the pacts, the gods were forbidden from such direct action in the world – had hollowed out the Pillars of the Gods.

A figure stood at the end of the tunnel, silhouetted against an opening that seemed as bright as noon, as though it opened onto the outside world. I took it for a man, but as my mind accommodated the scale of the tunnel I realised that it stood twice the height of any mortal. Its limbs were as thick around as my chest, its head like a boulder balanced on the cliff of its neck. So commanding was its presence that I did not note the figures gathered around it, seeming like a gaggle of children until one of them stepped towards me with an expression of astonishment.

'*Alder?*' the man said, and at once his features came into focus, though weathered by time and hardship, framed by the unruly length of his beard and the braids of his hair, so at odds with the careful grooming of a Sienese tutor. My heart leapt within me, habits drilled into me in childhood coming awake after long dormancy. I felt at once the urge to show him deference, as a student ought to bow to his former teacher, even as a thousand questions darted through my mind, chief among them being: how had he come into the company of a god?

Before I could muster a greeting, however, Koro Ha crossed the distance between us and, in a moment as shocking as any in my life, drove his fist into my jaw.

32
An Unexpected Reunion

Koro Ha

Koro Ha winced, massaging his bruised knuckles and aching, arthritic wrist while he offered Alder's companions an apologetic smile.

'You must understand,' he said. 'He had that coming.'

'Oh,' the old, wild-looking woman said, 'I am *blisteringly* certain that he did.'

It had taken Koro Ha a moment to recognise his erstwhile student, dressed as he was in Nayeni peasant's clothes, no longer a slim whip of a youth but a young man, broad of chest, with a wild tangle of red-tinted hair around his head and the first shadows of a beard outlining his jaw.

When the stone-faced god had warned of intruders, Koro Ha had feared Hands of the emperor marching at the head of a thousand Sienese soldiers. Yin Ila and the dozen warriors she had gathered carried knives and bows and prepared to hold the mouth of the tunnel, even if only long enough for Goa Eln and Tuo Pon to muster a more potent defence.

Even after the god's reassurance that the intruders claimed to be allies, enemies of the emperor, bearing a warning and an offer of help, the fear had persisted, needling the back of his mind. Bizarrely, he had not been entirely wrong. The intruders weren't soldiers but a Hand of the emperor – or at least a young man who had once been a Hand – leading an army made up of an angry-looking crone with bones in her hair and a gnarled root of a man who tugged at his beard so vigorously he seemed on the verge of tearing it out.

Alder rubbed the bruise blossoming on his cheek. Anger flashed in his eyes, and a chill of fear swept through Koro Ha. The boy was a sorcerer, after all, or had been at least. Nevertheless, he had failed Orna Sin in too many ways to go back on his final promise. And, he had to admit, he had harboured a slow-burning anger towards Alder for a long while, ever since the boy's rebelliousness had put the Toa Aloni school at risk. Yet that anger had faded now, leaving room for a warm reunion.

'A great deal has happened to both of us, it seems,' Koro Ha said, smiling despite the lingering tension between them. 'Before anything else, however, I must ask how you found this place, and why you have come.'

Alder's considered hesitancy reminded Koro Ha of their days in the garden, the interchange of questions and answers, debating the finer points of a doctrine that now seemed abhorrent to him – and presumably to his former student as well. Yet even after everything that had happened since then, the old rhythms returned, with Koro Ha acting as the questioner and Alder carefully formulating answers to his interrogations. Only now these were no mere exercises, no preparation for a performance, and that calculating light in Alder's eyes made Koro Ha wonder what the boy might try to hide in the careful wording of his answer.

'It would take a great deal of time to explain everything,' Alder said. 'Time we do not have to spare. I might deliver what you must know more quickly were I to transmit it into your mind, in much the same way this god speaks to you. Would that be acceptable?'

Koro Ha looked to the god.

<It is not without danger,> the god answered. <There are ways of twisting the mind with this magic, but we will protect you. Our mind is as unbending as granite.>

Alder nodded slowly. 'Prudent. When you are ready, Koro Ha.'

Not without a few still-burning embers of fear, Koro Ha agreed, though he wondered how the boy had learned magic that, to Koro Ha's understanding, belonged only to the gods. Though that was something he would presumably learn from the information Alder meant to share, as he might also learn how the boy had come to lose his right hand.

Alder's mind surged through Koro Ha like a flooding river, submerging him in sensations not his own. The cascade was composed of memories, he realised, a deluge of sounds and images that captured, in a handful of moments, Alder's life since their last meeting. Glimpses of his time with Hand Usher, the agony of a friend's blood on his hands, the soaring obelisks of a distant city glimmering in the sun and then shattered and collapsing. His reunion with the old man – the very same doctor, Koro Ha was astonished to learn, who had healed him from his strange illness in childhood, which he now understood to have been wrought as a consequence of ill-worked magic. His meeting with the old woman, and her nature as an ancient witch who had lived as long as the emperor, since before the pacts were made.

Even as he wanted to weep for all the suffering and hardship his student had endured, hope rose in Koro Ha. He felt Alder react, the flow of his memories slowing in a moment of questioning.

'Go on,' Koro Ha said. 'I will explain later.'

'It would be faster if you let me see,' Alder said gently, and Koro Ha felt a twinge of guilt that he still thought of the boy thus, for he had seen in those shared memories that he now lived under his Nayeni name. Yet the whirl of new information left him little time or opportunity to change his habits of thought. 'Simply call the memories to mind.'

They came easily, for the god's words weighed heavily on Koro Ha. He recalled an image of the towering column, lined with writing he could not comprehend and imbued with magic he could feel but not control. The river of Alder's thoughts roiled with sudden excitement, as though plunging into rapids.

'A weapon to carve apart the pattern of the world and weave it anew,' Alder breathed. He looked to the old crone – Hissing Cat – with the same bright-eyed enthusiasm he had so often worn during their most rigorous debates. 'The question then becomes whether Tenet intends to use it or destroy it.'

'I'm sorry, who?' Yin Ila interjected, stepping forwards from the stone-faced god's side, her hand still at the hilt of her knife. 'Koro Ha, this is your student, correct? The one whose treason, however delightful for its own sake, led to Orna Sin's capture, yes? How did he come to be here?'

The stone-faced god turned its gaze upwards, as though peering through layers of earth and stone. <There are others. Another presence. Mustering above us.>

Alder spat a curse. 'I'm sorry, there isn't time to explain. Koro Ha, take us to the weapon. Hissing Cat or I—'

Yin Ila shook her head, her eyes never leaving Alder. 'I don't think so. Whatever bastards are following you, you go and lead them away from here. This is the last safe haven our people have. I won't see it become a battlefield.'

'The emperor is not after us,' Alder pressed. 'He is after the same thing we are. And you have no way to defend yourselves against him. Take us to the weapon and we will.'

'We have *that*,' Yin Ila said, jerking her thumb at the stone-faced god. 'It dropped a tunnel on your heads, didn't he? I'm given to understand that's only the beginning of what it can manage.'

<We are not accustomed to war,> the stone-faced god said flatly. <Ours is to grow and build, not to destroy. But we will do what we can.>

'I honestly can't speak for Cur here, whose attitude towards violence seems to change like the bloody tides, but I am *very* accustomed to war,' said Hissing Cat. Her grin gleamed in the glow of the moss. 'Not *fond* of it. Bloody tired of it, in fact, and still not quite recovered after a thousand years of rest. But the thought of facing Tenet down does offer some satisfaction.'

Yin Ila met the old crone's stare, then burst out laughing. 'Gods, I wish you were my grandmother. What did you say your name was?'

'You'll let us see the weapon, then?' Doctor Sho asked. At Alder's description of the weapon, a desperate hunger had lit in the old doctor's eyes.

'You must,' Alder said firmly, the words carrying an unspoken threat. Koro Ha had seen the violence in the boy's past. What was he now willing to destroy to achieve his aim? Would he unleash his storm of fire and lightning here, in this sacred cavern, if he were opposed? Koro Ha saw no reason to press the issue.

'How long until these most recent intruders arrive?' he asked.

<It is difficult to say,> the stone-faced god answered. <They move more slowly. It seems they are greater in number. And I am better prepared for them. I will do what I can to slow their progress.>

'Then we should hurry.' Koro Ha turned towards the path into the cavern. 'The weapon is this way. Yin Ila, spread word that the danger is not past. We should gather defenders here, and the people should remain in their homes, where it is safe.'

Yin Ila grumbled that he was not her captain but went to do as he instructed. Koro Ha motioned for the newcomers to follow him. The stone-faced god, too, fell into step, the wake of its heavy, slow-moving presence still radiating upwards, into the mountain above their heads, opposing the emperor's advance.

For the first time since the Black Maw had risen from the sea, Koro Ha found himself able to believe, truly, that the world might be restored. That Toa Alon might endure, not hidden in obscurity beneath the earth but returned to its glory. Ambal Ora's weapon – his tool for crafting a better world – would create that future, he had to believe. Yet a new fear nagged at him: he had seen only fragments of Alder's memories and nothing of his intent for the weapon, nothing of what the better world he envisioned might entail. And he had seen the violence the boy was capable of unleashing. *But that violence was unleashed only in opposition to the empire*, he told himself.

He glanced over his shoulder at the strange party that followed him. Hissing Cat's gaze swept over the miracles of the cavern – the fields, planted only a week ago, already showing the first fruits of their harvest; the towering stalagmites dotted with windows full of flickering lamplight; the clouds swirling over their heads, one even then releasing a gentle mist of rain. Beside her, Doctor Sho kept his eyes fixed forwards, clutching at something tucked into his right sleeve. Alder seemed torn between the two, taken aback by the cavern's wonders but with a contemplative distance to his gaze, as though teasing out the intricacies of a tangled thought experiment.

That expression, more than anything else, quietened Koro Ha's fears. Alder had always been hasty, overflowing with ambition and courage, but uncommon insight and wisdom had always shown through the cloud of his foolishness. The memories he had shared with Koro Ha told the tale of a long, tortuous lesson in caution. In essence, it came down to a question of which would ultimately win out: caution or arrogance, ambition or compassion, the diligent student or the boy who had nearly killed himself in his desperation to learn what was forbidden.

Koro Ha turned back to the path. The looming stalagmite that housed Ambal Ora's weapon rose ahead. He could not use it himself, yet he could, one last time, serve as a teacher and guide Alder to using it well as best he could, as its creator had intended.

33

A Last, Desperate Measure

Foolish Cur

The wake of the weapon called to mind the obelisks of An-Zabat. Naphena's spell, anchored to the obelisks, had persisted for so long that the pattern of the world had rearranged itself around them, folding their wake into the natural interchange of energies. Then, still new in my power and constrained by the marks of pact and canon, it had taken unusual concentration to feel their slow churning deep beneath the earth, drawing up water to feed the city's great oasis.

At first the wake struck me only as a vague unease, a sense that the world danced around me to an awkward, uncommon rhythm, one that stumbled ever so slightly every few dozen steps. Had I not, by creating the canons of witchcraft, become familiar with the heavy, piercing wake anchoring a spell from the layer of the soul to the layer of the world, I might have shrugged off the feeling. This wake was far older, far subtler, and far more powerful than what Naphena had created. As we drew nearer to the vast stalagmite that dominated the centre of the chamber, the wake grew deeper, and my unease with it.

The scale of it staggered me. Thousands of tendrils plunged deep into the innermost mysteries of the pattern and grew outwards, like the roots of an ancient tree, tunnelling through the layers of the soul and the mind. Tracing them all to their ends would have consumed as much time as running a finger along every stroke of every logogram in the imperial library, and much more energy.

A weapon to undo the pattern of the world and weave it anew. A grandiose claim, and one I had assumed to be an exaggeration. Yet, as my mind charted even one of those tendrils of power, following its curling line through the deepest reaches of the pattern – that layer of the soul from which all else arises, in which dwell the gods and which we touch by our every exercise of freedom that deviates from the pattern's natural flow – I came to believe.

We cannot know which falling stone will trigger a landslide, which breath of wind will spark a thunderstorm, which droplet of water will overwhelm a riverbank. I had learned, and at great expense, the cost of unconsidered action. But how can one consider the consequences of an act on such a scale with the very fabric of reality, the pattern of the world itself, at stake? The greatest sage might sit in contemplation a thousand years and not arrive at any course of action. Yet such a task had, by some terrible contortion of the pattern, fallen to me.

I was too small for it, too true to my name. I needed counsel, guidance from one who had held such powers for longer, who better understood all their implications.

'Do you feel it?' I whispered to Hissing Cat, leaning close.

She gave me a quizzical look. Before I could put words to what I felt, to convey to her the enormity of it – the promise and the threat – the stone-faced god waved its hand, parting the surface of the stalagmite before us like a curtain. No wake of magic accompanied the act. I realised, with an unsettling start, that while I had felt the weight of the gods' minds when they spoke to me, their use of magic left no perceptible wake, save that first, wrenching agony at the breaking of the pacts and the resumption of their war. Only the twisting of the unwoven, the blurring of time and distance, the vibrations that shook the very foundations of the world, indicated that they used their power.

'Are you all right, Alder?' Koro Ha hesitated in the entryway. The others had already followed the stone-faced god into the chamber while my spiralling thoughts rooted me to the ground.

I smiled, hoping the expression veiled my confusion and mounting horror. There were too many unanswered questions, too many facets of magic, of the gods, of the world itself that I did not yet understand. The enormity of the power that radiated from this weapon could rewrite the very foundational maxims of the world, as though reconstructing Sienese doctrine not only from Traveller-on-the-Narrow-Way's first writings but from the first impulses and principles that had motivated him to dip his brush in ink.

'I'm fine,' I said. 'Let's see this weapon.'

The parallel to the obelisks of An-Zabat deepened, only rather than dozens of columns scattered throughout a city, here was one, at the heart of the world, decorated not in silver filigree but in carving so delicate I could imagine no tool capable of the work: a single knot encircling the column, spiralling upwards, towards the sky – or perhaps downwards, towards the centre of all things; it was impossible to say, illiterate in the script as I was. Hissing Cat stood at the base of the column, one fist digging into her hip, the other tugging at a matted lock of hair, making the ravens' skulls sway and clatter. Beside her, Doctor Sho gazed upwards, his expression unreadable as his eyes traced the swirling knotwork. The stone-faced god stood beside the entryway as though it were but a permanent decoration of the room, the column's counterpart and eternal reader.

<The weapon of Ambal Ora,> the god said, its voice

shattering the stillness of the sublime, as final and certain as the cornerstone of the world. <That which we were to protect and preserve until the coming of those who might wield it.>

'Well, if Tenet knew what this was, I can see why he nearly shat himself,' Hissing Cat said.

'Do *you* know what it is?' I pressed, suppressing a jolt of hope.

'No,' she said, 'but I knew Ambal Ora, for a while, during the last war. An odd man. In some ways, Ambal was like Tenet. Naphena tried to find a way to leave the world better for her people, and I … well, you know how I spent my time. But Tenet and Ambal were unconvinced that the pacts would bind the gods. They obsessed over the fear that their war would start again. You know what that fear drove Tenet to do. I bloody well hope Ambal's solution was less terrible.'

'But you can use it,' Koro Ha cut in. 'And you must. You cannot delay, Alder. I felt the magic you wielded in your journey here. In its wake, how many will transform into monsters? How many of my people will those monsters slaughter? We are safe here, but in the city above …' He shook his head. 'What could be worse than the nightmare we are now enduring? Put an end to the suffering, Alder. Please.'

The stone-faced god turned its head, a subtle movement but such a sudden and unexpected shattering of its stillness that it drew all of our attention – save Doctor Sho, who remained fixated on the column and its looping script.

<The interlopers draw nearer,> it said. <They are gaining speed. I will do what I can to oppose them.>

A distant tremor shook elsewhere in the cave, reaching us only by a slight vibration of the stone beneath our feet. Again, the god's use of magic without a pact disturbed me, yet I had no time to contemplate it.

'But I have no idea what it does,' I told Koro Ha. 'It reaches through the layers of the pattern, into the layers of the soul and the mind, from which thoughts and magic arise and where the gods dwell. It might end this nightmare only to birth another. It might strike at the gods and, in doing so, tear the pattern to shreds.'

Hissing Cat cocked her head at me. 'Could be, though I'd wager Ambal Ora wasn't one willing to risk so much.'

'It can't be only an attack on the gods,' Doctor Sho murmured, the first indication that he had been listening to our conversation. 'Why would Tenet be afraid of something that suits his agenda? Think. What would frighten him more than anything else in the world? Enough to derail whatever plans he had been concocting to rush here in an effort to seize or destroy it?' He brushed the fingers of his left hand along the column, tracing the ancient words, while his other hand clutched the hem of his sleeve. 'I never knew this Ambal Ora, but I travelled far, in my day. To the edges of the empire and beyond. Even to Toa Alon. This script would have been aged even in those days, but I can make sense of fragments.'

Tears wetted his cheeks and the wisps of his beard. He looked at me, all the disaffection of his centuries fallen away like dust shaken from a robe, his fatalism evaporated as though it had never been. He was no longer Doctor Sho the wandering physician who had abandoned his legacy and his past, overburdened by the fear that the wrongs he had unwittingly caused might never be put right. Who had taken up instead a medicine chest and walked the earth, knowing all the while that ten thousand lives saved from pox, ten thousand mended bones, ten thousand boils lanced or wounds stitched might never balance the scales.

But this ... What he had asked of Tenet, and been refused. What he had begged of me, and been ignored, for the scale of the treatment and its ramifications had been too monumental, too sublime, too much an affront to all I held dear and had hoped might be redeemed for me to face. What Ambal Ora, a stranger from another land, had dreamed in parallel, and devised, and left as his only legacy.

This could heal the world.

The thought carried in its wake a thunderous voice, a single, screaming howl of outrage. Dust cascaded down the walls as the chamber shook around us, seized by a sudden, violent quake.

'What are you doing?' Hissing Cat shouted, rounding on the stone-faced god, which had stretched out its hand and stepped between us and the doorway it had made.

For a millennium the stone-faced god had safeguarded this place, the column, and the weapon forged of magic that it anchored, never knowing its purpose: not a weapon meant for the destruction of the gods – not, then, something Tenet would wish us to use – but a scalpel to carve magic out of the world as a doctor carves out a tumour. Yet, for the stone-faced god, a being of the pattern of the soul, the consequences would be much the same.

The floor shook, nearly toppling me as I dashed for the column. Though far from certain I would use it, neither could I let it be destroyed. The smell of smoke filled the chamber and a roar like a forest fire shook me to my knees. The stone-faced god closed its hand and pulled a howling wolf – its face seamed with glowing scars, its fur as orange as the heart of a flame – from thin air, holding it by the scruff like a disobedient puppy.

Okara writhed in the grip of the stone-faced god, kicking out, his claws seeking his captor's flesh. Fire licked out from between his gnashing teeth and from the tufts of his fur. The stone-faced god held firm as heat and light washed off its body like water.

I found my feet, though the ground still shook beneath me. Only the column seemed firm, as though the weight of the spell anchored to it had armoured it against the gods' battle. I stumbled towards it even as I reached out with my phantom limb.

Okara howled, and a single word split my thoughts.

<NO!>

The air blurred before me. A second wolf, her fur the grey-black of billowing smoke, stepped into the world: Ateri, the she-wolf, Okara's mother and the mate of primordial fire by the old mythologies of Nayen. Behind her, white furred, springing to life like a spark struck from steel, emerged her daughter, Tollu, the wolf of wisdom, who once had argued on my behalf, sparing me the wrath of the other gods, only to preserve me for a purpose I had long since served.

<Think about what you mean to do, Foolish Cur,> Tollu's voice was an echo of Okara's but slower, not a raging forest fire but the churning heat at the heart of the world. <How much have you sacrificed to deny the emperor his victory? And now you lunge forwards, unthinking, to give him the world he wants? He is our enemy. He is *your* enemy.>

'He wants to destroy this place and this weapon,' I said, my heart thundering, my will carving deep into the pattern, making ready to create a seal to destroy these gods, whose stone gaze had followed me from my first leaping steps into knowledge of magic. Tollu certainly *seemed* present, here in the world, yet all three of the wolf gods had appeared as though from nothing, stepping between the layer of the soul and the mortal world as easily as over a crack in the street. If I attacked them, they might just as easily vanish, and reappear to destroy me the moment I dropped my guard. 'It seems to me your goals align with his, not with mine.'

<What was that tale your Sienese master told, of a cat who wanted to meddle in the affairs of men?> Tollu pressed on, padding towards me, a wave of heat rolling from her, drawing sweat that soon stung my eyes. <You are a child meddling in the affairs of gods. How dare you so blithely remake the world?>

Her words cut me to the heart, echoing my deepest terror – that

I would, once again, break the world in my attempt to heal it; that in wielding Ambal Ora's weapon, I might deal the world a wound to echo down through time, inflicting suffering that neither he nor I had imagined.

All the brazen confidence of my youth had been stripped away. Too many had suffered for my arrogance. And now I stood on the precipice of an act that would reshape every life in the world and every generation to come.

The floor shook again. The stone-faced god grunted, a sound like a splitting boulder. Okara contorted himself and closed his jaws around the god's forearm. Viscous black blood dripped between his gleaming teeth and spattered to the floor. The chamber shook as the stone-faced god slammed Okara against a wall and drove its fist into the side of his head, yet the wolf god clung on, his teeth sawing, his eyes wild and bright as stars.

'Well, well,' Hissing Cat's voice rasped. 'It's good to see you, old friends.' Dust rained down around her, shrouding her as she stepped towards Ateri and Tollu. The wolf gods hunched their backs and snarled.

Hissing Cat showed her teeth in a wide, eager grin. 'Do what needs doing, Cur. If you left it up to me, I'd go hide in a cave and think about it for another few thousand years. I'll keep them occupied.'

A wake like iron shackles fell upon me as power surged from Hissing Cat, slashing through the pattern of the world, tracing the edges of a seal with the agility of a duelling swordsman. Ateri screamed and began to blur, her body seeming to fade in and of existence as she dashed towards Hissing Cat. The seal burst into being, a hole falling out of the pattern of the world where Ateri had been a moment before, but the god had slipped its edges. Roiling flames spilled over Hissing Cat, splashing against defences whose frigid wake left me shivering, hardly able to move a limb.

<This is a fight that cannot be won, Foolish Cur,> Tollu pressed, her words like a dagger in my skull. She still faced Hissing Cat, though had not yet joined in the fray. <More, I wonder why you wish to win it. The war between the gods is nearly ended. You have led us to our last, greatest enemy, this stone-faced god who has slumbered beneath the earth, beyond our reach, armoured against the influence of other gods. But, though you hate us, you are still one of our people. Still named in the ancient way. Where you go, we go, and we could little allow you to give the emperor his victory.

<Let us fulfil our purpose, Foolish Cur. Let us destroy this rival and let the people of Nayen be safe and free from fear – of the empire, and of those older terrors we were born to face. The howls of unseen beasts and songs of rival tribes. The dark of night. The shadows between the trees.>

Hissing Cat's will darted through the pattern, carving out seals like ribbons that chased after Ateri's flickering, dancing steps, trying to encircle her and snuff her like a candle flame. In my grandmother's tales, the gods had been the protectors and benefactors of our people. Ateri's gift of fire had been the spark that begat civilisation. Tollu's gentle guidance had given rise to art and the heroic epics and all that was worth preserving. Okara's guile had kept us safe from those half-conceived nightmares – remembrances, it seemed to me now, of the unwoven – that crawled in the dark of night.

My short life had left such a wake of destruction. Of Oriole's life. Of the city of An-Zabat. Of the peace between the gods that had endured for generations. Would I destroy, too, the gods? These strange, ancient beings so long revered by my people?

I knew them for my enemies, but part of me – the same arrogant, festering part that raged against Doctor Sho's desire to rid the world of magic, that still, even after everything, longed for mastery as a child longs for a shiny bauble it cannot have – wanted to believe Tollu, to believe those old stories and return to the feeling of awe and wonder I had felt when the gods had first visited me in dreams.

Realisation dawned with the fury of the desert sun.

At once I put up walls within my mind, sealing myself off from magic, and thus from the influence of the gods, leaving only the barest window through which we might communicate. Their magic carried no wake, but its effects at once began to fade. The longing for mastery, that desperate desire to break every boundary and command magic in all its mystery and power – a desire that had led me down every step towards that fateful moment in Eastern Fortress when, with a desperate spell, I had shattered the ancient pacts – at once became only an ember, true to me yet no truer, no more driving, than any other facet of my being or any other desire of my heart.

How often had I cast aside friendship, or love, or comfort to chase my ambition? How long had I counted that ambition as core to my self, central to my being, when it had only ever alienated me – from my parents, from Atar – and carried danger in its wake?

Beneath my fury burned a new, deeper horror. How many times, at how many turning points, had the gods twisted my thoughts? Not mere arguments but a subtle influence upon my mind, impossible for me to discern from the conflicts of the heart that dwell in every soul?

Might I have stayed with the An-Zabati and Atar, if not for them? Might I have been satisfied to serve the empire, fulfilling my father's far simpler ambition for me, becoming only a local magistrate like Clear River?

Tollu snarled at me, her voice – muted now – echoing as from far away, full of hatred, no longer that of a wise councillor but of a god galled to outrage by my resistance.

<Arrogant boy. Do you think we would not have used some other, in time? You were no more than an opportunity, one we seized. Do not pretend you loathe us for all we have given you. Would one such as you, with such potential, be satisfied with an ordinary life?>

<Might the pacts remain unbroken, and the pattern of the world unscarred?> I countered.

She barked a laugh. <Perhaps, and Nayen would still lie beneath the boot of the empire. Tenet would have his way with the world. The pattern would be shaped for ever by his cruelty. Is that a better world, Foolish Cur?>

Doubt crept in, not from the god's influence – the armour around my mind held, fixed in place as it was by all the power I could muster – but born of truth and of wondering what would have been. I had caused great harm. But a scalpel, too, causes harm. The empire was a cancer. It would have grown until it consumed the world. If not for me, if not for my power …

No. That line of thought was born of true arrogance, true foolishness. The rebellion had existed before me and would have endured in spite of me. Perhaps I would have found my power and lent it to the rebellion without the influence of the gods. Perhaps I would have nonetheless carved a path of havoc, leaving suffering and ruin in my wake. One cannot blame oneself for failures in a world that never was.

The truth was this: the gods had, from my earliest, most profound memories, made me their puppet. When I had thought myself most free to chase my ambitions, I had only followed their lure. Whenever the pattern brought me to a place where I might have escaped their influence, be it on the deck of the *Spear of Naphena* or in Hissing Cat's cave, they had drawn me back to their purpose, not only by deception but by subtle manipulations of my deepest, most soulful desires.

A scream tore through the cave. Ateri faltered in her flitting war dance. Her body, as it flickered in and out of being, showed no injury, but she reeled like a drunkard, her grey-black fur ashen and sickly. Tollu wheeled towards her wounded mother as she howled and darted at Hissing Cat, whose will lashed out, enfolded Ateri, and sliced her out of the world.

The wolf god, the mate of fire, faded like a wisp of smoke.

Her children howled. The earth shook with their voices. Flames roiled from their throats. Okara writhed in the grip of the stone-faced god, sawing with his teeth until fingers of stone spasmed open. He joined his sister in their attack, their eyes blazing like stars, their teeth gleaming like the sickle moon. A heavy wake lashed out from Hissing Cat, whose shoulders heaved with exhaustion – too slow. The gods flickered and flitted, darting from the net she wove. Blood trickled from her ear, from the corner of her mouth. She might have put up a shield, sheltered behind it and let the gods stalk its edges, or let them turn their ferocity on the stone-faced god, or Doctor Sho, Koro Ha, and me. Her snarls matched those of the gods, as did her ferocity and her desperation for this all to be done with, for the ancient war to end.

Her eyes met mine. Without need of a word or a transmitted thought, her fury snapped me out of paralysed introspection and into action. I reached out towards the column at the heart of the chamber and the branching roots of magic anchored to it: Ambal Ora's weapon, which promised freedom, at last, from the influence of the gods, from the power of the empire, from every danger posed by magic itself. My phantom limb took hold of that power and it came alive, surging through me like liquid fire, like a fork of white lightning, desperate to be unleashed to serve its ancient purpose after a millennium buried latent beneath the earth. In that moment, I could feel the contours of what Ambal Ora meant to do, the subtle unravelling of the layers of the pattern, stripping away magic, and with it the gods, but leaving all else to flow as it had from the birth of the first star.

All it required was a motion of the will. An act of trust that the world would be a better place if humankind were forced by our frailty to live in alignment with the will of the pattern of the world rather than bending all things to our own desires. A deliberate choice on the part of one who wielded magic in the old way – one who understood all the wonder and potential, all the myriad possibilities magic promised, all that would be lost – to bow their head and submit, with total finality, to birth and death, growth and decay, heat and cold, light and shadow, peace and danger, all in eternal, inscrutable cycle.

Pinion, who perhaps understood Ambal Ora's vision as well as any man of our age, would have acted. Koro Ha had enough faith in those who came before him, in the legacy he carried, to do the same. Doctor Sho, who watched me, and begged me with tears charting the creases beneath his eyes, had never drawn so near his dream of harmony.

But fool that I am, arrogant to the end, desirous from childhood not of the freedom to act but of the freedom to bend the world to my will, I hesitated. And the world nearly lost its future.

34
Pursuit into Shadow

Ral Ans Urrera

Grinding nausea tears Ral Ans Urrera from sleep, from dreams of the broad dome of the sky, the sway of golden grass upon the plain, her father's smile. Dreams that leave her aching as they fade. And then the ache, too, fades as the labyrinth wrests control of her mind, save that small, screaming fragment that clings to memory, to hatred, to a hunger for vengeance that is her only shield against total annihilation by the emperor's will.

The nausea, too, vanishes. A wake of magic. The same as the strange power that delivered the emperor and his fists to do battle with the Skyfather; the same that carried her with him to the heart of the empire, and then to Toa Alon. She lies in the same small, windowless cell of plain stone where he delivered her upon their arrival. Has he abandoned her, cast her aside as a hunter will cast aside a blunted spear? If she had been quicker to learn, nimbler in her use of magic, more able to become the weapon he needs against the gods, she would still have a place at his side. She rises from her pallet and reaches deep into the pattern of the world, through the well at the heart of the labyrinth, the guiding star that directs her power towards the emperor's aims. She will succeed and prove her usefulness.

She will not fail him. She will not languish in this cell.

Even as she thinks this, the shred of her that survives rages and wails. Terrible thoughts – that the labyrinth will shatter if only she could focus, if only her mind were free – echo through her. Thoughts which her mind, constrained by the labyrinth, bound by its structures, cannot entertain lest she be driven mad.

Madness is better than slavery!

She remembers Atar, her An-Zabati, and the Red Bull band turning their backs on the emperor's offer of protection. The winddancer's voice rings in her ears: *We would sooner die.*

Ral trembles, shakes her head furiously, curls her hands tight until her wrists ache and blood beads beneath her nails. The labyrinth, too, quakes and shivers.

Which will break first, she wonders in a moment of rare lucidity: her mind or that which binds it?

The door creaks open. She opens her eyes, only then realising they have been clenched shut. The emperor stands over her, dressed in black scales of iron trimmed with gold, flanked by Fists in battle harness. Euphoria washes through her. She has not been abandoned. She has been given another chance.

'You felt it? Their arrival in the city? Their burrowing beneath the earth?' the emperor says, seething with rage. 'They out-manoeuvred me, hid their weapon where I would never think to look for it, distracted as I was by the idiocy of those I left to govern here. There is no more time. Either you will serve as I require or the world will die.'

'I will serve,' she says. 'Though it destroys me, I will serve.'

The emperor nods and brings her to her feet with a gesture. They leave behind her cell, buried beneath the gardens of the governor's estate. An escort falls in around them – ten more Fists, accompanied by dozens of men with crossbows or spears. Useless. One cannot kill a god with a crossbow, nor with a chemical grenade. Yet for all his power the emperor is a being of flesh, and there are yet fools in the world who would plunge a dagger into his back or put an arrow through his eye.

Blood runs in the streets of Toa Alon. The new governor has taken his work seriously. The heaped corpses of men, women, and children lie stacked in alleys, waiting their turn on the acrid pyre that burns in the square. Greasy soot clings to the carved facades of the buildings. Among the corpses are monsters with too many limbs, with claws and stranger appendages where arms and fingers ought to be, with bestial teeth below too-human eyes. A fate that awaits all of humankind if the emperor fails to bring the gods to heel.

Eerie howls and bestial screams rise over the city, and sounds of battle echo from the alleyways. Hands and Fists raise barriers of shimmering light that feel like holes torn in the world, resembling those that enfolded the surrendering Girzan on the plain. Behind them stand wild-eyed, trembling soldiers. The battle below the city will be fought with magic. These ranks of men with spears and crossbows and these scant few Hands and Fists are all that guard the emperor's back from the hordes of unwoven that will be drawn as certainly as flies to rotting meat.

They are doomed, unless Ral can fulfil her purpose.

The carnage in the street thins, then fades to old scars and broken facades as they draw near the towering mound at the centre of the city. The vastness of it astonishes Ral. The earth does not herald it with an undulation of foothills, as it would any other mountain. It rises, instead, from a downward slope, in opposition to geology. The emperor leads them to a gap in the low wall around the strange mound. The stone lies congealed and lumpy, like wax drippings on a long-cooled candle. Beyond the broken wall, a tunnel bores into the side of the mound, its depths soon swallowed by darkness.

Quick orders set the bulk of the spears and crossbows to guard the entrance to the tunnel. A scant handful follow the emperor, Ral, and the dozen Fists into its mouth, which plunges downwards at an angle, lit by a globe of fire that hangs above them, fed by a trickling, feverish wake from the emperor. Her time in the emperor's service has accustomed Ral to enclosed spaces – cells and locked rooms – but she still flinches when the sky vanishes from sight, haunted by the weight of stone and earth overhead.

The ground shakes beneath her feet. Chips of stone and dust cascade around her. She swallows against rising terror.

'It seems that, whatever lies below, it is far from inclined to welcome the Cur and the Cat,' the emperor muses, a smile quirking the corner of his mouth. He redoubles his pace, and Ral hikes up the skirt of her robe to match it. She is his sword, his spear, his bow and quiver. No fear of stumbling, of the dark, of the mountain collapsing on her head can dissuade her, not when she is willing to tear her soul apart to destroy his enemies.

A crack splits stone somewhere ahead and above them, and a wall of dust rushes upwards from further down the tunnel, nearly knocking Ral to her knees. Her lungs and throat burn as she gasps for breath. The emperor shouts orders that she barely hears. Ral's vision blurs as another wake, bright and searing as summer fire, tears through her. The emperor shouts again and the Fists behind her push her upright and onwards, carrying her on the current of their obedience.

She squirms in their grasp until they put her down. She is Ral Ans Urrera and she will not be so shamed. This is but the first leg of the trial. The true test lies ahead, in the depths of this mound, far from the light of the sky, where she will drown herself in the deepest fires of the pattern to burn the gods from the world. She will embrace her fate walking on her own two feet, though the ground shudders beneath her and a mountain threatens to bury her.

They press onwards, delayed time and again by piles of earth and stone that fall to block the tunnel, obstructions that dissolve beneath the emperor's will and power. Without the sun, with only the interminable walls of smooth stone to mark distance and time, Ral loses any sense of progress or of passage. There is only the downward march, the warmth of bodies around her, the thickening of the air, the emperor's orders and the wake of his power, and that shard of her buried screaming in the depth of the labyrinth.

This is her chance.

A bolt of lightning to carve through these dozen Fists, and through the emperor.

All she need do is reach out. All she need do is exert her will.

Better to die than be a slave.

The walls of the labyrinth, too, quake and shudder beneath the storm of such terrible thoughts, but they hold, and with them her sanity, her understanding of her purpose as the emperor's weapon. She is only afraid of the darkness and the confrontation to come. These doubts, these violent impulses, will seem so foolish when they reach the end of the tunnel and the gods are destroyed.

A laugh bubbles up within her and spills between her teeth like a splash of water from an overfull skin. One of the Fists eyes her worriedly, but she ignores him. What cares she, Ral Ans Urrera, the god-killing spear in the emperor's hand, for one of these dull daggers on his belt?

A spear in the emperor's hand, or in the hand of the Skyfather?

The Fist behind her bumps into her and snarls a curse, then pushes her onwards. She walks mechanically, her legs shaking like a newborn foal's.

How long has she conceived of herself as a weapon? She remembers no such notion when she first sat on sacred shale and learned to call lightning from the storm, nor when she imagined gathering other children like herself, to raise up a new generation of Stormriders, to secure the future for her people. A spear in the Skyfather's hand ... She remembers her father's face, bloated nearly beyond recognition. Remembers her horror, her rage. Remembers losing herself to it, to the point of abandoning Atar and Jhin – faithful companions – on the steppe. Rage that reduced her, that carved a singular purpose into her mind: vengeance. It is a purpose she has pursued with total determination, even in the face of her own death, even in the face of her people's destruction, spurred on all the while by the Skyfather's voice. A purpose and a pattern of thought well trodden by the time the emperor took her and filled in those furrows with the foundations of his walls.

She screams, her voice rebounding first through the labyrinth, then through the narrow confines of the tunnel. The earth quakes; the labyrinth trembles. Dust and chipped stone rain down, and she can feel, for the first time since the Skyfather's death – perhaps, now that she thinks of it, since long before that – a gust of freedom through the cracks in the labyrinth.

A fist thuds into her stomach, silencing her. She grits her teeth and doubles over, but her mind is only driven deeper into the heart of this terrible realisation. She had only ever wanted to preserve her people, to restore them as best she could. War had been brought to her, and with it her twofold enslavement: the shaping of her self to serve purposes other than her own.

The cracks widen. She can feel the walls tumbling, brick by brick, stone by stone, shattering as once the aurora that blinded her to her magic shattered. Her will reaches into those cracks and pries and twists and shakes. The labyrinth begins to tear, as the binding aurora in her mind tore while the tents and corpses of her people burned. She will break this bondage, too, and stand, and scour the emperor and all his cruelty from the world.

Pain sears through her, but it is only a matter of endurance, of pulling against the agony until it gives way. She stares at the back of the emperor's head, only a few paces in front of her, where she will plant a bolt of lightning the moment the labyrinth falls. She grits her teeth and pulls, until a terrible weight falls upon her.

<Enough.> The word thunders through her, drowning her wrath. The walls of the labyrinth redouble in size and strength, towering over her, blinding her, and reorient themselves into a new and stunning complexity. She remembers, vaguely, a terrible truth that needles her, but it fades as quickly as she can grasp it.

'We have wasted too much time,' the emperor snarls, somewhere ahead of her. 'Bind the girl and carry her, if you must.'

The aurora blooms within her, shining over the walls of the labyrinth, as chains of light crush her arms to her sides and bind her ankles, but she pays none of this any mind. Only one puzzle occupies her: that fleeting memory, that fog where outrage should be.

She grasps for it, again and again, while the emperor leads them to the end of the tunnel and into a strange cavern, like a mirror of the streets above them, and thence to a temple. At its heart they descend a seemingly interminable staircase, where Fists cast aside paltry resistance – men and women with little more than knives and farming tools – with gouts of lightning and fire. But her mind has been scoured clean, the walls that define it strengthened, the space they enclose reduced. That shredded fragment that remains of her cringes in a shadowed corner, where the light of the aurora does not touch, reaching over and over for the only clue she can recall: a name, but one that slips through her grasp as she reaches for it, until at last she is too exhausted, too worn down by fruitless struggle, to reach.

35
The Last Debate

Foolish Cur

Doctor Sho's voice rang meaninglessly in my ears. He shook me, his eyes wild, the wispy corona of his hair blackened and crisped where the flames of Hissing Cat's duel with the gods had singed it. They still did battle, behind him, while the stone-faced god gathered itself, the wounds dealt by Okara's flames and claws gradually sealing, the gush of black, oily blood slowing to a drip.

If I did as Doctor Sho desired, I would unmake the world as I knew it. The gods would vanish, no longer able to influence the pattern from the layer of the soul, no longer able to tear it to shreds in their constant, pointless war, born out of ancient, immutable rivalry. But magic, too, would vanish, with all its mystery and wonder, and with it all the good it could do. How many dozens had I healed? How many hundreds of wounds had Clear-River and Running Doe knit in their clinic? There had to be a way to preserve it. To keep what I loved while destroying what I hated.

The stone-faced god turned its head, a motion swift and sudden enough to draw my attention. With the grinding of stone on stone, it heaved itself, wounded and staggering, towards the entrance in the stalagmite's wall. Beyond, at the top of the winding trail leading back to the spiral stairwell that bound this strange cavern to the buried city, fire flashed and steel glinted. Shouts echoed down, echoing through the cavern. A thin wake – a brisk chill and a rush of fever – slipped through the hammering power of Hissing Cat's duel with the gods, and an explosion of flame and wind hurled down a dozen of the cavern's defenders, their bodies toppling from the path to break in the fields below.

The emperor rose like the dawn, carried on wings feathered in fractal light. Ribbons of fire and lightning swirled out from his hand, carving through the Toa Aloni.

Koro Ha wailed, throwing himself at the opening in the wall. With one hand the stone-faced god held him back, and with the other it sealed the opening shut. 'You have to help them!' he yelled, pounding his fists on stone. 'How can you let them die?'

Another storm of flames raged around Hissing Cat. The chilling wake of her defences still held but had faded from the bite of winter's heart to a gentle summer breeze. If only I had more time, if only I better understood the intricacies of Ambal Ora's design, I might manipulate it, leaving enough of a tie between the layers of the soul and mind and the pattern of the world to seal the gods away while letting magic trickle in. Not so much that it could be used to shatter mountains and birth seas, but enough to knit a wound or fly with an eagle hawk's wings.

Pain blossomed on my cheek. Doctor Sho flexed his hand, red from striking me. 'Are you as selfish as Tenet that you would prolong the suffering of countless innocents for fear of losing what you want? *Do what you know is right*, before it's too late! If Tenet reaches this place, we lose our—'

A wake of magic shook my bones. A deafening thunder and a cloud of shattered stone burst behind me. My knees cracked against the ground. Doctor Sho clung to my arm, sprawling as the shadows of bodies moved through the settling dust. Weight settled on my shoulders and power as heavy as the mountain above our heads hammered at my mind. I hurled my will at the column, at Ambal Ora's weapon, panic and desperation making my decision for me, and found only terrible, familiar walls.

I centred myself, became the sphere of jade hovering over the pattern, aligned my will, and hurled it against those walls. They cracked, and redoubled in strength.

'You see, I too am capable of new tricks,' the emperor said, his voice ringing. His wings of light cut through the dust, filling the chamber with blinding radiance.

The stone-faced god turned and raised its fist, whether to strike at the emperor or to work some magic, to collapse the chamber of Ambal Ora's weapon, or even bring the Pillars of the Gods down on our heads, I could not say. The wakes of the gods' powers are imperceptible, bound so deeply as they are to the deepest reaches of the pattern of the world.

The emperor met the gaze of the stone-faced god. Two Fists and a woman I did not at first recognise, the grime on her face riven with tears, appeared from thin air with a thunderclap and a wake of magic that tore at the world to surround the last of the stone-faced gods – the last god still to serve humanity rather than some twisted evolution of its first purpose.

As one, four overlapping seals punched through the pattern of the world, enfolding the god. It still stood, its arm raised to strike. Nothing seemed to vanish from the world. No light faded from its stone eyes, which had never held any sign of life. Yet the god now stood inert rather than merely frozen, a statue stripped of animation.

A howl of mingled rage and triumph pounded at my ears. Tollu arched her back, snarling, flames roiling around her, ready to lunge at the emperor. Okara dived in front of her.

Some unheard argument swirled between them as the emperor, with a gesture, readied to strike.

The wolf gods vanished, disappearing in a flash of heat and light.

'Ral!' the emperor roared.

The tear-streaked woman went to her knees. A wake of magic poured from her – thick and burning as molten stone, so potent I felt as though my own flesh bubbled and split – tearing down through the pattern into the layer of the soul, then cycling back up, like a needle drawing thread through layered cloth. The woman rocked back and forth, her jaw creaking, her eyes squeezed shut, a low wail rising in her throat. The wake of her spell mirrored Ambal Ora's weapon, drawing on its power but narrowing it, reforging it with more precision than had been worked into its design as it pierced the layers of the pattern.

Two impulses surged through me. The first was to rush her, to strike her down with my bare hands if need be, to prevent whatever it was the emperor intended, to oppose him at every turn as my grandmother would have done, or my uncle, Frothing Wolf, Burning Dog, Atar, all the Nayeni and An-Zabati and Toa Aloni and others who would have sooner died than allow him to succeed. The second was to let her rid the world of the scourge of the gods, to preserve magic, even if it meant leaving the world in the emperor's hands.

'Why are you hesitating?' the emperor roared, rounding on the woman. She only shook her head as the wail from between her grinding teeth deepened.

The dust had settled. Hissing Cat was slumped on the far side of the column, her body heaving with every breath, blood matting her singed hair and staining her clothes black, wrapped in the terrible light of binding sorcery and flanked by two Fists. Though weakened by her duel with the gods and unable to break the emperor's hold, fury and fire still burned in her eyes.

Near her, Koro Ha lay sprawled in the dust, unmoving. Doctor Sho crouched beside me, one hand cradling something in his sleeve, his eyes fixed on the emperor.

'One final aphorism, my boy,' he whispered, his voice trembling. 'One I should have written long ago. Harmony is found only in selflessness, by the wise who see the pain of others as their own.' He took a steadying breath. 'I can give you a chance. When you have the opportunity, strike. Bring this all to an end.'

He did not wait for an answer. Perhaps he feared, as I did even then, that the emperor and I were too alike. That, despite my new understanding of the depth of the god's manipulations, I would give way to the arrogance within me, the desire for control, for mastery, for that monstrous dream of domination I had for so long mistaken for freedom.

Doctor Sho stood, folded his hands in his sleeves, and crossed the rubble-strewn earth towards the emperor.

'Do you recognise me, Tenet, old friend?' he called, his voice echoing above the woman's wailing.

For a long moment the emperor scrutinised him, as though he were a familiar logogram written in strange calligraphy, making it near indecipherable. Then a laugh burst from him.

'Traveller!' He shook his head. Only when my sword pierced his chest had I before seen such a look of disbelief on the emperor's face. 'It must be quite the tale that brought you here. I'll be glad to hear it when this is done. Do you see?' He gestured to the corpse of the stone-faced god. 'I've done it! All we once dreamed. The dream you cast away, in your cowardice. You have, as I promised, lived to witness it.'

'I have,' Doctor Sho said, nodding solemnly. 'And I have, in that long life, travelled the length and breadth of the world. The length and breadth of your empire. I could compose a new treatise. A revised edition of Streams and Valleys, even of

Living and Dying. One with protections against what you have made of them.'

The emperor scowled. 'After all I have done for the world, you still come to me with these old complaints. Yes, our understandings are somewhat different, Traveller, perhaps because I am one cursed with the burden of power while you are only an old, ponderous man. Your aphorisms and moral tales carry kernels of potent truth, yes, but a man such as I must not only philosophise but act, must not only dream of a world but make one. And even with such power as I wield, the world can be *intractable*. But you see?' Again, the gesture towards the stone-faced god, like a child proudly showing off evidence of a new skill or a budding talent. 'I bend it to my will, Traveller. I will build a harmonious world if I must tear it down to the bedrock first. There is but one obstacle left to me. Let me finish my work, and then I will indulge this conversation.'

He turned his attention back to the woman, his scowl deepening and with it the weight of transmission that bound him to her. Her wail broke into a scream. Every bone in my body ached, as though filled with molten lead. My muscles spasmed and flashed with heat – a bare fraction, I knew, of the agony that seized her. Again I centred myself, felt into the pattern, but touched only the walls of the maze the emperor had made of my mind.

His attention whipped towards me. 'I've not forgotten you, Wen Alder – or Foolish Cur, or whatever you want to be called. This girl suffers as she does because of you. Working together, you and I and a host of Hands and Voices bearing the tetragram might have accomplished what she does now. It would have burdened us, but it would not have destroyed us as it will destroy her. You shattered my plans, and so I devised a new one. Crueller, perhaps, but necessary to restore the world *you* destroyed.'

'None of this is necessary, Tenet,' Doctor Sho said softly, taking another slow, measured step towards him. 'None of it has ever been necessary.'

'You wrote yourself that all things must align to their proper place for peace and harmony to reign,' the emperor said. 'What is the proper place of the gods, Traveller? You did not compose the Classic of Upright Belief, but surely you know. You have witnessed two of their wars now, haven't you?'

Doctor Sho gave no answer, and so the emperor forged on, carried by the current of his argument. 'They seem to believe they deserve a place atop the hierarchy, but they were our servants first, born of the first unwitting magic we worked upon this world. Conjured in answer to the terrors that tore through our souls.' He jabbed a finger at Hissing Cat. 'She knows. For a thousand years, she hid away in the very cave where her gods were born, where the chronicle of the world before their birth, in its aftermath, was written in stone. What did you seek there, Hissing Cat? What did you hope to read from your bones?'

'Fuck off,' Hissing Cat wheezed.

A laugh crackled from the emperor. 'I think I know you well enough to speak for you, fortunately. In the first days, before the gods, people like us – witches of the first sort – did not understand their power. They could feel the pattern around them but had no skill, no training, no understanding. They learned ways of making sense of what they felt. Marks cut in bone, or signs derived from the scattered entrails of slaughtered beasts, or the patterns in a flock of birds. After Naphena's death, you thought to join me in my purpose, didn't you, Cat? But your rage was too tempered by fear, by hesitation. You wanted a vision of what the world might be without the gods. And so you retreated to that deepest place and searched the bones, hoping for ... what? Permission? A salve for your conscience before you plunged ahead? A promise, perhaps, that we would succeed, and that the world would indeed be better off without their kind?'

'I caught a few glimpses,' Hissing Cat snarled. 'Enough to know you're a bloody lunatic.'

'Perhaps. If so, we must consider madness a reasonable reaction to an unjust world.' The emperor smiled. 'All I want is freedom from the chains our forebears shackled to our necks in their idiocy and fear. Our kind made these gods and, in making them, broke that harmony you so love, Traveller. Shattered for ever the possibility of peace. It is our duty to destroy them so that the world can, at last, align to the pattern, with all in its proper place.'

Doctor Sho took another step, shaking his head. I tensed, waiting for the opportunity he had promised, wondering what shape it would take.

'With you atop it all,' he said. 'Reigning in the gods' stead.'

'You say that as though it is hypocrisy, but someone must rule. Who better to lead the world into freedom than the one with the vision to grant it?'

'Until, as has already occurred, those beneath you chafe against your rule and rise up, and the world is plunged back into chaos.'

'Is it my fault if fools and barbarians cannot comprehend the world's design? My vision derives from *your* teachings, need I remind you.'

Doctor Sho sighed, his hand falling from within his sleeve. 'I was wrong, Tenet. About so many things. I hope that you can forgive me.'

He glanced over his shoulder, meeting my eye.

'Shatter the wheel.'

The emperor cocked his head. A wrinkle of confusion split his brow, and in that moment of opportunity Doctor Sho darted forwards, the tip of a needle between his fingers glinting in the glow of the moss that clung to the cavern. Despite his apparent age, Doctor Sho had always moved with surprising speed, a gift of whatever magic Tenet had woven to preserve him through time, to force him – as a final argument in the disagreement that had shattered their friendship – to witness the rise of the empire and the downfall of the gods. So it was that Doctor Sho crossed the distance in only a dozen steps, as swiftly as the emperor could raise his hand. Lightning burned out. Doctor Sho toppled backwards, screaming, his skin splitting in bursts of steam.

Tenet spat a curse and shook his hand. The needle clattered to the floor while he massaged his palm, wincing.

Doctor Sho's scream became a slow, cracking laugh.

Tenet stared at him, and the walls of the labyrinth within my mind began to shiver.

'What did you do?' Lightning crackled at the tips of Tenet's hand. 'Tell me or I will tear the knowledge from you!'

With a slow, deliberate smile, Doctor Sho – once Traveller-on-the-Narrow-Way – breathed a rattling gasp, and the walls of Tenet's transmission fell to dust.

Hissing Cat roared. Cinnamon scent and a wake of veering rolled from her, sending cramps down my arms. The Fists guarding her, deprived of the emperor's canon, came apart like paper dolls as she set upon them with a bear's blood-soaked teeth and claws. Tenet stared down at the needle, tipped with a droplet of his blood. I rushed him, reaching for wind and lightning, not knowing how long whatever drug Doctor Sho had injected him with might last.

His eyes snapped towards me, their pupils wide, dark, and full of terror.

A wake swept through me like a killing fever. Lightning darted up, knocking the emperor from his feet. The tear-streaked woman stood as he collapsed and pawed at the burned ruin of his stomach, gagging and gasping.

'I am Ral Ans Urrera, bastard,' she snarled in harsh Sienese, through bleeding gums and cracked teeth. 'I am the spear of the Girzan Steppe.'

The chamber shook as lightning tore through the emperor, rendering enamelled armour, golden filigree, and the eternal flesh of the emperor to a smear of greasy ash.

36
Decision

Foolish Cur

I dropped to Doctor Sho's side, pouring healing sorcery into his broken body.

Too late. Whether because of his wounds or because, with the emperor's death, the spell that had sustained him had faded, I did not know. I pressed trembling fingers to his eyes, easing them closed. He had been a man of peace. Disgusted by violence yet forced to endure it for the sake of a better world. That he had died in battle felt like a sick contortion, like a poem whose rhythm and evocation collapse into meaninglessness in its final lines.

With a grunt, Hissing Cat slumped against the wall of the chamber, her hair matted to her skull with blood – her own, and that of the four men she had ripped apart, whose remains lay scattered at her feet.

'He's dead?' she muttered. I nodded, and she shook her head. 'Poor bastard. Should have stayed behind. Though, if he had, we'd all be dead in his place, I suppose.'

Carefully, I picked up the needle. Beneath the blood, a few grimy particles of red-and-yellow dust clung to its tip. His sleeve held a small pouch filled with the same powder, and I recalled the mushrooms he had fed me in the forest to block my access to magic and, with it, the ability of the unwoven to hunt us as we made our way to Eastern Fortress.

'Who is this man?' said the tear-stained woman – the emperor's killer, the witch of the old sort Ral Ans Urrera, whom I now recognised from Atar's memories and a vision Okara had shown me. She spoke Sienese, and with little accent, though to my knowledge had spent her life hiding out upon the steppe – a result, I imagined, of the emperor's hold on her.

'A very wise and very old doctor,' I said. 'A friend of the emperor's, once. And a good friend of mine.'

She nodded, then looked around the chamber as though seeing it for the first time. 'That bastard wanted to stop you reaching this place almost as badly as he wanted to kill the gods. Why? Where are we?'

Her words drew me back to the task at hand – a task that, had I not hesitated to complete it, could have spared Doctor Sho his life.

No. That was far from certain. Unmaking magic would surely have unmade the spell that had sustained him. Which prompted another, terrible thought.

I looked to Hissing Cat, whose wounds were slowly knitting as she worked healing magic. She, too, had lived far longer than the pattern would have normally allowed. Would Ambal Ora's weapon destroy her along with the gods?

'Did I hear correctly?' Koro Ha said, coated in dust, his beard singed and a trickle of blood smeared along the side of his face. He knelt beside me, shocked and disbelieving. 'This man is Traveller-on-the-Narrow-Way?'

I nodded.

'Was he not the doctor who healed your … shall we say, childhood illness?'

'He was,' I answered.

Koro Ha shook his head. 'This world is too full of strange coincidences, my boy.' He looked to the remains of the emperor, his expression one of mingled grief and horror. 'Magic is a new thing to me. I little understand this weapon, or why the emperor sought to destroy it, or why you hesitate to wield it, but it is the legacy of my people. I fear the horrors of the gods' war have already torn through Toa Alon. The horrors of the empire certainly have. This may be our last gift to the world. I would not see it cast aside.'

'The grey-hair has a point,' Hissing Cat grunted, speaking Sienese – an odd tongue to hear from her mouth – for the benefit of Koro Ha and Ral. 'Not all this about legacy or what have you. Hateful as the empire was, Tenet's little band of sorcerers were all that held back the unravelling of the world – other than our little outpost in Eastern Fortress, of course. I can't imagine things are going well without him.'

'But the gods' war has ended,' I said, clinging to hope. 'Okara and Tollu claimed this stone-faced god was their last rival, save the emperor. Now the unravelling will cease.'

'I wouldn't count on it, Cur.' Hissing Cat heaved herself to her feet with a grunt. 'Remember those winged freaks above Eastern Fortress? They, too, were gods. I can't explain the mechanics of it – honestly, only Ambal Ora, and maybe Tenet, ever understood how any of this works well enough to explain it, or manipulate it as they did. Tollu and Okara have the advantage of still being remembered by their people. There are statues to them, temples hidden in the forest or deep in caves. They cling to their form and purpose. Those others are just raw fear and rage, lashing out blindly at anything that might threaten them. The forgotten gods of the old kingdoms of Sien, and of the Batir Waste from before Naphena stole their worship with her act of mercy. In time, Tollu and Okara will outwit and destroy them, but there's a long, bloody road from here to there.'

She gazed up at Ambal Ora's weapon for a moment, fear crawling out from the deep creases on her face. 'We could hunker down, put up seals and shields and whatnot, wait out the storm and preserve a remnant of humanity. Let the gods of Nayen win the war, and then see what happens next. It's an option. One not too dissimilar from what I did after Naphena died while Tenet built his little empire. Wait and see. Hope it'll all work out.'

'My people are scattered, some into imperial captivity,' Ral said, the hard planes of her face sharpened by dust and the furrows of her tears. 'Though perhaps they will free themselves, now that the empire has lost its magic. The rest escaped into the Waste and back to the plains, with no power to defend themselves from the terror that twists the world. Your people may endure if you let your gods chase their victory. Mine will be destroyed.'

Her words seared through me, sharp and burning as any battle sorcery, carving towards that part of me that clung to magic, to all the wonder and promise of it.

'Do none of you see the danger in this?' I said, conjuring one last argument as a shield against the harsh, unwavering truth. 'Not even you understand what this weapon will do, Hissing Cat. All we know is that it will separate the layers of the pattern. It will sever us from the influence of the gods, yes, and from magic, but what consequences might there be? Is magic not the extension of that spark in all of us that makes us greater than beasts, that gives us freedom, that makes us more than mere objects caught in the pattern's flow?'

'Tenet thought so,' Hissing Cat answered, 'and, I assumed, taught his Hands and Voices the same. Clearly, Ambal Ora disagreed, or thought that the risk Tenet was right was worth freedom from the influence of the gods.'

'But we can't know!' I insisted. 'If we do this, the world will change in ways we cannot anticipate. We may do far more harm than good!'

'Isn't that always the nature of an act?' Koro Ha said gently. 'We can never know, with anything like certainty, the outcomes of our deeds. The appeal of imperial doctrine, it seems to me, is that it guards against uncertainty by motivating and justifying action according to principles, disregarding consequence, and thus the crippling fear that an act will ripple out in unanticipated ways.'

'Crone, tell me how to wield this weapon and I will do what must be done,' Ral snapped. 'We can leave these Sienese to their pitiful worrying.'

The skulls in Hissing Cat's hair clattered in rhythm with her laughter. 'I like you, girl, but I spent the last few hundred years wondering if Tenet was right to build his empire, and if I should have joined him. I can indulge a little thoughtfulness.'

'While they *think*, the world unravels,' Ral snarled.

'You're not wrong. But neither is Cur. We know what happens if we wait, but we don't know what happens if we act. That's the agonising thing, isn't it? That uncertainty. I spent lifetimes trying to pierce through it, to read messages from the pattern in broken bone, to know whether Tenet's goal was worth the cost. But whenever I thought I'd glimpsed some hint of what might happen next, I tended to disregard it, to doubt myself, or doubt the message. Can't say for certain. What I *can* say is this.' She nodded towards the column of stone. 'This isn't our only option.'

Her words sent a shiver through me that built and built. Not from horror, but at how sweet they sounded, how they appealed, how they dug hooks into my deepest longings and dragged me towards a terrible path.

'You want to destroy the gods without destroying magic, while leaving the world as it is?' she asked. 'So did Tenet. Between the three of us, we have more than enough power, more than enough skill, to forge a canon as he did. It's something you've already begun, Cur. A path you're already walking. You need only follow it further. Not as quick a solution – people will suffer while we work to save them – but one we can better predict. No great leap into the unknown, only a recreation of what Tenet had already built, but stronger, better, without his cruelty and brutality.' She glanced at the broken corpses of the Fists. 'Or, at least, with less of it. You want to preserve the world as you know it? Take up the empire. Rebuild it.'

'After all our people have suffered, how could you suggest this?' Koro Ha clenched his fists in fury. 'Or are all your kind the same, callous and unfeeling towards we smaller folk without your power?'

Hissing Cat stared him down, her eyes dark. 'Would I have hidden myself away if I felt nothing?'

Ral's fist cracked against Ambal Ora's pillar. 'You talk and talk and talk. I can feel the power surging through this place. I will seize it and use it, with or without your guidance.'

'You would give up your power?' I asked her, this woman who had lived a life parallel to mine – similar, and yet profoundly different. Perhaps a life that had left her mind less clouded. 'More than that, you would leap into the unknown?'

'This world is a horror,' she answered. 'I will tear it down to its foundations, if I must, to build a better one.'

Her will plunged into the pattern of the world and seized the far-reaching, fractal roots of power anchored to the column. Stone shook. The glowing moss that clung to the walls pulsed with life. The air thrummed with unspent energy, reeking of a lightning storm.

Sparks lit between her blood-stained teeth. A scream bubbled in her throat, but she held, determined to do what I could not, trained as I had been by a lifetime of mistakes. Too often had

I plunged into depths beyond my ken, wielded powers without understanding. I remembered twisted limbs and brittle, hollow bones. The theft of the wind from the An-Zabati and the crumbling of their obelisks. The unfurling of the gods, mindless of anything but wrath and fear.

Doctor Sho's whisper, before he walked towards the emperor, wielding words and a needle to give us this chance to make a better world: *Shatter the wheel.*

Who can say what is right and what is wrong? I saw only that Ral Ans Urrera suffered, her body racked by ancient powers beyond her control.

I centred myself, became that sphere of jade, plunged deep into the pattern, and reached for her mind.

37
A Weapon

Ral Ans Urrera

The storm rages.

Its winds carry fire from one end of the world to the other.

Back again.

Whirling, full of grit and sand, tearing and scalding her.

She shrinks back, her grasp slipping. It hurts too much. Yet not more than the labyrinth. Not more than the bloated face of her father. The piled corpses of her kindred. The annihilation of her future, of all that she hoped to be and build.

She is Ral Ans Urrera. The storm is her spear.

She will drive it at the broken heart of the world, shatter the foundations on which all her suffering has been built.

Light cascades behind her eyes and bursts, like dying stars, within her skull. Her bones creak. Her muscles scream and froth like horses run to ground. Her tendons fray and tear like the strings of an over-taut bow.

Exhaustion is a pit at the core of her. The footing at its edge crumbles with every motion of her will, every pull against the power that howls within her. Too little time has passed since her struggle to contort this weapon to the emperor's purpose. There is a sick pride to be felt in his use of her, his belief that she might do what he could not, yet it has sapped her strength. This weapon – this ancient, buried power – will overwhelm what remains, even if she wields it to its intended design.

Let go. To live is to let go.

She feels it tunnelling through her, prying her apart muscle by muscle, sinew by sinew. Still she holds on. If she does not do this, no one will. Certainly not the Sienese boy, the coward, cringing from the loss of his power and influence.

It is not enough to live. She has a gift, a curse, one granted to her if not by the Skyfather then by fate, or by chance, or by some alignment of the stars at her birth. It does not matter. Power carries with it an impetus to act.

The emperor is dead, his empire broken. It is enough.

'No!' she wails. It will never be enough. Perhaps there could be peace, for a time, but as long as this power exists, as long as men can seize it and use it to shape the world at their whim, there will be another emperor, another empire, another hierarchy demanding obedience, another system breaking the world like a reluctant colt.

She herself became such a one, turning on the Red Bull, tired of their questioning, their reluctance, their unwillingness to be forged with the other bands into her weapon against the emperor.

It has to end.

You will destroy yourself and accomplish nothing.

The thought carries with it a wave of fear and a redoubling of the storm, of the pain. The firm ground at the edge of the emptiness crumbles. Exhaustion will swallow her and the power will tear her to dust. What is the point of such self-destruction, of such fury and determination, if it is doomed to failure?

She tastes blood, feels the roots of her teeth quake and loosen in the depths of her gums. A vessel bursts behind her eye. Blood and mucous pour past her lip. Her hold on the power that rages within her falters.

There is worth in trying. Even if failure is certain. Even if the attempt can only end in death.

A weight hammers at her mind and she howls. Was the emperor's death some trick? An illusion conjured of light and shadow? A work of some magic beyond her understanding? It seems impossible, but she knows this magic as she knows the face of her father's corpse.

Well. She can reverse the trap. She can hold his mind within her and let Ambal Ora's weapon tear them both apart.

<It is Foolish Cur, Ral!> A voice echoes within her, speaking as the Skyfather did. <The magic is killing you! You must—>

There is some relief in that. The boy seems weaker than the emperor. Less practised, certainly. It will be far easier to overpower him.

'Do not presume to order me, boy,' she snarls. 'I do not share your cowardice.'

<If you do this on your own, you will die. Let me help you!>

She curses the boy. It is far easier to be resigned to death when there is little hope for life. 'Why should I trust you, who argued against what is necessary? You have the empire's ambition.'

The weight of his mind deepens. Ral feels her strength buckle beneath it and groans. Her muscles fray. Her bones splinter.

<Once it has begun, I don't think it can be stopped,> he says at last, and she feels an echo of his regret. <It is only a question of whether Ambal Ora's weapon succeeds or fails. The power is there. A deep well, already shaped to a single end. I have made things like this before, but never so ambitious. *Nothing* has ever been so ambitious, not even the canon of sorcery.>

'Enough babbling!' Ral screams.

The boy's mind recoils, then returns. It ripples through the tortured pattern of her thoughts, tracing the fractals of the power that courses through her unchecked, digging into her like roots into the earth, prying her apart.

<I think I see what he was trying to do. It's meant to be subtle. A scalpel, not a—>

The word falls through Ral's mind.

The edge of the abyss crumbles away. Sound and sight fade to nothing. Her thoughts wheel out of her control.

Weeks in the labyrinth, howling, tearing at the walls.

She endured, even then.

She is Ral Ans Urrera, the spear of the Girzan steppe.

She holds on.

38
The Pattern

Foolish Cur

<Ral?> I prodded, digging at her thoughts, desperate for a response.

She stood beside me, feet planted wide, her fist against Ambal Ora's column all that prevented her collapse. Blood poured from her nose and ears and trickled from the corners of her eyes, which stared ahead, their pupils dilated to black, depthless pits. She had gone silent, and now no matter how deep my transmission reached, I could find no trace of her, only the raging torrent of magic that poured from that column, threatening to destroy her and, with her, the world.

'What the hell is going on, Cur?' Hissing Cat demanded.

There was no time to explain. Possibilities flitted through my mind.

Doctor Sho's needle, there on the stone floor. A dose of witch's eye would sever her from the pattern, saving her life.

No. The power within her would tear free without direction. A scalpel is still a blade, and unleashed to carve through the world undirected there was no telling what damage it might do. The war between the gods would seem a pathetic prelude to the horror and chaos unleashed.

If only I had not hesitated.

'Hissing Cat, if I black out, you need to reach into my mind and make sure this magic does what it's supposed to do,' I shouted, and plunged back into the howling depths.

Ambal Ora had made something like the canon of witchcraft, but vaster, overshadowing what I had done as a mountain overshadows an anthill. It was not enough to reach into the well of power he had left behind, to unleash the spell. To do so was, in fact, a paradox.

To unmake magic, one needed to wield magic. As the layers of the pattern came apart, so too would the power parting them. The blade would destroy itself even as it cut. Wielded without the right nuance, it would shatter long before its work was done.

The stone-faced god had said that only a witch of the old sort could wield Ambal Ora's weapon. Now I understood why. Our first gift was not the power to reshape the pattern, after all, but sensitivity to its eternal flow.

<It will be all right, Ral,> I thought, even as my heart thundered. I took deep, centring breaths, became as a sphere of jade hovering over the pattern of the world. <Everything will be all right.>

I traced the contours of Ambal Ora's weapon, branching outwards, unfolding in complexity towards infinity. Such complexity dashed my hope of taking the power into myself, relieving Ral of the torrent that burned through her. If I did, it would destroy me as surely as it was destroying her. In truth, I could little imagine how she had survived so long. The power of it was vaster than anything I had ever seen. Heavier than the emperor's transmission. More steadfast than Hissing Cat's will. Woven with more skill than the obelisks of An-Zabat. Alone, neither of us could wield it properly – I because I lacked her strength, she because she lacked my understanding – but together we stood a chance.

I enfolded Ral's mind within my own – and not her mind alone, but with it that part of her that drew from the layer of the soul, that phantom limb still clinging tightly to Ambal Ora's weapon even as her consciousness slipped away.

<Hold on, Ral,> I said. As long as she did, I could guide the weapon, untethering the layers of the pattern according to Ambal Ora's intricate design. But if she succumbed, the power of it would tear through me, and through the world. The terror of the gods' war would pale in comparison to the horror that would be unleashed.

I lowered myself into the pattern, bringing Ral and the weapon with me. My sixth sense felt the grinding of bedrock and the burning heart of the earth, the trickling of water down the stalactites above us and the accretion of stone it left behind, the bright life pulsing through the moss clinging to the cavern's walls. Koro Ha, Hissing Cat, even Ral and I, and those dozens of Toa Aloni and Sienese warriors who still battled on the stair, our pulses an asynchronous drumbeat to match the dance of the stars.

Deeper still, into the layer of the mind.

Memories darted through me like bolts of lightning: the scrape of shale on my knees as a child, dancing to the rhythm of rain and lightning, days on horseback, the wind tousling my hair, a face I did not know at first smiling kindly, then afraid, then contorted in death.

Ral's memories. The core of her self, to which she clung as Ambal Ora's weapon tore her apart.

Never in my life had I been so dependent upon the strength of another soul.

<Just hold on a little while longer,> I said, and plunged deeper still.

Every line of Sienese poetry, every aphorism of the classics, every song ever sung, every turn of Toa Aloni knotwork or curve of calligraphy, every brush stroke of every landscape painting, every step of the Soldiers' Dance – the Glassblowers', the Weavers', the Jewellers', the Windcallers', and every dance of An-Zabat that I had never had the joy to learn – every spark of curiosity, every thrill of wielding magic, every true word ever spoken is but a fleeting gesture towards all that I felt as the pattern of the soul washed over me.

A poet could better capture it, but I was never a particularly talented poet. Pinion might have done it justice.

Beauty itself, in all its unending refractions, glimpsed in an instant.

And with it a cold, gnawing terror.

Too late to retreat. Too late to give in to fear.

I let the sphere of jade dissolve. Let myself become one, truly, with the pattern of the world, of the mind, of the soul. Let Ambal Ora's weapon unfurl.

What cost, a better world?

Epilogue

Foolish Cur

This world is, indeed, an emptier place.

The claws of the unwoven no longer scrape stone and tear flesh. In that respect, at least, the emptiness is peaceful.

It is not, however, without lasting pain. Holes in hearts and homes where mothers, fathers, siblings, and friends should be. It will be a monumental task, spanning lifetimes, to count and tally the dead.

Perhaps someone will take up that burden. It lies beyond me, as so much does.

My chronicle of the world's ending, and its rebirth, is ended. I hope I have done justice to the voices of my fellows. They told their tales to me, in time – Koro Ha first, before Hissing Cat and I left Toa Alon on the *Swiftness of the South Wind*, returning to Nayen. No more tearing holes in the pattern for us, stepping from one place to another in a breath and a twist of nausea.

Already, as a wind and sea unbent by any human will carried us, Hissing Cat began to show her age. Clear-River, Running Doe, and I buried her in the painted cave where she spent so many years.

'Just toss me off a cliff,' she growled when I asked how she wished to be honoured, when the rattling cough and seizures grew severe and even Running Doe agreed that all herbs could do was offer comfort. 'Or pile a heap of bones on top of me. I've lived far too long to give a bloody damn.'

I feared, for a time, that I would suffer a similar fate. That we witches of the old sort, cut off from our power, might wither like flowers kept in darkness. But I am now only another man. One who carries his share of emptiness.

We left Ral behind in Sor Cala, strong enough to sit and speak for a time, despite her doctor's frustrated insistence that she rest. After hearing her tale, which knit together the fragments of memory I had witnessed, I know with as much certainty as I have ever known anything that, under her leadership, the Girzan will thrive in this new world, when she is hale enough to return to them.

I must confess that I go on writing because I fear that when I lift my brush from the final logogram, seal my pot of ink, put away the paperweights and inkstone, I will lose the last thread that binds me to that lost world, rich with magic and possibility, and to my childish dream of mastery and freedom.

An incompatible duality, I now believe. The emperor was master, but he was never free. Doctor Sho – perhaps the freest man I have ever known, with the length and breadth of the world open to him and even time itself no threat – claimed mastery of nothing, abandoning the right hand of the emperor to walk barefoot and carry medicine upon his back, bound only by his responsibility to others. Yet I, weak fool that I am, cannot forget that dream: that feverish wake, that first glimpse of magic pulsing through me. My name was a prophecy, in truth.

I sit now not far from that altar where I was named. Running Doe complains that I spend my days far from the house, but the quietness and solitude here comfort me. When I close my eyes and breathe deeply, I can almost feel ...

Only memory, surely, like the sense that the eyes of the wolf gods are watching me from their statues, or from the shadows between the trees on my nightly walks back to my father's estate.

My estate, now. Or perhaps my mother's. No one has yet come to collect taxes or register our deed to the place, at any rate, so it matters little. I'm sure they will, in time. Clear-River and his army of bureaucrats will see to that.

It is growing dark. The crickets are singing in the undergrowth. An owl cries. My mother and grandmother will have a meal ready, and Running Doe will plant her hands on her hips with a scowl to peel paint if I wander in when the food is already cold.

I will linger only a few moments more.

I asked Pinion, once, what he felt on that day when the pattern of the world, and our relationship to it, changed for ever.

He was, I now believe, a witch of the old sort too, though never with a chance to discover his gift. He felt no magic, he said, but he did not even think to reach for it, accustomed as he was to the shell I had built around Eastern Fortress and anchored to Hissing Cat's oracle bones. Yet a strange disquiet had gripped him, as though he had woken to find all the decorations in his room adjusted slightly, almost imperceptibly, by some malevolent visitor. It was like a feeling he had suffered at times in childhood, he said, when some matter of governance soured his father's mood and his frustration stalked their home, unseen, unsensed, yet potent nonetheless. Driven to investigate, he rose from his pallet, despite his aching wounds. At the very least, he would know if he was alone in this strange feeling.

The skies were clear, he noted first, empty of the strange, dark cloud that had hung over the harbour since the coming of the gods. He went to Oriole's tree, worried that his unease might be a symptom of the shell's failure, of the pattern beginning to unravel around him. There, beneath branches swaying in the gentle wind, he found Clear-River, who would soon be Sun King, with a canon of witchcraft in his trembling hand.

Clear-River removed his finger from the three lines where I had anchored the power to conjure flame. With tears streaming from his eyes and a broad smile, he passed the canon to Pinion, who pressed his thumb to each mark in turn, feeling nothing but furrows carved in old, dry bone.

'It's done,' Clear-River said. 'Whatever they found in Toa Alon, they put an end to it. And now we have a chance to build something new.'

I leave the world in their hands now, and in Ral's – they who have a vision for its future, with kinder, wiser souls than mine. Perhaps my own will find some gentler purpose, now that my record is written.

My grandmother once, long ago, suggested whittling.

END

Acknowledgments

In my classroom, at the end of a major project, I will often ask my students to reflect on their creative process. To take an accounting of where they began, and where they have ended, and what they learned along the way. It seems appropriate to do likewise here at the end of my first completed trilogy of novels.

Unlike my students, who are usually creating something simply because they are compelled to for the sake of their grades, we authors feel a deep, personal investment in the books we right. All the more so for a trilogy of novels (which is, in a way, simply one very long novel divided into rough thirds), the product of over six years of creative effort. When the kernel of an idea that would become *The Hand of the Sun King* was only beginning to sprout, circa 2015 and 2016, I was fortunate enough to find two groups of dedicated writers, one in Taipei and one in Spokane. Among them, I would like to particularly thank Dan Bocook, Pat Woods, Jenny Green, and Brad Williams, all of whom offered feedback that was instrumental in helping me grow and find my voice.

That kernel would not have developed from a short story into a full novel – and later into a trilogy, as I found questions and potentialities in the writing that I did not expect – I leaned heavily on help from Erin Cairns and Jon Ficke, fellow Writers of the Future winners who have been endlessly generous with their time as beta readers. As that novel found its shape, it also found its way to my agent Joshua Bilmes, who was instrumental in polishing it into the best it could be, and then to Stevie Finegan at the Zeno Literary Agency, who placed it in exactly the right hands at exactly the right moment. Those hands, fortunately, belonged to my editor Brendan Durkin, whose deep understanding of what these books are fundamentally about helped me shape the latter pieces of the trilogy into what they needed to be. I hope to continue working with him for a long time, and am thrilled by the conversation we have already had about the next project currently in progress.

Through it all, I could not have continued in the often perilous writing journey – as fraught with disappointment and frustration as it is filled with delight and excitement – without the support of my wife, Hannah, my parents, Ward and Jenny, and my brothers, Nathan and Seth. I am also incredibly grateful for the support, generosity, and tolerance of the booksellers and staff at Auntie's Bookstore, where I found a job I could tolerate some years ago and who have become something of a second family. Finally, I need to thank Clay Harmon, a good friend an an excellent writer in his own right, and the folks in the Write or Die Growlery, with whom I have been delighted to share in the joys and sorrows of the writing life for the past year or so.

As always, the map is not the landscape, the pacts are not the whole of magic, and the acknowledgments section is no complete accounting of all those who deserve to be thanked and recognized. But these things are only useful because they are simplifications of the whole. So we must leave it there at the end of what has been a very long journey full of good friends and fellow travelers.

Credits

J.T. Greathouse and Gollancz would like to thank everyone at Orion who worked on the publication of *The Pattern of the World* in the UK.

Editor
Brendan Durkin
Áine Feeney

Copy editor
Alan Heal

Proof reader
Andy Ryan

Audio
Paul Stark
Jake Alderson

Contracts
Dan Herron

Design
Nick Shah
Rachael Lancaster
Joanna Ridley

Editorial Management
Charlie Panayiotou
Jane Hughes

Finance
Nick Gibson
Jasdip Nandra
Sue Baker

Communications
Jenna Petts

Production
Paul Hussey

Sales
Jennifer Wilson
Esther Waters
Victoria Laws
Rachael Hum
Anna Egelstaff
Sinead White
Georgina Cutler

Operations
Jo Jacobs
Sharon Willis